CW00558546

A NEST OF GENTLEFOLK
AND OTHER STORIES

A NEST
OF
GENTLEFOLK

Ivan S. Turgenev

Translated from the Russian and with an Introduction by
Jessie Coulson

Preface by
Boris Dralyuk

riverrun

First published in Great Britain in 1959 by Oxford University Press
This edition published in Great Britain in 2020 by

riverrun

An imprint of

Quercus Editions Ltd
Carmelite House
50 Victoria Embankment
London EC4Y 0DZ

An Hachette UK company

Preface © 2020 by Boris Dralyuk
Boris Dralyuk asserts his moral right in the copyright of the preface.

A CIP catalogue record for this book is available
from the British Library

Paperback 978 1 52940 405 0
eBook 978 1 52940 404 3

10 9 8 7 6 5 4 3 2 1

Typeset by CC Book Production
Printed and bound in Great Britain by Clays Ltd, Elcograf S.p.A.

MIX
Paper from
responsible sources
FSC® C104740
www.fsc.org

Papers used by Quercus are from well-managed forests and other responsible sources.

Contents

Note

Lists of Characters are given before each story, and there is a 'Note on Pronunciation' of the Russian names at the end of the list for *A Nest of Gentlefolk*.

Preface

BORN JUST OVER TWO centuries ago, Ivan Turgenev was the first Russian author to become a celebrity in Europe, where he spent nearly half his life. He was, of course, more than a celebrity – he was a living link, a vital conduit to a society that remained largely hidden from Western eyes. It was, as Henry James wrote two decades after Turgenev's death, 'from his writings almost alone that we of English, French, and German speech have derived our notions . . . of the Russian people'.

Yet by the time James wrote those words in 1903, Turgenev was already ceding ground to his near contemporary, Tolstoy, whose 'baggy monsters' (to borrow another of James's vivid phrases) had been loosed upon the English-speaking world in various guises at the turn of the century. A decade later, Dostoyevsky and Chekhov would begin to appear, simultaneously, in Constance Garnett's influential translations, elbowing Turgenev farther and farther out of view. Still, he retained his admirers, including, somewhat surprisingly, Ernest Hemingway – but the ever-pugilistic American's ranking of influences on his own work is telling: 'I started out very quiet and I beat Mr Turgenev. Then I trained hard and I beat Mr de Maupassant. I've fought two draws with Mr Stendhal, and I think I had an edge in the last one. But nobody's going to get me in any ring with Mr Tolstoy unless I'm crazy or I keep getting better.' Such was Hemingway's scorecard in 1950; in the rough-and-tumble world of mid-century letters, Tolstoy was up and Turgenev was down, if not out.

One of the causes of Turgenev's unjust sidelining may be that his best writing, unlike the works of Tolstoy or Dostoyevsky, frustrates the reader on the hunt for big ideas. It isn't that his novels and stories are devoid of ideas – many are full of them. In fact, he was often the first to discern and capture in writing the ideas that came to define the Russian nineteenth century. He helped expose the cruelty and inanity of serfdom in *A Sportsman's Sketches* (1852); established the image of 'the superfluous man' – an idealist hopelessly stymied by a stagnant society and by his own obsessively contemplative nature – in *The Diary of a Superfluous Man* (1850) and *Rudin* (1856); anatomized the revolutionary materialism of a generation of Russian 'nihilists' in *Fathers and Sons* (1862); and made a keen study of a subsequent generation of populist radicals in *Virgin Soil* (1877).

Still, ideas themselves are never Turgenev's central concern. His focus is always on the beautifully individuated, perfectly imperfect human beings who cling to ideas for dear life, on the compromises, sacrifices, and self-deceit their convictions demand of them, and on the pain, relief, or deadening numbness that set in as these convictions crumble away. In Turgenev's work, ideas are fuel, propelling his characters in unforeseen directions before, in most cases, burning out. It's no surprise to learn, from James, that the 'first form in which a tale appeared to him was as the figure of an individual, or a combination of individuals, whom he wished to see in action, being sure that such people must do something very special and interesting'. Turgenev, who worshipped Shakespeare, had a dramatist's imagination. For all their talk, his people leave much unspoken, and what they do say – and sometimes rant – hints at deeper psychological motivations, conflicts more intimate and primal.

It takes a gifted translator to reproduce not only the hidden depths of Turgenev's characters, but also the famously crystalline surface of his prose – precise in its diction, subtle in its rhythms. 'This mastery, this delicacy and sureness of touch,' as Jessie Coulson puts it in her introduction, present 'a challenge at once stimulating and daunting.' Luckily, Coulson, who expresses a humble hope that her translation 'will succeed in giving pleasure', is more than up to the task.

Her excellent selection is meant to showcase Turgenev's strengths as a prose stylist and as a student of human nature, not of intellectual trends. All four pieces in this volume – the novel-length *A Nest of Gentlefolk* (1858), as well as the novellas *A Quiet Backwater* (1854), *First Love* (1860), and *A Lear of the Steppes* (1870) – are works of memory, set in the 1830s and early 1840s, the era of Turgenev's boyhood and youth. In them the stagnant social and political realities of the time form the background – rendered vividly and economically, without overt authorial judgement – for dramas of love thwarted and betrayed, of difficult maturation and embarrassed old age. In her introduction, Coulson elegantly sketches in the biographical sources of these stories, and also gives readers a sense, in her voice, of what she herself values in Turgenev's art.

But what impresses me most are the voices she lends to Turgenev's narrators – graceful yet earnest, meditative yet immediate. In places, she does not depart greatly from Constance Garnett's better-known versions; occasionally, her departures are not significant improvements. But her tone is consistently more alive, honest both to the stylistic norms of Turgenev's era and to the perennial freshness of his vision. Her rendering of a pivotal scene in *First Love* – in which the middle-aged Vladimir Petrovich tells of his earliest infatuation, at the age of sixteen, with his twenty-one-year-old neighbor Zinaida – reverberates like the crack of a whip. Vladimir Petrovich spots his strict, restrained father speaking to Zinaida through an open window:

My first impulse was to flee. 'If my father looks round,' I thought, 'I am lost . . .' but a strange feeling, a feeling stronger than curiosity, stronger even than jealousy, stronger than fear, stopped me. I began to watch, I strained my ears. My father seemed to be insisting on something, and Zinaida refusing to agree. As if it were now I can see her face – sad, serious, beautiful, bearing the inexpressible stamp of devotion, sorrow, love, and something like despair – I can find no other word. She spoke in monosyllables, without raising her eyes, but smiling – meekly and obstinately. From nothing but that smile I could have recognized my old Zinaida. My father shrugged his shoulders and straightened his hat on his head – always a sign of impatience with him. Then I heard the words: '*Vous devez vous séparer de cette* . . .' Zinaida sat up straight and stretched out her arm . . . Then something unbelievable happened before my eyes: my father suddenly raised his riding-whip with which he had been gently beating the dust from the skirts of his coat – and I heard a sharp blow on that arm, bare to the elbow. I could hardly refrain from crying out, and Zinaida started violently, looked at my father in silence and, slowly raising her arm to her lips, kissed the crimsoning weal.

A sensitive hand is at work, making myriad little choices in order to ensure that we feel the full shock of Vladimir Petrovich's trauma. It isn't only that 'crimsoning weal' is infinitely more suggestive than Garnett's version: 'the streak of red upon it'.

Unlike Garnett, Coulson cuts off her sentences at just the right moments: 'strained my ears', not 'strained my ears to listen'; 'can find no other word', not 'can find no other word for it'. Rhythms that, in Turgenev, do so much to emphasize the sense of a passage, are recreated faithfully yet artfully: the feeling that stops the young man from fleeing is 'stronger even than jealousy, stronger than fear', not 'stronger than jealousy, stronger even than fear'. And the nature of Zinaida's gaze remains a haunting paradox ('meekly and obstinately'), rather than being explained away ('submissively, but without yielding').

It is above all this last quality – this readiness to leave us without explanations – which sets Turgenev apart from the other nineteenth-century Russian giants and makes him, together with Chekhov, not just modern, but eternally contemporary. 'There are such moments in life,' he tells us at the end of the epilogue to *A Nest of Gentlefolk*, 'such feelings . . . We can only point to them – and pass by.' Seldom have such moments and feelings been pointed to with greater 'delicacy and sureness of touch'. Those who return to them by way of Coulson's translation will be richly rewarded.

Boris Dralyuk

Introduction

IN THE FIFTIES AND early sixties of the nineteenth century, a
time to which all but one of the works in this volume belong,
Ivan Sergeevich Turgenev enjoyed the position of the central
figure of the Russian literary world. His first considerable work
in prose, *A Sportsman's Sketches*, which began to appear in 1847,
had been published in book form in 1852; it was acclaimed
not only for its literary quality but also for the social criticism
implicit in its pictures of peasants as human beings and of their
greedy, stupid, brutal, or ineffectual masters. The criticism is
implied, not openly expressed, but in the novels that followed
social and political ideas are usually discussed at some length;
indeed, the presence or absence of this kind of discussion is one
of the principal distinctions between the stories Turgenev classed
as novels and those, not very much shorter or greatly different
in structure, he called 'tales' (long-short stories or *nouvelles*).

Now, a hundred years later, the old controversies are faded

and forgotten, the discussions that once seemed vital have dwindled into mere dullness and are seen as rather tiresome excrescences, often with no organic relationship to the work to which they are attached. Even in the eyes of Turgenev's contemporaries, more than one of his novels was seriously impaired by political or social arguments that seem forced and unnecessary; in several, characters appear to have been created solely as pegs to hang discussions on. Mikhalevich, in *A Nest of Gentlefolk*, might fairly be classed as such a character: his connexion with the plot is tenuous, and certainly there seems no reason for the introduction of his visit to Vasilyevskoe except to allow him to argue all night with Lavretsky. In this instance we are told very little of the substance of the dicussion; indeed, the allusions throughout the novel to Lavretsky's concern with the problem of the serf-owning landlord and to his personal solution of it are so vague and cursory that it is quite possible for a modern reader without much detailed knowledge of the period never to discover, or to care, what that solution is, or even to be more than faintly aware what problems have been raised.

Generally speaking, it is those novels that, like *A Nest of Gentlefolk*, have comparatively little material of social significance, and the long-short stories, from which it is absent, that still retain the charm that first attracted the western reader to Turgenev, in the days when he was regarded by the outside world as the only voice of 'mute Russia'. These novels and stories have a nostalgic, evocative quality which, while it owes something to the mere passage of time, owes still more to Turgenev's own attitude and circumstances and the poetic precision of his writing. When he wrote the *Sportsman's Sketches* he had already broken finally with the mother on whose estate he had seen exemplified the worst aspects of serfdom – or rather, she had broken with him; even earlier he had spent years abroad, first as a student in Berlin and later in his infatuated pursuit of Pauline Viardot; after 1861 he never went back to Russia except for short periods. The first sentence of *A Nest of Gentlefolk* tells us that the events it narrates took place in 1842, *A Quiet Backwater* appears to belong roughly to the same period, while *First Love* and *A Lear of the Steppes* relate to the author's childhood and youth, about 1833 or earlier; these two stories were written in 1860 and 1870 respectively, *A Quiet Backwater* in 1854 and *A Nest of Gentlefolk* in 1858. In all the stories in this volume, then, Turgenev was as it were looking backward towards what he had left behind in time and place, towards the quiet, unchanging life of the old gentry in the remote countryside. In these placid-seeming surroundings, like jewels on velvet, are set those charming and delightful young girls whose portraits Turgenev so excelled in drawing.

If we say that all, or nearly all, of Turgenev's heroines, like so many other young girls in nineteenth-century Russian literature, are to be regarded as having descended from Pushkin's Tatyana (in *Eugene Onegin*), this is not to imply that they are all alike, though they may have a family resemblance, or that they produce any impression of being purely literary creations. On the contrary, they are remarkably real and human, solid flesh and blood. Two of the most enchanting of all are Liza in *A Nest of Gentlefolk* and Masha in *A Quiet Backwater*, and they remain as vivid in our memory as though we had known them ourselves. We remember as if we had seen them with our own eyes Masha leaning against a birch-tree with her hands behind her, her gaze fixed on the distance and her dark head uncovered, or again in the drawing-room, her proud shy reserve conquered for the moment, singing her Ukrainian songs with all the warmth and passion of her nature ringing in her voice; or Liza, with 'that pale, fresh complexion, eyes and lips so serious, that honest and innocent look', sitting silent and still in the warm summer evening, wrapped in a happy dream, by the open window through which the song of the nightingale, 'almost impertinently loud', pours in a great flood. Zinaida, in *First Love*, although her kittenishness makes her less appealing to many readers, has in common with these two great emotional depth and a force of character that enables her to pursue, in her own unaided strength, the course she has decided on for herself. Martyn Petrovich's daughters, Anna and Evlampia (in *A Lear of the Steppes*), do not belong to this gallery of dark and true and tender women, and we are given rather the slightest of sketches than full-length studies of them, but they, too, plainly have deep and powerful emotional possibilities, and in them strength of will has hardened into steeliness.

With some exceptions Turgenev's general tendency, to put it simply and perhaps too crudely, is to portray strong women and weak men. In the essay *Hamlet and Don Quixote* he divided men, or rather those high-minded and well-educated intellectuals who were worthy to be made the heroes of books, into two types: the Hamlets, introspective, irresolute, and ineffectual, and the Don Quixotes, equally idealistic, but men of action, courageous and even rash – the types, in fact, that are now often distinguished as introverts and extraverts. It was the second type that Turgenev was often reproached for not portraying, and in spite of many efforts, he succeeded only once or twice in producing a convincing representation of one. This is perhaps partly because he himself, like Veretyev in *A Quiet Backwater* and Lavretsky in *A Nest of Gentlefolk*, can best be classified among the Hamlets. Veretyev might be called the typical Turgenev hero; he is a finished example of the 'superfluous man'. Intelligent, gifted, charming, he consciously and uselessly fritters away his talents, drifting lazily through a life without value for society or meaning for himself. We are given more detail about Lavretsky and about the influences and upbringing that have formed him, but somehow the outlines of this character seem curiously blurred, like those of a figure looming up large and out of focus, too close to the camera, in the foreground of a photograph. It is as if the author had looked not directly at Lavretsky, but only at the other characters through his eyes, and it is not unreasonable to suppose that this inner view comes from the fact that the character is to a large extent a self-portrait. Lavretsky shares many of Turgenev's qualities and opinions, for example, his taste for music and feeling about the church, and certainly Lavretsky's relations with and attitude to his wife are a reflection of Turgenev's with Madame Viardot.

Pauline Viardot was an opera singer of considerable reputation and what must have been remarkable attractions. Turgenev met and fell in love with her when she came to St Petersburg with the Italian opera company, and he followed her back to her home in Paris and all over Europe. She accepted him as her lover, but only for a very short time, and Turgenev, like Lavretsky in similar circumstances, fled from her to Italy. He could not long remain apart from her, however, and returned to become a permanent member of her household for the rest of his life. It is tempting to inquire whether, if Lavretsky is indeed a partial portrait of Turgenev, Varvara Pavlovna represents Pauline Viardot. Varvara Pavlovna is portrayed as a beautiful, elegant, talented, and vivacious creature, whom men and women alike find almost irresistible when she sets herself to charm them for her own ends, but whose emotions are shallow and trivial and who pursues her selfish aims by sly intrigue. Whether or not she resembles Pauline Viardot, she is representative of a type to which Turgenev frequently returns, and to which Veretyev's sister, Nadezhda Alexeevna, also belongs.

There is no doubt about the originals of the principal characters in the long-short story, *First Love*: it was acknowledged by the author to be based on his own adolescence, and the narrator, Vladimir Petrovich, is himself. A woman friend, N. A. Ostrovskaya, tells us that in a discussion of the story, his favourite among all his works, with him towards the end of his life, she asked, '"And the boy – surely he is a real person?" "That boy was your humble servant." "What? Were you really in love like that?" "Yes, I was." "And did you go about with a knife?" "Indeed I did."' Vladimir's father and mother were drawn from Turgenev's own father and mother. His mother was an extraordinary woman – passionate, self-willed, domineering, jealous, embittered by an unhappy childhood and by marriage to a handsome and dashing young officer, younger than herself, whom she adored, but who had married her only to retrieve his family's fortunes, and did not pretend to be anything but indifferent to her. She treated her serfs and servants with brutal despotism and often with extreme cruelty; over the sons she loved she tyrannized in the same way, and when her mounting disapproval of Ivan's associates and way of life reached a climax in 1845 she broke with him completely, cut off his allowance and never saw him again until 1850, when she was dying. The woman depicted in *First Love*, however, is less the harsh domestic tyrant than the jealous, unhappy wife who is bitterly conscious that she is neither loved nor liked by the husband she adores and fears. 'My mother led a sad life: she was in a perpetual state of agitation, jealousy and anger – but not in my father's presence; she was very much afraid of him, and he was always stern, cold and distant . . .' The story, although told in the first person, is remarkably objective in feeling, as much so as *A Lear of the Steppes*, which is also based on recollections from its author's youth, but earlier and less intimately personal ones.

Comparison of this story with the memoirs of a contemporary shows how closely Turgenev adhered to the essentials of the original happenings, which occurred in 1840 in a small village near his mother's estate of Spasskoe-Lutovinovo. The village belonged to Stepan Ivanovich Yaryshev, who 'gave away to his daughters all his land, leaving himself nothing but a little cottage. Stepan Ivanovich was of tall stature and ungainly build, but phenomenal strength; he led the simplest of lives, and in winter invariably wore a short sheepskin coat, in summer an ample frock-coat of homespun cloth . . . When his sons-in-law turned him out of his little house, he came in terrible distress to Varvara Petrovna Turgeneva at Spasskoe, bewailing the heartlessness of his daughters and asking for permission to live at Spasskoe; this Varvara Petrovna of course gave . . . One Sunday morning he disappeared from Spasskoe, and less than three hours afterwards a rider galloped over from Merkulovo with the news that Stepan Ivanovich had killed himself falling from the roof of his house, which he had begun to pull down.' Turgenev took immense pains to ensure that the bare bones of this story should be clothed in living flesh, inquiring from the steward of his estate all the legal details involved in the transfer of property, the necessary witnesses, and the police and government officials whose presence would be required and, with his usual care and precision in the use of language, asking also for the exact local terminology to describe the construction and timbers of a roof. What, however, makes this one of his most successful stories is, as always in his best work, the gallery of memorable and lifelike portraits, of a large number of minor characters as well as of the protagonist, Martyn Petrovich.

In all Turgenev's work it is the actors rather than the action that make the greatest impression and are best remembered. They are drawn with what seems remarkable economy and simplicity of means; where Turgenev excels is in the skill with which these apparently slight and almost casual strokes create not only the characters but their setting and the very atmosphere in which they live, the art which makes the reader's own imagination cooperate in that creation. Turgenev's first writings were in verse, and his prose at its best is the prose of a poet. This is not to say that it is 'poetical' prose, although it is true that some of his early writing and also some of his last is studied, elaborate, and rhapsodical; but in his best works, those that are still living today, the poet's precision in the use of language, the rhythms that please the poet's ear, are beautifully employed to render what is seen by the poet's eye. This mastery, this delicacy and sureness of touch, are felt perhaps even more clearly in the evocation of landscapes or the moods of nature than in the description of people. One example may be chosen from the many in the present volume: Lavretsky, driving to his estate, with the field-enclosures wheeling past like the spokes of a fan and 'a thin mist spreading like milk through the air', finds his dark mood turned to sweet, if melancholy, placidity, by 'the fresh, fertile, solitary bareness of the steppes, the greenness, the long lines of the hills, the fluid delicacy of the birches, the ravines with their stunted bushy oaks, the little grey hamlets'.

Writing like this offers the translator a challenge at once stimulating and daunting. The immediate appreciation of Turgenev when he was first introduced to the western world, however, shows that the challenge can be successfully met, and makes it possible to hope that this new translation will succeed in giving pleasure to English readers.

Jessie Coulson

A Nest of Gentlefolk

Characters

KALÍTINA, Maria Dmítrievna, *a widow*

"   Elizavéta Mikháylovna: Líza, *and*

"   Eléna Mikháylovna: Lénochka, *her daughters*

PESTÓVA, Martha Timoféevna, *her aunt*

PESTÓV, Dmítri Timoféich (Timoféevich), *Martha Timofeevna's brother*

GEDEÓNOVSKY, Sergéy Petróvich, *a neighbour*

PÁNSHIN, Vladímir Nikoláich (Nikoláevich)

LEMM, Christopher Fëdorych (Fëdorovich)

Shúrochka

OGÁRKOVA, Nastásya Kárpovna

LAVRÉTSKY, Fëdor Iványch (Ivánovich): Fédya, Fedyúsha

"   Iván Petróvich, *his father*

"   Peter Andréich (Andréevich), *his grandfather*

3

LAVRÉTSKAYA, Varvára Pávlovna (*née* KORÓBYINA), *Fëdor Ivanych's wife*

"   Malánya Sergéevna, *his mother*

"   Glafíra Petróvna, *his aunt*

"   Ánna Pávlovna, *his grandmother*

KOROBYÍN, Pável Petróvich, *his father-in-law*

KOROBYINÁ, Calliope Kárlovna, *his mother-in-law*

MIKHALÉVICH, *his university friend*

KUBÉNSKAYA, *Princess*

Vasílyevna

Antón

Apraxéya

A Note on Pronunciation

If the reader will remember (i) to give strong stress to the syllable marked with an accent in this list, (ii) to give the vowels their 'continental' value and pronounce the consonants as in English, a rough approximation to the Russian pronunciation will be obtained. The consonant translated 'kh' sounds rather like Scottish 'ch' in 'loch'; 'zh' represents a sound like 's' in 'measure'; 'ë' (always stressed) is pronounced roughly 'yo'; 'y' as a vowel is like English 'short i'; and the final '-v' is pronounced '-f'.

The patronymics ('middle' names) are frequently given a shorter pronunciation in colloquial speech, and this form is usually written by Turgenev, although when he is reporting more formal speech he gives the conventional spelling. In this list the shorter form is given first and the longer, in brackets, follows.

A Nest of Gentlefolk

I

THE BRIGHT SPRING DAY was declining towards evening and the little rosy clouds high in the clear sky seemed to be not so much floating past as retreating into the farthest recesses of the blue.

Before the open window of a very fine house on the outskirts of the provincial capital of O—— (this was in 1842), two women were sitting, one about fifty, the other an old woman of seventy.

The first was called Maria Dmitrievna Kalitina. Her husband, who had been the procurator of the province, and noted in his day for his business abilities, a quick-witted and determined man with an obstinate, bilious disposition, had died ten years before. He had received an exceptionally good education and studied at the university, but since he had been born in poor circumstances, he early realized the necessity of making his own way in the world and amassing money. Maria Dmitrievna had married him for love: he was clever and fairly good-looking and could be very attentive when he liked. Maria Dmitrievna, whose maiden name was Pestova, had lost her parents when she was still a child; after several years at school in Moscow she returned to the family estate of Pokrovskoe, some fifty versts from O——, where she lived with her aunt and her elder brother. Not long afterwards, the brother's duties in the service removed him to St Petersburg, and he kept his sister and his aunt in straitened circumstances until his career was brought to an end by his sudden death. Maria Dmitrievna inherited Pokrovskoe, but she did not live there long; a year after her marriage to Kalitin, who had succeeded in capturing her heart in the course of a few days, Pokrovskoe was exchanged for another estate, more profitable but unattractive, and with no house on it; at the same time Kalitin acquired a house in the town of O——, where he settled down to live with his wife. The house had a large garden, and on one side gave directly on to the country outside the town. 'Consequently,' decided Kalitin, who had very little relish for rural peace, 'there is no need for us ever to go trailing into the country.' In her heart Maria Dmitrievna many times regretted her pretty Pokrovskoe, with its cheerful little stream, wide meadows, and green groves; but she never crossed her husband in anything, and stood in awe of his intellect and knowledge of the world. When he died, after fifteen years of marriage, leaving a son and two daughters, Maria Dmitrievna had grown so used to her house and to town life that she had no desire to go away from O——.

In her youth Maria Dmitrievna had enjoyed the reputation of a very pretty little blonde, and at fifty her features, though somewhat overblown and less clear-cut, had not lost all their attractiveness. She was more sentimental than kind-hearted and in her riper years still preserved the habits of her schooldays; she indulged all her own whims and would fret and even cry when her routine was disturbed; but she was very sweet and charming when all her wishes were complied with and nobody opposed her in anything. Her house was one of the pleasantest in the town. She was well off, thanks not so much to what she had inherited from her family as to her husband's acquisitions. Both her daughters lived with her; her son was being educated in one of the best State academies in St Petersburg.

The old lady who was sitting at the window with Maria Dmitrievna was the same aunt, her father's sister, with whom she had shared several years of solitude in Pokrovskoe. She was called Martha Timofeevna Pestova. She was considered eccentric, had an independent temper, always spoke her mind without fear or favour and, with very scanty means, behaved as though she could dispose of thousands. She had not been able to abide the late Mr Kalitin and, as soon as her niece married him, removed herself to her own little estate, where she lived for ten years in a peasant's hovel so wretched it had not even a chimney. Small, sharp-nosed, still dark-haired and bright-eyed

9

in her old age, Martha Timofeevna moved briskly, held herself erect, and spoke rapidly and clearly in a shrill, penetrating voice. She always wore a white cap and blouse.

'What is it, niece?' she now asked abruptly. 'Why do you sigh?'

'Oh, nothing,' murmured the other. 'What wonderful clouds!'

'I suppose they make you feel sad, eh?'

Maria Dmitrievna did not answer.

'Why doesn't Gedeonovsky come?' said Martha Timofeevna, busy with her needles (she was knitting a large woollen scarf). 'He would be able to sigh with you – or else tell you some of his lying stories.'

'You are always so hard on him! Sergey Petrovich is a very worthy man.'

'Worthy!' repeated the old lady reproachfully.

'And he was so devoted to my dear husband!' said Maria Dmitrievna. 'To this day he cannot speak of him without emotion.'

'I should think not! It was your husband who dragged him out of the gutter!' grumbled Martha Timofeevna, the needles in her hands clicking still more rapidly.

'He looks so meek and mild,' she began again, 'with his grey hair, but every time he opens his mouth it's to tell a lie or slander somebody. And he a State Councillor! Well, of course he's only a priest's son!'

'Everybody has faults, auntie. Of course, that is his failing.

Sergey Petrovich, of course, is not well educated, and he can't speak French; but you must admit he's a nice man.'

'Yes, he's always kissing your hand. As for not speaking French – what a tragedy! That lingo isn't exactly my strong point, either. It would be better if he couldn't speak any language at all, then he wouldn't tell lies . . . Talk of the devil, there he is,' added Martha Timofeevna, glancing into the street. 'Here he comes, your nice man. Such a long, lean creature, just like a stork!'

Maria Dmitrievna patted her hair. Martha Timofeevna watched her with amusement.

'What is that, niece, surely not a grey hair? You should give your Palashka a good talking-to. What can she be thinking of?'

'Oh, auntie, you are always . . .' murmured Maria Dmitrievna, vexed, her fingers beating a tattoo on the arm of her chair.

'Sergey Petrovich Gedeonovsky!' squeaked a red-cheeked page, darting in through the door.

II

The tall man entering the room wore a neat frock-coat, shortish pantaloons, grey chamois gloves, and two stocks, a white one underneath and a black on top. Everything about him breathed propriety and decorum, from his handsome face and hair combed flat over the temples to his heel-less, noiseless boots. He bowed first to the mistress of the house and then to Martha Timofeevna, slowly drew off his gloves, advanced to take Maria Dmitrievna's hand, kissed it reverently twice, unhurriedly took his seat in an arm-chair and, rubbing the tips of his fingers together, inquired with a smile:

'And is Elizaveta Mikhaylovna well?'

'Yes,' replied Maria Dmitrievna; 'she is in the garden.'

'And Elena Mikhaylovna?'

'Lenochka is in the garden too. Is there any news?'

'Indeed there is, indeed there is,' answered the visitor, slowly blinking his eyes and thrusting out his lips. 'Hm! . . . this really is something new and very surprising: Fëdor Ivanych Lavretsky is here.'

'Fedya!' exclaimed Martha Timofeevna. 'Wait a minute, you're making this up, my good man, aren't you?'

'Not at all. I saw him with my own eyes.'

'Well, that still does not prove it.'

'He seems very flourishing,' continued Gedeonovsky, pretending that he had not heard Martha Timofeevna's comment. 'His shoulders are broader than ever, and his cheeks are full of colour.'

'Flourishing,' pronounced Maria Dmitrievna with great deliberation. 'I wonder what cause he has to be flourishing.'

'Yes,' answered Gedeonovsky. 'Any other man in his position would be ashamed to show his face.'

'Why, pray?' broke in Martha Timofeevna. 'What nonsense is this? A man comes back home – where do you want him to go? Besides, how is he to blame?'

'I venture to state, madam, that a husband is always to blame when his wife behaves badly.'

'You say that, my good man, because you are not married.' Gedeonovsky's smile was forced.

'Allow me to inquire,' he resumed after a short pause, 'for whom that charming scarf is intended.'

Martha Timofeevna threw him a rapid glance.

'It is intended,' she retorted, 'for someone who is neither a gossip, nor a hypocrite, nor a liar, if such a person exists on this earth. I know Fedya well. There is only one thing he can be blamed for – spoiling his wife. Well, he married for love, and no good ever comes of love matches,' added the old lady as she rose, with a side glance at Maria Dmitrievna. 'And now, my good man, you may sharpen your teeth on anybody you fancy – me if you like; I am going, I shall not hinder you.' And Martha Timofeevna departed.

'There, she's always like that,' said Maria Dmitrievna, following her aunt with her eyes, 'always!'

'It's her age! It can't be helped,' remarked Gedeonovsky. 'You know she said "somebody who isn't a hypocrite". But aren't we all hypocrites nowadays? It's the times we live in. A. friend of mine, a very respectable man and, I may tell you, an official not of the lowest rank, was saying that nowadays even a hen acts the hypocrite with a grain of corn and makes a dart at it, so to speak, from one side. But when I look at you, dear lady, your disposition is truly angelic; allow me to kiss your snow-white hand.'

Maria Dmitrievna smiled weakly and extended her plump hand with the little finger stuck stiffly out. He applied his lips to it and she moved her chair nearer to him and, bending slightly forward, asked in a lower tone:

'So you have seen him. Is he really all right, well and cheerful?'

'Yes, he's quite cheerful, he's all right,' Gedeonovsky answered in a whisper.

'Have you heard where his wife is now?'

'She was in Paris recently; now, I hear, she has gone to Italy.'

'It is terrible, really, Fedya's situation; I don't know how he puts up with it. Misfortunes can happen to anybody, of course, but his, you may say, have been published all over Europe.'

Gedeonovsky sighed.

'Ah, yes, yes. They say, you know, that she associates with artists and pianists and lions, as they call them in their language, and other wild beasts. She has quite lost all shame . . .'

'I feel very, very sorry for him,' said Maria Dmitrievna. 'As a relative; after all, as you know, he is my second cousin.'

'Yes, yes indeed. How could I fail to know something connected with your family? Of course I know.'

'Will he come to see us, do you think?'

'I should expect so; but I hear that he is making plans to go to his estate in the country.'

Maria Dmitrievna raised her eyes to heaven.

'Ah, Sergey Petrovich, Sergey Petrovich, when I think how carefully we women must behave!'

'There are women and women, Maria Dmitrievna. Unfortunately, there are some whose nature is flighty . . . and there are indiscreet ages, too; then some have not had the right principles drilled into them when they are young.' Sergey Petrovich took a blue check handkerchief from his pocket and began to unfold it. 'Such women certainly do exist.' Sergey Petrovich raised a corner of his handkerchief to each eye in turn. 'But generally speaking, if we judge rightly, that is . . . There is an extraordinary amount of dust in the streets,' he concluded.

'*Maman, maman,*' cried a pretty girl of about eleven, running into the room, 'Vladimir Nikolaich is coming on horseback!'

Maria Dmitrievna rose; Sergey Petrovich, also rising, bowed. 'My best respects to Elena Mikhaylovna,' he said, and, retreating for propriety's sake into a corner, applied himself to blowing his long and well-shaped nose.

'He's got such a marvellous horse!' the little girl continued. 'He was at the garden gate just now, and he told Liza and me he would ride up to the porch.'

There was a trampling of hoofs and a handsome rider on a beautiful bay horse appeared in the street and stopped before the open window.

III

'Good morning, Maria Dmitrievna,' the rider exclaimed in pleasant ringing tones. 'How do you like my new purchase?'

Maria Dmitrievna went to the window.

'Good morning, Woldemar! Oh, what a beauty! Who did you buy him from?'

'From the remount officer . . . Charged me a pretty penny, the robber.'

'What is his name?'

'Orlando . . . But it is a stupid name; I shall change it . . . *Eh bien, eh bien, mon garçon* . . . He is terribly restive.'

The horse was snorting, pawing the ground, and shaking its foam-flecked muzzle.

'Stroke him, Lenochka, don't be afraid . . .'

Lenochka stretched her hand out of the window, but Orlando suddenly reared and pranced away to one side. The rider, unperturbed, gripped the horse tighter with his knees, stretched the whip along his neck and, in spite of his resistance, brought him back before the window.

'*Prenez garde, prenez garde,*' Maria Dmitrievna repeated again and again.

'Stroke him, Lenochka,' said the horseman, 'I won't let him prance.'

The little girl again stretched out her hand and timidly

touched Orlando's trembling nostrils, while he quivered and champed his bit.

'Bravo!' exclaimed Maria Dmitrievna. 'Now dismount and come in.'

Skilfully the rider turned his horse, gave him a touch of the spurs, passed along the street at a hand-gallop and entered the courtyard. A minute later, waving his whip, he ran through the hall door into the drawing-room, and at the same time there appeared on the threshold of the other door a tall, graceful, black-haired girl of some nineteen years – Maria Dmitrievna's elder daughter Liza.

IV

The young man with whom we have just made our readers acquainted was called Vladimir Nikolaich Panshin. He was a civil servant in St Petersburg, in the Special Missions Department of the Foreign Office. He had come to O—— on a temporary government mission and was in attendance on the Governor, General Zonnenberg, whose distant relative he was. Panshin's father, a retired cavalry officer and a noted gambler, a man with wheedling eyes, a wrinkled face, and a nervous twitch of the lips, had rubbed shoulders all his life with the best society, frequented the English Clubs of both capitals, and passed for a shrewd, not very reliable, but genuine and decent chap. In spite of all his shrewdness, he found himself almost constantly on the very brink of beggary, and he left his only son a meagre and mismanaged fortune. On the other hand, he had done his best, in his own way, for his education; Vladimir Nikolaich spoke excellent French, good English, and bad German. This is as it should be: well-brought-up people would be ashamed to speak German well, but to let fall an odd German phrase in certain, for the most part humorous, circumstances, is permissible; *c'est même très chic*, as St Petersburg Parisians say. At the age of fifteen Vladimir Nikolaich already knew how to enter any drawing-room without embarrassment, circulate in it in a pleasing manner, and take himself off at the appropriate moment. His father had made many connexions for him; shuffling the cards between rubbers or relaxing after a successful grand slam, he missed no opportunity of putting in a word for his 'Volodka' to some important person with a taste for games of skill. On his side, Vladimir Nikolaich, while he attended the university, which he left with a not very distinguished degree, made the acquaintance of several young people of high rank and began to be received in the best houses. He was always welcome; he was handsome, easy-mannered, amusing, always in good health and ready for anything; where necessary, deferential, where possible, insolent, an excellent companion, *un charmant garçon*. Panshin early mastered the secret of dealing with the great world; he contrived to feel genuine respect for it, he knew how to treat trivialities with half-humorous gravity and appear to regard all weightier matters as trivialities; he danced remarkably well and dressed like an Englishman. Within a short time he had gained the reputation of one of the cleverest and most delightful young men in St Petersburg. He really was very clever, no less so than his father; he was also very talented. Everything came easily to him: he sang agreeably, drew skilfully, wrote verses, and was not at all bad as an actor. He was no more than twenty-two, and already he held an office at court and high rank in the service. Panshin firmly believed in himself, his own intellectual powers and his penetration; he forged ahead gaily and confidently; his life ran on well-oiled wheels. He was used to being liked by all, young and old, and saw himself as one who understood people, especially women: what he did know very well was their everyday weaknesses. As a devotee of the arts he felt within himself some of the fervour, impulsive ardour, and enthusiasm of the artist, and consequently allowed himself some deviation from the ordinary rules: dissipation, association with persons not belonging to good society, and free and easy manners; but at heart he was coldly hypocritical, and in the midst of the most abandoned self-indulgence the intelligent brown eye was always watchful, always on the alert; this free and daring youth could never quite forget himself or yield wholly to impulse. To his credit it must be said that he never boasted of his conquests.

On his arrival in O——, Panshin had quickly found his way to Maria Dmitrievna's house, and was soon completely at home there. Maria Dmitrievna would not hear a word against him. Now he bowed amiably to the whole room, pressed the hands of Maria Dmitrievna and Lizaveta Mikhaylovna, tapped Gedeonovsky lightly on the shoulder, then turned and took Lenochka's head between his hands and kissed her on the forehead.

'Aren't you afraid to ride such a vicious horse?' Maria Dmitrievna asked him.

'Oh, no, excuse me, he's very quiet. But I'll tell you what I am afraid of, and that is playing preference with Sergey Petrovich; yesterday at the Belenitsyns' he cleaned me out.'

Gedeonovsky's laugh was thin and servile: he always fawned upon the brilliant young St Petersburg official, the Governor's favourite. In conversation with Maria Dmitrievna he frequently referred to Panshin's remarkable capabilities. After all, he argued, how could one help praising him? The young man was a success in the highest social spheres, an exemplary official, and not in the least proud. Indeed, even in St Petersburg he was accounted a capable civil servant: work entrusted to him fairly bustled along; he spoke of it lightly, as befits a man of the world who does not take his labours too seriously, but he 'got things done'. The authorities like such subordinates; there was no doubt that if he chose he would in time be given a Ministry.

'You are pleased to say that you lost money to me,' said Gedeonovsky, 'but who was it who won twelve roubles from me last week? And again . . .'

'Ah, you wicked villain,' interrupted Panshin, with amiable

but slightly contemptuous lack of ceremony, and, paying him no further attention, went up to Liza.

'I haven't been able to get hold of the overture to *Oberon* here,' he began. 'Mme Belenitsyna was only boasting when she said she had all the classical music. In fact she has nothing but polkas and waltzes; but I have already written to Moscow, and within a week you shall have your overture. By the way,' he continued, 'I wrote a new ballad yesterday; the words are my own as well. Would you like me to sing it to you? I don't know how it has turned out; Mme Belenitsyna thought it charming, but what she says means nothing – I want your opinion. But perhaps it might be better to wait till later on.'

'Why later on?' put in Maria Dmitrievna. 'Why not now?'

'As you will,' said Panshin, with his own bright, sweet smile, which both appeared and vanished with great suddenness, and, moving up a chair with his knee, he sat down at the piano, struck a chord or two, and began to sing, articulating the words with great precision:

'Mid silver clouds remote the pale moon rides,
O'er earth and ocean;
Yet from on high its magic draws the tides
And gives them motion.
So my heart's tides, submissive to your reign,
Own you their moon;
So are they moved, in rapture or in pain,
By you alone.

Ah, racked by all the agonies of love
And sick at heart,
I see you, pitiless as that moon above,
Serene, apart.

The second couplet was sung by Panshin with particular expression and force; in the stormy accompaniment the tossing of the sea could be heard. After the words 'sick at heart' he sighed lightly, cast down his eyes and lowered his voice, *morendo*. When he finished, Liza praised the air, Maria Dmitrievna said 'Very pretty,' and Gedeonovsky exclaimed: 'Delightful! The poetry and the melody – both equally delightful!' Lenochka gazed with childish awe at the singer. In short, everybody in the room was very pleased with our young dilettante's composition; but outside the drawing-room door there stood a new arrival, an old man to whom, judging by the expression on his downcast face and the movement of his shoulders, Panshin's ballad, even if it was very pretty, gave no pleasure. After pausing for a moment to dust his boots with a pocket-handkerchief of coarse quality, this man, screwing up his eyes, sullenly compressing his lips, and stooping still further his bowed shoulders, slowly entered the room.

'Ah, Christopher Fëdorych, how are you?' exclaimed Panshin, before anybody else could speak, hurriedly jumping up from his chair. 'I had no idea you were here; nothing would have induced me to sing my ballad in your presence. I know you are not fond of light music.'

'I listened not,' the new-comer answered in bad Russian, bowing to all the company and then stopping awkwardly in the middle of the room.

'Have you come to give Liza her music-lesson, Monsieur Lemm?' asked Maria Dmitrievna.

'No, not Lissafet Mikhaylovna, Elen Mikhaylovna.'

'Oh. Well, that's very nice. Lenochka, go upstairs with Mr Lemm.'

The old man was following the little girl when Panshin stopped him.

'Don't go away after the lesson, Christopher Fёdorych,' he said. 'Lizaveta Mikhaylovna and I are going to play Beethoven's Sonata for four hands.'

The old man grumbled something under his breath, and Panshin continued in German, with a very bad accent:

'Lizaveta Mikhaylovna has shown me the sacred cantata you dedicated to her – a beautiful thing! Please do not think I am incapable of appreciating serious music. On the contrary: it may sometimes be tedious, but then it is good for us.'

The old man coloured to the roots of his hair, cast a sidelong glance at Liza, and hurried out of the room.

Maria Dmitrievna requested Panshin to repeat his ballad, but he declared that he did not wish to offend the ears of the learned German and proposed to Liza that they should tackle the Beethoven sonata. Maria Dmitrievna sighed and suggested that Gedeonovsky should walk with her in the garden. 'I want to talk about our poor Fedya,' she said, 'and ask your advice.' Gedeonovsky smirked, bowed, with two fingers took up his hat, on the brim of which his gloves were neatly laid, and went off with Maria Dmitrievna. Panshin and Liza remained in the drawing-room; she took out the music and opened it, and both sat down at the piano without a word. From above floated down the hesitant notes of a scale played by Lenochka's stumbling little fingers.

V

Christopher Theodore Gottlieb Lemm, the son of poor musicians, was born in 1786 in the town of Chemnitz in the kingdom of Saxony. His father played the French horn, his mother the harp. He himself was practising three different instruments by his fifth year. He was orphaned at the age of eight, and when he was ten began to earn his bread by his art. For a long time he led a wandering life, playing everywhere – in taverns, at fairs, at country weddings, and at balls; finally, he joined an orchestra and, steadily gaining promotion, attained the position of conductor. He was a rather poor executant, but his knowledge of music was profound. In his twenty-eighth year he removed to Russia, at the summons of a great nobleman who could not bear music but maintained an orchestra out of vanity. Lemm spent seven years with him in the capacity of *Kapellmeister* and left his service empty-handed; the nobleman was ruined, and though he at one time proposed to give him a note of hand, he subsequently refused him even that – in short, he did not pay him a copeck. Lemm was advised to leave the country, but he did not wish to return home a pauper from Russia, great Russia, that gold-mine for artists; he resolved to stay and try his luck. The poor German tried his luck for twenty years: he served various masters, lived both in Moscow and in provincial towns, endured and suffered much, knew destitution, struggled like a fish on dry land; but in the midst of all his misfortunes, the dream of returning to his own country never left him; indeed, it alone supported him. But it did not please the fates to grant him this first and last happiness: in his fifties, old before his time, and ill, he came to anchor in the town of O—— and remained there for good, finally deprived of all hope of leaving the Russia he hated and somehow contriving to support his meagre existence by giving lessons. Lemm's outward appearance did not dispose people in his favour. He was short and stooping, with crooked shoulders, shrunken belly, large flat feet, and livid nails at the ends of the strong, permanently bent fingers of his muscular red hands; he had a wrinkled face with hollow cheeks and compressed lips, whose constant mumbling motion, combined with his habitual taciturnity, produced an almost sinister effect; his grey hair hung in tufts over his low forehead; his tiny eyes with their fixed expression glowed dimly like the embers of a dying fire; with every ponderous step his ungainly body lurched from side to side. Some of his movements recalled the clumsy scufflings of a caged owl which feels it is being watched but can itself hardly see with its great yellow eyes, blinking with fear and somnolence. Ancient, inexorable griefs had set their ineradicable mark on the poor musician, deforming and disfiguring his already unprepossessing person; but anybody who was capable of going beyond first impressions would see something good and honest, something out of the ordinary, in this half-derelict creature. A devotee of Bach and Handel, an expert in his own subject, gifted with a lively imagination and that speculative boldness which is attainable only by the German race, Lemm might – who knows? – have become one of the great composers of his people, if his life had led him into other places; but he had not been born under a lucky star. He had written much in his time – and had never had the good fortune to see one of his compositions published: he did not know how to set about it properly, recommending himself in the right quarters and choosing the opportune moment for action. Once, a very long time previously, it had happened that a friend and admirer of his, also a German and also poor, had published two of his sonatas at his own expense – but even they remained undisturbed in the cellars of the music-shops; they disappeared silently and without trace, as though they had been dropped by night into the river. Lemm had finally come to regard all this with a shrug of indifference; besides, age had also taken its toll of him: just as his fingers had grown rigid, he had grown hard and stiff. Alone with an old cook whom he had rescued from the poor-house (he had never married), he lived in a small house in O——— not far from

26

Maria Dmitrievna's; he went for many walks and read the Bible, a Lutheran psalm-book, and Schlegel's translation of Shakespeare. He had written nothing for a long time, but evidently Liza, his best pupil, had been able to inspire him: it was for her that he had composed the cantata Panshin had mentioned. He had taken the words from his psalter and himself written a few additional verses. It was meant to be sung by two choruses, one of those blest by fortune and the other of the ill-starred; both joined in harmony at the end and sang together: 'Merciful God, forgive us sinners and deliver us from all evil thoughts and worldly hopes.' On the title-page, written with elaborate care and even ornamented with flourishes, stood the words 'Only the Righteous are Justified. A sacred cantata. Composed and dedicated to my dear pupil, Miss Elizaveta Kalitina, by her teacher, C. G. T. Lemm.' The words 'Only the Righteous are Justified' and 'Elizaveta Kalitina' were haloed with radiating lines. Underneath was written: 'For you alone: *für Sie allein.*' This was why Lemm had crimsoned and looked askance at Liza; he was deeply hurt that Panshin should speak to him of his cantata.

VI

Panshin loudly and firmly struck the first notes of the sonata (he was playing the bass part), but Liza did not begin. He stopped and looked at her. Liza's eyes, gazing straight at him, expressed displeasure; her lips did not smile, her whole face looked stern and sad.

'What is the matter?' he asked.

'Why did you not keep your word?' she said. 'I showed you Christopher Fëdorych's cantata on condition that you should not speak of it to him.'

'I am sorry, Lizaveta Mikhaylovna. I was carried away.'

'You have offended him – and me as well. Now he will not trust even me.'

'What would you have, Lizaveta Mikhaylovna? I've never been able to stand Germans since I was so high: so I couldn't resist teasing him.'

'How can you say that, Vladimir Nikolaich? This German is a poor, lonely, broken man – and you are not sorry for him? You feel obliged to torment him?'

Panshin was taken aback.

'You are right, Lizaveta Mikhaylovna,' he said. 'My eternal thoughtlessness is to blame for everything. No, don't contradict me: I know myself well. My thoughtlessness has done a great deal of harm. It is thanks to it that I have acquired the reputation of an egoist.'

Panshin paused. Whatever the subject with which he began a conversation, he usually ended by talking about himself, and the effect was somehow one of pleasant and endearing, apparently spontaneous, intimacy.

'Even here in your house,' he went on, 'your mother is, of

course, very kind to me – she is so good; you – but I don't know your opinion of me; your aunt, on the other hand, simply cannot bear me. I must have offended her, too, by some stupid, thoughtless word. She doesn't like me, you know, does she?'

'No,' said Liza, with a slight hesitation, 'she doesn't care for you.'

Panshin ran his fingers rapidly over the keyboard; an almost imperceptible sneer touched his lips.

'And you?' he said. 'Do you think I am an egoist, too?'

'I don't know you very well yet,' answered Liza, 'but I don't consider you an egoist; on the contrary, I ought to thank you . . .'

'I know, I know what you are going to say,' Panshin interrupted, again running his hand over the keys, '– for the music, for the books I bring you, for the bad drawings I beautify your album with, and so on, and so forth. I can do all this – and still be an egoist. I make bold to imagine that I do not bore you and that you don't consider me a bad fellow, but all the same you assume that I – how the devil does the phrase go? – would spare neither father nor friend to make a bad joke.'

'You are careless and forgetful, like all men of the world, that is all,' said Liza.

Panshin frowned slightly.

'Listen,' said he, 'let us not talk about me any longer, let us begin to play our sonata. But one thing I beg of you,' he added, flattening with his hand the sheets of music on the stand, 'think what you will of me, call me an egoist even, if you like – so be it! but don't call me a man of the world: I cannot endure that name . . . *Anch'io sono pittore*. I too am an artist, if a bad one, and I will prove it to you – that I am a bad artist, I mean, and prove it now, in practice. Let us begin.'

'Very well, let us begin,' said Liza.

The first *adagio* went fairly well, although Panshin made more than one mistake. His own compositions and things he had studied he played very nicely, but he was bad at reading music. But the second movement, a fairly quick *allegro*, did not go at all: at the twentieth bar Panshin, who was two bars behind, broke down and laughingly pushed back his chair.

'No!' he exclaimed, 'I can't play today. It is a good thing Lemm didn't hear us; he would have swooned away.'

Liza stood up, closed the piano, and turned to Panshin.

'What shall we do, then?' she asked.

'How like you that question is! You are quite unable to sit still and do nothing. Well, if you like, we can do some drawing before the light has quite gone. Perhaps another muse, the muse of painting – what's her name? I've quite forgotten – will be kinder to me. Where is your album? I seem to remember there is a landscape in it I didn't finish.'

Liza went into the other room for her album and Panshin, left alone, took a cambric handkerchief from his pocket, polished his fingernails with it, and squinted admiringly at his hands. They were very white and beautiful; on his left thumb he wore a spiral gold ring. Liza returned and Panshin sat down by the window and opened the album.

'Ah!' he exclaimed. 'I see you have begun to copy my landscape – and very well too. Excellent! Only just here – give me a pencil – the shadows are not quite strong enough. Look.'

And Panshin added several long sweeping strokes of the pencil. He always drew one and the same landscape: a foreground of large trees with untidy masses of foliage, a glade in the middle distance and jagged mountain-peaks on the horizon.

'In drawing – and in life generally –' said Panshin, tilting his head first to the right and then to the left, 'ease and boldness are of the first importance.'

At this moment Lemm entered the room and, bowing coldly, attempted to make his escape; but Panshin laid aside the album and pencil and barred his way.

'Where are you going, my dear Christopher Fëdorych? Aren't you staying for tea?'

'I am going home,' morosely answered Lemm. 'I have a headache.'

'What nonsense is this? Do stay. We will argue about Shakespeare.'

'I have a headache,' repeated the old man.

'We had a shot at the Beethoven sonata while you were not here,' went on Panshin, laying his arm amiably round the other's shoulders and smiling brightly, 'but nothing went right. Imagine, I couldn't strike two consecutive notes without a mistake.'

'You would better haf again played your ballad,' retorted Lemm, removed Panshin's arm and went out.

Liza ran after him. She overtook him in the porch.

'Christopher Fëdorych, listen to me,' she said in German, accompanying him over the short green grass of the courtyard to the gate. 'I behaved badly to you – forgive me.'

Lemm did not answer.

'I showed Vladimir Nikolaich your cantata; I was sure he would appreciate it – and indeed, he did like it very much.'

Lemm stopped.

'It does not matter,' he said in Russian, and then added in his native tongue, 'but he cannot understand anything; why can you not see that? He is a dilettante – nothing more.'

'You are unjust to him,' Liza replied. 'He understands everything, and he can do nearly everything himself.'

'Yes, second-rate light stuff, tossed off in a moment. People like it, and they like him, and he is pleased with that; well and good. But I am not angry; my cantata and I are both old fools; I am a little ashamed, but it does not matter.'

'Forgive me, Christopher Fëdorych,' said Liza again.

'It does not matter, it does not matter,' he repeated in Russian. 'You are a good girl – and here is somebody coming to see you. Goodbye. You are a very good girl.'

And Lemm quickened his steps towards the gate, by which a gentleman unknown to him, in a grey overcoat and wide straw hat, had just entered. Bowing politely (he bowed to all new-comers in the town, but he turned away when he met acquaintances – this was the rule he had made for himself), Lemm passed him and disappeared beyond the fence. The stranger's eyes followed him in astonishment, and then he saw Liza and walked towards her.

VII

'You do not recognize me,' he said, taking off his hat, 'but I knew you at once, although eight years have gone by since I last saw you. You were a child then. I am Lavretsky. Is your mother at home? May I see her?'

'Mother will be very glad,' answered Liza. 'She heard you were here.'

'Your name, I think, is Elizaveta, isn't it?' said Lavretsky, mounting the steps to the front door.

'Yes.'

'I remember you well. You already had the kind of face that is not forgotten. In those days I used to bring you sweets.'

Liza blushed and thought, 'How odd he is!' In the hall Lavretsky stopped for a moment, and Liza went into the drawing-room, where Panshin could be heard talking and laughing; he was retailing some of the town gossip to Maria Dmitrievna and Gedeonovsky, who had returned from the garden, and laughing loudly at his own remarks. At Lavretsky's name Maria

Dmitrievna, turning pale, rose in confusion and went towards him.

'How do you do, how do you do, my dear cousin?' she exclaimed in a languid and almost tearful voice. 'How glad I am to see you!'

'How do you do, my kind cousin?' answered Lavretsky, affectionately clasping her outstretched hand. 'How are things with you?'

'Sit down, sit down, dear Fëdor Ivanych. Oh, how glad I am! Allow me first to introduce my daughter Liza to you . . .'

'I have already introduced myself to Lizaveta Mikhaylovna,' Lavretsky interrupted.

'Monsieur Panshin – Sergey Petrovich Gedeonovsky . . . But do sit down! I look at you and really I can hardly believe my eyes. How are you?'

'As you see, I am flourishing. And you too, cousin – touch wood! – have not grown any thinner in these eight years.'

'When you think how long it is since we saw each other,' mused Maria Dmitrievna. 'Where have you come from now? Where did you leave – that is,' she amended hastily, 'I meant to say, are you here for long?'

'I have just come from Berlin,' answered Lavretsky, and tomorrow I am going into the country – probably for some time.'

'You will live at Lavriki, of course?'

'No, not at Lavriki; I have a small estate about twenty-five versts from here. I shall go there.'

'Is that the estate Glafira Petrovna left you?'

'Yes, that is the one.'

'But really, Fëdor Ivanych! You have such a wonderful house at Lavriki!'

Lavretsky's frown was barely perceptible.

'Yes . . . but there is a small house on the other estate, and that is all I need for the time being. It is the most convenient place for me just now.'

Maria Dmitrievna was at a loss, and could only sit up straight and fling out her hands. Panshin came to her aid and entered into conversation with Lavretsky. Maria Dmitrievna grew calmer, leaned back in her chair, and only put in a word here and there; but at the same time she looked at her visitor with such commiseration, sighed so significantly and shook her head so mournfully that he grew tired of it at length and asked her with some asperity if she were not well.

'Yes, thank God,' answered Maria Dmitrievna. 'But why?'

'Oh, I thought you did not seem yourself.'

Maria Dmitrievna took on a dignified and somewhat injured expression. 'Well, if that is how you feel,' she thought, 'I am sure it makes no difference to me. Evidently, my dear sir, it is all like water off a duck's back to you. Anybody else might be pining away with grief, but you seem to thrive on it.' When she talked to herself, Maria Dmitrievna did not mince matters; aloud, she expressed herself more elegantly.

Lavretsky really did not resemble a victim of fate. From his red-cheeked, purely Russian face with its wide white forehead, thickish nose and big straight mouth there seemed to breathe the health of the steppes and a vigorous, lasting strength. He was extraordinarily strongly built and his fair hair curled over his head like a boy's. Only his prominent, rather fixed blue eyes revealed something between weariness and thoughtfulness, and his voice sounded somehow too level.

Meanwhile, Panshin continued to sustain the conversation. He turned it to the profits of sugar-refining, on which he had recently read two French pamphlets, and with quiet modesty set himself to expound their contents without, however, saying a single word about the pamphlets themselves.

'But surely that is Fedya!' suddenly said Martha Timofeevna's voice from beyond the half-open door of the next room, 'Fedya himself!' And the old lady darted into the drawing-room. Before Lavretsky had time to rise from his chair, she was embracing him. 'Let me look at you, let me look at you,' she said, moving far enough away to see his face. 'Well! You look splendid! You are older, but still just as handsome. But why do you kiss my hand? Kiss me, if you don't find my wrinkled cheeks too repellent. I'm sure you didn't even ask if old auntie was still alive. And yet I held you in my arms when you were born, and a rare little rascal you were! Well, that doesn't matter; why should you remember about me? But you did right to come. Well, my dear,' she added, turning to Maria Dmitrievna, 'have you given him anything to eat?'

'I don't want anything,' said Lavretsky hastily.

'Why, you must at least have some tea, my dear. Good God! Here he arrives from heaven knows where, and they don't offer him so much as a cup of tea! Liza, go and see to it, as quick as you can. I remember he was terribly greedy when he was little, and no doubt he still likes his food.'

'My respects to you, Martha Timofeevna,' said Panshin, coming up to the excited old lady and bowing low.

'Excuse me, my dear sir,' replied Martha Timofeevna, 'in my excitement I didn't notice you. You have grown like your darling mother,' she continued, again addressing Lavretsky, 'only you always had your father's nose, and you have it still. Well – are you here for long?'

'I am going away tomorrow, auntie.'

'Where to?'

'To my place at Vasilyevskoe.'

'Tomorrow?'

'Yes, tomorrow.'

'Well, if it must be tomorrow, tomorrow it must be. I suppose you know best. Only see you come and say goodbye!' The old lady tapped his cheek. 'I didn't think I should live to see you again; not that I am thinking of dying; no, I am good for perhaps ten years yet: all we Pestovs are long-lived; your late grandfather used to say we were indestructible; but after all, God only knows how long you might have gone on wasting time abroad. Well, you look splendid, splendid; I suppose you can still lift ten poods with one hand? Your poor father, excuse my saying so, was a terrible fool, but he did the right thing when he engaged that Swiss for you; do you remember how you used to fight him with your fists? – gymnastics they call that, don't they? But I mustn't go running on like this; I am preventing Mr Panshín' (she would never give his name the correct pronunciation, Pánshin) 'from giving us one of his clever talks. Let us have tea, and let us go out on the terrace for it, my dear. We have some marvellous cream, not like you get in your Londons and your Parises. Come along, come along! and you, Fedyusha, give me your arm. Oh, how solid it is! You certainly would never let one fall.'

Everybody stood up and went out on the terrace, with the exception of Gedeonovsky, who quietly stole away. During the whole of Lavretsky's conversation with their hostess, Panshin, and Martha Timofeevna, he had sat in the corner blinking attentively and pouting with childish curiosity; now he was in a hurry to carry the news of the visitor all over the town.

At eleven o'clock that evening the situation in Maria Dmitrievna's house was this: downstairs at the drawing-room door, Vladimir Nikolaich had seized a favourable opportunity and was holding Liza's hand as he bade her goodnight and saying: 'You know who it is that brings me here; you know why I am always visiting this house; what need is there for words, when everything is clear without them?' Liza did not answer; she stood gazing unsmiling at the floor, with slightly raised eyebrows and a flush on her cheeks, but she did not take away her hand. Upstairs, in Martha Timofeevna's room, by the faint light of the lamp hanging before the dim, ancient icons, Lavretsky sat in an arm-chair with his elbows on his knees and his head in his hands; the old lady, standing before him, smoothed his hair from time to time in silence. He had spent more than an hour with her after taking leave of his hostess; but he had told his good old friend almost nothing, and she had not asked him any questions . . . And indeed, what was there to say, and what need for questions? She understood well enough as it was, and felt for him in everything that filled his heart to overflowing.

VIII

Fëdor Ivanych Lavretsky (we must ask the reader's permission to break the thread of our story for a time) came from an ancient noble family. The founder of the Lavretskys came from Prussia in the reign of Basil the Blind and was granted two hundred chetverts of land on the Upper Bezhetsk. Many of his descendants served in various departments of State or under princes and famous men in remote provinces, but none of them raised himself to very high office or amassed any great fortune. The richest and most distinguished of all the Lavretskys was Fëdor Ivanych's great-grandfather Andrey, a cruel, bold, wise and subtle man. To this very day men still talk of his tyranny, his fierce temper, his extravagant generosity and his insatiable cupidity. He was very tall and heavily built, with a swarthy, beardless face, a burr in his voice, and a sleepy look; but the more gently he spoke, the more those around him quaked. He found himself a wife who was a good match for him. Of gipsy stock, goggle-eyed, hawk-nosed, yellow-skinned, round-faced, hot-tempered and vindictive, she held her own in every way with her husband, who all but killed her, and whom she did not long survive, although her quarrels with him had been incessant. Andrey's son Peter, Fëdor's grandfather, was not like his father: he was a simple gentleman of the steppes, rather hare-brained, loud-voiced, sluggish, boorish but not ill-natured, hospitable, and fond of hunting. He was over thirty when he inherited an estate of two thousand souls, in admirable order, from his father, but he had soon dispersed the peasants, sold part of the land, and demoralized his domestic serfs. Like cockroaches, swarms of insignificant little people, acquaintances and strangers alike, came crawling from everywhere into his spacious, warm and untidy house; the whole collection ate their fill of what they could get, drank themselves drunk, and carried off whatever they could, extolling and glorifying their bountiful host; and their host, when he was out of humour, glorified his guests, too – as spongers and scoundrels; but without them he was bored. Peter Andreich's wife was a submissive creature; he had taken her from a neighbouring family, by the choice and at the command of his father; her name was Anna Pavlovna. She interfered in nothing, cordially welcomed guests and herself went out very willingly, although, in her own words, it was death to her to be powdered. They would put, she used to tell in her old age, a felt bandeau round your head, comb all your hair upwards, smear it with grease, sprinkle it with flour and stick steel pins into it – you couldn't wash it clean afterwards; but to go out in society without powder was impossible – people would be offended. Sheer torture! She liked driving behind fast horses, and was prepared to play cards from dawn till dark; if her husband approached the card-table, she would always cover up with her hand the note of the few copecks she might have won, but she had placed her dowry and all her money absolutely at his disposal. She had two children: a son, Ivan, Fëdor's father, and a daughter, Glafira. Ivan was not brought up at home but with a rich old aunt, Princess Kubenskaya: she had named him her heir (otherwise his father would not have let him go to her); she dressed him up like a doll, engaged all kinds of instructors for him, and appointed a tutor, a certain Frenchman, formerly an abbé, Monsieur Courtin de Vaucelles. He had been a pupil of Jean-Jaques Rousseau's and was an adept and subtle intriguer and the absolute *fine fleur*, as the Princess expressed it, of the emigration; she ended by marrying the *fine fleur* when she was almost seventy years old, transferred all her property to him and soon afterwards, painted and powdered, scented *à la Richelieu*, surrounded by negro pages, elegant little dogs, and screeching parrots, she died, lying on a curly, silk-covered Louis-Quinze sofa, with an enamel snuff-box by Petitot in her hand – and died deserted by her husband: the plausible M. Courtin had chosen to remove himself, and her fortune, to Paris. Ivan was only twenty when this unexpected and crushing blow – we are speaking of the Princess's marriage, not her death – fell on him; he had no desire to remain in his aunt's house, where he had been suddenly transformed from the rich heir to a needy hanger-on; in St Petersburg the society in which he had grown up was closed to him; he loathed the idea of the obscure and laborious life of a clerk in the lower grades of the civil service (all this took place at the beginning of the reign of the Emperor Alexander); he was forced, willy-nilly, to return to the country and to his father. Dirty, poverty-stricken, squalid – this was how the family nest appeared to him; the life of the steppes offended him at every step by its stagnant and primitive quality; he was ravaged by boredom; to crown all, everybody in the house, except his mother, regarded him with hostility. His father did not like his city ways, his frock-coats and jabots, his books, his flute, or his cleanness and neatness, in which he scented, not without reason, fastidious disgust: every now and then he complained and grumbled at his son. 'Nothing is right for him here,' he would say; 'he's too dainty at table and only picks at his food, he can't endure the way the servants smell, he thinks our rooms are stuffy, the sight of a drunken man upsets him, you daren't strike anybody when he's about, and he won't work: his health is too delicate, you see; pah, what a milksop! And all because his head is full of Voltaire.' The old man particularly disliked

Voltaire and 'that fanatic' Diderot, although he had not read a word of their writings: reading was not in his line. Peter Andreich was not mistaken: his son's head was indeed full of Diderot and Voltaire, and not only of them, but of Rousseau and Raynal and Helvetius, and many similar writers besides – but only his head. Ivan Petrovich's old tutor, the former abbé and encyclopaedist, was satisfied that he had steeped his pupil in all the enlightenment of the eighteenth century, and his pupil was indeed saturated with it; but it simply existed in him, without mingling with his blood, or penetrating to his soul, or expressing itself in strong convictions . . . How, indeed, could one expect convictions in a young man of fifty years ago, when even now we have not acquired them? The guests in his father's house also found Ivan Petrovich in the way; he loathed them and they feared him. With his sister Glafira, who was twelve years older than he, he did not get on at all. This Glafira was a strange creature: plain, round-shouldered, lean, with stern, wide-open eyes and thin, compressed lips, she was reminiscent in her face, voice, and quick, angular movements of her gipsy grandmother, Andrey's wife. Stiff-necked and power-loving, she refused even to consider marriage. Ivan Petrovich's return was not at all to her liking; while Princess Kubenskaya kept him at her side, she could hope to inherit at least half of her father's estate: cupidity was another respect in which she resembled her grandmother. Besides, Glafira was jealous of her brother; he was so well-educated and spoke such good French, with a Parisian accent, whereas she

43

could barely say 'bon joor' and 'commong vous portay-vous?' It is true that her parents did not speak French at all, but this made things no better for her. Ivan Petrovich did not know what to do for boredom and misery; he had spent a year in the country without a break and it felt like more than ten. Only with his mother could he find distraction, and he used to sit for hours in her low-ceilinged rooms, eating preserves and listening to the good woman's simple chatter. It happened that among Anna Pavlovna's servants there was a very pretty girl, with meek, bright eyes and delicate features, called Malanya; she was a modest and sensible girl. She caught Ivan Petrovich's eye from the very beginning, and he fell in love with her: he loved her timid gait, her shy speech, her soft voice and gentle smile; every day she became dearer to him. And she was devoted to Ivan Petrovich, as only Russian girls can be devoted, with all the strength of her soul – and gave herself to him. In a country house no secret can be kept for long; soon everybody knew of the tie between the young master and Malanya; news of the attachment came at last to the ears of Peter Andreich himself. At another time he would probably have paid no attention to a matter of such minor importance; but he had long been nursing his irritation with his son and was glad of the opportunity to put the clever St Petersburg dandy to shame. There was a tremendous hue and cry: Malanya was locked in a store-room; his father sent for Ivan Petrovich. Anna Pavlovna also came running at the uproar. She made some attempt to pacify her husband, but Peter Andreich was past hearing anything. He pounced on his son like a hawk, accusing him of immorality, atheism, and hypocrisy; he seized the chance of venting on him all his accumulated spite against Princess Kubenskaya, and heaped him with insults. At first Ivan Petrovich steeled himself and said nothing, but when his father took it into his head to threaten him with humiliating punishment, he could endure it no longer. 'That fanatic Diderot has been brought up again,' he thought; 'so I will let fly with him too, just wait. I'll surprise you all!' And then and there, in a quiet, even tone, although with an inward tremor in every limb, Ivan Petrovich declared that his father had no cause to reproach him with immorality; that although he did not intend to justify his fault, he was prepared to rectify it, the more willingly as he felt himself to be superior to all prejudice – and, specifically, was ready to marry Malanya. With these words, Ivan Petrovich certainly achieved his purpose: Peter Andreich was so taken aback that his eyes started out of his head and he was momentarily struck dumb; but he recovered himself immediately, and just as he was, in his squirrel-trimmed jacket, with slippers on his bare feet, flung himself with flailing fists on Ivan Petrovich who, as though by design, had that day dressed his hair *à la Titus* and put on a new, dark-blue, English frock-coat, tasselled boots and foppish, tight-fitting buckskin breeches. Anna Pavlovna screamed with all the power of her lungs, while her son fled through the house, darted into the yard, and rushed through the garden and the kitchen-garden and out into the street, running all the time without a backward glance until he ceased to hear behind him the heavy drumming of his father's feet and his violent, spasmodic cries . . . 'Stop, you scoundrel!' he bawled. 'Stop! My curse on you!' Ivan Petrovich took refuge in the house of a poor neighbouring gentleman, and Peter Andreich returned home exhausted and sweating, announced almost before he had got his breath back that he would deprive his son of both his parental blessing and his inheritance, and gave orders that all his damfool books should be burnt and the girl Malanya sent to a distant estate. Kind friends sought out Ivan Petrovich and informed him of all this. Shamed and furiously angry, he vowed to be revenged on his father, and that same night he lay in wait for the peasant's cart in which Malanya was being conveyed, snatched her away by force, galloped off with her to the nearest town, and married her. He had been supplied with money by the neighbour, a good-hearted and perpetually drunken retired sailor, with a passionate interest in any kind of 'well-bred' (as he called it) story. The next day Ivan Petrovich wrote a bitingly cold and polite letter to Peter Andreich and betook himself to the village where his cousin Dmitri Pestov lived with his sister, already known to the reader, Martha Timofeevna. He told them everything, explained that he meant to go to St Petersburg to look for a position, and begged them to give his wife asylum at least for a time. At the word 'wife' he shed bitter tears and, in spite of his St Petersburg education and his philosophy, he knelt at his relatives' feet like the poor, humble

Russian suppliant that he was, and even knocked his forehead on the ground. The Pestovs, good, compassionate people, willingly consented; he stayed with them for three weeks, secretly hoping for an answer from his father; but no answer came – and none was possible. When Peter Andreich learned of his son's marriage, he took to his bed and forbade Ivan Petrovich's name to be mentioned in his presence; but his mother, unknown to her husband, borrowed five hundred paper roubles from the archdeacon and sent them, with a small icon, to her son's wife; she was afraid to write, but sent word to Ivan Petrovich by a scrawny peasant messenger, who could cover up to sixty versts a day on foot, that he must not be too distressed, that, God willing, everything would come right and his father's anger turn to kindness; that she too could have wished for another daughter-in-law, but that evidently it was God's will and therefore she sent Malanya Sergeevna her blessing. The scrawny peasant, rewarded with a rouble, asked permission to see the new mistress, whose godfather it seemed he was, kissed her hand, and hastened home.

Ivan Petrovich went off to St Petersburg with a light heart. An unknown future awaited him; poverty, it might be, threatened him; but he had said goodbye to the detested life in the country and, most important, had not betrayed his teachers but really 'let fly with' and justified in action Rousseau, Diderot, and the *Déclaration des droits de l'homme*. Feelings of duty accomplished, of triumph and of pride, filled his soul; and the parting from his wife held no distress for him; he would have found more disturbing the necessity of living permanently with her. That matter had been dealt with; it was necessary to turn to others. In St Petersburg, contrary to his own expectations, he had a stroke of luck: Princess Kubenskaya – who had already been deserted by M. Courtin but was not yet on her death-bed – tried to make some amends to her nephew by recommending him to all her friends, and by giving him five thousand roubles, almost the very last of her money, and a watch by Lepic, bearing his initials in a wreath of cupids. Before three months had passed, he had been given a post in the Russian legation in London and set sail (steamships had not yet been invented) in the first English vessel to leave. A few months later he received a letter from Pestov, in which the good gentleman congratulated him on the birth of his son, who first saw the light on 20 August, 1807, in the village of Pokrovskoe, and was named Fëdor in honour of the blessed martyr Theodore Stratilatus. Because she was still very weak, Malanya Sergeevna added only a few lines, but even those few lines astonished Ivan Petrovich: he did not know that Martha Timofeevna had taught his wife to read and write. Ivan Petrovich, however, did not long give himself up to the gratifying emotions of fatherhood; he was paying court to some famous Phryne or Lais of the time (classical names were still in vogue in those days); the peace of Tilsit had just been concluded and the whole world was hastening to enjoy itself; everything was caught up in a sort of mad whirl, and the black eyes of his bold beauty set his head, too, whirling. He had very little money, but he was lucky at cards, made many acquaintances, took part in all kinds of festivity, in short, he was launched on prosperous seas.

IX

For a long time old Lavretsky could not pardon his son's marriage; if Ivan Petrovich had gone to him after six months, full of contrition and fallen at his feet, he might perhaps have forgiven him, having first abused him roundly and given him a rap with his stick to frighten him; but Ivan Petrovich was living abroad and, to all appearances, cared not a straw. 'How dare you? Be quiet!' Peter Andreich would repeat, every time his wife tried to incline him towards leniency. 'The puppy! He ought never to stop thanking God that I haven't laid my curse on him; my old father would have killed the good-for-nothing scoundrel with his own hands, and he would have been right!' Anna Pavlovna, at these terrible words, could only cross herself stealthily. As for Ivan Petrovich's wife, Peter Andreich refused at first even to hear her spoken of, and when Pestov mentioned his daughter-in-law in a letter, ordered him to be told in answer that he knew nothing of any so-called daughter-in-law, but thought it his duty to warn him that the law forbade the harbouring of runaway wenches. Later, learning of the birth of his grandson, he relented a little, gave orders that the health of the mother should be inquired after, casually, and sent her a little money, but as though it did not come from himself. Fedya was not yet a year old when Anna Pavlovna sickened with a mortal illness. Some days before the end, when she could no longer rise from her bed, she revealed to her husband, in the presence of her confessor, and with apprehensive tears in her dimming eyes, her wish to see and say farewell to her daughter-in-law and give her blessing to her grandson. The grief-stricken old man comforted her and immediately sent his own carriage for his daughter-in-law, whom for the first time he referred to as Malanya Sergeevna. She arrived with her son and Martha Timofeevna, who would not for the world have let her go alone or be insulted. Half-dead with fear, Malanya Sergeevna entered Peter Andreich's study. Behind her the nurse carried Fedya. Peter Andreich looked at her in silence; she approached his hand and her trembling lips barely closed on it in a soundless kiss.

'Well, my jumped-up fine lady,' he said at last, 'how do you do? Let us go to the mistress.'

He rose and bent over Fedya; the baby smiled and held out his pale little hands to him. The old man's mood was changed.

'Oh,' he said, 'poor little thing! You plead your father's cause well; I will not forsake you, my little bird.'

As soon as Malanya Sergeevna entered Anna Pavlovna's bedroom she fell on her knees by the door. Anna Pavlovna beckoned her to the bedside, embraced her, and blessed her son; then, turning her face, ravaged by her cruel illness, to her husband, she tried to speak . . .

'I know,' said Peter Andreich, 'I know what you want to ask me. Don't grieve: she shall stay here with us, and I will pardon Vanka for her sake.'

Anna Pavlovna, with an effort, took her husband's hand and pressed her lips to it. That same evening she died.

Peter Andreich kept his word. He informed his son that by his mother's dying wish and for the sake of the baby he would no longer withhold his blessing, and would keep Malanya Sergeevna in his house. She was assigned two rooms in the attic; he introduced her to his most honoured guests, one-eyed Brigadier Skurekhin and his wife; and he gave her two maids and a boy to run errands. Martha Timofeevna said goodbye to her; she had taken a violent dislike to Glafira, and quarrelled with her no less than three times in the course of one day.

It was an awkward and difficult life for the poor woman at first, but afterwards she learned to endure it and grew used to her father-in-law. He grew used to her, too, and even fond of her, although he hardly ever talked to her and even at his most affectionate displayed a certain involuntary disdain. Malanya Sergeevna had most to endure from her sister-in-law. While her mother was still alive, Glafira had managed to get the whole control of the household gradually into her own hands; everybody, from her father down, deferred to her; without her permission not so much as a piece of sugar could be doled out; she would rather have died than shared her authority with another mistress of the house – and such a mistress! She had been even more outraged than Peter Andreich by her brother's marriage; she set herself to school the upstart, and from the first moment Malanya Sergeevna was her slave. Indeed, how could she, meek, always troubled and fearful, and in poor health, resist the wilful and imperious Glafira? Not a day passed but Glafira reminded her of her former condition and praised her for not forgetting it. Malanya Sergeevna would willingly have resigned herself to these reminders and praises, bitter though they were ... but Fedya was taken away from her: this was what broke her. On the pretext that her health did not permit her to undertake his education, she was hardly ever permitted to see him; Glafira took charge and the boy came completely under her control. In her grief, Malanya Sergeevna began to implore Ivan Petrovich in her letters to return as soon as he could, and Peter Andreich himself wished to see his son, but Ivan Petrovich only went on writing to thank his father for having received his wife and for the money he sent, and promising to come shortly – but he did not come. It was 1812 that finally brought him home from abroad. Meeting for the first time after six years of separation, father and son embraced and said not a word of their former differences; there was no time for that now: all Russia was rising against the enemy, and both felt that Russian blood ran in their veins. Peter Andreich equipped a whole regiment of militia at his own expense. But the war ended, the danger passed, Ivan Petrovich again grew bored and longed to be far away, in that world with which he had identified himself and in which he felt at home. Malanya Sergeevna had no power to hold him back; she meant too little to him. Even what she had hoped for had not come about: her husband also considered it much more suitable that Fedya's education should be entrusted to Glafira. Ivan Petrovich's poor wife could not endure this blow and the renewed separation from her husband; within a few days, without a murmur, she pined away and died. Throughout her life she had never offered resistance to anything and she did not struggle against her illness. When she was already past speech, and the shadows of the grave lay on her face, her features still expressed her former patient perplexity and enduring humility; with the same dumb submission as before she looked at Glafira, and as Anna Pavlovna on her death-bed had kissed Peter Andreich's hand, she kissed Glafira's, entrusting to her her only son. So a quiet and gentle creature, torn, God knows why, from her native soil and immediately abandoned, like a sapling dragged out of the ground and left lying with its roots in the sun, ended her earthly course; she faded and vanished without leaving a trace, this poor creature, and nobody mourned for her. Only her maids regretted Malanya Sergeevna, and Peter Andreich. The old man missed her silent presence. 'Forgive – and farewell, my gentle dear!' he whispered, taking his last leave of her, in the church. He was weeping as he threw a handful of earth into her grave.

He survived her by only five years. In the winter of 1819 he died peacefully in Moscow, where he had gone with Glafira and his grandson: he left directions that he should be buried beside

Anna Pavlovna and 'Malasha', At the time, Ivan Petrovich was in Paris, for his own pleasure; he had retired from the service after 1815. When he learned of his father's death, he decided to return to Russia. He must think about the organization of the estate; besides, Fedya, as a letter from Glafira pointed out, was twelve years old and the time had come to take a serious interest in his education.

X

Ivan Petrovich returned to Russia an Anglomaniac. His close-cropped hair, high starched collar, long-skirted many-caped pea-green coat, his sour expression, something both harsh and indifferent in his manner, his way of speaking through his teeth, his abrupt, wooden-sounding laughter, his absence of smiles, his conversation exclusively concerned with politics and political economy, his love of underdone beef and port wine – everything about him spoke of Great Britain; its spirit seemed to have completely permeated him. But strange to say, in turning Anglomaniac, Ivan Petrovich had also turned patriot, or at least he called himself a patriot, although he knew little of Russia, did not observe Russian customs, and expressed himself very oddly in the Russian language: in ordinary conversation his languid and halting speech was diversified with many Gallicisms; but as soon as the talk turned on subjects of importance, Ivan

Petrovich began to use expressions like 'exercise new experiments in self-diligence', 'out of agreement with the circumstantial nature', and so on. He had brought back with him various manuscript schemes relating to the organization and improvement of the government; he was very displeased with everything he saw, and the lack of system especially aroused his sour disapprobation. When he met his sister, his first words to her were a declaration that he intended to introduce radical reforms and that henceforth all his affairs were to be regulated according to a new system. Glafira Petrovna did not answer him, only clenched her teeth and wondered: 'What is to become of *me*?' When, however, she returned to the country with her brother and nephew, she was soon reassured. Some changes were indeed effected in the house: the parasites and hangers-on quickly found themselves turned out of doors; among the victims of this eviction were two old women, one blind and the other paralysed, and a decrepit old major of Catherine the Great's day who, because of his really remarkable greed, was fed exclusively on black bread and lentils. Orders were given also that none of the former guests were to be received: their place was taken by a distant neighbour, a blonde, scrofulous baron, highly educated and extremely stupid. New furniture from Moscow made its appearance; so did spittoons, bells, and wash-hand-stands; luncheon was served in a different way; foreign wines replaced the vodkas and cordials; new liveries were made for the servants; the family coat of arms had added to it the motto 'In recto virtus' . . . In substance, though,

Glafira's power was no whit less: all the stores and purchases depended on her, as before; the Alsatian house-steward, imported from abroad, tried conclusions with her – and lost his place, in spite of being the master's own protégé. As for the farming and management of the estates (Glafira Petrovna had a share in this, too), although Ivan Petrovich had repeatedly expressed the intention of breathing new life into the chaos, everything remained as before, except that here and there rents were raised, or the compulsory work on the master's land increased, or the peasants forbidden to approach Ivan Petrovich directly: the 'patriot' heartily despised his fellow countrymen. Ivan Petrovich's system was applied in its full force only to Fedya: his education really did undergo 'radical reform'; all his father's attention was concentrated on him.

XI

Until Ivan Petrovich's return from abroad, Fedya, as has been said, was entirely in Glafira Petrovna's charge. He was not eight years old when his mother died; he had not seen her every day, but he loved her passionately: the memory of her still, pale face, her sad looks, and her timid caresses, was imprinted for ever in his heart; but he dimly understood her position in the house; he felt that between himself and her there was a barrier which she dared not and could not break down. He fought shy of his father, and Ivan Petrovich never displayed any affection for him; his grandfather occasionally smoothed his hair and allowed him to kiss his hand, but called him a little savage and considered him stupid. After Malanya Sergeevna's death his aunt was entirely responsible for him. Fedya was afraid of her, afraid of her bright sharp eyes and her strident voice; he dared not utter a sound in her presence; if he so much as stirred, she snapped out, 'Where are you going? Sit still!' On Sundays, after church, he was allowed to play; that is, he was given a thick book, a mysterious book, the work of one Maximovich-Ambodik, entitled *Symbols and Emblems*. The book contained something like a thousand drawings, some of them highly enigmatical, with equally cryptic comments in five languages. A plump and naked Cupid played a large part in these drawings. To one of them, called 'Saffron and Rainbow' was appended the commentary: 'This possesses great efficacy'; opposite another, representing 'A Heron flying with a Violet in its Beak', was written 'All these are known to you'. 'Cupid and a She-bear licking her Cub' signified 'Little by little'. Fedya pored over these drawings; he knew them down to the smallest detail; some, always the same ones, plunged him into day-dreams and stirred his imagination; he had no other amusements. When the time came to teach him music and languages, Glafira Petrovna engaged, for a trifling salary, an elderly spinster, a Swede with timorous eyes, who spoke indifferent French and German and played the piano after a fashion, but who made excellent pickled cucumbers. In the society of this preceptress, his aunt, and an old house-serf, Vasilyevna, Fedya spent four whole years. He used to sit in a corner with his 'Emblems' – sit for hours; the low-ceilinged room smelt of geraniums, the one tallow candle gave a feeble light, a cricket chirped away on one note as though it were bored, a mouse scrabbled and gnawed stealthily behind the wallpaper, and the three old women, like the three Fates, rapidly and silently plied their knitting-needles, while the shadows from their hands fled up the walls or wavered strangely in the half-light, and thoughts equally strange and equally shadowy thronged the child's mind. Nobody would have called Fedya an interesting child: he was rather pale, but thickset, clumsy, and awkward – a regular peasant, in Glafira Petrovna's words; the pallor would soon have disappeared from his cheeks if he had been allowed out in the fresh air a little oftener. He was fairly good at his lessons, although he was often lazy; he never cried; on the other hand, he had occasional fits of mulish obstinacy; at such times he was completely unmanageable by anybody. Fedya did not love any of the people surrounding him . . . Woe to the heart that does not know love in youth!

Such was the state in which Ivan Petrovich found him, and he set himself without delay to put his new system into operation. 'I want above all to make a man of him, *un homme*,' he said to Glafira Petrovna, 'and not only a man, a Spartan.' Ivan Petrovich's first step towards the fulfilment of his intention was to dress his son in the Scottish fashion: at twelve years old the boy began to go about with bare knees and a cock's feather in his Glengarry bonnet; the

Swedish instructress was replaced by a young Swiss tutor, who was an expert in gymnastics; music, as a pursuit unworthy of a man, was banished for ever; the natural sciences, international law, mathematics, the carpenter's craft, in accordance with Jean-Jaques Rousseau's advice, and heraldry, to foster knightly sentiments – these were to be the pursuits of the future 'man'; he was awakened at half-past four in the morning, given a cold shower, and made to run round a high pole on a rope; he had one meal a day, consisting of a single dish; he rode on horseback and shot with a cross-bow; on every suitable occasion, with his parent as a model, he practised strength of will, and every evening he entered in a special book his account of the past day and the impression it had made on him; Ivan Petrovich, on his side, wrote him edifying screeds in French, in which he called him *mon fils* and addressed him as *vous*. In Russian Fedya called his father thou, but he dared not sit down in his presence. The 'system' bewildered the boy, planted confusion in his mind and cramped it; but the new way of life had, on the other hand, a beneficial effect on his health; at the beginning he caught a feverish cold, but he soon recovered and developed into a fine upstanding lad. His father congratulated himself and called him, in his strange idiom, 'a son of nature and my creation'. When Fedya was sixteen, Ivan Petrovich judged it his duty to implant contempt for the female sex in him in good time – and the young Spartan, with bashfulness in his heart and the first down on his upper lip, full of sap, strength, and red blood, strove to appear indifferent, cold, and churlish.

Meanwhile, time passed steadily. Ivan Petrovich spent the greater part of the year at Lavriki (this was the name of the principal family estate), and in the winter travelled to Moscow alone, stayed in a very modest hotel, diligently frequented his club, held forth in drawing-rooms, developing his plans, and remained more of an Anglophile, a grumbler, and a man of politics than ever. But the year 1825 came, and brought much sorrow with it. Many of Ivan Petrovich's acquaintances and close friends suffered trying ordeals. Ivan Petrovich hurriedly retired to the country and shut himself up in his house. Another year passed and Ivan Petrovich suddenly began to be weak, sickly, and ill; his robust health had deserted him. The freethinker began to go to church and order prayers for himself; the European began to steam himself for long periods in the bath, dine at two o'clock, go to bed at nine, and fall asleep to the sound of the old steward's ramblings; the political thinker burned all his plans and correspondence, trembled before the Governor, and fidgeted in the presence of the chief of police; the man of iron will whined and whimpered when he had a boil or his soup was cold. Once more Glafira ruled the whole house; once again stewards, bailiffs, and simple peasants began to come to the back door to talk to the 'old battle-axe', as the house-serfs called her. The change in Ivan Petrovich made a powerful impression on his son; he was nineteen and was beginning to think for himself and shake off the oppressive weight of his father's hand. Even before this he had noticed the difference between his father's words and his deeds, between his generous liberal theories and his harsh petty despotism; but he had not expected so abrupt a transformation. All at once the inveterate egoist stood completely revealed. Young Lavretsky was getting ready to go to Moscow, to prepare for the university, when a new and unexpected misfortune came down on Ivan Petrovich's head: he went blind, without any hope of recovery, in a single day.

Not trusting the skill of Russian doctors, he began making strenuous efforts to get permission to go abroad. He was refused. Then, taking his son with him, he spent three years travelling all over Russia from one doctor to another, journeying ceaselessly from town to town and reducing his doctors, his son, and his servants to despair by his cowardice and impatience. He returned to Lavriki a fearful, lachrymose and capricious child. In the painful days that followed, everybody had much to bear from him. Ivan Petrovich subsided only at meal-times; he had never eaten so much or so greedily; all the rest of the time he gave neither himself nor anybody else any peace. He prayed incessantly, railed at his fate, cursed himself, his system, everything he had taken pride in and boasted of, everything he had once set before his son as an example; he insisted that he had no faith in anything, and then returned to his prayers; he could not bear a moment's solitude and demanded that the members of his household should sit by his chair constantly, day and night, and entertain him with stories, which he interrupted every now and then with exclamations of 'Don't tell so many lies! – what rubbish!'

It was especially hard on Glafira Petrovna; he simply could not get on without her – and to the end she fulfilled every whim of the invalid, although sometimes she could not answer him at once lest the sound of her voice should betray the bitter anger that choked her. In this way he creaked along for a further two years and died early in May, when he had been carried out on the balcony in the sunshine. 'Glasha, Glashka! My beef-tea, my beef-tea, you old idi—,' his stiffening tongue stammered out and, without finishing the last word, fell silent for ever. Glafira Petrovna, who had just taken the cup of beef-tea from the steward's hands, stopped, looked into her brother's face, crossed herself with a slow, sweeping gesture, and retreated without a word; his son, who was present, also said nothing, but leaned on the balcony railing and for a long time contemplated the garden, all green and scented, sparkling in the rays of golden spring sunshine. He was twenty-three years old; with what terrible and unnoticed swiftness those twenty-three years had passed! ... Life was opening out before him.

XII

Having buried his father and entrusted to the changeless Glafira Petrovna the management of the estate and the supervision of the bailiffs, young Lavretsky, driven by an obscure but powerful emotion, departed for Moscow. He was conscious of the defects of his education and intended as far as possible to remedy its deficiencies. During the past five years he had read much and seen something; many ideas were fermenting in his brain; any professor might have envied some of his knowledge, but at the same time he was ignorant of much that had long been familiar to every schoolboy. Lavretsky recognized that he was not free; secretly he felt that he was an oddity. It was a sorry joke that the Anglomaniac had played on his son; his eccentric upbringing had borne fruit. For long years he had submitted without question to his father; when at last he saw through him, the mischief was done, the habits had taken root. He could not get close to people: twenty-three years old, with an unquenchable thirst for love in his shy heart, he had never dared to look any woman in the face. With his intelligence, clear and sound but a little ponderous, with his tendency to stubbornness, contemplation, and indolence, he ought to have been plunged from his earliest years into the maelstrom of life, and instead he had been kept in artificial solitude . . . Now that the charmed circle was dissolved, he continued to stand in the same spot, imprisoned within himself. To adopt the uniform of a student at his age was ludicrous; but he was not afraid of ridicule: his spartan training had served at least one purpose, that of developing in him a contempt for other people's opinions – and he donned the student's uniform without embarrassment. He enrolled in the faculty of physics and mathematics. Robust, taciturn, red-cheeked, with a beard already bushy, he produced a strange effect on his fellow students; they did not suspect that within the stern man arriving punctually for lectures in a wide country sledge with a pair of horses there was concealed almost a child. He seemed to them some odd sort of pedant, they wanted and expected nothing from him, and he avoided them. During the first two years he spent at the university, he made friends with only one student, from whom he took lessons in Latin. This student, Mikhalevich by name, an enthusiast and a poet, was sincerely attached to Lavretsky, and quite by accident became responsible for a major change in his fate.

One night at the theatre (Mochalov was then at the height of his fame and Lavretsky never missed a performance) he saw a young girl in one of the boxes of the grand tier – and although not a single woman ever passed by his gloomy figure without making his heart quiver, it had never quivered so violently before. The young lady sat without moving, leaning her elbows on the velvet of the box-ledge; there was a lively play of youth and sensitivity in her dark, round, pretty face; a refined intelligence shone in the beautiful eyes, with their soft, attentive gaze from under the delicate brows, in the quick smile of the expressive mouth, in the very posture of the head, arms, and neck; she was charmingly dressed. Next to her sat a yellow, wrinkled woman of some five and forty, decolletée, wearing a black toque, with a toothless smile on her intent yet empty face; an elderly man, in a wide frock-coat and a high collar, with a wheedling yet suspicious look in his little eyes, with a dyed moustache and whiskers, great meaningless forehead and withered cheeks – to all appearances a retired general – was visible in the back of the box. Lavretsky did not take his eyes off the girl who had captured his attention; suddenly the door of the box opened and Mikhalevich walked in. The appearance of this man, almost the only person he knew in the whole of Moscow, his appearance in the company of this one girl who absorbed all his attention, seemed to Lavretsky startling and strange. He continued to watch the box and saw that all the persons in it treated Mikhalevich as an old friend. What was happening on the stage ceased to interest Lavretsky; even Mochalov himself, although he was in form that evening, did not produce his usual effect on him. At one very pathetic passage, Lavretsky involuntarily looked at his beauty: she was leaning forward, her cheeks flushed; under the influence of his persistent gaze her eyes, which had been fixed on the stage, slowly turned and rested on him . . . All night he saw those eyes before him. The artificially constructed dam had given way at last: he trembled, he was on fire. The next day he sought out Mikhalevich. From him he learned that the beauty's name was Varvara Pavlovna Korobyina; that the older man and woman sitting in the box with her were her father and mother and that he, Mikhalevich, had made their acquaintance a year before, while he was a tutor in the household of Count N——, near Moscow. The enthusiast spoke with the highest praise of Varvara Pavlovna. 'That, my boy,' he exclaimed, with his characteristic warbling voice and fitful emphasis, 'that girl is an astounding creature, a genius, an artist in the true sense of the word, and extremely good-hearted besides.' Seeing from Lavretsky's questions what an impression Varvara Pavlovna had made on him, he offered to introduce him to her, adding that he was perfectly at home in their house, that the general was not at all proud, and that the mother was so silly that she was all but weak-minded. Lavretsky blushed, mumbled something inarticulate, and fled. For five whole days he struggled with his shyness; on the sixth the young Spartan donned a new uniform and put himself at the disposal of Mikhalevich, who, being his own servant, confined himself to brushing his hair – and both took themselves off to the Korobyins'.

XIII

Varvara Pavlovna's father, Pavel Petrovich Korobyin, a retired major-general, had spent all his life in the service in St Petersburg. As a young man he had the reputation of a good dancer and a military expert, was obliged by his poverty to serve as adjutant to two or three insignificant generals, married the daughter of one of them, with a dowry of some twenty-five thousand, developed to a fine art his skill in parades and reviews, toiled and drudged, toiled and drudged, and at last, after about twenty years, attained the rank of general and got his regiment. Now he might have rested on his oars and, without haste, consolidated his prosperous position; indeed, this was what he had counted on, but he managed matters a little carelessly: he invented a new method of putting government funds to good use; the method proved to be excellent, but he failed to be generous at the right moment and was informed against: the consequence was a more than unpleasant, indeed a very nasty, scandal. The general struggled out of his difficulties somehow, but his career was ruined; he was advised to hand in his resignation. For a year or two he hung about in St Petersburg, in the hope that a snug little civilian job would fall into his lap; but the job did not materialize; his daughter had left school, his expenses were increasing every day . . . Reluctantly he made up his mind to go to Moscow, where the cost of living was low, rented a tiny, low-pitched house in Old Stable Street, with a seven-foot-high coat of arms on the roof, and settled down to the life of a retired general on 2,750 roubles a year. Moscow is a hospitable town, glad to welcome all and sundry, especially generals; Pavel Petrovich's figure, corpulent but still retaining its military bearing, soon made its appearance in the best Moscow drawing-rooms. The back of his bald head, with its few sparse dyed hairs, and the soiled ribbon of the Order of St Anne on his raven-black cravat, became familiar to the pale, languid, young men who loitered listlessly about the card-tables during the dancing. Pavel Petrovich knew how to establish himself in society; he spoke little but, from old habit, with condescension – not, of course, to those of higher rank; he was a cautious card-player; at home he ate frugally, but at other people's tables enough for six. Of his wife there is almost nothing to say: her name was Calliope Karlovna; her left eye was inclined to water, and on the strength of this Calliope Karlovna (who was, moreover, of German origin) considered herself a woman of refined sensibility; she was always in fear of something, always looked as though she had not enough to eat, and wore narrow velvet dresses, toques, and tarnished pinchbeck bracelets. The only daughter of Pavel Petrovich and Calliope Karlovna, Varvara Pavlovna, was just turned seventeen when she left her boarding-school, in which she had been considered, if not the most beautiful, certainly the cleverest girl and the best musician, and where she had won the Empress's prize for the best pupil; she was not yet nineteen when Lavretsky saw her for the first time.

XIV

The Spartan's knees were buckling under him when Mikhalevich led him into the Korobyins' rather poorly furnished drawing-room and presented him to his hosts. But his overwhelming shyness soon vanished; in the general the good nature inborn in all Russians was intensified into that special kind of affability peculiar to those whose reputations have been slightly blown upon; the general's wife soon effaced herself; as for Varvara Pavlovna, she was so tranquil and sweetly self-possessed that in her presence everybody immediately felt at home; besides, from her whole captivating being, her smiling eyes, her faultlessly sloping shoulders and pink-tinged white hands, her light but yet languid-seeming movements, from the very sound of her voice, lingering and sweet, there breathed an ingratiating charm, as unseizable as a subtle perfume, a soft and as yet timid voluptuousness, something difficult to express in words, but both touching and provocative – and it was not, of course, shyness that it provoked. Lavretsky led the conversation to the theatre and the previous day's performance; she immediately began to speak of Mochalov, and did not confine herself to mere exclamations and rapturous sighs, but commented judiciously and with feminine perception on his acting. Mikhalevich mentioned music; she sat down at the piano without any fuss and played, accurately, several of Chopin's mazurkas, then just becoming fashionable. It was the dinner-hour; Lavretsky would have left, but they made him stay; at table, the general regaled him with a good Lafitte, for which his manservant had been sent galloping off to Desprez's in a cab. When Lavretsky reached home, late that night, he sat for a long time without undressing, his hand over his eyes, in a trance of fascination. It seemed to him that he was realizing for the first time what made life worth living; all his plans and hypotheses, all that stuff and nonsense, had disappeared in an instant; his whole being was fused into one emotion, one desire, the desire for happiness, for possession, for love, the sweet love of a woman. From that day he began to haunt the Korobyins'

house. Six months later he declared his love to Varvara Pavlovna and offered her his hand. The offer was accepted; long
before, almost before Lavretsky's first visit, the general had
inquired of Mikhalevich how many serfs Lavretsky owned; and
Varvara Pavlovna herself, who had preserved throughout the
young man's courtship, and indeed in the very moment of his
declaration of love, her habitual serenity and clarity of mind,
Varvara Pavlovna herself was very well aware that her fiancé
was rich; and Calliope Karlovna thought, '*Meine Tochter macht
eine schöne Partie*' – and bought herself a new toque.

XV

Lavretsky's offer, then, was accepted, but on certain conditions.
First, he must leave the university immediately: who ever heard
of marrying a student? and indeed, what an odd idea for a rich
man, a landowner, to be learning lessons at twenty-six years old
like a schoolboy! Second, Varvara Pavlovna charged herself with
the ordering and buying of her dowry and even the choosing of
the bridegroom's presents. She had much practical ability, a great
deal of taste, an immense love of comfort, and a great capacity
for procuring it for herself. This capacity seemed particularly
striking to Lavretsky when, immediately after the wedding,
he and his wife set off together for Lavriki in the comfortable
travelling-carriage she had purchased. What care, forethought,

and anticipation were disclosed by everything surrounding him! What charming travelling dressing-cases in various cosy niches, what delightful toilet-boxes and equipment for making coffee, and how prettily Varvara Pavlovna herself made coffee in the mornings! Lavretsky, however, at that time had little attention to spare for such things: he was blissfully happy, he revelled in happiness, he gave himself completely up to it, like a child . . . He was, indeed, innocently child-like, this youthful Alcides. It was not for nothing that the whole being of his young wife had radiated fascination, not for nothing that it promised to the senses the secret luxury of unexplored delights: it concealed even more than it promised.

Arriving at Lavriki in the full blaze of summer, Varvara Pavlovna found the house dark and dirty and the servants antiquated and ridiculous, but she did not consider it necessary even to hint at this to her husband. If she had been disposed to settle at Lavriki, she would have altered everything in it, beginning, needless to say, with the house; but the idea of remaining in those remote regions of the steppes never for one moment entered her head; she lived there as if she were camping out, uncomplainingly putting up with all the inconveniences, and making fun of them very amusingly. Martha Timofeevna came to see her nursling; Varvara Pavlovna liked her very much, but she did not like Varvara Pavlovna. The new mistress of the house did not get on with Glafira Petrovna either; she would have left her in peace, but old Korobyin wanted to have a hand in his son-in-law's affairs; to manage the estates of so close a relative, he said, was no disgrace even to a general. It must be supposed that Pavel Petrovich would not have shown any reluctance to occupy himself with the estate even of a complete stranger. Varvara Pavlovna conducted her campaign very skilfully; without revealing her hand in advance, and while she was apparently engrossed in honeymoon bliss, peaceful country life, music and reading, she gradually drove Glafira to the point where, one morning, she burst like a madwoman into Lavretsky's study and, flinging a bunch of keys on the table, announced that she had not the strength to go on looking after things and that she refused to stay any longer. Having been duly prepared beforehand, Lavretsky immediately agreed to her departure. Glafira Petrovna had not expected this. 'Very well!' she said, and her eyes darkened, 'I see I am not wanted here! I know who is driving me away from the nest I was born in. Only remember my words, nephew: you are not fated to build yourself a nest anywhere, you must be a wanderer for ever. That is my last word to you.' The same day she removed herself to her little property, and a week later General Korobyin arrived and, with good-humoured resignation in his looks and gestures, took the management of the whole estate into his hands.

In September Varvara Pavlovna took her husband away to St Petersburg. There she spent two winters (they removed to Tsarskoe Selo for the summer) in a fine, light, elegantly furnished flat; they made many acquaintances in the middle and even higher social circles, went out and received a great deal, and gave the most charming musical evenings and dances. Varvara Pavlovna attracted guests like moths to a light. Fëdor Ivanych was not altogether pleased with a life so aimless. His wife advised him to enter the civil service; the memory of his father and his own ideas prevented him from doing so, but to please Varvara Pavlovna he remained in St Petersburg. He soon realized, however, that nobody wished to prevent him from leading his own solitary life, that it was not for nothing that he had the quietest and most comfortable study in the whole of St Petersburg, and that his solicitous wife was even ready to assist him to preserve his solitude – and from that moment everything went swimmingly. He applied himself once more to his own education, which had been left, in his opinion, unfinished, began to read again, and even started the study of the English language. It was strange to see his powerful, broad-shouldered form for ever stooping over a desk and his round, whiskered, ruddy face half hidden in a dictionary or a notebook. He spent every morning working, dined excellently (Varvara Pavlovna was an unsurpassed housekeeper), and in the evening entered an enchanting, brightly lighted, scented world, inhabited by gay young people, the central point of which was that same careful housekeeper, Varvara Pavlovna. She gratified him by bearing him a son, but the poor boy did not live long; he died in the spring, and in the summer, on the advice of his doctors, Lavretsky took his wife abroad to a spa. Distraction was essential to her after such a misfortune, and besides, her health required a

73

warm climate. They spent the summer and autumn in Germany and Switzerland and, as was to be expected, went to Paris for the winter. In Paris, Varvara Pavlovna blossomed like a rose, and contrived to make a little nest for herself as quickly and adroitly as she had done in St Petersburg. She found a pretty little flat in a quiet but fashionable street, ordered her husband such a dressing-gown as he had never worn before, engaged a chic maid, an excellent cook, and a smart manservant, and acquired a delightful little carriage and a charming little upright piano. Before a week had passed, she could cross the street, wear a shawl, open an umbrella, or put on her gloves like a Parisian born. She very quickly acquired acquaintances also. At first only Russians came to call on her, but then Frenchmen began to appear, all highly agreeable, polished, unmarried, with beautiful manners and euphonious names; they all talked a great deal, and very fast, bowed with easy grace, and grimaced very pleasantly; every one had white teeth that flashed beneath rosy lips – and how well they knew how to smile! Each one brought his friends, and soon *la belle Madame de Lavretsky* was known from the Chaussée d'Antin to the Rue de Lille. In those days (this was in 1836) the tribe of reporters and gossip-writers, who now swarm everywhere like ants in an overturned ant-heap, had not yet appeared; but even then a certain M. Jules, a gentleman of unprepossessing exterior and scandalous reputation, base and impudent, like everybody who fights duels or gets horse-whipped, used to be seen in Varvara Pavlovna's salon. This M. Jules was loathsome to Varvara Pavlovna, but she received him because he wrote for various newspapers and constantly mentioned her, referring to her now as *Mme de L . . . tₓki*, now as *Mme de* ——, *cette grande dame russe si distinguée, qui demeure rue de P.*, and informing the world (that is, some hundreds of subscribers who had not the slightest interest in *Mme de L . . . tₓki*) how gracious and amiable a lady she was, a true Frenchwoman in mind (*une vraie française par l'esprit*) – the French know no higher praise – what an unusually accomplished musician she was, and how marvellously she waltzed (Varvara Pavlovna really did waltz in a fashion that drew all hearts after the flying gossamer hems of her skirts); in short, he spread abroad her fame to the world, and that, whatever one may say, is pleasant. Mlle Mars had already left the stage, Mlle Rachel had not yet appeared on it; nevertheless, Varvara Pavlovna assiduously attended the theatres. She went into raptures over Italian music and laughed at the ruins of Odri, yawned decorously at the Comédie Française, and wept at the performance of Mlle Dorval in some ultra-romantic melodrama. And, most important of all, Liszt played for her twice, and he was so kind, so unassuming – charming! Amid such pleasant sensations the winter passed; towards the end of it, Varvara Pavlovna was even presented at court. Fëdor Ivanych, for his part, was not bored, although at times life weighed a little heavy on his hands – heavy, because empty. He read the newspapers, attended lectures at the Sorbonne and the Collège de France, followed the debates in the Assembly, and undertook the translation of a well-known scientific work on irrigation. 'I am not wasting time,' he thought;

'all this is useful; but before next winter I must return to Russia and set to work.' It is difficult to say whether he had any clear conception of what exactly that work would consist in, and God only knows whether he would have managed to return to Russia before the winter; meanwhile he was going to Baden-Baden with his wife ... An unexpected happening destroyed all his plans.

XVI

Going into Varvara Pavlovna's room one day in her absence, Lavretsky saw on the floor a small piece of paper, carefully folded. He automatically picked it up, just as automatically unfolded it, and read the following note, written in French:

My angel Betsy (I cannot bring myself to call you *Barbe* or Varvara).

I waited for you in vain at the corner of the boulevard; come tomorrow to our little apartment at half-past-one. Your good, fat husband (*ton gros bonhomme de mari*) is usually buried in his books about then; we will sing that song you taught me, by your poet *Puskin* (*de votre poète Pouskine*): 'Old husband, stern husband!' – I kiss your hands and feet a thousand times. Awaiting you.――

ERNEST

Lavretsky did not at once realize what he had read; he read it a second time – and his head began to whirl and the floor to sway under his feet like the deck of a rolling ship. He cried out, and gasped, and wept, all in one breath.

He was beside himself. He had trusted his wife so blindly; the idea of deceit or treachery had never been present to his thoughts. This Ernest, this lover of his wife's, was a fair-haired, pretty boy of about twenty-three, with a turned-up nose and a thin little moustache, almost the most insignificant of all her acquaintances. Several minutes passed, half an hour; Lavretsky still stood, clenching the fatal note in his hand and staring mindlessly at the floor; he saw pale faces glimmering through a swirling darkness; his heart faltered agonizingly; he seemed to be falling, falling, falling . . . endlessly falling. The familiar light rustle of silken clothes roused him from his stupor; Varvara Pavlovna, in hat and shawl, was hurrying back from her walk. Lavretsky trembled all over and flung himself from the room; he felt that at that moment he could rend her to pieces, beat her half to death, like a peasant, or strangle her with his own hands. Varvara Pavlovna, in consternation, tried to stop him; he could only whisper 'Betsy!' – and rush from the house.

Lavretsky took a carriage and ordered it to drive out of the city. All the rest of that day, and all through the night, he wandered about on foot, constantly stopping and throwing up his hands in despair: at times he was quite out of his mind, at others he seemed amused and almost cheerful. In the morning, chilled through and through, he went into a wretched little out-lying inn, asked for a room, and sat down in a chair before the window. He experienced a fit of spasmodic yawning. He could hardly stand, his body was completely exhausted, but he did not even feel his weariness; fatigue, however, had its way: he sat staring before him, thinking of nothing; he did not understand what had happened to him, or why he found himself alone, with stiff limbs, a bitter taste in his mouth, and a heavy load on his heart, in an unfamiliar empty room; he did not understand what had made her, Varya, give herself to that Frenchman or how, knowing herself to be unfaithful, she had been able to be as calm as ever, as affectionate and trustful as ever, with him. 'I don't understand it!' he whispered with dry lips. 'Who can assure me now that in St Petersburg . . . ?' He did not finish the question, but yawned again, shivering violently and shrinking into himself. Bright and dark memories alike tormented him; suddenly it came into his mind that some days earlier, when he and Ernest were both present, she had sat down at the piano and sung 'Old husband, stern husband!' He remembered the expression on her face, the strange glint in her eyes and the red flush on her cheeks – and he got up from the chair, seized with a desire to go and say to them: 'You should not have played with me; my great-grandfather used to hang up his peasants by the ribs, and my grandfather was a peasant himself' – and kill them both. Then all at once it seemed to him that everything that was happening to him was a dream, and not even a dream, but simply some kind of jest; that he had only to shake himself and look around . . . He looked around and, like a hawk driving its talons into its prey, anguish struck deeper and deeper into his heart. To crown all, Lavretsky had been hoping to be a father in a few months' time . . . The past, the future, his whole life, were poisoned. He returned at last to Paris, stopped at an hotel, and sent Varvara Pavlovna M. Ernest's note with the following letter:

The enclosed paper will explain everything. I must say, by the way, that this was most unlike you: you, always so careful, to leave such an important paper lying about!

Poor Lavretsky spent several hours composing and brooding over this sentence.

I cannot see you again; I assume that you also have no wish for an interview with me. I am assigning fifteen thousand francs a year to you; I cannot give you more. Send your address to the office on the estate. Do as you please; live where you please. I wish you happiness. No answer is necessary.

Lavretsky had written that he did not require an answer . . . but he waited, he hungered, for an answer, an explanation of this incomprehensible, inconceivable thing. Varvara Pavlovna sent him a long letter in French that same day. It made his wretchedness complete; his last doubts vanished – and he was ashamed that he had had any doubts remaining. Varvara Pavlovna did not attempt to justify herself: she wished only to see him, and begged him not to condemn her irrevocably. The letter was strained and cold, although traces of tears were visible here and there. Lavretsky laughed bitterly and sent a verbal reply by the messenger that everything was all right. Three days later he was no longer in Paris: but he had gone, not to Russia, but to Italy. He himself did not know why he had chosen Italy; it was all the same to him where he went – so long as it was not home. He sent instructions to his bailiff for the payment of his wife's allowance, and ordered him at the same time to take over all the management of the estate from General Korobyin immediately, without waiting for the accounts to be made up, and to arrange also for His Excellency's departure from Lavriki; before his mind rose a vivid picture of the discomfiture and futile dignity of the dismissed general, and in spite of his own sorrow, he felt a certain amount of malicious satisfaction. Then he wrote a letter to Glafira Petrovna asking her to return to Lavriki, and sent off a power of attorney in her name; Glafira Petrovna refused to return to Lavriki, and she printed a notice in the papers announcing the cancellation of the power of attorney, which was quite unnecessary. Skulking in a small Italian town, for a long time Lavretsky could not refrain from following his wife's movements. From the newspapers he learned that, as she had intended, she had gone from Paris to Baden-Baden; her name soon reappeared in a paragraph signed by the same M. Jules. Through the usual jocosity there could be discerned in this paragraph something like friendly commiseration; reading it produced a very nasty impression on Fëdor Petrovich's mind. Later, he learned that a daughter had been born to him; some two months after this he received the information from his bailiff that Varvara Pavlovna had demanded the first instalment of her allowance. Then worse and worse rumours began to be current, until at last a tragi-comic story in which Varvara Pavlovna had played an inglorious part made a great stir in all the newspapers. This was the end: Varvara Pavlovna had become 'notorious'.

Lavretsky ceased to follow her career, but it was long before he could become reconciled to himself. Sometimes he was seized with such longing for his wife that he thought he would give anything, even, perhaps . . . forgive her, only to hear her caressing voice again and feel her hand in his once more. But the passing of time had its effect. He was not born to be a martyr; his healthy nature came to his aid. Many things became clear to him; the very blow that had struck him down no longer seemed to him unforeseen; he now understood his wife – you can fully understand a person very near to you only when you part from him. He became capable of regarding everything with equanimity. Four years went by, and he felt strong enough to return to his own country and meet his friends. Without delaying either in St Petersburg or in Moscow, he arrived in the town of O——, where we left him, and to which we now request the indulgent reader to return with us.

XVII

On the day after that we have described, some time before ten o'clock, Lavretsky entered the porch of the Kalitins' house. There Liza met him, wearing a hat and gloves.

'Where are you going?' he asked her.

'To mass. Today is Sunday.'

'And do you actually go to mass?'

Liza looked at him in silent surprise.

'Please forgive me,' Lavretsky resumed. 'I . . . that was not what I wanted to say. I came to say goodbye to you; I am leaving in an hour's time.'

'But you won't be very far from here?' asked Liza.

'About twenty-five versts.'

Lenochka, accompanied by a maid, appeared on the threshold.

'See that you don't forget us,' said Liza, as she went down the steps.

'Don't you forget me, either. And listen,' he added, 'you are going to church: perhaps you will say a prayer for me too.'

Liza stopped and turned to him.

'If you wish it,' she said, looking into his face. 'I will say a prayer for you, too. Come along, Lenochka.'

In the drawing-room Lavretsky found Maria Dmitrievna alone. She smelt of eau-de-cologne and peppermint. She had, she said, a headache, and had had a restless night. She received him with her usual languid civility and indulged in a little conversation.

'Don't you agree,' she asked him, 'that Vladimir Nikolaich is such a nice young man?'

'And who is Vladimir Nikolaich?'

'Panshin, of course; you know, he was here yesterday. He liked you enormously, and I will tell you a secret, *mon cher cousin*, he is quite mad about my Liza. Well, he comes from a good family, and he is doing very well in the service; he's clever, too, and he has a position at court, and if it is God's will – for my part, as her mother, I shall be very glad. It's a great responsibility, of course; of course, children's happiness depends on their parents, and, you know, I must say this: up to now, whether for good or ill, after all, it's been me all the time, absolutely nobody but me. I've brought the children up and educated them, and everything . . . I've just written to Mme Bolius for a French governess . . .'

Maria Dmitrievna was well launched into a description of her worries, her endeavours, and her maternal feelings. Lavretsky listened to her silently, turning his hat in his hands. His cold serious look disconcerted the chattering lady.

'And what do you think of Liza?' she asked.

'Lizaveta Mikhaylovna is a very beautiful girl' replied Lavretsky, and he stood up, bowed himself out and went off to Martha Timofeevna's room. Maria Dmitrievna looked after him with displeasure and thought, 'What a bear, a real peasant!

83

Well, now I understand why his wife could not remain faithful to him.'

Martha Timofeevna was sitting in her room, surrounded by her suite. It consisted of five persons, almost the only ones she was fond of: a thick-necked educated bullfinch, whom she loved because he had forgotten his tricks of whistling and drawing water; a very quiet and timid little bitch, Roska; a cross-grained tom-cat, Matros; a swarthy, fidgety, nine-year-old girl with enormous eyes and a sharp little nose, who was called Shurochka; and an elderly woman of about fifty-five, wearing a white cap and a short brown jacket over her dark-coloured dress, named Nastasya Karpovna Ogarkova. Shura was the orphan daughter of tradespeople. Martha Timofeevna had taken charge of her, as she had of Roska, out of pity; she had found both the child and the dog in the street; both were thin and hungry, both were soaked with the autumn rain; nobody came to claim Roska, and Shurochka was very willingly yielded up to Martha Timofeevna by her uncle, a drunken shoemaker, who had not enough to eat, and who, instead of feeding his niece, struck her over the head with his last. Martha Timofeevna had made Nastasya Karpovna's acquaintance on a pilgrimage, in a monastery; she had approached her in the church (Martha Timofeevna was attracted to her because, in her own words, she so much enjoyed praying), struck up a conversation with her, and invited her to her room for a cup of tea. From that day she had never parted from her. Nastasya Karpovna was a woman of the most cheerful and gentle disposition, a childless widow, from a family of poor gentlefolk; she had a round head of grey hair, soft white hands, a soft face with large, kindly features and a slightly comical upturned nose; she was devoted to Martha Timofeevna, who was very fond of her, although she chaffed her for her soft-heartedness: Nastasya Karpovna had a weakness for all young people, and involuntarily blushed like a girl at the most innocent pleasantry. Twelve hundred paper roubles formed the whole of her little capital; she lived at Martha Timofeevna's expense, but on a footing of equality with her: Martha Timofeevna would not have endured servility.

'Ah, Fedya!' she began, as soon as she saw him. 'Yesterday evening you did not see my family: now you can admire them. We have all come together for a cup of tea; this is our second, because it is Sunday. You may stroke everybody; only Shurochka won't allow it and the cat will scratch you. So you're leaving today?'

'Yes.' Lavretsky squatted down on a low stool. 'I've already said goodbye to Maria Dmitrievna. I saw Lizaveta Mikhaylovna as well.'

'Call her Liza, my dear. Why on earth should she be Mikhaylovna to you? And sit still, or you will break Shurochka's chair.'

'She was going to mass,' Lavretsky continued. 'She isn't religious, is she?'

'Yes, Fedya, very. More than you or I, Fedya.'

'But you are religious, aren't you?' remarked Nastasya

Karpovna in a whisper. 'You didn't go to early mass today, but you'll go to the late one.'

'No, I shan't, you'll be going alone: I'm lazy, my dear,' answered Martha Timofeevna, 'and I've been indulging in too much tea.' She said 'thou' to Nastasya Karpovna, although they lived together as equals: after all she was a Pestov, and three Pestovs had been among Ivan the Terrible's victims, and Martha Petrovna did not forget it.

'Tell me something, please,' Lavretsky began again. 'Maria Dmitrievna was talking to me just now about that . . . what's his name? . . . Panshin. What sort of man is he?'

'She talks a good deal too much, God forgive me,' grumbled Martha Timofeevna. 'I suppose she confided in you as a great secret that an eligible young man has turned up. She could have whispered it all over with her friend the priest's son; but no, evidently that's not enough for her. And you know, there is nothing in it yet, and thank God for that! but she must be talking already.'

'But why thank God?' asked Lavretsky.

'Because I don't like that young man; and what would there be to be so pleased about, anyhow?'

'You don't like him?'

'No. He can't captivate everybody. He'll have to be satisfied with having made Nastasya Karpovna here fall in love with him.'

The poor widow was filled with confusion.

'How can you say that, Martha Timofeevna?' she exclaimed, and her cheeks and neck were momentarily flooded with red.

'And he knows quite well, the wretch,' Martha Timofeevna interrupted her, 'he knows how to get round her: he has given her a snuff-box. Fedya, ask her for a pinch of snuff; you will see what a fine snuff-box it is: it has a picture of a mounted hussar on the lid. And you, my dear, had better not try to make excuses for yourself.'

Nastasya Karpovna could only throw up her hands.

'Well,' asked Lavretsky, 'but is Liza quite indifferent to him?'

'I think she likes him, but the Lord only knows! Another man's mind, you know, is a dark forest, and even more when it's a girl's. Take Shurochka's mind – try to decipher that! Why has she been keeping out of sight, but not going far away, ever since you came?'

Shurochka snorted with suppressed laughter and bounded away, and Lavretsky rose from his place.

'Yes,' he said slowly, 'a girl's mind is not to be read.'

He began to say his goodbyes.

'Well, now, shall we see you soon?' asked Martha Timofeevna.

'Whenever you feel the need, auntie: after all, it's not far from here.'

'Oh, yes, of course, you're going to Vasilyevskoe. You don't want to live at Lavriki – well, that's your affair; only you must look in there and pay your respects to your mother's grave, and your grandmother's as well. Abroad there, you acquired all kinds of understanding, and who knows? perhaps in their graves they will feel that you came to see them. And don't forget, Fedya, to have a requiem said for Glafira Petrovna as well; here is a rouble. Take it, take it, it is *I* who want to have the mass said. I didn't like her when she was alive, but say what you like, she was a lass with character. She was a clever woman; and she didn't forget you. Now get along with you, or I shall be boring you.'

And Martha Timofeevna embraced her nephew.

'And Liza won't marry Panshin, don't worry; he's not the husband she deserves.'

'But I am not in the least worried,' answered Lavretsky, and took himself off.

XVIII

Four hours later, he was on his way home. His tarantass rolled along a soft-surfaced country road. The weather had been dry for about two weeks; a thin mist spread like milk through the air and veiled the distant forest; from it came a smell of burning. A multitude of darkish clouds with blurred edges drifted over the pale blue sky; a rather strong wind blew in a dry and steady stream that did not disperse the sultry heat. Lying back with his head on the cushions and his arms folded over his breast, Lavretsky watched the field-enclosures wheeling past like an opened fan, the slow appearance and disappearance of the withies, the stupid rooks and crows, with their sidelong looks of dull suspicion at the moving carriage, the long boundary-strips between the fields, overgrown with tansy, wormwood, and wild parsnip, watched . . . until the fresh, fertile, solitary bareness of the steppes, the greenness, the long lines of the hills, the fluid delicacy of the birches, the ravines with their stunted bushy oaks, the little grey hamlets – the whole Russian scene, which he had not seen for so long, filled his heart to overflowing with sweet, yet almost melancholy, feelings and weighed on his breast with a pleasurable oppression. His thoughts wandered idly; their outlines were as vague and confused as those of the high clouds which seemed to be drifting just as idly. He remembered his childhood, his mother, remembered how he had been carried to her when she was dying and she, pressing his head to her breast, had begun to wail feebly above his head, and looked at Glafira Petrovna – and fallen silent. He remembered his father, vigorous at first, always dissatisfied, with his metallic voice, then blind and lachrymose, his beard unkempt; remembered how once, at table, when he had drunk a glass of wine too many and spilt sauce on his table-napkin, he had suddenly begun to laugh and talk about his amorous conquests, growing red in the face and winking his unseeing eyes; he remembered Varvara Pavlovna – and winced involuntarily, as a man winces at a momentary twinge of inward pain, and shook his head. Then his thoughts dwelt on Liza.

'Here,' he thought, 'is a new being, just entering upon life. A fine person, will she make something of herself? She is pretty, too. That pale fresh complexion, eyes and lips so serious, that honest and innocent look. It is a pity that she seems a little over-pious. Her height is just right, and she walks so lightly, and her voice is quiet. I like the way she stands suddenly still, listening intently, without a smile, then falls into profound thought and tosses back her hair. Panshin, though, it seems to me, is not worthy of her. But what is wrong with him? Why do I let my thoughts ramble on like this, though? She will hurry along the same path as all the rest of them. I'd do better to go to sleep.' And Lavretsky shut his eyes.

He could not sleep, but he lost himself in the drowsy dullness of the traveller. As before, images of the past rose before him, floating unhurriedly upwards to the surface of his mind, mingling and blending with other images. For no reason at all, Lavretsky began to think of Robert Peel . . . of French history . . . of how he would win a battle if he were a general; he imagined he could hear shots and cries . . . His head slipped to one side; he opened his eyes . . . Still the same fields, the same views of the same steppes; the worn shoes of the side-horses gleamed one after the other through the eddying dust; his driver's yellow shirt, with its red gussets, ballooned in the wind . . . 'A fine state I am coming home to my own country in!' flashed through Lavretsky's mind, and he shouted, 'Get on!', huddled down into his overcoat, and pressed his head deeper into the cushions. The tarantass jolted: Lavretsky sat up and opened his eyes wide. Before him a very small village lay stretched up the slope of a little hill; a short distance to the right could be seen a small and ancient manor-house with closed shutters and a curving flight of steps; the wide courtyard was overgrown to the very gates with nettles as thick and green as hemp; in it stood a small barn built of oak and still sound. This was Vasilyevskoe.

The driver wheeled towards the gates and stopped the horses; Lavretsky's servant raised himself on the box, as though preparing to jump down, and shouted, 'Hello there!' A hoarse, muffled barking could be heard, but nobody came, not even the dog; the servant once more prepared to jump down and once more shouted, 'Hello there!' The feeble barking was repeated and after a moment a man in a nankeen caftan, with a head as white as snow, ran into the courtyard from somewhere out of sight; shading his eyes from the sun, he looked at the tarantass, clapped both his hands to his thighs and, after a few irresolute dashes from side to side, rushed to open the gates. The tarantass drove into the yard, its wheels rustling through the nettles, and stopped before the door. The white-haired man, who seemed to be extremely nimble, was already standing on the lowest step, with his legs planted crookedly far apart; he unfastened the apron, plucking and twitching at the leather, and kissed his master's hand as he helped him to alight.

'Greetings, greetings, brother,' said Lavretsky. 'Your name is Anton, I think. And so you are still alive?'

The old man bowed without speaking and ran to fetch the keys. Meanwhile, the coachman sat motionless on his box with arms akimbo and gazed at the locked door, while Lavretsky's manservant stood as he had jumped down, in a picturesque pose with one arm flung over the box. The old man brought the keys and, with his elbows raised high and a good deal of unnecessary bending and curving of his body, unlocked the door, stood to one side and again bowed from the waist.

'So here I am, at home; so I have come back,' thought Lavretsky, as he walked into the tiny hall, while one after another the shutters opened with a screech and a bang and daylight penetrated into the deserted rooms.

XIX

The little house to which Lavretsky had come, where Glafira Petrovna had died two years before, had been built in the previous century of durable pine timber; it looked tumbledown but was still capable of standing another fifty years or more. Lavretsky went through all the rooms and, to the great discomfort of the ancient, sluggish flies, with white dust on their backs, sitting motionless under the door-lintels, ordered the windows to be opened everywhere: nobody had unfastened them since the day of Glafira Petrovna's death. Everything in the house remained as it had been then: the slender-legged white sofas in the drawing-room, upholstered in shiny grey brocade, threadbare and broken-springed, were reminiscent of the days of Catherine the Great; in the drawing-room, too, there stood the favourite arm-chair of the mistress of the house, with a high straight back against which she had never leaned, even in her old age. In the place of honour hung an old portrait of Fëdor's great-grandfather, Andrey Lavretsky; the dark, bilious face was hardly distinguishable from the cracked and blackened background; the malicious little eyes gleamed sullenly from under pendulous, swollen-looking eyelids; the black, unpowdered hair rose like a crest above the heavy, furrowed forehead. On a corner of the frame hung a wreath of dusty immortelles. 'It was Glafira Petrovna herself who had that made,' announced Anton. In the bedroom stood a narrow bed, under a canopy of ancient striped material of excellent quality; a pile of discoloured pillows and a thin quilted cover lay on the bed, and near its head hung an icon of the Presentation of the Blessed Virgin, the same to which the old spinster, dying alone and forgotten by everybody, had for the last time pressed her lips already growing cold. An inlaid dressing-table with brass ornaments and a warped looking-glass in a tarnished gilt frame stood by the window. Next to the bedroom was an oratory, a small room with bare walls and a heavy icon-case in the corner; on the floor lay a threadbare carpet, spotted with wax; on it, Glafira Petrovna used to bow down to the ground.

Anton went away with Lavretsky's servant to open the stables and coach-house; in his place appeared an old woman, all but his equal in age, with her head bound up in a kerchief that came down to her eyebrows; her head trembled ceaselessly and her eyes, dim as they were, expressed diligent zeal, the long habit of unquestioning service, and at the same time respectful commiseration. She came and kissed Lavretsky's hand and then stood by the door to await his orders. He simply could not remember her name, could not even remember whether he had ever seen her: it appeared that she was called Apraxeya; some forty years earlier, Glafira Petrovna had sent her away from the house and set her to look after the poultry; she spoke little, as though age had taken away her wits, and her looks were obsequious. Besides these two old people and three pot-bellied children in long shirts, Anton's great-grandchildren, there lived in the house a one-armed, semi-independent moujik; he muttered and grumbled like a blackcock and was no good at anything; not much more useful was the decrepit old dog whose barking had greeted Lavretsky's arrival: for ten years it had been kept on a heavy chain, bought by Glafira Petrovna's orders, and was barely able to drag its burden or indeed move at all. When he had looked round the house, Lavretsky went out into the garden, and was pleased with what he found. It was all overgrown with burdock and other weeds, and with gooseberries and raspberries; but there was a great deal of shade in it, provided by many ancient limes, remarkable for their enormous size and strangely distorted branches; they had been set too close together and had once – some hundred years earlier – been cut back. The garden ended in a small clear pond bordered by tall reddish reeds. The traces of human occupation are very soon obliterated: Glafira Petrovna's estate had not yet run completely wild, but it seemed already sunk in that tranquil doze in which everything slumbers whenever the restless plague of mankind is absent. Fëdor Ivanych walked through the village as well; the women watched him from the thresholds of their huts, their cheeks resting on their hands; the peasants bowed from a distance, the children ran away, the dogs barked indifferently. Finally, he felt the desire to eat, but he was not expecting his cook and domestic servants till evening, the cart-load of provisions from Lavriki had not yet arrived: he had to turn to Anton. Anton set about matters at once; he caught, killed, and plucked an old hen; Apraxeya spent a long time scraping and cleaning it, and washed it as though it were linen, before she put it in the saucepan; when it was cooked at last, Anton spread the cloth and laid the table, setting in front of his master's place a three-legged salt-cellar of tarnished plate and a cut-glass decanter with a round stopper and a narrow neck; then in a sing-song voice he announced that the meal was ready, and stationed himself behind the chair with a napkin wound round his right hand, diffusing a strong and ancient odour like cypress wood. Lavretsky ate his soup and applied himself to the hen; the skin was covered with large pimples; a thick sinew ran down each leg; the flesh tasted of wood and lye. When he had dined, Lavretsky said that he would like tea, if . . . 'I will bring it at once, sir,' the old man interrupted – and he was as good as his word. He found a pinch of tea, wrapped up in a scrap of red paper; he found a small but very fierce and noisy samovar; he even found sugar in extremely small pieces that looked half-melted. Lavretsky drank his tea from a large cup; he remembered the cup from when he was a child: there was a picture of playing-cards on it, and only guests used to drink from it; now he was drinking from it like a guest. Late in the afternoon the servants arrived; Lavretsky did not want to sleep in his aunt's bed, so he ordered them to make up a bed for him in the dining-room. When he had put out the candle, he lay for a long time looking round him and thinking sad thoughts; he experienced the sensations familiar to every man who has to sleep for the first time in a place long uninhabited; it seemed to him that the darkness which surrounded him on every side could not get used to the new-comer, that the very walls of the house were perplexed. At last he sighed, pulled the blanket tight over himself and fell asleep. Anton sat up later than anybody else; he whispered with Apraxeya for a long time, crossing himself and moaning and groaning in an undertone; neither of them had expected that the master would come back to live at their Vasilyevskoe, when he had such a fine estate ready to hand, with an excellently organized house; they did not suspect that it was precisely the house that was repugnant to Lavretsky; it aroused painful memories in him. When he had had his fill of whispering, Anton took his watchman's stick, drummed on the long-silent board hanging by the barn, and lay down there in the courtyard, without any covering for his white head. The May night was still and mild, and the old man slept sweetly.

XX

The next day Lavretsky got up fairly early, had a talk with the village elder, paid a visit to the threshing-floor, ordered the chain to be taken off the yard-dog – which only uttered a few barks, but did not leave its kennel – and returned to the house, where he remained all the rest of the day sunk in a kind of peaceful numbness, from which he did not rouse himself all day. More than once he said to himself: 'The time has come when I have sunk to the very bottom of the river.' He sat unmoving by the window and listened, as it were, to the tranquil current of the life all round him and to the infrequent sounds of this remote countryside. Somewhere beyond the nettles somebody began to hum in a thin thread of sound; a gnat seemed to echo the humming. This stopped, but the gnat continued to whine; through the concerted, importunate, plaintive buzzing of the flies came the drone of the fat bumble-bee which from time to time bumped its head against the ceiling; a cock crowed in the village street, hoarsely prolonging the last note, cart-wheels rumbled past, a yard-gate creaked. A woman's jarring voice cried suddenly: 'What?' 'Ah, my little princess,' said Anton to the two-year-old child he was dandling in his arms. 'Bring the kvass,' came the same peasant-woman's harsh voice again – and suddenly a dead silence fell: not a sound, not a motion; not a leaf stirred in the wind; one after another the swallows skimmed silently over the ground and their noiseless flight made the heart ache. 'The time has come when I am at the bottom of the river,' thought Lavretsky again. 'But here, at whatever time, life is always quiet and unhurried,' he thought; 'whoever enters its charmed circle must yield to it: here there is no reason for agitation, nothing to cause disturbance; here success comes only to the man who lays down his path with deliberation, as the ploughman draws his furrow. And what vigour all around, what strength in this inactive stillness! Here, by the window, a sturdy burdock pushes its way through the thick grasses, above it the willow-herb stretches its juicy stalk, and lady's-tears shakes out its pink tresses higher still; farther off, there in the field, the rye is glossy, the oats have already pushed up their shoots, and every leaf on every tree, every blade of grass on its stalk, has expanded to its full extent. My best years have gone in the love of a woman,' Lavretsky's thoughts continued; 'now let the placid tedium of life here restore me to sobriety, calm my nerves, and make it possible for me to do what I have to do without haste.' And once more he began to listen to the silence, expecting nothing – and yet at the same time, it would seem, in constant expectation of something: the stillness was all around him, the sun rolled quietly through the quiet blue sky and the clouds quietly floated in it; they seemed to know where they were going and why. Meanwhile, in other places on the earth's surface, life seethed and bustled and made thunderous noises; here, the same life flowed silently, like water among marsh grasses; until the evening, Lavretsky could not drag himself away from the contemplation of this life flowing past, slipping past; in his heart sorrow for what was gone melted away like the spring snows and, strangely enough, he had never had so deep and strong a feeling for his native country.

XXI

In two weeks, Lavretsky had restored Glafira Petrovna's house to order and cleaned up the courtyard and garden; comfortable furniture had been brought from Lavriki and wine, books, and newspapers from the town; horses had appeared in the stables; in short, Fëdor Ivanych had provided himself with everything necessary and begun to live as something between a landowner and a hermit. His days were all passed in the same manner; but he was not bored, although he saw nobody; he applied himself diligently and intently to managing his estates, rode about the countryside, and read. He did not, however, read very much: he found it pleasanter to listen to old Anton's stories. Usually, Lavretsky sat by the window with a pipe and a cup of cold tea; Anton stationed himself by the door, clasping his hands behind him, and embarked on leisurely tales of the long-distant past, those fabulous days when oats and rye were sold not in measures but in great sacks, at two or three copecks a sack; when pathless forests and inviolate steppes stretched on all sides right up to the very outskirts of the town. 'But now,' complained the old man, who had already passed his eightieth birthday, 'there has been so much ploughing-up and cutting-down everywhere that you can't go anywhere any more.' Anton had a great deal to tell about his mistress, Glafira Petrovna, too: how sensible and thrifty she had been; how a certain gentleman, a young neighbour, had won her favour and begun to pay frequent visits, and how she had even condescended to wear her Sunday cap with the magenta ribbons and her yellow twilled silk dress for him; but how afterwards, angry with the young gentleman for his indelicate question: 'How much, madam, would you say your capital might amount to?', she forbade him the house, and at the same time gave orders that after her death everything, down to the smallest scrap, should go to Fëdor Ivanych. And indeed Lavretsky found all his aunt's possessions intact, not excluding the Sunday cap with the magenta ribbons and the yellow twilled silk dress. But there were none of the old papers or curious documents on which Lavretsky had reckoned, except one ancient little manuscript book in which his grandfather, Peter Andreich, had written, here 'Celebration in St Petersburg of the peace with the Turkish Empire, concluded by His Excellency Prince Alexander Alexandrovich Prozorovsky'; here a recipe for a pectoral *decocktion* with the note: 'This precept was given to Mme General Praskovya Fëdorovna Saltykova by Theodore Avksentyevich, Archpriest of Holy Trinity Church'; now a piece of political news of the following kind: 'Talk of the French tigers has somewhat died down'; now, side by side with this last: 'The Moscow Gazette announces the passing of Senior

Major Michael Petrovich Kolychev. Is this not Peter Vasilyevich Kolychev's son?' Lavretsky also found a few old almanacs and dream-books, and Mr Ambodik's mysterious work: the sight of the long-forgotten but familiar *Symbols and Emblems* awakened many memories. In Glafira Petrovna's toilet-table Lavretsky came across a small packet bound with a black ribbon, sealed with black wax, and thrust into the farthest corner of the drawer. In the packet, face to face, lay a pastel portrait of his father in his youth, with soft curls tumbling over his forehead, long, languid eyes and half-open lips, and another portrait, almost effaced, of a pale woman in a white dress with a white rose in her hand – his mother. Glafira Petrovna would never allow a portrait of herself to be made.

'Yes, sir, Fëdor Ivanych,' Anton used to tell Lavretsky, 'even if I didn't use to live in the big house in those days, still I do remember your great-grandfather, Andrey Afanasyevich, and why shouldn't I? – I must have been eighteen when he passed away. One time I met him in the garden, and my knees were knocking together; only he didn't say anything, he only asked me what I was called and sent me to his room to fetch him a handkerchief. He was a gentleman all right, I can tell you – and he called no man master. Because, I must tell you, your great-grandfather had a magic talisman; it was a monk from Mount Athos that gave it him. And this monk said to him, "I am giving you this, sir, for your kind welcome; wear it, and never be afraid of what may come to you." Well, after all, sir, you know what the times were like then: if the master wanted to do anything, he did it. Sometimes, one of the other gentlemen would try to stop him, and he would just look at him and say: "You're not big enough" – and that was his favourite saying. And he lived, your great-grandfather, God rest his soul, in a little wooden house; and what didn't he leave behind him? such silver, and all kinds of stores, all the cellars were cram-full. He was a good manager. That decanter you liked, that was his: he used to drink vodka out of it. But your grandfather, Peter Andreich, built himself a stone house, and he didn't make any money; nothing he did never came to any good; he didn't never live so well as his father and he never had no pleasures – and he lost all his money and there's nothing left to remember him by, he didn't leave no silver spoons; but then, thank goodness, Glafira Petrovna took it all in hand.'

'Is it true,' interrupted Lavretsky, 'that they called her the old battle-axe?'

'But look at who called her it!' retorted the old man, displeased.

On one occasion, Anton plucked up courage to ask:

'How is the young mistress, sir, if I may make so bold? Where is she, sir?'

'I have parted from my wife,' said Lavretsky with an effort. 'Please do not ask about her.'

'No, sir,' answered the old man mournfully.

After three weeks Lavretsky rode over to the Kalitins' at O—— and passed the evening with them. Lemm was there, and Lavretsky took a great liking to him. Although, thanks to his father, he did not play any instrument, he was passionately fond of music, serious, classical music. Panshin was not present that evening. The Governor had sent him somewhere out of the town. Liza played alone, with great correctness; Lemm became animated, let himself go, rolled up some paper into a baton and conducted. Maria Dmitrievna at first laughed to see him, then she went to bed; she said Beethoven was too exciting for her nerves. At midnight Lavretsky walked back with Lemm to his rooms and sat with him until three o'clock in the morning. Lemm talked a great deal; his back grew straighter, his eyes opened wider and began to shine; the very hair above his forehead seemed to spring up straight. It was a very long time since anybody had shown any sympathy with him, but Lavretsky was clearly interested and questioned him with thoughtful intentness. The old man was touched; he ended by showing the guest his music, and played and even sang in a ghost of a voice excerpts from his compositions, including the whole of Schiller's ballad 'Friedolin', which he had set to music. Lavretsky praised him, made him repeat some things and, when he left, invited him to spend a few days with him. Lemm, accompanying him to the door of the house, agreed at once and wrung his hand, but, left alone in the fresh damp air of early dawn, he looked round, screwing up his eyes, seemed to shrivel into himself and wandered back to his little room like a guilty man. '*Ich bin wohl nicht klug*' (I am out of my mind), he muttered, as he lay down on his short, hard bed. He tried to say that he was ill when, a few days later, Lavretsky came to fetch him in his carriage, but Fëdor Ivanych went to his room and persuaded him to change his mind. What most strongly influenced Lemm was the fact that Lavretsky had had a piano sent to his house from the town especially for his visitor. The two went off to the Kalitins' and spent the evening there, but not quite as pleasantly as on the previous occasion. Panshin was there, and he had a great deal to say about his trip and gave very amusing imitations of the landed proprietors he had met; Lavretsky laughed, but Lemm remained obstinately in his corner and said never a word, quivering all over like a spider, looking morose and stupid, and rousing himself only when Lavretsky began to make his farewells. Even in the carriage the old man's unsociable and shrinking mood continued; but the warm, tranquil air, the slight breeze, the delicate shadows, the scent of grass and budding birch-trees, the peaceful radiance of the starry, moonless sky, the harmonious drumming of hoofs and the snorts of the horses – all the enchantment of the road, and the spring, and the night sank into the soul of the poor German, and he began of his own accord to talk to Lavretsky.

XXII

He talked of music, of Liza, and of music again. His words seemed to be uttered more slowly when he spoke of Liza. Lavretsky led the conversation to his compositions and, half in jest, offered to write a libretto for him.

'Hm, a libretto!' answered Lemm; 'no, that is not for me. I have not the liveliness or the play of imagination that are essential for opera. I have lost all my powers now . . . But if I could still do something, I should be content with a romance; of course I should want the words to be good . . .'

He sat silent and motionless for a long time, with his eyes raised to the sky.

'For example,' he said at last, 'something like this: Oh, stars, you chaste stars . . .'

Lavretsky turned his face towards him and watched him.

'Oh, stars, you chaste stars,' repeated Lemm . . . 'You look down on innocent and guilty alike . . . but only the pure in heart – or something like that . . . understand you – or no – love you. I'm no poet, how should I be? But something of that kind, something elevated.'

Lemm pushed his hat to the back of his head; in the thin dusk of the clear night his face looked paler and younger.

'And you, too, know,' he continued in a voice growing gradually softer, 'you know who loves, who is capable of loving, for you, chaste stars, you alone can give consolation . . . No, that's not it at all! I am no poet,' he said, 'but something of that sort . . .'

'Unfortunately, I am not a poet either,' remarked Lavretsky.

'Empty dreams,' replied Lemm, and sank back into the corner of the carriage. He closed his eyes as though preparing for sleep.

Some moments passed . . . Lavretsky listened . . . 'Stars, chaste stars, love,' whispered the old man.

'Love,' repeated Lavretsky to himself, musing – and his heart was heavy.

'The music you wrote for *Friedolin* is splendid, Christopher Fëdorovich,' he said aloud, 'but what is your opinion: this Friedolin, when the count brought him to his wife, I suppose he became her lover there and then, eh?'

'You think so,' answered Lemm, 'because, probably, experience . . .' He stopped abruptly and turned away in confusion. Lavretsky's smile was constrained and he too turned away and began to watch the road.

The stars were growing pale and the sky was silver when the carriage drew up at the steps of the little house at Vasilyevskoe. Lavretsky took his guest to the room assigned to him, returned to his study and sat down by the window. In the garden a nightingale was singing its last song before the break of day. Lavretsky remembered that a nightingale had sung in the Kalitins' garden also; he remembered too the quiet movement of Liza's eyes as she turned towards the window at the first notes. He began to think about her, and his heart grew still. 'A pure young girl,' he said, half aloud; 'chaste stars,' he added with a smile, and peacefully lay down to sleep.

Lemm sat on his bed for a long time with a music manuscript book on his knees. It seemed to him that some sweet, unimaginable melody was about to visit him; already he was on fire with excitement, already he felt the languor and sweetness of its approach . . . but he waited in vain . . .

'No poet – and no musician either!' he whispered at last.

And his weary head drooped heavily to his pillow.

XXIII

On the following day host and guest were drinking tea in the garden under an old lime-tree.

'Maestro!' said Lavretsky in the course of the conversation, 'soon you will have to compose a triumphal cantata.'

'For what occasion?'

'For the occasion of Liza's marriage to Mr Panshin. Did you notice how attentive he was yesterday? It looks as though they were on very good terms already.'

'That will never be!' exclaimed Lemm.

'Why not?'

'Because it is impossible. However,' he added after a pause, 'on this earth everything is possible. Especially among you people here, in Russia.'

'We will leave Russia out of it for the moment; what fault have you to find with this marriage?'

'Everything, everything. Lizaveta Mikhaylovna is a young lady of high principles and elevated sentiments, and serious, and he . . . he is a dilettante, in one word.'

'But I suppose she loves him?'

Lemm got up from the garden-seat.

'No, she does not love him; that is to say, she is very pure in heart and does not understand what the word "love" means. Madame von Kalitin tells her that he is a nice young man, and she listens to Madame von Kalitin because she is still only a child, even though she is nineteen years old: she still says her prayers night and morning – and that is quite right; but she does not love him. She can only love the beautiful, and he is not beautiful; I mean, his soul is not beautiful.'

Lemm pronounced all this speech fluently and warmly, taking short strides backwards and forwards beside the tea-table and searching the ground with his eyes.

'Dearest maestro!' exclaimed Lavretsky suddenly, 'it seems to me that you are in love with my cousin yourself.'

Lemm stopped abruptly.

'Please,' he began in a trembling voice, 'don't laugh at me like that. I am not out of my mind: I look forward to the dark grave, not to a rosy future.'

Lavretsky felt sorry for the old man and asked his forgiveness. After tea, Lemm played his cantata, and at dinner, prompted by Lavretsky, he talked about Liza again. Lavretsky listened with attention and curiosity.

'What do you think, Christopher Fëdorych?' he said at length. 'We seem to have things straight here now, and the garden is in full flower . . . What if I invited her here for the day with her mother and my old auntie, eh? Would you like that?'

Lemm bowed his head over his plate.

'Yes, do,' he said in a barely audible voice.

'But we needn't have Panshin?'

'No, we needn't,' answered the old man, with an almost childlike smile.

Two days later Fëdor Ivanych went to town, to the Kalitins'.

XXIV

He found them all at home, but he did not at once reveal his plans; he wished to discuss them first with Liza. Chance came to his aid: they were left alone together in the drawing-room. They talked freely; she had had time to grow used to him – but, indeed, she was not usually shy with anybody. He listened to her, and watched her face, mentally repeating Lemm's words and finding himself in agreement with them. It sometimes happens that two people, who are already acquainted but not intimate, suddenly and rapidly draw near to one another in the space of a few moments, and the consciousness of this nearness is expressed in their looks, in their quiet, friendly smiles, in their very movements. This was just what had happened to Lavretsky and Liza. 'So this is what he is like,' she thought, looking at him affectionately. He too was thinking, 'So this is what you are like.' Thus he was not very surprised when she, not without some slight faltering, told him that she had long had it in her heart to say something to him, but she was afraid he would be angry.

'Don't be afraid; say it,' he answered, standing before her.

Liza raised her clear eyes to his.

'You are so good,' she began (and at the same time she was thinking, 'Yes, he really is good . . .'). 'Forgive me – perhaps I ought not to speak of it to you . . . but how could you . . . why did you leave your wife?'

Lavretsky started, glanced at Liza, and sat down beside her.

'My child,' he said, 'please do not probe that wound: your hands are tender, but all the same it will give me pain.'

'I know,' went on Liza, as if she had not heard him, 'that she wronged you, and I don't want to excuse her; but how is it possible to sunder what God has joined?'

'Our beliefs on this subject are too widely different, Liza Mikhaylovna,' said Lavretsky rather sharply. 'We shall not understand one another.'

Liza turned pale; her whole body trembled slightly, but she did not stop.

'You ought to forgive,' she said quietly, 'if you wish to be forgiven.'

'Forgive!' Lavretsky caught her up. 'You ought to know first who you are pleading for. Forgive that woman, take her back into my house, that empty, heartless creature! And who told you that she wants to come back to me? Believe me, she is quite satisfied with her situation . . . But what is the use of talking? You ought not even to pronounce her name. You are too innocent, you are not in a position to understand such a creature.'

'Why be abusive?', said Liza with an effort. The shaking of her hands was becoming visible. 'It was you who left her, Fëdor Ivanych.'

'But I tell you,' retorted Lavretsky, with an involuntary flash of impatience, 'you don't know what kind of creature she is!'

'Then why did you marry her?' whispered Liza, and cast down her eyes.

'Why did I marry her? I was young then, and inexperienced; I was deceived, I fell in love with a beautiful exterior. I didn't know women, I knew nothing. God grant you may make a happier marriage! but, believe me, you can rely on nothing.'

'I may be unhappy too,' said Liza (her voice had begun to shake), 'but then I should have to submit; I don't know how to say it, but if we do not submit . . .'

Lavretsky clenched his teeth and tapped his foot.

'Don't be angry, forgive me,' said Liza hastily.

At this moment Maria Dmitrievna entered the room. Liza rose and went towards the door.

'Stop,' Lavretsky called after her unexpectedly. 'I have a great favour to ask of your mother and you: that you will pay me a visit in my new home. You know I have acquired a piano; Lemm is staying with me; the lilacs are in flower; you will be able to breathe the country air, and you can return the same day – will you?'

Liza looked at her mother, and Maria Dmitrievna put on an air of suffering; Lavretsky did not give her time to open her mouth but at once kissed both her hands. Maria Dmitrievna, always susceptible to flattering attentions and not expecting such extreme politeness from the 'bear', was touched and accepted. While she was considering which day to name, Lavretsky went up to Liza and, still agitated, whispered aside to her, 'Thank you, you are a good girl; I was wrong . . .' Her pale face flushed and she gave him a bright shy smile; her eyes smiled too. She had been afraid until that moment that she had offended him.

'May we bring Vladimir Ivanych with us?' asked Maria Dmitrievna.

'Of course,' answered Lavretsky, 'but wouldn't it be better with just our own small family circle?'

'But, you know, it seems . . .' began Maria Dmitrievna. 'However, as you wish,' she added.

It was decided to take Lenochka and Shurochka. Martha Timofeevna declined to undertake the journey.

'Too hard for me, love,' she said; 'it would make my old bones ache; and then I don't suppose you have anywhere for us to sleep, and besides, I can't sleep in a strange bed. Let the young things enjoy themselves.'

Lavretsky found no further opportunity of being alone with Liza; but he looked at her in such a way that she felt happy, and a little shy, and sorry for him. When he said goodbye, he gripped her hand tightly; left alone, she was thoughtful.

XXV

When Lavretsky returned home he was met at the door of the drawing-room by a tall thin man in a worn blue frock-coat, with a lined but lively face, untidy grey whiskers, a long straight nose and inflamed little eyes. This was Mikhalevich, his old university friend. Lavretsky did not recognize him at first, but embraced him warmly as soon as he named himself. They had not seen each other since Moscow. They rained questions and exclamations on each other; long-buried memories were brought into the light of day again. Hurriedly puffing pipe after pipe, swallowing cups of tea in a single gulp, and waving his long arms, Mikhalevich related his adventures to Lavretsky; there was nothing very cheerful about them, he could not boast of success in his enterprises, but he laughed ceaselessly in nervous, husky guffaws. A month earlier he had obtained a position in the private office of a rich tax-farmer, some thirty versts from the town of O——, and, learning of Lavretsky's return from abroad, had made a detour in order to see his old friend. Mikhalevich's speech was as jerky and disconnected as in his youth, and he was as noisy and excitable as ever. Lavretsky tried to touch upon his own present circumstances, but Mikhalevich interrupted him with a hasty murmur: 'I heard about it, old man, I heard; who could have expected it?' and immediately turned the conversation to general topics.

'I must leave tomorrow, old man,' he said; 'today, if you will excuse me, we will sit up late. I simply must know what you are doing, and what your opinions are, and your beliefs, what you have become, what life has taught you.' (Mikhalevich still clung to the phraseology of the thirties.) 'As for me, I have changed a great deal, old man: the waves of life have beaten against my breast – who the devil said that? – although in the important, the essential things I haven't changed; I still believe in the good and the true, as I always did; but now I do more than believe – I have faith now, yes, I have faith, faith. Listen, you know I occasionally write verse; there is no poetry in it, but there is truth. I will read you my latest piece; it expresses my sincerest convictions. Listen.' And Mikhalevich proceeded to read his verses; they were rather long and ended with the following lines:

'I am imbued with feelings new,
A childlike spirit now is mine;
My old gods to the flames I threw,
What once I burned seems now divine.'

As he uttered the last two lines, Mikhalevich was almost in tears; a slight tremor – the sign of strong feeling – twitched his wide mouth, his unbeautiful face lit up. Lavretsky listened to him . . . and the spirit of contradiction stirred in him: he was irritated by the ever-ready, always overflowing enthusiasms of the Moscow student. Before a quarter of an hour had passed, they were hotly engaged in an argument, one of those endless arguments of which only Russians are capable. After many years of separation, passed in two different worlds, without any clear understanding of each other's ideas, or even of their own, they had plunged headlong into a wrangle on the most abstract subjects, clinging to words and arguing solely over words – and arguing as though it were a matter of life and death for both: they so roared and shouted that all the servants were in a flurry and poor Lemm, who had shut himself up in his own room on Mikhalevich's arrival, was quite bewildered and even began to experience a hazy feeling of alarm.

'What are you, then? – a disillusioned man?' Mikhalevich was shouting at midnight.

'Are disillusioned people like me?' retorted Lavretsky. 'They are all pale and sickly – would you like me to lift you with one hand?'

'Well, if you're not disillusioned, you're a sceptic, and that's even worse.' (Mikhalevich's pronunciation testified to the region he came from, Little Russia.) 'And what right have you to be a sceptic? You have had bad luck in your life, we'll suppose; that was no fault of yours: you were born with a passionate, loving nature, and you were forcibly kept away from women: the first woman you came across was bound to take you in.'

'She took you in, too,' remarked Lavretsky morosely.

'All right, all right; I was the instrument of fate – or no, why am I talking such nonsense? – fate doesn't come into it; I express myself inexactly from old habit. But what does that prove?'

'It proves that I was warped from childhood.'

'Straighten yourself out then! that's why you were born a human being, a man; you have energy enough. But however that may be, is it possible, is it permissible, to raise a private, so to speak, fact, into a general law, and unalterable rule?'

'What rule are you talking about?' interrupted Lavretsky. 'I don't admit . . .'

'Yes, your rule, your rule,' interrupted Mikhalevich in his turn.

An hour later, he was thundering: 'You're an egoist, that's what it is! You wanted self-enjoyment, you wanted happiness in life, you wanted to live only for yourself . . .'

'And what, pray, is "self-enjoyment"?'

'And everything deceived you, everything crumbled away beneath your feet.'

'I ask you again, what is "self-enjoyment"?'

'And it must needs crumble away. For you sought a foothold where there was none to be found, for you built your house on the shifting sands . . .'

'Speak more plainly, without metaphors, *for* I don't understand you.'

'For – all right, laugh – for there is no faith in you, no warmth of heart; intellect, nothing at all but a ha'porth of intellect . . . you're simply a pitiful, out-of-date Voltairean, that's what you are!'

'Me, a Voltairean?'

'Yes, just like your father, and you don't suspect it yourself.'

'After that,' exclaimed Lavretsky, 'I have the right to call you a fanatic!'

'Alas,' contritely answered Mikhalevich, 'unfortunately I have not yet earned so exalted a title . . .'

'Now I've found the right word for you,' the same Mikhalevich was crying at two o'clock in the morning; 'you're not a sceptic, not a disillusioned man, not a Voltairean, you're a sluggard, and a vicious sluggard, a conscious sluggard, not a naïve sluggard. Naïve sluggards lie about on the stove and do nothing, because they are incapable of doing anything; they don't think anything either, but you are a thinking man – and yet you lie there; you could do something – and you do nothing; you lie with your well-filled belly upwards and say: "This is the right thing, to lie here, because whatever people do is all useless rubbish and leads nowhere."'

'And what gave you the idea that I lie and do nothing?' repeatedly demanded Lavretsky. 'Why do you assume that I have such thoughts?'

'And on top of that,' pursued the indefatigable Mikhalevich, 'you are all, all your sort, learned sluggards. You know what is the Germans' heel of Achilles, you know what is wrong with the English and the French – and your pitiful learning comes to your assistance, and justifies your shameful sloth and your base inactivity. Some of you even boast of being, as you say, the clever ones, taking your ease while the other fools do all the rushing about. Yes! Or we have certain gentlemen – however, I am not referring to you now – who spend all their lives in a sort of trance of boredom, quite used to it, sitting in it like . . . like a mushroom in sour cream.' Mikhalevich himself laughed at the comparison as he pounced on it. 'Oh, that trance of boredom is the bane of Russia! Our disgusting sluggards spend their whole lifetime just getting ready to work . . .'

'What's all this railing for?' shouted Lavretsky in his turn. 'Work . . . act . . . Better tell us what to do without all this abuse, you Demosthenes from Poltava!'

'So that's all you want! No, I won't tell you that, brother; everyone ought to know that for himself,' ironically retorted Demosthenes. 'A landowner, a gentleman – and not know what to do! You've no faith, or else you would know; no faith – and no inspiration.'

'At least let me have a rest, devil; give me time to look round,' begged Lavretsky.

'Not a moment's rest, not a second!' retorted Mikhalevich, with a peremptory wave of the arm. 'Not one second! Death doesn't wait, and life mustn't wait either.'

'And when and where did people take it into their heads to idle about?' he was shouting at three o'clock in the morning, in a voice by now somewhat hoarse. 'Here! now! in Russia! when there lies on every single individual a duty, a great responsibility to God, to the people, and to himself! We are asleep, and time is passing; we are asleep . . .'

'Allow me to remark,' said Lavretsky, 'that we are certainly not asleep now, but rather preventing other people from sleeping.

We are crowing as loud as the cocks. Listen, that's the third time already.'

This sally amused and appeased Mikhalevich. 'Till tomorrow,' he said with a smile, thrusting his pipe into his pouch. 'Till tomorrow,' repeated Lavretsky. But the friends went on talking for more than an hour longer . . . Now, however, their voices were no longer raised, and their talk was quiet, sad, and kindly.

Mikhalevich left the next day, in spite of Lavretsky's efforts to detain him. Although Fëdor Ivanych failed to persuade his friend to stay on, he talked to his heart's content with him. It appeared that Mikhalevich had not a penny to bless himself with. The evening before Lavretsky had already been saddened to notice in him all the marks and habits of inveterate poverty: his boots were down at heel, there was a button missing from the back of his coat, his hands were innocent of gloves, there were bits of fluff in his hair; when he arrived, he did not think of asking if he might wash, and at supper he ate like a shark, tearing the meat with his hands and noisily cracking the bones with his strong, discoloured teeth. It also appeared that he had not prospered in his occupation, and that all his hopes now rested in the tax-farmer, who had taken him on solely in order to have an 'educated man' in his office. With all this, Mikhalevich had not lost heart, but pursued his course, as cynic, idealist, and poet, sincerely rejoicing or sorrowing over the fates of mankind and his own vocation – and very little concerned with how to avoid dying of hunger. Mikhalevich was unmarried, but he had been in love times without number, and written verses to all his loves: he had hymned with particular ardour one mysterious aristocratic Polish lady with a head of black curls . . . There were, it is true, rumours that the Polish aristocrat was simply a common little Jewess, well known to many cavalry officers . . . but does that really make any difference, when you come to think of it?

Mikhalevich did not get on well with Lemm: his noisy talk and rough ways scared the German, who was not used to them . . . One poor wretch instantly scents another from far away, but in old age rarely gets on with him, and this is not at all surprising: he has nothing to share with him, not even hope.

Before he left, Mikhalevich had much more talk with Lavretsky, prophesied his ruin, if he did not pull himself together, begged him to occupy himself seriously with the welfare of his peasants, held himself up as an example, stating that he had been purged in the furnace of misfortune – and at the same time more than once referred to himself as a happy man and compared himself with the birds of the air and the lilies of the field . . .

'A black lily, at all events,' remarked Lavretsky.

'Eh, my dear chap, don't take that snobbish tone,' good-naturedly retorted Mikhalevich, 'but rather thank God that honest plebeian blood flows even in your own veins. But I see that what you want now is some pure, heavenly creature who would force you out of your apathy . . .'

'No, thank you, my dear fellow,' said Lavretsky. 'I've had enough of heavenly creatures.'

'Silence, cynic!' exclaimed Mikhalevich.

Even sitting in the tarantass, when his flat, yellow, strangely light portmanteau had been carried out to it, he still talked; wrapped in a sort of Spanish cloak with a rusty collar and lions' paws for clasps, he was still developing his views on the fate of Russia and waving his sunburnt hands about as though he were sowing the seeds of future prosperity. At last the horses moved off . . . 'Remember my three last words,' he shouted, thrusting his whole body out of the tarantass and swaying as he stood, '– religion, progress, humanity! . . . Goodbye!' His head, with its cap pulled well down over the eyes, disappeared. Lavretsky remained standing alone on the porch, staring down the road until the tarantass was out of sight. 'Perhaps, after all, he is right,' he thought, going back into the house; 'perhaps I am a sluggard.' Many of Mikhalevich's words had irresistibly penetrated his mind, although he had not agreed with them and had argued against them. Let a man only be good – nobody can resist him.

XXVI

Two days later, Maria Dmitrievna, in accordance with her promise, was at Vasilyevskoe with all her young people. The little girls at once ran into the garden, and Maria Dmitrievna languidly walked through all the rooms and languidly commended them.

She considered her visit to Lavretsky a token of the greatest condescension, almost an act of charity. She smiled graciously when Anton and Aproxeya, according to the custom of old-fashioned house-serfs, advanced to kiss her hand, and she asked for tea in a faint, nasal voice. To the great disappointment of Anton, who had put on white knitted gloves, tea was served to the visitors not by him but by Lavretsky's hired valet, who, in the old man's words, had no idea of how to do things properly. But at dinner Anton came into his own; he stood firmly behind Maria Dmitrievna's chair and yielded his place to nobody. The presence of guests at Vasilyevskoe, so long unused to them, both flustered and pleased the old man: he was delighted to see that his master was acquainted with people in good society. He was not the only one, however, to be agitated that day: Lemm also was flustered. He had put on his short, snuff-coloured, swallow-tail coat and pulled his neckerchief tight, and now, incessantly clearing his throat, he hovered in the background with a cordial and ingratiating expression. Lavretsky saw with satisfaction that the friendship between him and Liza continued; as soon as she entered she warmly extended her hand to him. After dinner Lemm extracted from the back pocket of his tail-coat, into which he had from time to time thrust his hand, a small roll of music-paper, which he silently and with compressed lips laid on the piano. This was a drawing-room ballad which he had composed the day before to old-fashioned German words, in which reference was made to the stars. Liza immediately sat down at the piano and unrolled the song . . . Alas! the music proved to be complicated and disagreeably strained; it was apparent that the composer had been striving to express something passionate and profound, but nothing had come of it: the striving remained no more than striving. Lavretsky and Liza both felt this – and Lemm knew it: without a word he put the song back in his pocket and, in answer to Liza's offer to play it again, merely remarked significantly, with a shake of his head: 'Now – that is enough!' and walked away, shrunken and stooping.

Late in the afternoon the whole company went fishing. The pond beyond the garden was full of carp and loach. Maria Dmitrievna was installed in an arm-chair on the bank, in the shade, a rug was spread under her feet and she was given the best rod; Anton offered her his services as an old, experienced fisherman. He zealously put on the worms, slapped them with his hand, spat on them, and even made the casts himself, with a graceful inclination of his whole body. Maria Dmitrievna remarked of him that same day to Fëdor Ivanych, in schoolgirl French: '*Il n'y a plus maintenant de ces gens comme ça comme autrefois.*' Lemm and the two little girls went farther along, right to the dam; Lavretsky took his stand by Liza. The fish were biting all the time; as they were pulled from the water, the sides of the carp gleamed constantly, now gold, now silver; the joyful exclamations of the little girls never ceased; even Maria Dmitrievna once or twice uttered a delicate little scream. Liza and Lavretsky least frequently landed anything; this was probably because they paid less attention than anybody else to their fishing, and allowed their floats to drift back close to the bank. The tall red-tinged reeds rustled peacefully round them, before them the still water shone peacefully bright, and their talk was quiet and peaceful. Liza stood on a small raft; Lavretsky sat on the slanting trunk of a willow; Liza's dress was white, caught around the waist with a wide ribbon, also white; her straw hat hung from one arm, the other, with some effort, supported the flexible rod. Lavretsky watched her pure, somewhat severe profile, the hair swept back behind her ears, and her soft cheeks, sunburnt like a child's, and thought: 'Oh, how sweetly you stand there above my pond!' Liza did not turn towards him, but looked at the water, now frowning and now smiling. The shadow of a lime-tree close at hand fell on them both.

'You know,' Lavretsky began, 'I have been thinking a lot about our last talk and I have come to the conclusion that you are more than ordinarily good.'

'It wasn't in the least with that intention . . .' Liza began to reply, and stopped in shy confusion.

'You are good,' repeated Lavretsky. 'I am a rough, clumsy fellow, but I feel that everybody must love you. Take Lemm, for instance: he is simply in love with you.'

Liza did not exactly frown, but her brows twitched; this always happened when she heard something she did not like.

'I was very sorry for him today,' went on Lavretsky hastily, 'when his song turned out a failure. To be young and to lack skill, that is bearable; but to be old and to have lost one's powers – that is hard. And what really hurts is that one doesn't realize it, when one's powers are failing. It is hard for an old man to bear such blows! . . . Look out, you've got a bite . . . They say,' Lavretsky added after a pause, 'that Vladimir Nikolaich has written a very nice little song.'

'Yes,' answered Liza, 'it's only a trifle, but it's quite good.'

'And is he, in your opinion,' Lavretsky asked, 'a good musician?'

'I think he has a great talent for music, but up till now he hasn't applied himself to it as he should.'

'Indeed? And is he a good man?'

Liza laughed and cast a quick glance at Fëdor Ivanych.

'What a strange question!' she exclaimed, and she drew out her line and made a long cast.

'Why strange? I am asking you as somebody who has not been here long, and as a relative.'

'A relative?'

'Yes. After all, I think I'm your second cousin, aren't I?'

'Vladimir Nikolaich has a good heart,' said Liza; 'he is clever; *maman* is very fond of him.'

'And do you like him?'

'He is a nice man; why shouldn't I like him?'

'Ah!' said Lavretsky, and was silent. An expression half-sad, half-humorous, crossed his face. His fixed gaze embarrassed Liza, but she continued to smile. 'Well, God grant they may be happy!' he muttered at last as though to himself, and turned away his head.

Liza blushed.

'You are mistaken, Fëdor Ivanych,' she said. 'There is no reason for you to think . . . Don't you like Vladimir Nikolaich?' she asked abruptly.

'No, I don't.'

'But why?'

'I don't think he has a heart.'

Liza's face lost its smile.

'You are used to judging people severely,' she said after a long silence.

'I don't think so. What right have I to judge others severely, when I stand in need of leniency myself? Or have you forgotten that everybody who isn't too indolent laughs at me? . . . Well,' he added, 'did you keep your promise?'

'What promise?'

'Did you pray for me?'

'Yes, I prayed for you and I do pray for you every day. But please do not speak lightly about it.'

Lavretsky assured Liza that such an idea had never entered his head and that he profoundly respected any conviction; then he began to talk about religion, its significance in the history of mankind, and the meaning of Christianity . . .

'One must be a Christian,' Liza began, not without some effort, 'not in order to know things heavenly . . . there . . . and earthly, but because every man must die.'

With involuntary astonishment Lavretsky raised his eyes to Liza's and met her gaze.

'What words to have spoken!' he said.

'They are not mine,' she answered.

'Not yours . . . But why did you speak of death?'

'I don't know. I often think of it.'

'Often?'

'Yes.'

'One would not say so, to look at you now: your face is so bright and happy, you are smiling . . .'

'Yes, I'm very happy now,' replied Liza simply.

Lavretsky felt the wish to take both her hands in his and press them warmly . . .

'Liza, Liza,' cried Maria Dmitrievna, 'come here and look what a wonderful carp I have caught.'

'At once, *maman*,' answered Liza, and went to her, leaving Lavretsky sitting on his willow-trunk. 'I am talking to her as if my life was not over,' he thought. As she went, Liza had hung her hat on a branch; Lavretsky gazed at that hat, with its long, slightly rumpled ribbons, with strange, almost tender, emotion. Liza soon returned and took up her position on the raft.

'Why do you think Vladimir Nikolaich has no heart?' she asked some moments later.

'I have already said I may be mistaken; however, time will tell.'

Liza was thoughtful. Lavretsky began to talk about his life at Vasilyevskoe, and Mikhalevich, and Anton; he felt a need to talk to Liza, to tell her everything that came into his mind: she was so sweet and attentive a listener, and her infrequent comments seemed to him so simple and wise. He even told her so.

Liza was astonished.

'Really?' she said. 'And I thought I was like my maid Nastya, and had no words *of my own* to say. She once told her sweetheart: "You must find it dull with me; you talk to me so nicely, and I've no words of my own."'

'And thank God for that!' thought Lavretsky.

XXVII

Meanwhile, evening had come and Maria Dmitrievna expressed the wish to go home. The little girls were with difficulty torn away from the pond and got ready. Lavretsky announced that he would escort his guests halfway and ordered his horse to be saddled. Settling Maria Dmitrievna in the carriage, he suddenly remembered Lemm, but the old man was nowhere to be found. He had disappeared as soon as they finished fishing. Anton, with a strength surprising at his age, slammed the doors and called sternly: 'Drive on, coachman!' The carriage moved off. On the back seat were Maria Dmitrievna and Liza, on the front one the little girls and the maid. The evening was calm and warm, and the windows on both sides were let down. Lavretsky rode at a trot beside the carriage on Liza's side, with his hand on the door (he had dropped the reins on the neck of his even-paced horse), and from time to time exchanged a word with her. The twilight vanished, night fell, but the air grew even warmer. Maria Dmitrievna was soon dozing; the little girls and the maid had also fallen asleep. The carriage rolled smoothly and swiftly along; Liza was leaning forward; the newly risen moon shone in her face, and the scented night-breeze breathed against her eyes and cheeks. She was happy. Her hand rested on the carriage-door beside Lavretsky's. He too was happy: he was carried along through the tranquil warmth of the night, never taking his eyes off the young face so full of simple goodness, and listening to the musical young voice whispering good, simple words; he did not even notice how he had reached the halfway point. He did not wish to waken Maria Dmitrievna, but lightly pressed Liza's hand and said, 'We are really friends now, aren't we?' She nodded her head and he reined up his horse. The carriage rolled on, quietly swaying and bouncing; Lavretsky turned homewards at a walk. The bewitching influence of the summer night embraced him; everything around seemed so unexpectedly strange and at the same time so long and so sweetly familiar; far and near – and the distance was visible, although much of what the eye could see it could not make out clearly – everything was steeped in quiet; young life in full flower revealed itself in that very quiet. Lavretsky's horse moved briskly, with a rhythmical swaying to right and left; there was something mysteriously pleasant in the clatter of the hoofs, something joyful and wonderful in the jingling cry of the quails. The stars were disappearing in a bright haze; the moon, not yet full, shone with steady brilliance; its light washed over the sky in a pale blue flood and threw a misty golden stain on the thin clouds sailing near it; the freshness of the air made the eyes slightly moist, caressingly enveloped all the limbs, and poured in a free stream into the breast. Lavretsky revelled in it and rejoiced to find himself doing so. 'Well, life isn't over for us yet,' he thought, 'We are not yet completely devoured by . . .' He did not specify by whom or what . . . Then he began to think about Liza, that it was unlikely that she loved Panshin, that if only he had met her in different circumstances, God only knew what might have come of it, that he could understand Lemm's feelings, even if she had no words 'of her own'. But that was not true: she had words of her own . . . 'Do not speak lightly of it,' Lavretsky remembered. He rode for some time with hanging head, then straightened his back and slowly pronounced:

'My old gods to the flames I threw,

What once I burned seems now divine . . .'

– then immediately gave his horse a blow with the whip and galloped the rest of the way to the house.

Dismounting, he gave a last look round, with an involuntary smile of gratitude. Night, silent and tender, lay on the hills and valleys; from far away in its fragrant depths came a lingering breath, God knows whether from earth or heaven, of still, mild warmth. Lavretsky sent a last greeting to Liza and ran up the steps.

The next day seemed somewhat flat. Rain fell from early

morning on; Lemm, with a lowering face, compressed his lips tighter and tighter, as though he had taken an oath never to open them again. When Lavretsky went to bed, he took with him a whole pile of French newspapers, which had lain unopened on his table for more than a fortnight. Indifferently he began to tear off the wrappers and skim through their columns, in which, however, he found nothing new. He was on the point of abandoning them when he started up from the bed as though he had been stung. In one of the papers M. Jules, with whom we are already acquainted, informed his readers of the 'melancholy news that that charming and delightful lady from Moscow, that queen of fashion, that ornament of Parisian salons,' as he wrote, Madame de Lavretsky, had died very suddenly, and that this information, unfortunately but too true, had only then reached him, M. Jules. He could, he continued, describe himself as a friend of the deceased lady . . .

Lavretsky dressed, went out into the garden, and paced backwards and forwards up and down the same tree-lined walk until morning.

XXVIII

Next morning at breakfast, Lemm asked Lavretsky for horses to return to the town. 'It is time I applied myself to work, I mean to lessons,' remarked the old man. 'I am only wasting time here.'

Lavretsky did not answer immediately; he seemed preoccupied. 'Very well,' he said at last, 'I will go with you myself.' Without the help of the valet Lemm, groaning and cursing, packed his small box and tore up and burnt several sheets of music-paper. The horses were brought. Lavretsky, as he left his study, put into his pocket the newspaper he had read the previous day. During the journey Lemm and Lavretsky spoke little; each was occupied with his own thoughts and each was glad not to be interrupted by the other. Their parting, too, was rather cool; this, however, often happens between friends in Russia. Lavretsky took the old man to his little house, where he alighted, reached down his box and, without holding out his hand (he was clasping his box to his breast with both arms) or even looking at his friend, said in Russian, 'Goodbye!' 'Goodbye,' repeated Lavretsky, and ordered the coachman to drive to his rooms. He had taken lodgings in the town in case of need. After writing some letters and dining hurriedly, Lavretsky went to the Kalitins'. In the drawing-room he found only Panshin, who declared that Maria Dmitrievna was coming immediately and at once, with the most charming amiability, struck up a conversation. Until that day Panshin had treated Lavretsky, if not patronizingly, at least condescendingly; but Liza, telling Panshin of the previous day's excursion, had spoken of Lavretsky as a splendid and intelligent person; it was enough: the 'splendid' person must be won over. Panshin began by paying Lavretsky compliments, then described the raptures with which, according to him, all Maria Dmitrievna's family had spoken of Vasilyevskoe, and after that, in his usual way, adroitly switched to the subject of himself, and began to speak of his duties and of his views on life, society, and the government service, said a word or two about the future of Russia and about the best way of keeping Governors under one's thumb, then cheerfully laughed at himself and added that among other things he had been entrusted in St Petersburg with the task '*de popular-iser l'idée du cadastre*'. He talked for quite a long time, solving all difficulties with careless self-confidence and juggling with the most important administrative and political problems with practised ease. Expressions like 'That's what I should do if I were the government', or 'You, as an intelligent man, will instantly agree with me', were constantly on his lips. Lavretsky listened coldly to these flights of eloquence: he had no liking for this handsome, intelligent man with his easy elegance, bright smile, urbane voice, and inquisitive eyes. Panshin, with his peculiarly swift understanding of other people's feelings, soon realized that he was not affording his companion any great pleasure and made some plausible excuse for disappearing, having decided in his own mind that Lavretsky might indeed be a splendid man, but he was unsympathetic, '*aigu*', and '*en somme*' rather ridicu-lous. Maria Dmitrievna made her appearance, accompanied by Gedeonovsky; then Martha Timofeevna arrived with Liza, and after them the rest of the household. They were followed by an amateur musician, Madame Belenitsyna, a small thin woman with an almost babyish face, tired and pretty, in rustling black clothes, carrying a painted fan and wearing heavy gold bracelets; with her came her husband, a chubby, red-cheeked man with big hands and feet, white eyelashes, and a fixed smile on his thick lips (in company, his wife never spoke to him, but at home, in tender moments, she called him her pigling); Panshin returned; the rooms were full of noise and people. Such a crowd was not to Lavretsky's taste; he found Madame Belenitsyna, who gazed at him now and then through her lorgnette, particularly irritating. He would have left immediately, if it had not been for Liza: he wanted to have a word with her alone, but it was a long time before he could find a suitable opportunity, and he had to be content with the secret delight of following her with his eyes; her face had never seemed to him sweeter or more noble. She gained greatly from the proximity of Madame Belenitsyna, who was always fidgeting in her chair, shrugging her narrow little shoulders, laughing affectedly, and now narrowing her eyes, now suddenly opening them wide. Liza sat still, looked straight at people, and did not laugh at all. The hostess sat down to play cards with Martha Timofeevna, Belenitsyna, and Gedeonovsky, who played very slowly and made innumerable mistakes, blinking incessantly and wiping his face with his hand-kerchief. Panshin adopted a melancholy air and spoke briefly, meaningfully and gloomily – the living image of the frustrated artist – but in spite of the pleading of Madame Belenitsyna, whose manner to him was full of coquetry, he declined to sing his romance: he felt constrained in Lavretsky's presence. Fëdor

Ivanych also had little to say; the peculiar expression of his face had struck Liza as soon as she entered the room: she felt at once that he had something to tell her but, without knowing why, she was afraid to question him. Finally, as she crossed into the large drawing-room to pour tea, she involuntarily turned her head in his direction. He followed her immediately.

'What is the matter?' she asked, setting the teapot on the samovar.

'Have you noticed something?' said he.

'You are not the same today as I have always seen you before.'

Lavretsky leaned over the table.

'I wanted,' he began, 'to tell you a piece of news, but it is not possible now. However, read what is marked with pencil in this article,' he added, giving her the copy of the newspaper he had brought with him. 'Please keep it to yourself. I will call tomorrow morning.'

Liza was at a loss . . . Panshin appeared on the threshold; she put the paper in her pocket.

'Have you read Obermann, Lizaveta Mikhaylovna?' Panshin asked her pensively.

Liza gave some sort of answer and went out of the room and upstairs. Lavretsky returned to the drawing-room and approached the card-table. Martha Timofeevna, red in the face and with her cap-ribbons untied, began to complain about her partner, Gedeonovsky, who, according to her, did not know how to lead.

'It's clear that playing cards is not the same thing as making up untrue stories,' she said.

Gedeonovsky went on blinking and wiping his face. Liza entered the room and sat down in a corner. Lavretsky looked at her, she looked at him – and both became almost afraid. He read perplexity and a certain mysterious reproach in her face. He could not talk to her as he would have liked; to remain in the same room with her, one guest among others, was too difficult; he resolved to leave. Saying goodbye, he managed to repeat that he would come the next day, and added that he trusted in her friendship.

'Yes, come tomorrow,' she answered, with the same look of perplexity.

Panshin brightened on Lavretsky's departure; he began to advise Gedeonovsky, flirted playfully with Madame Belenitsyna and, at last, sang his romance. But he talked to Liza, and looked at her, as before, meaningfully and a little mournfully.

Again Lavretsky passed a sleepless night. He felt neither grief nor agitation, he was completely calm, but he could not sleep. He was not even remembering the past, he was simply looking deep into his own life: his heart beat strongly and evenly, the hours sped past, the thought of sleep did not enter his head. Only at times the idea rose to the surface of his mind: 'But it is not true, all this is nonsense' – and he paused, drooped his head, and resumed the contemplation of his life.

XXIX

Maria Dmitrievna did not receive Lavretsky very cordially when he appeared at her house the following day. 'He seems to make a habit of it,' she thought. She did not like him very much, and Panshin, under whose influence she was, had, with great artfulness, praised him carelessly the day before. Since she did not regard him as a guest and did not think it necessary to concern herself with a relative, almost a member of the household, within less than half an hour he and Liza were walking under the trees in the garden. A few steps away from them, Lenochka and Shurochka were running about among the flower-beds.

Liza was as quiet as usual, but more than usually pale. She took from her pocket and held out to Lavretsky the page of newspaper folded small.

'It is terrible,' she said.

Lavretsky did not answer.

'And, perhaps, it is not even true,' added Liza.

'That is why I asked you not to speak of it to anybody.'

Liza walked on.

'Tell me,' she began, 'are you not grieved? just a little?'

'I don't know myself what I feel,' answered he.

'But you loved her once, didn't you?'

'Yes.'

'Very much?'

'Very much.'

'And her death does not grieve you?'

'She was dead to me already.'

'What you say is sinful . . . Don't be angry with me. You say I am your friend: a friend may say anything. To me, truly, it seems terrible . . . Your face had lost its goodness yesterday . . . Do you remember being so bitter about her the other day? – and perhaps she was no longer on this earth at that moment. It is frightening. Just as though it had been sent to punish you.'

Lavretsky smiled wryly.

'Do you think so? . . . At least, I am free now.'

Liza shuddered slightly.

'Stop, don't say such things. What good is your freedom to you? You must not think of that now, but of forgiveness . . .'

'I forgave her long since,' he interrupted, with a wave of his hand.

'No, I don't mean that,' replied Liza, blushing. 'You misunderstand me. You ought to be anxious for forgiveness yourself.'

'Who is to forgive me?'

'Who? God. Who can forgive us but God?'

Lavretsky seized her hand.

'Ah, Lizaveta Mikhaylovna, believe me,' he exclaimed, 'I have been punished enough even as it is. I have paid for everything, believe me.'

'That is something you cannot know,' said Liza in a low voice.

'You have forgotten – not long ago, when you were talking to me, you were not willing to forgive her.'

Both walked on silently.

'But what about your daughter?' Liza asked suddenly, and stopped.

Lavretsky started.

'Oh, don't worry. I have sent letters everywhere already. The future of my daughter, as you call . . . as you say . . . is assured. Don't worry.'

Liza's smile was sad.

'But you are right,' Lavretsky continued. 'What am I to do with my freedom? What good is it to me?'

'When did you receive this newspaper?' said Liza, not answering his question.

'The day after your visit.'

'And didn't you . . . didn't you even shed a tear?'

'No. I was thunderstruck, but why should I weep? Weep for the past? – but for me it has been burnt to ashes! . . . Her fault itself did not destroy my happiness, it merely showed me it had never existed. What was there to weep for there? But who knows? Perhaps I might have grieved more if I had received the news two weeks earlier . . .'

'Two weeks?' objected Liza. 'But what has happened in these last two weeks?'

Lavretsky did not answer, and Liza suddenly blushed more than ever.

'Yes, yes, you have guessed it,' Lavretsky burst out abruptly. 'During these two weeks I have learned the meaning of a woman's pure heart, and the past seems remoter than ever.'

Liza grew confused and moved quietly away towards Lenochka and Shurochka among the flowers.

'I am glad I showed you that newspaper,' said Lavretsky, following her. 'Already I am used to hiding nothing from you, and I hope that in return you will have the same trust in me.'

'Do you think so?' said Liza, standing still. 'In that case I ought to . . . but no! That is not possible.'

'What? Tell me, tell me.'

'Really, I think I ought not to . . . However,' Liza added, turning with a smile towards Lavretsky, 'what is frankness worth if it goes only halfway? Do you know, I received a letter today?'

'From Panshin?'

'Yes . . . How did you know?'

'To ask for your hand?'

'Yes,' said Liza, looking directly and seriously at Lavretsky. He in his turn looked seriously at Liza.

'Well, and what was your answer?' he asked at last.

'I don't know what to answer,' Liza returned, letting fall her clasped hands.

'What? You love him, don't you?'

'Yes, I like him; I think he is a good man.'

'You told me the very same thing in the very same words

three days ago. I should like to know if you love him with that strong, passionate feeling we are used to calling love.'

'Not as *you* understand it, no.'

'You are not in love with him?'

'No. But is that necessary?'

'What?'

'Mama likes him,' Liza went on, 'he is kind, I have nothing against him.'

'But still you hesitate?'

'Yes . . . and perhaps . . . you, your words, are the cause of it. Do you remember what you said the day before yesterday? But this is weakness . . .'

'Oh, my child!' exclaimed Lavretsky suddenly, and his voice trembled. 'Don't try to be subtle and philosophical, don't call the cry of your heart, which does not want to give itself without love, weakness. Don't take on yourself such a terrible responsibility to a man you do not love and to whom you are willing to belong . . .'

'I am only obeying, not taking anything on myself,' Liza began.

'Obey your heart; only it can tell you the truth,' Lavretsky interrupted. 'Experience, judgement – all that is dust and ashes! Don't deprive yourself of the best, the only, happiness on earth.'

'Do *you* say that, Fëdor Ivanych? You married for love yourself – and were you happy?'

Lavretsky flung up his arms.

'Oh, don't talk about me! You can't begin to understand what a young, inexperienced, badly brought-up boy can take for love! . . . Besides, after all, why should I misrepresent myself? I told you just now that I had not known happiness . . . but no! I was happy!'

'I think, Fëdor Ivanych,' said Liza slowly, lowering her voice (when she disagreed with what somebody else said, she always lowered her voice; besides, she felt greatly moved), 'happiness in this world does not depend on us . . .'

'It does, it does, believe me' (he seized both her hands in his; Liza turned pale and looked at him almost fearfully but still with close attention), 'unless we ourselves have spoiled our own lives. For other people a marriage for love might be unhappy, but not for you, with your tranquil disposition and your serene spirit! I implore you, do not marry without love, from a feeling of duty, self-sacrifice, what not . . . That is the same as lack of faith, the same as calculation – and even worse. Believe me – I have the right to say this: I have paid dearly for it. And if your God . . .'

At this moment Lavretsky noticed that Lenochka and Shurochka were standing beside Liza and staring at him in mute bewilderment. He released Liza's hands, hastily murmured: 'Please excuse me' and walked away towards the house.

'I ask only one thing of you,' he said, returning again to Liza; 'don't decide at once, wait, think over what I have said. Even if you didn't believe me, if you decided to make a marriage of convenience – even then you couldn't marry Panshin: he is not the husband for you . . . You will promise me not to be in a hurry, won't you?'

Liza wanted to answer Lavretsky – and could not utter a word, not because she had decided to 'be in a hurry', but because her heart was beating too violently and something resembling terror stopped her breath . . .

XXX

As he left the Kalitins', Lavretsky met Panshin; they bowed coldly to one another. Lavretsky returned to his rooms and shut himself in. He was experiencing a sensation such as it is doubtful if he had ever experienced before. Was it so long since he had found himself in a condition of 'peaceful numbness'? was it so long since he had felt that he was, as he expressed it, at the very bottom of the river? What had changed his situation? what had carried him up to the surface? was it that most ordinary, inevitable, although always unlooked-for, happening, death? Yes; but he had not thought so much of his wife's death and his own freedom as of what answer Liza would give Panshin. He felt that in the course of the last three days he had begun to see her with different eyes; he remembered how, returning home and thinking of her in the quiet of the night, he had said to himself: 'If only! . . .' That 'if only', referred by him to the past, to the impossible, had come about, although not in the way he had supposed – but his freedom alone was not enough. 'She will obey her mother,' he thought, 'and marry Panshin; but even if she refuses him, does that make any difference to me?' Passing in front of a looking-glass, he threw a glance at his own face and shrugged his shoulders.

The day had passed swiftly in these reflections; evening had come. Lavretsky set off for the Kalitins'. He walked swiftly, but slowed his pace as he approached the house. Panshin's droshky stood before the porch. 'Well,' thought Lavretsky, 'I won't be an egoist' – and he entered the house. He saw nobody in the house, and the drawing-room seemed very quiet; he opened the door and saw Maria Dmitrievna playing piquet with Panshin. Panshin bowed silently, but his hostess exclaimed, 'This is an unexpected pleasure!' and just perceptibly frowned. Lavretsky sat down beside her and began to look at her cards.

'Do you know how to play piquet?' she asked, with some concealed irritation, and immediately declared that she had discarded.

Panshin scored ninety and politely and calmly proceeded to take the tricks, with a severe and dignified expression. So diplomats ought to play; that was probably the way he used to play in St Petersburg with some powerful dignitary, whom he wished to impress with a favourable opinion of his soundness and maturity. 'A hundred and one, a hundred and two, hearts, a hundred and three', came his measured tones, and Lavretsky could not decide whether their sound conveyed reproach or self-satisfaction.

'Is Martha Timofeevna at home?' he asked, noticing that Panshin, with even greater dignity, was now beginning to shuffle the cards. Not so much as a shadow of the artist could now be seen in him.

'I think so. She is upstairs, in her room,' answered Maria Dmitrievna. 'Go and see.'

Lavretsky went upstairs. He found Martha Timofeevna also at cards: she was playing Old Maid with Nastasya Karpovna. Roska barked at him, but both old ladies appeared pleased to see him, and Martha Timofeevna especially seemed in good spirits.

'Ah, Fedya! Come in!' she said. 'Sit down, my dear. We'll have finished our game in a minute. Would you like some jam? Shurochka, get him a jar of strawberry jam. Won't you have any? Well then, just sit there; but – don't smoke: I can't bear your dreadful tobacco, and besides, it makes Matros sneeze.'

Lavretsky hastened to declare that he had no wish to smoke.

'Have you been downstairs?' went on the old lady. 'Whom did you see there? Is Panshin still hanging about? Did you see Liza? No? She was going to come here . . . And here she is; talk of the devil.'

Liza came into the room, and blushed when she saw Lavretsky.

'I've only come for a minute, Martha Timofeevna,' she was beginning.

'Why only for a minute?' answered the old lady. 'Why is it

all you young girls are so fidgety? You can see I have a visitor: talk to him, keep him amused.'

Liza sat down on the edge of a chair, raised her eyes to Lavretsky – and felt that she could not but let him know the outcome of her interview with Panshin. But how was she to do it? She felt both ashamed and awkward. She had not known him long, this man who hardly ever went to church and who had taken the death of his wife so calmly – and here she was confiding her secrets to him . . . He was, it is true, full of sympathetic interest in her; she trusted him and felt drawn to him; but all the same, she felt ashamed, as though a stranger had entered her pure, virginal room.

Martha Timofeevna came to the rescue.

'If you aren't going to keep him amused, you know,' she began, 'who *will* amuse him, poor dear? I am too old for him, he is too clever for me, and he is too old for Nastasya Karpovna: give her young men every time.'

'How can I amuse Fëdor Ivanych?' said Liza. 'Perhaps I had better play him something on the piano, if he likes,' she added hesitantly.

'Splendid; that's clever of you,' answered Martha Timofeevna. 'Go downstairs, my dears; come back when you have finished. I've been made the old maid, and I resent that; I want to have my revenge.'

Liza rose and Lavretsky followed her. As she went down the stairs, Liza stopped.

'What they say is quite true,' she began; 'the human heart is full of contradictions. Your example might have frightened me, made me mistrustful of love-marriages, but I . . .'

'You refused him?' interrupted Lavretsky.

'No; but I didn't accept him, either. I told him all I felt, and asked him to wait. Are you pleased?' she added with a fleeting smile and, lightly brushing the rail with her hand, ran downstairs.

'What shall I play for you?' she asked, raising the lid of the piano.

'What you like,' answered Lavretsky, and sat down where he could see her.

Liza began to play and for a long time did not lift her eyes from her fingers. When at last she looked at Lavretsky, she stopped playing, so marvellous and strange did his face appear.

'What is the matter?' she asked.

'Nothing,' he replied. 'I am very happy; I am glad for you, I am glad to see you; go on playing.'

'It seems to me,' said Liza, some moments later, 'that if he really loved me, he would not have written that letter; he must have felt that I couldn't give him an answer now.'

'That doesn't matter,' said Lavretsky. 'What matters is that you don't love him.'

'Stop! This is a strange kind of conversation. I seem to see your poor wife all the time, and you frighten me.'

'Don't you think my Lisette plays nicely?' Maria Dmitrievna was asking Panshin at that very moment.

'Yes,' he replied, 'very nicely.'

Maria Dmitrievna looked fondly at her young partner; but he assumed an air even weightier and more preoccupied, and declared a quatorze of kings.

XXXI

Lavretsky was not a young man; he could not long deceive himself on the score of the feelings inspired in him by Liza; that same day he finally convinced himself that he loved her. This conviction did not bring him much joy. 'Could I really,' he thought, 'find nothing better to do at thirty-five years old than give my heart once again into the keeping of a woman? But Liza is not like *her:* she would not demand shameful sacrifices of me; she would not tempt me away from my work; she would herself inspire me to strict, honest labour, and we should both go forward to a noble goal. Yes,' he concluded his meditation, 'this is all very well, but what is not well is that she will have no desire to go with me at all. It does not count for nothing that she said I frightened her. On the other hand, she does not love Panshin either . . . Poor consolation!'

Lavretsky went to Vasilyevskoe; but he could not endure to stay there longer than three days, so heavy did the time hang on his hands. He was weary too with vain expectation: the news conveyed by M. Jules required confirmation, and he had received no letters.

He returned to the town, and spent an evening at the Kalitins'. It was easy to see that Maria Dmitrievna had been set against him; but he managed to mollify her to some extent by losing fifteen roubles to her at piquet, and he passed about half an hour alone with Liza, in spite of her mother's having advised her the previous day not to be too familiar with a man '*qui a un si grand ridicule*'. He found a change in her: she seemed to have become more pensive, reproached him with his absence, and asked him whether he would not go to church the following day. (The next day was Sunday.)

'Do come,' she said, before he had time to answer, 'we will pray together for the repose of *her* soul.' Then she added that she did not know what to do, she did not know whether she had the right to make Panshin wait any longer for her decision.

'But why not?' asked Lavretsky.

'Because,' said she, 'I begin to suspect already what that decision will be.'

She declared that her head ached and went upstairs to her own room, hesitantly giving Lavretsky the tips of her fingers.

On the following morning, Lavretsky went to mass. Liza was in the church when he arrived. She saw him, although she did not turn towards him. She was praying fervently: her eyes shone softly, softly she bent and raised her head. He felt that she was praying for him as well – and a wonderful tenderness filled his heart. He was both happy and a little conscience-stricken. The simple people standing sedately there, the faces of his own people, the harmonious singing, the scent of incense, the long rays slanting from the windows, the very darkness of the walls and arches – all spoke to his heart. It was long since he had been in church, long since he had turned to God: and even now he uttered no word of prayer, nor did he pray without words – but, if only for a moment, not physically but with his whole mind, he prostrated himself and bowed in submission to the ground. He remembered how, when he was a child, he always prayed in church until he felt on his forehead, as it were, the touch of something fresh and cool; that, he thought now, was my guardian angel accepting me and laying on me the stamp of election. He glanced at Liza . . . 'You brought me here,' he thought; 'touch me then, touch my soul.' She was quietly praying, as before; her face seemed to him to be full of joy, and again he was deeply moved, and sought peace from another's soul, and forgiveness from his own . . .

They met in the church porch; she greeted him with cheerful and affectionate gravity. The sun brightly lit up the young grass in the churchyard and the coloured dresses and handkerchiefs of the women; the bells of the neighbouring churches hummed overhead; sparrows twittered in the garden hedges. Lavretsky stood smiling with uncovered head; the light breeze lifted his hair and the ends of the ribbons on Liza's hat. He handed Liza and Lenochka, who was with her, into their carriage, distributed all his money among the beggars, and quietly strolled home.

XXXII

Difficult days set in for Fëdor Ivanych. He was in a constant fever. Every morning he turned his steps to the post-office, broke the seals of his letters and newspapers in agitation – and found nothing anywhere either to confirm or to refute that fateful rumour. Sometimes he became loathsome to his very self: 'What am I doing,' he thought, 'waiting like a carrion crow for trustworthy information of my wife's death?' He was at the Kalitins' every day, but even there things were no easier for him: he was clearly out of favour with his hostess, who received him only out of forbearance; Panshin addressed him with exaggerated courtesy; Lemm affected misanthropy and barely acknowledged his presence – and, worst of all, Liza seemed to be avoiding him. if, however, she happened to be left alone with him, she showed confused embarrassment in place of her former trustfulness; she did not know what to say to him and he himself felt at a loss. Within a few days, Liza had ceased to be the girl he had known: in her movements, her voice, her very smile, there was to be remarked a secret perturbation, an unsteadiness not present in her before. Maria Dmitrievna, like a true egoist, suspected nothing; but Martha Timofeevna began to watch her favourite closely. More than once Lavretsky reproached himself for having shown Liza the newspaper he had received: he could not but be conscious that there had been in his mental state something profoundly disturbing to a pure emotion. He supposed also that the alteration in Liza arose from her struggle with herself and her doubt as to what reply she should give Panshin. On one occasion she brought him a book, a novel by Sir Walter Scott, which she had asked him to lend her.

'Have you read the book?' he asked.

'No; I am not interested in books now,' she answered, and would have moved away.

'Stay a moment; it is so long since I was alone with you. You seem to be afraid of me.'

'Yes.'

'Why, for pity's sake?'

'I don't know.'

Lavretsky paused.

'Tell me,' he began, 'have you decided yet?'

'What do you mean?' she asked, without raising her eyes.

'You understand me . . .'

Liza's cheeks flared crimson.

'Don't ask me any questions,' she said swiftly; 'I don't know anything; I don't know myself . . .'

And she moved away immediately.

The following day Lavretsky went to the Kalitins' after dinner and found preparations going forward for an evening service. In a corner of the dining-room was a square table covered with a clean cloth, and on it small icons, with gold overlay and small tarnished diamonds set in the haloes, leaned against the wall. An old servant, in a grey frock-coat and wearing shoes, walked unhurriedly down the length of the room, careful that his heels should make no sound on the floor, set two wax candles in silver candlesticks in front of the icons, crossed himself, bowed, and went out noiselessly. The unlighted drawing-room was empty. Lavretsky walked about the dining-room for a time, and then inquired if it were somebody's name-day. He received the whispered answer: no, but an evening service was to be held at the wish of Lizaveta Ivanovna and Martha Timofeevna; they had wanted to do honour to a miracle-working icon, but that had gone thirty versts away, to a sick person. Soon the priest, a man no longer young, with a large bald patch, arrived with his deacons, and noisily cleared his throat in the hall; the ladies immediately filed out of the study and went to receive his blessing; Lavretsky bowed to them in silence; they silently bowed to him. The priest waited a little, cleared his throat once more, and his bass voice said in an undertone:

'Do you wish me to begin?'

'Yes, begin, father,' replied Maria Dmitrievna.

He began to put on his vestments; a surpliced deacon obsequiously asked for a live coal; the scent of incense rose. The maids and menservants entered from the hall and stood crowded together by the door. Roska, who had never come downstairs before, suddenly appeared in the dining-room; they tried to drive her out and she became scared, scurried round and round, and sat down; one of the servants picked her up and carried her out. The service began.

Lavretsky squeezed himself into a corner; his sensations were strange, almost mournful; he himself could hardly tell what he felt. Maria Dmitrievna stood in the very front, before the chairs; she crossed herself in an elegantly perfunctory fashion, like a fine lady, and now looked around her, now cast her eyes up: she was bored. Martha Timofeevna seemed troubled; Nastasya Karpovna prostrated herself to the ground and stood up again with a kind of soft, discreet rustle; Liza stood where she had first placed herself, without moving; from her expression of concentration it was possible to guess that she was praying intently and fervently. When she kissed the cross at the end of the service she kissed also the priest's large, red hand. Maria Dmitrievna invited him to drink tea; he took off his stole, assumed a somewhat worldly expression and went into the drawing-room with the ladies. The conversation was not very lively. The priest drank four cups of tea, repeatedly mopped his bald patch with his handkerchief, mentioned in passing that the merchant Avoshkinov had given seven hundred roubles for gilding the 'cuppola' of the church, and told them of a reliable means of preventing freckles. Lavretsky would have sat down by Liza, but she remained severe, almost stern, and did not once glance at him. She seemed purposely not to notice him; a kind of cold, grave exaltation had descended on her. For some reason Lavretsky kept wanting to smile and say something amusing; but there was confusion in his heart and he went away at last full of secret perplexity . . . He felt that there had been something in Liza to which he could not penetrate.

On another occasion Lavretsky, sitting in the drawing-room and listening to Gedeonovsky's smooth-flowing but dull spate of conversation, suddenly, without knowing why, turned round and caught a profound, attentive, questioning look in Liza's eyes . . . It was fixed on himself, that enigmatic look. Afterwards, Lavretsky pondered over it all night long. He was not in love like a boy, it was not his way to sigh and languish, and indeed Liza herself did not arouse that kind of emotion; but love at any age has its sufferings – and he experienced them to the full.

XXXIII

One day Lavretsky, as was his habit, was sitting at the Kalitins'. The hot weary day had been followed by such a beautiful evening that Maria Dmitrievna, in spite of her loathing of draughts, had ordered all the windows and doors into the garden to be opened and declared that she was not going to play cards, that it was sinful to play cards in such weather, and that one ought to be enjoying the beauties of nature. Panshin was the only other guest. Inspired by the evening, and not wishing to sing in Lavretsky's presence, but overcome by a surge of artistic feeling, he had recourse to poetry: he read, well but with too-conscious artistry and unnecessary refinements, some of Lermontov's poems (Pushkin had not yet come back into fashion) – and suddenly, as though ashamed of his enthusiasm, began, apropos of the well-known 'Elegy', to reproach and upbraid the new generation; nor did he lose the opportunity of stating how he would rearrange things to his taste, if the supreme power were in his hands. 'Russia,' he said, 'has lagged behind the rest of Europe; we must catch up. They say we are a young people – that's rubbish; and besides, we have no inventive skill; Khomyakov himself confesses that we haven't even invented a mousetrap. Consequently, we have to borrow from others. We are sick, says Lermontov – I agree; but we are sick because we have only half become Europeans; and we must cure ourselves with a hair of the dog that bit us.' (*'Le cadastre,'* thought Lavretsky.) 'Our best heads,' he continued, '– *nos meilleures têtes* – have long been convinced of this; all peoples are essentially the same; only introduce the right institutions – that's all. I dare say we can adapt ourselves to the present national way of life; that is our business, the business of us servants . . .' (he had almost said 'members') 'of the government; but in case of need, don't worry, the institutions will themselves transform the way of life.' Maria Dmitrievna assented with feeling to everything Panshin said. 'What a clever man,' she thought, 'to have talking in my house!' Liza was silent, leaning against the window; Lavretsky was also silent; Martha Timofeevna, playing cards in a corner with her friend, grumbled something under her breath. Panshin walked about the room as he talked, very well but with an undercurrent of irritation; he seemed to be attacking, not a whole generation, but a few people personally known to him.

In the Kalitins' garden, in a lilac-tree, lived a nightingale; its first evening notes sounded through the pauses in the eloquent discourse; the first stars were kindling in the sky, flushed with pink, above the motionless crests of the lime-trees. Lavretsky got up from his seat and began to answer Panshin; an argument developed. Lavretsky defended the youth and independence of Russia; he sacrificed himself and his own generation, but championed the new, its convictions and its desires; Panshin retorted harshly and irritably, declared that it was the duty of men of intelligence to change everything, and finally was so carried away that, forgetful of his official position and his career in the service, he called Lavretsky an out-of-date reactionary and even alluded – very distantly, it is true – to his false position in society. Lavretsky did not lose his temper, did not raise his voice (he remembered that Mikhalevich had also called him out-of-date, but a Voltairean) – and quietly defeated Panshin at all points. He proved to him the impossibility of sudden leaps forward and high-handed changes, unjustified either by knowledge of one's own country or true faith in an ideal, even a negative one, adduced his own upbringing as an example, demanded first of all recognition of the truth of the people and submission to it – without which even the courage to oppose the lie is impossible – and, finally, did not defend himself against the reproach, which he thought he deserved, of frivolous waste of his time and energies.

'That's all very well!' exclaimed Panshin, now thoroughly

vexed. 'Here you have returned to Russia – and what do you intend to do?'

'Cultivate the soil,' replied Lavretsky, 'and try to do it as well as possible.'

'Very praiseworthy, no doubt,' retorted Panshin, 'and I am told that you have already achieved great success in that field; but you will agree that not everybody can undertake such forms of activity . . .'

'*Une nature poétique*,' said Maria Dmitrievna, 'can't be expected to plough . . . *et puis*, you, Vladimir Nikolaich, are called to do everything *en grand*.'

This was too much even for Panshin: he lost the thread – and cut short the conversation. He made some attempt to turn it upon the beauty of the starry sky and Schubert's music, but somehow it dragged, and he ended by offering to play piquet with Maria Dmitrievna. 'What? On such a night?' she protested weakly; but she ordered the cards to be brought.

Panshin noisily tore open a new pack of cards, and Liza and Lavretsky, as though by arrangement, both got up and took seats near Martha Timofeevna. They both felt suddenly so happy that they were almost afraid to sit alone together – and both at the same time felt that the embarrassment and confusion they had experienced in the past few days had disappeared and would not return. The old lady stealthily tapped Lavretsky's cheek, slyly narrowed her eyes, and nodded her head several times as she said in a whisper: 'Thank you for finishing off that clever creature.' The room grew quiet; they could hear only the faint crackle of the wax candles, the occasional rap of a hand on the table, an exclamation, or the reckoning up of points and, pouring in a wide torrent through the window, together with the dewy freshness of the night, the strong, almost impertinently loud, clear song of the nightingale.

XXXIV

Liza had not said a word during the argument between Lavretsky and Panshin, but she had followed it closely and was entirely on Lavretsky's side. Her interest in politics was very slight, but the worldly young official's overweening tone (he had not expressed himself in such a way before) repelled her; his contempt for Russia outraged her. It did not enter Liza's mind to think of herself as a patriot, but she was heart and soul with the Russian people; the Russian turn of mind delighted her; she would talk for hours, without standing on ceremony, with the bailiff from her mother's estate, when he came to the town, and talk as to an equal, with no trace of superior condescension. Lavretsky felt all this: he would not have troubled to answer Panshin for his own sake; he had talked only for Liza. To each other they said nothing, and even their eyes only rarely met; but both understood that they had come very close together that evening, and that their likes and dislikes were the same. There was only one point on which they differed; but Liza secretly hoped to bring him to God. They sat near Martha Timofeevna and appeared to be following her game; indeed, they really were following it – but both of them felt their hearts swell in their breasts, and nothing was lost to them: it was for them that the nightingale sang, and the stars shone, and the trees whispered softly, lulled to sleep by warmth and the voluptuousness of summer. Lavretsky gave himself completely to the tide that carried him along – and was glad; but words cannot express what passed in the girl's pure heart: it was hidden from herself; let it remain hidden from the rest of the world also. Nobody can know, nobody has seen or will ever see how the seed, obeying the summons to live and blossom, swells and ripens in the bosom of the earth.

Ten o'clock struck. Martha Timofeevna went upstairs to her rooms with Nastasya Karpovna; Lavretsky and Liza crossed the room, stopped before the open door into the garden, looked far out into the darkness and then at one another – and smiled; they seemed ready to take one another by the hand and talk to their hearts' content. They turned to Maria Dmitrievna and Panshin, sitting over their protracted game of piquet. The last *partie* came to an end at length, and the hostess rose, sighing and groaning, from her cushioned arm-chair; Panshin took his hat, kissed Maria Dmitrievna's hand, remarked that nothing now prevented some happy creatures from sleeping or enjoying the beauties of the night, but that *he* would have to sit at his stupid papers till morning, bowed coldly to Liza (he had not expected that her answer to his proposal would be to ask him to wait, and consequently was sulking) – and took himself off. Lavretsky followed him. At the gate they parted; Panshin roused his driver by poking him in the neck with the end of his cane, got into the droshky and drove away. Lavretsky had no wish to go home: he walked out of the town into the open country. The night was clear and tranquil, although there was no moon; Lavretsky wandered for some time over the dewy grass; he chanced upon a narrow path; he followed it. It led him to a long fence and to a gate; he tried, without knowing why, to push this open; it creaked faintly and opened, as though it had been awaiting the touch of his hand. Lavretsky found himself in a garden, took a few steps along a lime-tree walk, and stopped in sudden amazement: he had recognized the Kalitins' garden.

He stepped at once into the patch of black shadow cast by a bushy hazel, and stood there a long time motionless, marvelling and perplexed.

'This can't be for nothing,' he thought.

All round him everything was still; no sound of any kind reached him from the house. He moved cautiously forward. Here, from a turn in the path, the dark façade of the whole house suddenly confronted him; only from two upstairs windows was there a gleam of light: a candle was burning behind Liza's white curtains, and in Martha Timofeevna's bedroom a lamp glimmered faintly before the icon, its little red flame reflected with a steady glow from the gold of the overlay; downstairs, a door left wide open yawned on to the verandah. Lavretsky sat down on a wooden bench, propped his head on his hand, and began to watch this door and Liza's window. In the town it struck midnight; a small clock in the house thinly chimed twelve; a watchman beat a tattoo on his board. Lavretsky was not thinking of anything, nor expecting anything; he was content to feel near to Liza and to sit in her garden on a bench where she herself had often sat . . . The light in Liza's room vanished.

'Goodnight, my dear girl,' whispered Lavretsky, still sitting motionless with his eyes fixed on the darkened window.

Suddenly a light appeared in one of the windows of the lower floor, passed to another, and then to a third . . . Somebody was walking through the rooms with a candle. 'Can it be Liza? Impossible! . . .' Lavretsky half rose . . . He caught a glimpse of the familiar face, and Liza appeared in the drawing-room. In her white dress, with her hair, still plaited, hanging down on her shoulders, she moved quietly to the table, stooped over it, set down her candle, and searched for something; then, turning to face the garden, she approached the open door and stood, all white, lightly poised and graceful, on the threshold. A tremor ran through Lavretsky's limbs.

'Liza!' escaped almost inaudibly from his lips.

She started and tried to penetrate the darkness with her eyes.

'Liza!' Lavretsky repeated more loudly, and emerged from the shadow of the trees.

Liza lifted her head in fright and then swayed back: she had recognized him. He called her a third time and stretched out his hands to her. She left the door and stepped into the garden.

'You?' she said. 'You here?'

'I . . . I . . . listen to me,' whispered Lavretsky, and, taking her hand, led her to the bench.

She followed him unresistingly; her pale face, her fixed gaze, all her movements expressed her unspoken bewilderment. Lavretsky seated her on the bench and placed himself in front of her.

'I had no idea of coming here,' he began. 'I was guided . . . I . . . I . . . I love you,' he said with an involuntary pang of fear.

Liza slowly turned her gaze on him; she seemed only at this moment to understand where she was and what was happening. She tried to get up, failed, and covered her face with her hands.

'Liza,' said Lavretsky. 'Liza,' he repeated, and stooped at her feet.

Her shoulders had begun to tremble slightly, and the fingers of her pale hands were pressed more closely to her face.

'What is the matter?' said Lavretsky, and heard a quiet sob. His heart seemed to stop beating . . . He understood what those tears meant. 'Can you possibly love me?' he whispered, and touched her knees.

'Get up,' he heard, 'get up, Fëdor Ivanych. What are we doing?'

He rose and sat down beside her on the bench. She was no longer crying, and she gazed at him searchingly with eyes still moist.

'I am afraid; what are we doing?' she repeated.

'I love you,' he said again. 'I am ready to devote my whole life to you.'

She started again as though she had been stung, and raised her eyes to the sky.

'That is all in God's hands,' she said.

'But do you love me, Liza? Are we to be happy?'

She lowered her eyes; he quietly drew her towards him, and her head fell on his shoulder . . . He turned his head slightly and touched her pale lips.

Half an hour later Lavretsky stood before the garden gate. He found it locked and was obliged to jump over the fence. He returned to the town and walked through the sleeping streets. A feeling of great, unlooked-for joy filled his heart; all his doubts had fled. 'Let the dark spectre of the past vanish!' he thought. 'She loves me, she will be mine.' Suddenly it seemed to him that he heard a stream of marvellous, triumphant sound in the air above his head; he stopped: the sounds pealed out still more magnificently; they poured forth in a powerful flood of melody – and he thought that all his happiness spoke and sang in them. He looked around: the sound came from the two upper windows of a small house.

'Lemm!' cried Lavretsky, and ran towards the house. 'Lemm! Lemm!' he repeated in a shout.

The music ceased and the figure of the old man, wearing a

dressing-gown open over his breast, and with disordered hair, appeared at the window.

'Ah!' he said with dignity. 'It is you, is it?'

'Christopher Fëdorych, what marvellous music! Let me in, for God's sake.'

The old man said not a word, but with a magnificent gesture threw the door-key from his window into the street. Lavretsky ran swiftly upstairs and into the room, and would have rushed to Lemm, but the other pointed imperiously to a chair, said jerkily in Russian, 'Sit, and hear,' himself sat down at the piano, threw a stern, proud glance all round, and began to play. It was long since Lavretsky had heard anything like this: the sweet, sensual melody took the heart captive from the first note; it was radiant and languorous with the inspiration of happiness and beauty; it swelled up and died away; it touched on all that is dear, mysterious and sacred on earth; it breathed immortal sadness and it died away among the stars. Lavretsky rose and stood cold and pale with rapture. This music pierced his very soul, so recently shaken with the happiness of love; the music too blazed with love. 'Again,' he whispered, as soon as the last note sounded. The old man looked at him with his eagle's gaze, tapped himself on the breast and, speaking with deliberation in his native tongue, said: 'I did this, for I am a great musician.' Then he played his wonderful composition once more. There were no candles in the room; the light of the newly risen moon slanted in at the window; the responsive air throbbed aloud; the poor little room seemed a shrine, and the old man's head was lifted high with inspiration in the silvery half-light. Lavretsky went over to him and embraced him. At first Lemm did not respond to his embrace, even pushed him away with his elbow; for a long time, without moving a muscle, he sat with the same fixed, stern, almost harsh gaze, only uttering once or twice in a muted growl: 'Aha!' At length his transfigured face grew calm and relaxed, and in reply to Lavretsky's fervent congratulations he first smiled a little and then burst into tears, feebly whimpering like a child.

'It is wonderful,' he said, 'that you came just at this moment; but I know, I know everything.'

'You know everything?' said Lavretsky in confusion.

'You heard me,' retorted Lemm, 'and surely you must have understood that I know everything?'

Lavretsky could not sleep that day; all night he sat on his bed. Liza did not sleep either: she was praying.

XXXV

The reader knows how Lavretsky grew and developed; we must say a few words of Liza's upbringing. She was ten years old when her father died; but he had not taken much interest in her. Full of the cares of business, always preoccupied with increasing his wealth, jaundiced, irritable, curt, he gave money ungrudgingly for the teachers, tutors, clothes, and other needs of his children; but he could not bear, as he expressed it, to wet-nurse mewling infants – and indeed he had no time to nurse them: he worked, fretted over business deals, slept little, played a very occasional game of cards, and worked again; he used to compare himself to a horse harnessed to a threshing-machine. 'My life has slipped away very quickly,' he said on his death-bed, with a little smile on his parched lips. Maria Dmitrievna concerned herself almost as little as her husband with Liza, in spite of her boasts to Lavretsky of having brought up her children all alone: she dressed her up, like a doll, stroked her head when there were visitors, and called her a good little girl and pretty darling to her face – and that was all: any kind of continued care was too fatiguing to the indolent lady. During her father's life, Liza was in the charge of a governess from Paris, Mademoiselle Moreau, and after his death she passed into Martha Timofeevna's keeping. The reader knows Martha Timofeevna; Mademoiselle Moreau was a tiny shrivelled creature with a bird's tiny claws and a bird's tiny brain. In her youth she had led a frivolous life, and when she was approaching old age she had only two remaining passions – for the pleasures of the table and for cards. When she had eaten her fill and was not playing cards or chattering, her face immediately took on an almost corpse-like expression: she would sit, her eyes would be open, she would be breathing, but it was quite evident that no thought of any kind passed through her head. She could not even be called good: birds, after all, are not virtuous. In consequence either of her frivolously spent youth or of the Parisian atmosphere she had breathed since she was a child, she nursed within herself a kind of cheap, universal scepticism, usually finding expression in the words: '*Tout ça c'est des bêtises.*' She spoke an incorrect but authentically Parisian jargon, neither gossiped nor indulged in whims – and what more could one wish for in a governess? On Liza she had very little influence; so much the greater therefore was the influence of her nurse, Agafya Vlasyevna.

This woman's history was remarkable. She came from a peasant family and at sixteen had been married off to a moujik, but she was sharply distinct from her peasant sisters. Her father had been a bailiff for twenty years, acquired a good deal of money, and spoiled her. She was an outstanding beauty, the most strikingly dressed of the girls of the whole region, clever, talkative, and bold. Her master, Dmitri Pestov, Maria Dmitrievna's father, a quiet and unassuming man, saw her once at threshing-time, talked to her, and fell passionately in love. She became a widow soon afterwards; Pestov, although he was a married man, took her into his house and dressed her like a house-serf. Agafya was at once at home in her new situation, as though she had known no other in her whole life. She grew white-skinned and plump; the arms under her muslin sleeves were 'fine-grained' like those of a merchant's wife; the samovar never left her table; she would wear nothing but silk or velvet and slept on a feather-bed. This beatific existence continued for five years, but Dmitri Pestov died; his widow, a kind woman, out of respect for her husband's memory was unwilling to deal unfairly with her rival, especially since Agafya had never forgotten herself in her presence; but she married her to a cow-herd and banished her out of sight. Three years passed. Once, on a hot summer's day, the mistress visited her cow-sheds, and Agafya refreshed her with such marvellous cool cream, behaved so modestly, and was so neat, cheerful and content with everything, that her mistress signified her forgiveness and allowed her to return to the house; in about six months' time she had become so attached to her that she promoted her to housekeeper and entrusted her with the management of the whole household. Agafya had returned to power, and again she grew plump and white-skinned; her mistress trusted her completely. So passed some five years more. For the second time misfortune struck at Agafya. Her husband, who had come with her as a manservant in the house, took to drink, began to disappear from the house, and ended by stealing six of his mistress's silver spoons, which he hid – until there was a chance to remove them – in his wife's box. This was discovered. He was sent away to become a cow-herd once more, and Agafya was disgraced; she was not turned out of the house, but she was reduced from housekeeper to sewing-maid, and instead of a cap she must now wear a kerchief on her head. To everybody's surprise, Agafya took the blow that had been dealt her with humble submission. She was then over thirty years old, all her children had died, and her husband did not long survive. The time had come for her to face realities: she faced them. She became very silent and pious, never missed matins or mass, and gave away all her fine clothes. For fifteen years she lived quietly, meekly, and soberly, quarrelling with nobody, yielding to everybody. If people were offensive to her, she only bowed and thanked them for the lesson. Her mistress had long since forgiven her and restored her to favour, and even given her the cap from her own head; but she refused to discard her kerchief and always wore sombre clothes. After her mistress's death she became even quieter and more humble. It is easy to rouse a Russian's fear or win his affection, but difficult to earn his respect: that is not given quickly or to everybody. Agafya was deeply respected by everybody in the house; nobody remembered her past sins, any more than if they had been buried with the old master.

When he became Maria Dmitrievna's husband, Kalitin wished to entrust the management of the household to Agafya, but she declined 'on account of the temptations'; he stormed at her: she bowed low and went out. Kalitin was sensible and understanding; he understood Agafya and did not forget her. When he removed to the town he installed her, with her consent, as nurse to Liza, who was just five years old.

Her new nurse's stern and serious face terrified Liza at first; but she soon grew used to her and began to love her. She herself was a serious child; her face recalled Kalitin's sharp and regular features; only her eyes were not her father's; they shone with a quiet goodness and attentiveness seldom seen in children. She did not care for playing with dolls, never laughed much or boisterously, and behaved with great propriety. She was not often thoughtful, but it was almost always to some purpose if she was; after a period of silence she usually ended by turning to some older person with a question that showed she had been pondering over a new impression. She early lost all her childish mispronunciations and was already speaking quite correctly before she was four years old. She was afraid of her father; her feeling for her mother was indeterminate – she was neither afraid of her nor demonstratively affectionate; but neither was she demonstrative with Agafya, the only person she really loved. Agafya never left her. It was strange to see them together, Agafya all in black, a sombre-coloured kerchief on her head, with her emaciated face, as transparent as wax, but still beautiful and expressive, sitting bolt upright and knitting a stocking, while Liza, in a little arm-chair at her feet, also worked diligently with her needle or, raising her grave, shining eyes, listened to the stories Agafya told her; but the stories Agafya told her were not fairy-tales: in measured, even tones she would relate the life of the blessed Virgin, the lives of hermits, holy saints, and blessed martyrs. She told Liza how holy men lived in the wilderness, how they were saved, how they suffered hunger and want – and how they did not fear emperors, but confessed Christ; how the birds of the air brought them food and the beasts obeyed them; and how, wherever drops of their blood had fallen, flowers sprang up. 'Wallflowers?' Liza, who loved flowers, asked once . . . Agafya talked to Liza gravely and humbly, as though she felt it was not for her to utter such high and holy words. Liza listened, and the image of omniscient, omnipresent Godhead lodged itself with a kind of sweet forcefulness in her soul and filled her with pure, reverent awe, and Christ became for her something near, well-known, almost familiar. Agafya had also taught her to pray. Sometimes she would wake Liza at dawn, dress her hastily and take her secretly to early mass; Liza would follow her on tiptoe, holding her breath; the chill and half-light of the morning, the freshness of the empty church, the very secrecy of these unheralded absences from home, the cautious return to the house and to bed – the whole mingling of the forbidden, the strange, and the sacred, agitated the child and penetrated to the utmost depths of her being. Agafya never judged others, and never scolded Liza for being naughty. When she disapproved, she merely was silent; and Liza knew what her silence meant; with the quick insight of childhood she also under-stood very well when Agafya disapproved of others – whether Maria Dmitrievna or Kalitin himself. Agafya looked after Liza for something over three years; Mademoiselle Moreau replaced her; but the frivolous Frenchwoman with her cold ways and her exclamation: '*Tout ça c'est des bêtises*' – could not dislodge Liza's beloved nurse from her heart: the seeds already sown had put forth roots too deep for that. Besides, Agafya, although she had ceased to look after Liza, remained in the house and often saw her nursling, who trusted her as before.

Agafya, however, did not get on well with Martha Timofeevna, when the latter came to live in the Kalitins' house. The stern dignity of the former peasant-girl was not to the impatient and self-willed old woman's liking. Agafya asked for leave to go on a pilgrimage, and did not return. There were vague rumours that she had retired into a community of schismatics. But the imprint she had left in Liza's soul was not effaced. Liza, as before, went to church as though to a festival, and prayed with delight, with a kind of suppressed and shamefaced ecstasy, at which Maria Dmitrievna secretly marvelled; and Martha Timofeevna herself, although she put no restraints on Liza, did try to moderate her fervour and would not allow her to bow down to the ground too many times: such tricks, she said, were not for ladies. Liza was good, that is to say diligent, at her lessons; God had not given her any particularly brilliant talent or a great intellect; she achieved nothing without hard work. She played the piano well, but only Lemm knew what pains it had cost her. She read very little; she had no 'words of her own', but she had thoughts of her own, and she followed her own path. It was not for nothing that she resembled her father: he had not asked other people what to do, either. So she grew up – quietly, without haste, and so she reached the age of nineteen. Without knowing it herself, she was very charming. Every one of her movements expressed an involuntary, slightly coltish, grace; her voice rang with the silver sound of untouched youth; the least feeling of pleasure summoned a delightful smile to her lips and gave her shining eyes a profound lustre and a mysterious sweetness. Filled with consciousness of her duty and with the fear of hurting anybody whatever, with her kind and gentle heart, she loved everybody in general and nobody in particular; she loved God alone with a rapturous, timid, tender love. Lavretsky had been the first to disturb her peaceful, inward life.

This was Liza.

XXXVI

The next day, between eleven and twelve o'clock, Lavretsky returned to the Kalitins'. On the way he met Panshin, who rode past him at a gallop with his hat pulled right down to his eyebrows. At the house, Lavretsky was not admitted – for the first time since he had known them. Maria Dmitrievna was 'resting', so the servant affirmed; 'madam' had a headache. Martha Timofeevna and Lizaveta Mikhaylovna were not at home. Lavretsky, with a vague hope of meeting Liza, took a turn about the garden, but he saw nobody. He went back again two hours later and received the same answer, while the manservant seemed to look at him rather oddly. Lavretsky thought it would not do to inquire a third time the same day, and resolved to go over to Vasilyevskoe, where he had in any case some business to attend to. He passed the journey in constructing plans, each more splendid than the last; but in his aunt's little village melancholy descended on him; he began talking with Anton, but every idea in the old man's head seemed wilfully gloomy. He told Lavretsky of how Glafira Petrovna, before her death, had bitten her own hand, and, after a silence, added with a sigh, 'Every man, dear master, is bound to devour himself.' It was already late when Lavretsky started on the return journey. The sounds of evening lapped around him; the image of Liza rose before his mind in all its gentle brightness; he was moved by the thought that she loved him, and he approached his little house in the town in a mood of peaceful happiness.

The first thing that struck him as he entered the house was the scent of patchouli, which he detested; there in the hall stood several large trunks and boxes. The face of his valet, hurrying towards him, seemed strange. Without formulating his impressions, he stepped across the threshold of the drawing-room . . . A lady in a flounced black silk dress rose to meet him from the sofa and, raising a batiste handkerchief to her pale face, took a few steps towards him, inclined her beautifully dressed, perfumed head – and fell at his feet . . . It was only then that he knew her: the lady was his wife.

His breath failed . . . He leaned against the wall.

'*Théodore*, don't send me away!' she said in French, and her voice was like a knife cutting into his heart.

He looked at her mindlessly, although involuntarily he noticed that she had grown pale and puffy.

'*Théodore*,' she went on, from time to time casting up her eyes and carefully wringing her astonishingly beautiful hands with their polished pink nails, '*Théodore*, I have wronged you, wronged you deeply – I will go further, I have sinned against you; but hear me out; I am tormented by remorse, I have become a burden to myself, I could bear my situation no longer. How many times I have thought of appealing to you, but I was afraid of your anger. I made up my mind to break every tie with the past . . . *puis, j'ai été si malade*, I was so ill,' she added, passing her hand over her forehead and cheek. 'I took advantage of the rumours that got about of my death; I abandoned everything, I hurried here without stopping day or night. For a long time I hesitated to appear before you, my judge – *paraître devant vous, mon juge*; but at last, remembering how good and kind you have always been, I decided to come to you; I found out your address in Moscow. Believe me,' she continued, rising very quietly from the floor and seating herself on the extreme edge of a chair, 'I often thought of dying, and I might have found enough courage to take my own life – alas, life for me is now an intolerable burden! – but the thought of my daughter, my Adochka, stopped me; she is here, asleep in the next room, poor child! She is tired. – You will see her: she at least is innocent, and I am so unhappy, so unhappy!' exclaimed Madame Lavretsky, and burst into tears.

Lavretsky had at last recovered himself: he left the wall and turned towards the door.

'Are you going?' said his wife in despair. 'Oh, that is cruel! Without one word, without even a reproach . . . Your contempt is killing me; this is terrible!'

Lavretsky stopped.

'What can you want to hear from me?' he said in an almost inaudible voice.

'Nothing, nothing,' she broke in rapidly. 'I know I have no right to ask anything of you. I am not insane, believe me; I do not hope, I dare not hope, for your forgiveness. I dare only ask you to tell me what I must do and where I must live. I will obey your orders, whatever they are, like a slave.'

'I have no orders to give you,' Lavretsky replied, in the same tone. 'You know that all is over between us . . . and now more than ever. You may live where you like; and if your allowance is too small . . .'

'Oh, don't say such terrible things,' Varvara Pavlovna interrupted him. 'Take pity on me, if only . . . if only for the sake of this angel . . .' And with these words Varvara Pavlovna rushed headlong into the next room and immediately reappeared with a little girl, very elaborately dressed, in her arms. Her fair hair fell in big curls over her pretty, rosy little face and her large, sleepy, dark eyes; she was smiling and screwing up her eyes against the light, and propping herself with her chubby little hand on her mother's neck.

'*Ada, vois, c'est ton père*,' said Varvara Pavlovna, brushing the curls away from the little girl's eyes and kissing her fervently, '*prie-le avec moi*.'

'*C'est ça, papa?*' lisped the little girl.

'*Oui, mon enfant, n'est-ce pas que tu l'aimes?*'

But here Lavretsky could bear no more.

'Which melodrama does this scene come out of?' he muttered, and left the room.

Varvara Pavlovna stood where she was for some time, then she shrugged her shoulders slightly, carried the little girl into the next room, undressed her and put her to bed. Afterwards she took up a book, sat down by the lamp, waited for about an hour, and at last went to bed herself.

'*Eh bien, madame?*' asked the French maid she had brought with her from Paris, as she took off her stays.

'*Eh bien, Justine,*' she replied, 'he has aged a good deal, but he seems to be as kind as ever. Give me my gloves for the night, and lay out the grey, high-necked dress for tomorrow; and don't forget to get mutton cutlets for Ada . . . Of course, it is difficult to get them here, but you must try.'

'*À la guerre comme à la guerre,*' answered Justine, and put out the candle.

XXXVII

For more than two hours Lavretsky wandered about the streets of the town. There came into his memory the night he had spent in the outskirts of Paris. His heart laboured and in his head, empty and as it were stunned, the same thoughts went round and round, sombre, meaningless, bitter. 'She is here, she is here,' he whispered, with constantly renewed amazement. He felt that he had lost Liza. Rage choked him; the blow had fallen with too-crushing suddenness. How could he so easily have believed ridiculous newspaper gossip, a scrap of paper? 'Well, but if I had not believed it,' he thought, 'what difference would it have made? I should not have known that Liza loved me; she would not have known it herself.' He could not banish from his mind the image, the voice, the eyes, of his wife . . . and he cursed himself and cursed everything on earth.

Exhausted, he came just before dawn to Lemm's house. For a long time he could not make his knocking heard; finally, the old man's head appeared in the window, wearing a nightcap, looking sour and wrinkled and no longer bearing the least resemblance to that inspired, austere head that had looked majestically down on Lavretsky twenty-four hours earlier from the full height of its artistic greatness.

'What do you want?' asked Lemm. 'I can't play for you every night. I have taken some medicine.'

But evidently Lavretsky's face was very strange: the old man hooded his eyes with his hand, peered at his nocturnal visitor, and admitted him.

Lavretsky entered the room and sank into a chair. The old man stood before him, pulling the skirts of his ancient, bright-coloured dressing-gown tighter round him, huddling into himself and chewing his lips.

'My wife has come,' said Lavretsky, lifted his head and suddenly, involuntarily, began to laugh.

Lemm's face showed his astonishment, but he did not even smile, only wrapped his dressing-gown closer round him.

'Of course, you didn't know,' went on Lavretsky. 'I imagined . . . I read in the papers that she was dead.'

'O-oh, you saw that recently?' asked Lemm.

'Yes.'

'O-oh,' repeated the old man, raising his eyebrows. 'And she has come here?'

'Yes. She is at my house now; and I . . . I am an unlucky man.'

And he began to laugh again.

'You are an unlucky man,' repeated Lemm slowly.

'Christopher Fëdorych,' began Lavretsky, 'would you undertake to deliver a note?'

'Hm. May I know to whom?'

'Lizav—'

'Ah, yes, yes, I understand. Very well. And when must the letter be delivered?'

'Tomorrow, as early as possible.'

'Hm. I could send Katrin, my cook. No, I'll go myself.'

'And will you bring me an answer?'

'Yes, I will bring an answer.'

Lemm sighed.

'Yes, my poor young friend; you are indeed an unlucky young man.'

Lavretsky wrote a few words to Liza: he informed her of the arrival of his wife and asked her to appoint a time when he might see her – and then threw himself down on the narrow sofa, with his face to the wall; the old man lay down on the bed and tossed and turned for a long time, coughing and sipping his medicine.

Morning came; they both got up. They looked at one another strangely. At that moment Lavretsky wanted to kill himself. Katrin, the cook, brought them atrocious coffee. It struck eight. Lemm put on his hat and left, saying that he was giving a lesson at the Kalitins' at ten o'clock, but that he would find a suitable pretext for going earlier. Lavretsky threw himself down again on the sofa, and again rueful laughter welled up from the bottom of his soul. He thought of how his wife's presence had driven him from the house; he pictured Liza's plight to himself, and he closed his eyes and lay with his hands behind his head. Lemm returned at last and brought a scrap of paper on which Liza had traced the following words in pencil: 'We cannot meet today; perhaps tomorrow evening. Goodbye.' Lavretsky thanked Lemm drily and absent-mindedly, and went home.

He found his wife at breakfast; Ada, wearing a white frock with blue ribbons and with her hair in long curls, was eating her mutton cutlet. Varvara Pavlovna rose as soon as Lavretsky entered the room and went towards him with a submissive expression. He requested her to follow him to his study, closed the door, and began to pace up and down the room; she sat down, modestly folded her hands together, and began to follow him with her still beautiful, although slightly made-up eyes.

It was a long time before Lavretsky could speak: he felt that he was not in control of himself; he saw clearly that Varvara Pavlovna was not in the least afraid of him, but was pretending that she might swoon at any moment.

'Kindly listen to me, madam,' he began, breathing heavily and occasionally clenching his teeth; 'there is no need for us to pretend. I do not believe in your remorse, but even if it were genuine, for me to go back to you again, to live with you, would be impossible.'

Varvara Pavlovna compressed her lips and narrowed her eyes. 'He loathes me,' she thought. 'It is all over. For him I am not even a woman at all.'

'Impossible,' repeated Lavretsky, buttoning his coat to the top. 'I do not know why you have honoured me with your presence here: probably you had no money left.'

'Oh! You hurt me,' whispered Varvara Pavlovna.

'However that may be, you are still, unfortunately, my wife. I cannot turn you out . . . and so I make you this offer. You may, if you care to do so, go to Lavriki today, and live there; the house there, as you know, is a good one; you shall be provided with all necessities, in addition to your allowance . . . Do you agree to that?'

Varvara Pavlovna raised an embroidered handkerchief to her eyes.

'I have already told you,' she said, with a nervous twitching of her lips, 'that I will agree to anything, whatever you wish to do with me; now it only remains for me to ask you to allow me at least to thank you for your magnanimity.'

'No gratitude, I beg you, it is better so,' said Lavretsky hastily. 'That means,' he continued, moving to the door, 'that I may rely . . .'

'I shall be in Lavriki tomorrow,' said Varvara Pavlovna, politely rising from her place. 'But, Fëdor Ivanych,' (she no longer called him *Théodore*) . . .

'What is it?'

'I know I have done nothing to earn your forgiveness yet; may I at least hope that with time . . . ?'

'Oh, Varvara Pavlovna!' interrupted Lavretsky, 'you are a clever woman, but after all I'm no fool, either. I know that isn't what you want at all. And I forgave you long ago; but there has always been a great gulf between us.'

'I shall know how to resign myself,' replied Varvara Pavlovna. 'I have not forgotten my sin; I should not have been surprised to learn that you were even glad of the news of my death,' she added meekly, with a slight gesture of the hand to the copy of the newspaper lying forgotten on the desk.

Fëdor Ivanych started: the column was marked with pencil. Varvara Pavlovna still looked at him with immense humility. She was very beautiful at that moment. The grey Paris gown moulding her shapely, supple, almost girlish waist, the slender, delicate neck embraced by a white collar, the breast regularly rising and falling, the hands and arms innocent of bracelets or rings – the whole figure, from the shining hair to the just visible tips of the shoes, was so elegant . . .

Lavretsky threw her a look of loathing, all but cried, 'Brava!', all but struck that head with his fist – and went out. An hour later he was already on the way to Vasilyevskoe, and two hours later Varvara Pavlovna sent for the best carriage in the town, put on a simple, black-veiled straw hat and an unpretentious mantle, left Ada in Justine's care and betook herself to the Kalitins': she had learned by questioning the servants that her husband went to see them every day.

XXXVIII

The day of Lavretsky's wife's arrival in O——, not a happy day for him, was a painful day for Liza also. She had not had time to go downstairs and say good morning to her mother before the sound of hoofs was heard under the window, and with secret terror she saw Panshin riding into the courtyard. 'He has come so early because he wants a final explanation,' she thought – and she was not mistaken; after an uneasy interval in the drawing-room he suggested that she should go with him into the garden, and there demanded the decision of his fate. Liza took her courage in both hands and declared that she could not be his wife. He heard her out, presenting to her his profile, with his hat pulled down over his eyes; politely, but in a changed voice, he inquired whether this was her last word and whether he had given her any cause for such a change in her views, then he pressed his hand to his eyes, uttered a short, broken sigh, and drew his hand away from his face.

'I did not want to follow the beaten track,' he said tonelessly, 'I wanted to follow the promptings of my heart in finding a wife; but evidently that was not to be. Farewell, my dream!' He bowed low and returned to the house.

Liza hoped that he would go away at once, but he went to Maria Dmitrievna in the study and sat with her for about an hour. As he left, he said to Liza: '*Votre mère vous appelle; adieu à jamais . . .*', mounted his horse, and broke at once into a full gallop. Liza went to Maria Dmitrievna and found her in tears: Panshin had informed her of his ill-success.

'Do you want to kill me? Do you want to kill me?' – thus the widow, chagrined, began her lament. 'What more can you want? What is wrong with him as a husband for you? He has a position at court, he's no fortune-hunter. In St Petersburg he could marry any lady-in-waiting he liked. And *I, I*, had such hopes! You must have changed towards him very recently! What brought that cloud into our sky? – it didn't come of its own accord. It was that stupid creature, wasn't it? A fine adviser you've found for yourself!'

'But he, poor darling,' continued Maria Dmitrievna, 'how polite he is, and how attentive even in his grief! He has promised not to desert me. Oh, I shall never be able to bear this! Oh, I have a splitting headache! Send Palasha to me. It will kill me, if you don't change your mind; do you hear?' And with a few accusations of ingratitude, Maria Dmitrievna dismissed Liza.

She went to her room. But before she had had time to recover from the interviews with Panshin and her mother, another storm burst about her ears, and that from a quarter where she least expected it. Martha Timofeevna came into her room and slammed the door behind her. The old lady's face was pale, her cap askew, her eyes blazed and her lips trembled. Liza was astounded: she had never before seen her sensible, reasonable aunt in such a state.

'Excellent, miss!' began Martha Timofeevna in a broken and trembling whisper, 'excellent! Who taught you such goings-on, though, miss? . . . Give me some water: I can't speak.'

'Calm yourself, aunt; what is the matter?' said Liza, giving her a glass of water. 'After all, you did not seem to like Mr Panshin yourself.'

Martha Timofeevna set down the glass.

'I can't drink it: I shall knock out the few teeth I have left. Why Panshin? What has Panshin to do with this? You had better tell me who taught you to make midnight assignations, eh, miss?'

Liza turned pale.

'And don't try to deny it, if you please,' went on Martha Timofeevna. 'Shurochka saw you herself, and she told me. I have forbidden her to talk so much, but she is not a liar.'

'I am not trying to deny it, aunt.' Liza's voice was hardly audible.

'Aha! So, my fine young lady, you did have a rendezvous with him, eh, that old sinner, that hypocrite?'

'No.'

'What?'

'I went down into the drawing-room for a book: he was in the garden – and he called me.'

'And you went? Excellent. And you love him, I suppose, do you?'

'Yes, I love him,' answered Liza in a low voice.

'Oh, my God! she loves him!' Martha Timofeevna plucked off her cap. 'She loves a married man, eh? She loves him!'

'He told me . . .' began Liza.

'What did he tell you, the darling, eh?'

'He told me his wife was dead.'

Martha Timofeevna crossed herself.

'Rest her soul,' she whispered. 'She was a shallow, worthless creature – may she be forgiven. So: that means he's a widower. And I see he's equal to anything. No sooner has he got rid of one wife than he's after the next. Still waters run deep. But I can tell you this, niece: in my day, when I was young, girls were made to smart for such tricks. Don't be angry with me, miss; only fools are angry at the truth. I gave orders that he was not to be admitted today. I am fond of him, but this I can never forgive him. So, he's a widower! Give me some water. As for sending Panshin away with a flea in his ear, I'm delighted with you for that. Only don't go sitting with men at night, they're not to be trusted. I'm an old woman, don't make me suffer so. Or you may find I'm not all sweetness – I can bite too . . . Widower!'

Martha Timofeevna went out, and Liza sat down in the corner and cried. She was filled with bitter sorrow; she had not deserved to be so humiliated. Her love had not revealed itself in joy: this was the second time since yesterday that she had been in tears. This new, strange feeling had barely awakened in her heart, and how dearly she had already paid for it, how rudely alien hands had touched her cherished secret! She felt ashamed, and bitter, and hurt: but there was no shadow of doubt or fear in her – and Lavretsky had grown dearer than ever to her. She had hesitated, before she understood herself; but after that meeting, that kiss, she could no longer hesitate; she knew that she loved – and loved honestly and in good earnest; the ties that bound her would last all her life – and she feared no menaces: she felt that nothing could break those ties.

XXXIX

Maria Dmitrievna was thrown into panic by the announcement of Varvara Pavlovna Lavretskaya's call; she did not even know whether or not to receive her: she was afraid of offending Fëdor Ivanych. Curiosity finally prevailed. 'After all,' she thought, 'she is a relative, too,' and, taking her seat in an arm-chair, she said to the manservant: 'Show her in!' A few moments passed; the door opened; Varvara Pavlovna approached Maria Dmitrievna with quick, almost noiseless steps and, without giving her a chance to rise, almost kneeled down before her.

'Oh, thank you, my dear aunt,' she began in Russian, in a quiet voice, full of emotion, 'thank you; I did not hope for such kindness from you; you are an angel of goodness.'

With these words, Varvara Pavlovna unexpectedly seized one of Maria Dmitrievna's hands and, lightly pressing it between her lavender-coloured kid gloves, humbly raised it to her full rosy lips. Maria Dmitrievna, seeing a woman so beautiful and so charmingly dressed almost at her feet, was quite at a loss; she did not know what to do first: she wanted to take her hand away, and to offer her guest a chair, and to say something affectionate to her; she ended by raising Varvara Pavlovna to her feet and kissing her smooth, scented forehead. Varvara Pavlovna was deeply moved by this kiss.

'Good morning, *bon jour*,' said Maria Dmitrievna, 'of course I did not imagine . . . however, I am, of course, very glad to see you. You understand, my dear, it is not for me to judge between husband and wife . . .'

'My husband is completely in the right,' interrupted Varvara Pavlovna. 'I alone am to blame.'

'Your feelings do you credit,' replied Maria Dmitrievna, 'great credit. Have you been here long? Have you seen him? But do sit down, please.'

'I arrived yesterday,' answered Varvara Pavlovna, obediently taking a chair. 'I saw Fëdor Ivanych and talked to him.'

'Ah! Well, and what did he do?'

'I was afraid my unexpected arrival would make him angry,' continued Varvara Pavlovna, 'but he did not refuse to see me.'

'That means, he did not . . . Yes, yes, I understand,' said Maria Dmitrievna. 'He is only a little rough on the surface, but his heart is soft.'

'Fëdor Ivanych has not forgiven me; he refused to hear what I had to say . . . But he was kind enough to assign Lavriki to me to live in.'

'Ah, a beautiful estate!'

'I am leaving for there tomorrow, in accordance with his wishes; but I thought it was my duty to come and see you first.'

'I am very, very much obliged to you, my dear. One ought never to forget one's relatives. But do you know, I am astonished at how well you speak Russian. *C'est étonnant.*'

Varvara Pavlovna sighed.

'I have been abroad too long, Maria Dmitrievna, and I know it; but my heart has always been Russian and I have never forgotten my own country.'

'Yes, yes, that is best. But Fëdor Ivanych was not expecting you at all . . . Yes, trust my experience, *la patrie avant tout*. Oh, do please let me see your charming mantle.'

'Do you like it?' Varvara Pavlovna promptly slipped it from her shoulders. 'It is very simple indeed; it is from Madame Baudran.'

'You can tell that at once. From Madame Baudran . . . How nice, and in such good taste! I am sure you brought a lot of exciting things with you. If only I could have seen them!'

'All my wardrobe is at your service, dearest auntie. If you

will allow me, I can show your maid some things. I have my maid from Paris with me – a wonderful needlewoman.'

'You are very kind, my dear. But really, I'm quite ashamed . . .'

'Ashamed . . .' repeated Varvara Pavlovna reproachfully. If you want to make me happy, treat me as if I were your own property.'

Maria Dmitrievna had quite thawed.

'*Vous êtes charmante*,' she said. 'But why not take off your hat and gloves?'

'Oh, may I?' asked Varvara Pavlovna, and lightly clasped her hands, as though under the stress of emotion.

'Of course; after all, you are dining with us, I hope. I . . . I will introduce my daughter to you.' Maria Dmitrievna felt some embarrassment, but 'Well, it can't be helped,' she thought. She added aloud, 'I am afraid she is not very well today.'

'O, *ma tante*, how good you are!' exclaimed Varvara Pavlovna, raising her handkerchief to her eyes.

The page announced that Gedeonovsky had called. The old gossip entered, smirking and performing a series of low bows. Maria Dmitrievna introduced him to her visitor. At first he was a little disconcerted, but Varvara Pavlovna treated him with such a blend of coquetry and deference that his ears grew as red as fire, and fictitious anecdotes, gossip, and compliments poured out of his mouth like honey. Varvara Pavlovna listened to him, smiled discreetly and little by little began to talk freely herself. She spoke modestly of Paris, of her travels, and of Baden; once or twice she made Maria Dmitrievna laugh and each time she sighed slightly and seemed to be inwardly reproaching herself for her unsuitable gaiety; she asked for permission to bring Ada; she took off her gloves and demonstrated with her smooth hands, scented with soap *à la guimauve*, how and where flounces, ruches, lace, and choux were worn; she promised to bring a flask of the new English scent, 'Victoria Essence', and rejoiced like a child when Maria Dmitrievna agreed to accept it as a gift; she shed a tear at the remembrance of the emotion she had felt the first time she heard Russian church bells: 'They struck so deep, into my very heart,' she said.

At that moment Liza came in.

Since that morning, from the minute when, cold with dismay, she had read Lavretsky's note, Liza had been preparing herself for a meeting with his wife. She had a presentiment that she would see her and she had resolved, as a punishment for what she called her guilty hopes, not to try to avoid her. The abrupt change in her destiny had shaken her to the root; in the space of two hours her face had grown thin; but she had not shed a tear. 'It serves me right,' she said to herself, in her agitation finding it difficult to repress certain impulses of bitter hatred in her soul that frightened even herself. 'Well, I shall have to go down,' she thought, as soon as she heard of Madame Lavretsky's arrival, and she went down ... She stood for a long time before the drawing-room door, trying to summon up enough resolution to open it. Thinking, 'I have wronged her,' she crossed the threshold and made herself look at

Varvara Pavlovna, made herself smile. Varvara Pavlovna advanced as soon as she saw her, and made her a slight but courteous bow. 'Allow me to introduce myself,' she began in an insinuating voice. 'Your *maman* is so indulgent to me that I hope you too will be as . . . kind.' The expression of her face as she uttered this last word, her sly smile, her glance, cold yet sweet, the movements of her shoulders and arms, her very clothes, her whole being – awoke such a feeling of repulsion in Liza that she was incapable of answering and had to compel herself to hold out her hand. 'My lady thinks herself too good for me,' thought Varvara Pavlovna, firmly grasping Liza's cold fingers; then, turning to Maria Dmitrievna, she said aloud, '*Mais elle est délicieuse!*' Liza flushed faintly: to her the exclamation sounded derisive and insulting; but she decided not to trust this impression and sat down at her embroidery-frame by the window. Even here Varvara Pavlovna did not leave her in peace: she went up to her and began to praise her taste and artistry . . . Liza's heart throbbed heavily and painfully: she could hardly force herself to remain in her place. It seemed to her that Varvara Pavlovna knew everything and was mocking her with secret triumph. Fortunately for her, Gedeonovsky began to talk to Varvara Pavlovna and distracted her attention. Liza bent over her work and covertly watched her. 'This,' she thought, 'is the woman *he* loved.' But she immediately banished the thought of Lavretsky from her mind: she was afraid of losing control of herself, and felt as though her head were quietly spinning round. Maria Dmitrievna led the conversation to music.

'I have heard, my dear,' she began, 'that you are a remarkably accomplished performer.'

'I have not played for a long time,' replied Varvara Pavlovna, promptly sitting down at the piano and running her fingers smartly over the keys. 'Would you like me to play for you?'

'Please do.'

Varvara Pavlovna played a difficult and brilliant étude by Hertz like a master. She had great power and agility.

'Ravishing!' exclaimed Gedeonovsky.

'Extraordinary!' agreed Maria Dmitrievna. 'Well, Varvara Pavlovna, I confess you have surprised me,' she said, using the name for the first time. 'You might even give concerts. We have a musician here, an old German, eccentric but very clever; he gives Liza lessons. He will be simply mad about you.'

'Is Lizaveta Mikhaylovna musical too?' asked Varvara Pavlovna, half-turning her head towards her.

'Yes, she's not a bad player and she loves music; but what's that compared to you? But we have a young man here as well; you ought to make his acquaintance. He has the soul of an artist, and he writes very nice music. He is the only one who could really appreciate you.'

'A young man?' said Varvara Pavlovna. 'Who is he? A poor young man?'

'Good gracious! – the most eligible young man here, and not only here – *et à Petersbourg*. A *kammerjunker*, and received in the best society. You have probably heard of him: Vladimir

Nikolaich Panshin. He is here on an official mission . . . a future Minister, I assure you!'

'And an artist?'

'An artist at heart, and so charming. You will meet him. He has come to see us very often during all this time, and I have asked him here this evening. I *hope* he will come,' added Maria Dmitrievna, with a little sigh and a wryly bitter smile.

Liza understood the meaning of that smile; but such things could not concern her now.

'And young?' repeated Varvara Pavlovna, delicately modulating the tones of her voice.

'Twenty-eight, and of a most pleasing appearance. *Un jeune homme accompli*, really.'

'A model youth, one might say,' remarked Gedeonovsky.

Varvara Pavlovna abruptly launched into a noisy Strauss waltz, beginning with such a rapid and powerful trill that Gedeonovsky actually jumped; in the very middle of the waltz she switched to a mournful air, and ended with the aria '*Fra poco . . .*' from *Lucia*. She had come to the conclusion that cheerful music was not suitable in her position. Maria Dmitrievna was very much touched by the aria from *Lucia*, with its sentimental passages emphasized.

'What soul!' she said aloud to Gedeonovsky.

'Ravishing!' repeated Gedeonovsky, raising his eyes to heaven.

Dinner-time came. Martha Timofeevna came downstairs

when the soup was already on the table. Her manner to Varvara Pavlovna was very dry; she answered her civilities in monosyllables and would not look at her. Varvara Pavlovna soon realized that she would not get any response from the old lady and ceased talking to her; Maria Dmitrievna, on the other hand, redoubled her attentions to her visitor: her aunt's discourtesy angered her. It was not only at Varvara Pavlovna, however, that Martha Timofeevna would not look: she did not look at Liza either, although her eyes absolutely blazed. She sat as if made of stone, looking pale and jaundiced, with compressed lips, and ate nothing. Liza appeared calm, as indeed she was: her heart had grown still, and a strange numbness, the numbness of the condemned, had descended on her. Varvara Pavlovna said little during the meal: she seemed to have become shy once more, and had adopted an expression of retiring melancholy. Only Gedeonovsky enlivened the conversation with his stories, although occasionally he glanced apprehensively at Martha Timofeevna and coughed nervously – his throat always felt parched if he was going to utter lies in her presence; but she did not hinder or interrupt him. After dinner, it appeared that Varvara Pavlovna was a great lover of the game of preference; this so delighted Maria Dmitrievna that she thought to herself, quite moved: 'What a fool, though, Fëdor Ivanych must be, not to understand a woman like this!'

She sat down to play cards with Varvara Pavlovna and Gedeonovsky, and Martha Timofeevna took Liza upstairs with her, saying that she did not look well and must have a headache.

'Yes, she has a dreadful headache,' said Maria Dmitrievna, turning to Varvara Pavlovna and rolling her eyes. 'I myself am subject to such migraines . . .'

'Are you really?' replied Varvara Pavlovna.

Liza entered her aunt's room and sank exhausted into a chair. Martha Timofeevna gazed at her for some time in silence, then quietly knelt down and began, still in silence, to kiss each of her hands in turn. Liza leaned forward, flushed, and burst into tears, but she did not raise Martha Timofeevna, nor take away her hands: she felt she had no right to take them away, no right to prevent the old lady from showing her remorse and sympathy, and seeking forgiveness for what had happened the day before. Martha Timofeevna could not stop kissing those poor, pale, nerveless hands, and the tears flowed silently from her eyes and from Liza's, while Matros, the cat, purred in a deep arm-chair by a half-knitted stocking, the long flame of the lamp wavered very faintly before the icon, and in the next room Nastasya Karpovna stood just inside the door and stealthily wiped her eyes with a checked pocket-handkerchief rolled into a ball.

XL

Meanwhile, in the drawing-room, they were playing preference; Maria Dmitrievna was winning and was in good spirits. A man-servant entered to announce Panshin's arrival.

Maria Dmitrievna dropped her cards and fidgeted in her chair; Varvara Pavlovna looked at her with a half-smile and then turned her eyes to the door. Panshin made his appearance in a black frock-coat, with a high English collar buttoned up to the top. 'I found it hard to obey you, but you see I have come,' was what his unsmiling, newly shaven face conveyed.

'Why, Woldemar,' exclaimed Maria Dmitrievna, 'you have always come in without being announced before!'

Panshin answered Maria Dmitrievna with a look, bowed politely to her, but did not kiss her hand. She introduced him to Varvara Pavlovna; he retreated a step, bowed to her equally politely but with a hint of additional elegance and respect, and sat down by the card-table. The game of preference soon ended. Panshin inquired after Lizaveta Mikhaylovna, learned that she was slightly indisposed, and expressed his sympathy; then he began to talk to Varvara Pavlovna, weighing and emphasizing every word like a true diplomat and deferentially listening to every word of her answers. But his portentously diplomatic tone did not impress Varvara Pavlovna or influence her own. On the contrary: she watched his face with amused attention and talked easily, while her delicate nostrils quivered slightly, as though with suppressed laughter. Maria Dmitrievna began to extol her talent; Panshin politely inclined his head, as far as his collar would allow, declared that 'he had been convinced of it beforehand', and almost contrived to lead the conversation to the topic of Metternich himself. Varvara Pavlovna narrowed her velvety eyes and said in a low voice, 'You, of course, are an artist too, *un confrère;*' then added, still lower, '*Venez!*' and nodded towards the piano. In an instant, as though by magic, that one word '*Venez!*' flung at him changed Panshin's whole appearance. His preoccupied manner disappeared; he became smiling and animated, unbuttoned his coat and, repeating, 'Not much of one, I am afraid, but you, I hear, are a genuine artist,' followed Varvara Pavlovna to the piano.

'Make him sing his romance – about the moon gliding along,' exclaimed Maria Dmitrievna.

'You sing?' said Varvara Pavlovna, flashing her bright eyes at him. 'Sit down.'

Panshin began to make excuses.

'Sit down,' she persisted, tapping the back of the chair.

He sat down, coughed, tugged at his collar, and sang the song.

'*Charmant,*' said Varvara Pavlovna. 'You sing extremely well, *vous avez du style.* Sing it again.'

She walked round the piano and stood directly in front of Panshin. He repeated the romance, putting a melodramatic tremor into his voice. Varvara Pavlovna watched him closely, with her elbows on the piano and her white hands raised to the level of her lips. Panshin ended the song.

'*Charmant, charmante idée,*' she said, with the calm confidence of the connoisseur. 'Tell me, have you written anything for a woman's voice, a mezzo-soprano?'

'I write hardly anything at all,' replied Panshin. 'This is

only something I jotted down, you know, at odd moments . . . But do you sing?'

'Yes.'

'Oh, do sing something for us,' said Maria Dmitrievna.

Varvara Pavlovna pushed her hair away from her flushed cheeks and tossed back her head.

'Our voices ought to go together,' she said, turning to Panshin; 'let us sing a duet. Do you know *"Son geloso"* or *"La ci darem"* or *"Mira la bianca luna"*?'

'I have sung *"Mira la bianca luna"*,' answered Panshin, 'but it was a long time ago, and I have forgotten it.'

'Never mind, we'll try it over softly first. Let me come.'

Varvara Pavlovna sat down at the piano. Panshin placed himself beside her. They sang the duet over softly, while Varvara Pavlovna corrected him several times, then they sang it aloud, then they repeated it twice: *'Mira la bianca lu-u-una.'* Varvara Pavlovna's voice had lost its freshness, but she used it very skilfully. Panshin was shy at first, and sang a little out of tune, then he let himself go, and if his singing was not above reproach, he lifted his shoulders, swayed his body, and raised his arm from time to time like a real singer. Then Varvara Pavlovna played two or three things by Thalberg and coquettishly 'recited' a little French air. Maria Dmitrievna did not know how to express her delight; several times she was on the point of sending for Liza; Gedeonovsky could not find words either, and contented himself with nodding his head – but then he yawned so suddenly that he hardly had time to cover his mouth with his hand. The yawn did not escape Varvara Pavlovna's notice; she swung round with her back to the piano, folded her hands, and said, '*Assez de musique comme ça*, let us talk.' '*Oui, assez de musique,*' repeated Panshin cheerfully, and plunged into conversation with her. The talk was dashing, gay, and in French. 'Just the same as in the best Paris salons,' thought Maria Dmitrievna, listening to their clever, inconsequential chatter. Panshin felt complete satisfaction; his eyes shone and he smiled; at first, whenever he chanced to meet Maria Dmitrievna's eyes, he passed his hand over his face, frowned, and uttered broken sighs, but afterwards he entirely forgot her and gave himself wholly up to the enjoyment of the half-worldly, half-artistic talk. Varvara Pavlovna revealed herself as a great philosopher: she had an answer ready for everything, never hesitated over anything, never had any doubts; it was clear that she had talked much and often with clever people of all kinds. All her thoughts and feelings were centred in Paris. Panshin turned the conversation to the subject of literature: it appeared that, like him, she read only French books; George Sand roused her to indignation, she respected Balzac, although he wearied her, in Sue and Scribe she discerned great knowledge of the human heart, she adored Dumas and Féval; in her heart she preferred Paul de Kock to all of them, but of course she did not even mention his name. To tell the truth, she was not much interested in literature. She skilfully avoided anything that might have any reference, however remote, to her situation; there was no mention of love in anything she said: on the contrary, she expressed rather severity, disillusionment, and resignation towards the impulses of passion. Panshin disputed with her; she disagreed with him . . . but, strange to say, while words of censure, frequently severe, issued from her lips, the sound of those words was like a tender caress and her eyes said – it would be difficult to state exactly what those charming eyes said, but it was something not stern but veiled and sweet. Panshin tried to understand this hidden meaning, tried to express with his own eyes what he was feeling, but he had no success; he was conscious that Varvara Pavlovna, in her quality of a real lioness from abroad, stood high above him, and consequently he was not entirely in command of himself. Varvara Pavlovna had the habit of laying her hand, ever so lightly, on the sleeve of her companion while she was talking, and this momentary contact very much disturbed Vladimir Nikolaich. She had the gift of easy intimacy with everybody; before two hours had passed it seemed to Panshin that he had known her all his life, and Liza, the Liza whom he nevertheless loved and to whom he had offered his hand the day before, was fading into a kind of mist. Tea was brought in; the conversation grew still more easy and natural. Maria Dmitrievna rang for her page and told him to ask Liza to come downstairs, if her head was better. Panshin, hearing Liza's name, began to talk of self-sacrifice, and of whether men or women were the more capable of it. Maria Dmitrievna at once became very excited, began asserting that women had the greater capacity for sacrifice, declared that she could prove it in two words, got into a muddle and ended by producing some rather unconvincing analogy. Varvara Pavlovna, as she ate a biscuit, took up a music-book, half concealed herself behind it and, leaning towards Panshin, said in an undertone, with a quiet smile on her lips and in her eyes, *'Elle n'a pas inventé la poudre, la bonne dame.'* Panshin was a little startled and amazed at her audacity; but he did not understand how much contempt for himself was concealed in this unexpected outburst and, forgetting Maria Dmitrievna's kindness and affection, the dinners she had given him, the money she had lent him, replied (unhappy man!) with the same slight smile and in the same tone of voice, *'Je crois bien'*, or rather, not even *'Je crois bien'*, but *'J'crois ben!'*

Varvara Pavlovna threw him a friendly glance and rose. Liza entered; Martha Timofeevna had tried in vain to keep her away: she had made up her mind to endure her trials to the end. Varvara Pavlovna moved towards her with Panshin, whose face had resumed its former diplomatic expression.

'How are you?' he asked Liza.

'Better now, thank you,' she answered.

'We have been having a little music; it is a pity you did not hear Varvara Pavlovna. She sings beautifully, *en artiste consommée.'*

'Come over here, *ma chère,'* came Maria Dmitrievna's voice.

Varvara Pavlovna, with childlike obedience, immediately went to her and sat down on a low stool at her feet. Maria

Dmitrievna had called her in order to leave her daughter, if only for a moment, alone with Panshin: she still secretly hoped that she would come to her senses. Besides, an idea which she felt she must communicate had come into her head.

'Do you know,' she whispered to Varvara Pavlovna, 'I should like to try to reconcile you with your husband; I will not answer for my success, but I will try. He has a great respect for me, you know.'

Varvara Pavlovna slowly raised her eyes to Maria Dmitrievna and folded her hands in a beautiful gesture.

'You would be my preserver, *ma tante*,' she said in a melancholy voice. 'I do not know how to thank you for your kindness; but I have done Fëdor Ivanych too great a wrong, he cannot forgive me.'

'But did you . . . really . . .' Maria Dmitrievna was beginning inquisitively.

'Don't ask me,' interrupted Varvara Pavlovna, lowering her eyes. 'I was young, thoughtless . . . However, I won't make excuses for myself.'

'But all the same, why not try? You must not despair,' replied Maria Dmitrievna, and would have tapped her cheek, but glanced at her face and did not venture. 'She is modest,' she thought, 'modest, but she is a real lioness.'

'Are you ill?' Panshin was saying meanwhile to Liza.

'Yes, I am not very well.'

'I understand you,' he said, after a rather prolonged pause. 'Yes, I understand you.'

'What do you mean?'

'I understand you,' significantly repeated Panshin, who simply did not know what to say.

Liza was taken aback, but then she thought, 'Oh, let it pass!' Panshin adopted an air of mystery and was silent, looking sternly past her.

'But I think it has already struck eleven,' remarked Maria Dmitrievna.

Her guests understood the hint and began to take their leave. Varvara Pavlovna was made to promise to come to dinner the next day and bring Ada with her; Gedeonovsky, who had been sitting in a corner all but asleep, offered to take her home. Panshin bowed solemnly to everybody and at the door, handing Varvara Pavlovna into the carriage, he pressed her hand and called after her, '*Au revoir!*' Gedeonovsky sat beside her; she amused herself all the way by placing the tip of her shoe as if accidentally against his foot; he was covered with confusion and paid her compliments; she giggled and made eyes at him every time the light of a street lamp fell into the carriage. The waltz she had played still rang excitingly in her head; wherever she was, she had only to imagine lights, a ball-room, rapid whirling to the sound of music – and her heart was aflame, her eyes flashed strangely, a smile strayed over her lips, her whole body was imbued with a sort of bacchantic grace. When they arrived at the house, Varvara Pavlovna leapt lightly from the carriage, as only lionesses can leap, turned to Gedeonovsky and suddenly burst into a ringing laugh straight in his face.

'A fetching creature,' thought the State Councillor, making his way to his apartment, where his servant was waiting with a flask of opodeldoc. 'It's just as well that I am not a susceptible man . . . but what was she laughing at?'

Martha Timofeevna sat all night by Liza's bedside.

XLI

Lavretsky passed a day and a half at Vasilyevskoe, and spent almost all the time wandering about the neighbourhood. He could not stay long in one place: he was gnawed by anguish; he suffered all the torments of incessant, violent, and impotent fits of passion. He remembered the feeling that had possessed him on the day after his first arrival there; he remembered the resolves he had made then and was bitterly angry with himself. What had wrenched him from the path of what he recognized as his duty and the sole task of his future? The thirst for happiness – once again the thirst for happiness! 'Evidently Mikhalevich was right,' he thought. 'You wanted to know happiness for the second time in your life,' he said to himself, 'and you forgot that it is a luxury, an undeserved blessing, if it visits a man only once. It was not perfect, it was false, you will say; but prove your right to perfect, genuine happiness! Look round you, and who is happy, who enjoys life? There is a peasant going to the mowing; perhaps he is content with his lot . . . What then? would you want to change places with him? Remember your mother: how pitifully small her demands were, and what fell to her lot! You were obviously only showing off to Panshin when you told him you had come to Russia to till the soil; you came to run after girls in your old age. The news of your freedom came, and you abandoned everything, you forgot everything; you chased off like a boy after butterflies . . .' The image of Liza was constantly before him in the midst of his brooding; he tried to force it away, like that other importunate image, those other impassive, subtle, beautiful and hateful features. Old Anton saw that his master was not himself; he breathed a few sighs outside the door, a few more on the threshold, and then, his mind made up, went up to his master and counselled him to take plenty of hot drinks. Lavretsky shouted at him, ordered him out of the room, and afterwards apologized to him; but this made Anton still more distressed. Lavretsky could not sit in the drawing-room: he imagined that his great-grandfather Andrey was looking contemptuously down from his canvas at his feeble descendant. 'You! You are very small fry!' he seemed to say, with his wryly distorted mouth. 'Surely,' thought Lavretsky, 'I am not incapable of mastering myself, surely I shan't succumb to this . . . nothing?' (In war, the seriously wounded always call their wounds 'nothing'. A man must deceive himself, or he could not live on this earth.) I'm not a mere child, am I? Well, it is true that I came very close to, I almost grasped in my hands, the possibility of happiness for my whole life – and suddenly it has vanished; but after all, in a lottery, too – let the wheel turn ever so little farther, and the beggar might become a rich man. If it is not to be, it is not to be – and that is the end of the matter. I must grit my teeth and set to work, and I will make myself be silent; luckily, this is not the first time I have had to take myself in hand. And why did I run away, why am I staying here like an ostrich burying its head in the sand? Is it so terrible to look misfortune in the face? – nonsense!' 'Anton!' he shouted aloud, 'have the horses put in the tarantass at once.' 'Yes,' he thought again, 'I must make myself be silent, I must rule myself with a rod of iron . . .'

With such words Lavretsky tried to help his grief, but it was great and violent; and Apraxeya herself, who had outlived not so much her mental faculties as all her capacity to feel, shook her head and mournfully followed him with her eyes when he got into the tarantass to drive into the town. The horses bounded forward; he sat erect and unmoving, gazing with unseeing eyes at the road ahead.

XLII

Liza had written to Lavretsky the day before, telling him to call on them that evening; but first he went to his lodging. He found neither his wife nor his daughter at home; from the servants he learned that they had gone to the Kalitins'. He was astounded and enraged by the news. 'Evidently Varvara Pavlovna has made up her mind to make life impossible for me,' he thought, with a storm of fury in his heart. He began to pace backwards and forwards, his hands and feet constantly striking the toys, books, and various feminine belongings that lay in his path; he called Justine and ordered her to clear away all this 'rubbish'. '*Oui, monsieur,*' she said with a grimace, and began to tidy up the room, stooping gracefully and with every movement giving Lavretsky to understand that she considered him an uncouth bear. He watched with hatred her mocking Parisian face, lined with dissipation but still 'piquante', her white cuffs, silk apron, and frivolous little cap. He sent her away at last, and after much hesitation (Varvara Pavlovna had still not returned), resolved to go to the Kalitins' to see, not Maria Dmitrievna (he would not for the world have entered her drawing-room, the drawing-room that held his wife) but Martha Timofeevna; he remembered that a back staircase led directly to her room from the servants' entrance. This plan he followed. Chance aided him: in the yard he met Shurochka, and she took him to Martha Timofeevna. He found her, contrary to her habit, alone; she was sitting huddled in a corner, without a cap, her hand crossed on her breast. When she saw Lavretsky the old lady, startled, sprang quickly to her feet and began to wander about the room as though seeking her cap.

'Ah, there you are, there you are,' she began, avoiding his eyes as she bustled about. 'Well, what now? What is to be done? Where were you yesterday? Well, she has come, yes, she's here. Well, we must do something . . . somehow or other.'

Lavretsky sank into a chair.

'Well, sit down, sit down,' the old lady went on. 'Did you come straight upstairs? Well, yes, of course you would. Well, so you came to take a look at me, did you? Thank you.'

The old woman paused; Lavretsky did not know what to say to her; but she understood him.

'Liza . . . yes, Liza was in here just now,' went on Martha Timofeevna, twisting and untwisting the cords of her reticule. 'She is not very well. Shurochka, where are you? Come here, my dear; why can't you sit still for a little? My head aches too. It must be from all that singing and playing.'

'What singing, auntie?'

'Oh, we had those what-you-may-call-'ems – duets, here. And in Italian all the time: chee-chee, cha-cha – regular magpies. Singing away with those drawn-out notes, as if they wanted to pull your soul out of your body. That Panshin and that wife of yours. And how smoothly everything went, right from the start: just like members of one family, no ceremony. But, indeed, even a dog will try to find a home for itself, and it won't starve, because people haven't the heart to drive it away.'

'All the same, I confess I didn't expect this,' replied Lavretsky. 'It needed great effrontery.'

'No, my dear, it wasn't effrontery, it was calculation. Well, good luck to her! They say you are sending her to Lavriki; is that true?'

'Yes, I am putting the estate at Varvara Pavlovna's disposal.'

'Has she been asking for money?'

'Not yet.'

'Well it won't be long before she does. But I have only just taken a good look at you. Are you well?'

'Quite well.'

'Shurochka,' exclaimed Martha Timofeevna suddenly, 'go and tell Lizaveta Mikhaylovna – or no, ask her . . . I suppose she is downstairs?'

'Yes, ma'am.'

'Well; then ask her where she has put my book. She will know.'

'Yes, ma'am.'

The old lady began fussing about again and opening drawers. Lavretsky sat without moving.

Suddenly there was the sound of light steps on the stairs, and Liza came in.

Lavretsky stood up and bowed; Liza stopped by the door.

'Liza, my darling,' began Martha Timofeevna busily, 'where did you put my book, where is my book?'

'What book, auntie?'

'Goodness gracious, my book! However, I didn't call you . . . Well, it makes no difference. What are you doing down there? Fëdor Ivanych has come, you see. How is your head?'

'All right.'

'You always say "all right". What's going on down there, music again?'

'No, they are playing cards.'

'Well, after all, she can turn her hand to anything. Shurochka, I can see you want to go and play in the garden. Run along.'

'I don't want to, Martha Timofeevna . . .'

'Don't argue, please, run along. Nastasya Karpovna went into the garden by herself: keep her company for a while. You must be considerate to an old woman.' Shurochka went out. 'Where on earth is my cap? Really, where can it have got to?'

'Let me look,' said Liza.

'Sit still, sit still; I've not lost the use of my legs yet. It must be in my bedroom.'

And Martha Timofeevna departed, with a frowning glance at Lavretsky. She was leaving the door open, but all at once she returned and shut it.

Liza leaned against the back of the arm-chair and quietly lifted her hands to her face; Lavretsky stayed where he was.

'So this is how we were to meet,' he said at last.

Liza took her hands away from her face.

'Yes,' she said dully. 'We were quickly punished.'

'Punished,' said Lavretsky. 'But why should you be punished?'

Liza raised her eyes to his. They showed neither sorrow nor agitation: they looked smaller and less lustrous. Her face was pale; her slightly parted lips were pale, too.

Lavretsky's heart throbbed with pity and love.

'You wrote to me that all was over,' he whispered. 'Yes, all is over – before it has begun.'

'We must forget all that,' said Liza. 'I am glad you came; I wanted to write to you, but it is better this way. But we must hurry if we are to take advantage of these few minutes. It remains only for both of us to do our duty. You, Fëdor Ivanych, ought to be reconciled to your wife.'

'Liza!'

'I ask this of you; it is the only way to efface . . . everything that has happened. You will consider – and not refuse me.'

'Liza, for God's sake, you are demanding the impossible. I am ready to do everything you tell me; but to be reconciled to her *now*! . . . I will agree to anything, I have forgotten everything; but I cannot compel my heart . . . For pity's sake, this is cruel!'

'I do not even ask . . . what you say; don't live with her if you cannot; but be reconciled,' replied Liza, and again lifted her hands to her eyes. 'Remember your daughter; do this for me.'

'Very well,' said Lavretsky through his clenched teeth, 'suppose I do this; by doing it I shall be doing my duty. Well, but you – what does your duty consist in?'

'I know that.'

Lavretsky gave a sudden start.

'Surely you don't intend to marry Panshin?' he asked.

Liza just perceptibly smiled.

'Oh, no!' she said.

'Ah, Liza, Liza,' exclaimed Lavretsky, 'how happy we might have been!'

Again Liza looked at him.

'Now you see, Fëdor Ivanych, that happiness depends not on ourselves but on God.'

'Yes, because you . . .'

The door from the neighbouring room opened quickly and Martha Timofeevna came in with a cap in her hand.

'I've managed to find it,' she said, standing between Lavretsky and Liza. 'I had put it down myself. That's what it means to be old, alas! However, being young is no better. Tell me, are you going to Lavriki with your wife?' she added, turning to Fëdor Ivanych.

'To Lavriki with her? I? I don't know,' he said after a moment.

'Are you going downstairs?'

'Not today.'

'Very well, just as you please; but you, Liza, must go down, I think. Oh, heavens above, I've forgotten to feed the goldfinch, too. Wait a moment, I'll just . . .'

And Martha Timofeevna, still without putting on her cap, ran out.

Lavretsky stepped quickly close to Liza.

'Liza,' he began in an imploring voice, 'we are parting for ever, my heart is breaking – give me your hand in goodbye.'

Liza raised her head. Her weary eyes, their light almost extinguished, rested on him.

'No,' she said, drawing back the hand she had already extended, 'no, Lavretsky' (this was the first time she had called him by that name), 'I will not give you my hand. What good would it do? Go away, I beg you. You know I love you . . . yes, I love you,' she added with an effort, 'but no . . . no.'

And she raised her handkerchief to her lips.

'At least give me your handkerchief.'

The door creaked . . . The handkerchief slipped to Liza's knees. Lavretsky snatched it up before it could reach the ground, thrust it hastily into his side pocket and, turning, met Martha Timofeevna's eyes.

'Lizochka, I think your mother is calling you,' said the old lady.

Liza at once got up and went away.

Martha Timofeevna sat down again in her corner. Lavretsky began to take his leave of her.

'Fedya,' she said suddenly.

'What, auntie?'

'Are you an honourable man?'

'What?'

'I asked you if you were an honourable man.'

'I hope so.'

'Hm. Give me your word of honour that you are an honourable man.'

'If you wish. But why all this?'

'I know why. And you yourself, my dear boy, if you think well, because after all you're not stupid, you will know why I ask you. Now goodbye, my dear. Thank you for coming; and remember you gave your word, Fedya, and kiss me. Oh, my dear, it is hard for you, I know; but you know it isn't easy for anybody. How much I used to envy flies: there, I used to think, that's the way to live; but once, at night, I heard one whining in the clutches of a spider – no, I thought, they have their tragedies too. There's nothing to be done, Fedya. All the same, remember your word. Go now!'

Lavretsky left by the back door and was already nearing the gate when a manservant overtook him.

'Maria Dmitrievna told me to ask you kindly to come in,' he announced.

'Say that I can't now . . .' Fëdor Ivanych was beginning.

'Madam said to ask you specially,' went on the servant. 'Madam said to say she was alone.'

'Have her visitors gone?' asked Lavretsky.

'Yes indeed, sir,' replied the servant, grinning.

Lavretsky shrugged his shoulders and followed him.

XLIII

Maria Dmitrievna was sitting alone in her study, in a high-backed arm-chair, sniffing at eau-de-cologne and with a glass of orange-flower water beside her on a little table. She was agitated and seemed apprehensive.

Lavretsky went in.

'You wished to see me,' he said, bowing coldly.

'Yes,' replied Maria Dmitrievna, and drank a little water. 'I heard you had gone straight up to aunt; I told them to ask you to see me: I must talk to you. Sit down, please.' Maria Dmitrievna drew a deep breath. 'You know,' she continued, 'that your wife has been here.'

'I am aware of it,' said Lavretsky.

'Well, that is, I wanted to tell you: she came to see me and I received her; that is what I wanted to talk to you about, Fëdor Ivanych. I may say, thank God, that I have earned everybody's respect, and I would not for the world do anything unseemly. Although I foresaw that you would not like it, still I could not bring myself to refuse her, Fëdor Ivanych. She is related to me – through you. Put yourself in my position; what right had I to forbid her the house? Do you agree with me?'

'You are worrying needlessly, Maria Dmitrievna,' replied Lavretsky. 'You acted quite rightly; I am not in the least angry. I have absolutely no intention of depriving Varvara Pavlovna of the possibility of seeing her friends; I did not come to you today, simply because I did not wish to meet her – that is all.'

'Oh, how pleased I am to hear that from you, Fëdor Ivanych,' exclaimed Maria Dmitrievna, 'but I always expected as much from your gentlemanly feelings. As for worrying, that is not surprising: I am a woman and a mother. And your wife . . . of course, I cannot judge either of you, as I told her; but she is such a charming woman that she must bring everyone pleasure.'

Lavretsky smiled and played with his hat.

'And this is what I wanted to say to you besides, Fëdor Ivanych,' went on Maria Dmitrievna, moving slightly nearer to him, 'if only you could have seen how modestly she behaved and how respectful she was! Really, it is quite touching. And if you could have heard how she refers to you! I have done him a very great wrong, she says; I did not know, she says, how to appreciate him; he is an angel, she says, not a man. Really, that is what she says: an angel. She is so full of remorse . . . Really, I have never seen such remorse!'

'Well, Maria Dmitrievna,' said Lavretsky, 'perhaps you will allow me to inquire: I hear Varvara Pavlovna sang for you; did she sing while she was being remorseful, or what?'

'Oh, surely you are ashamed to talk like that! She only sang and played to please me, because I insisted on it, almost made her. I could see she was depressed, so very depressed; I wondered how to distract her – and I had heard she had such a wonderful talent! Believe me, Fëdor Ivanych, she is quite crushed, you ask Sergey Petrovich; a broken woman *tout à fait*; how can you say such things?'

Lavretsky only shrugged his shoulders.

'And what a little angel your Adochka is, such a darling! How sweet she is, and what a clever little girl; she speaks French so well; and she understands Russian too – she called me auntie in Russian. And you know, as for being shy, like nearly all children of her age – not a bit of it! She is so like you, Fëdor Ivanych, terribly like. Her eyes, her forehead . . . they are you, absolutely you. I am not very fond of children, I confess; but I simply fell in love with your daughter.'

'Maria Dmitrievna,' said Lavretsky suddenly, 'may I ask why you are kind enough to tell me all this?'

'Why?' Maria Dmitrievna again sniffed at her eau-de-cologne and sipped her water. 'I am telling you, Fëdor Ivanych, because . . . after all, I am related to you, I have the deepest concern for you . . . I know you have the kindest of hearts. Listen to me, *mon cousin*, I am a woman of experience, after all, and I won't beat about the bush: forgive your wife, forgive her.' Maria Dmitrievna's eyes suddenly filled with tears. 'Think: youth, inexperience . . . and, perhaps, a bad example: she had not the kind of mother who would set her on the right path. Forgive her, Fëdor Ivanych, she has been punished enough.'

The tears rained down Maria Dmitrievna's cheeks; she did not wipe them away: she enjoyed crying. Lavretsky felt as though he were sitting on live coals. 'My God,' he thought, 'what torture! What a day I've had today!'

'You don't answer,' Maria Dmitrievna began again. 'How am I to take that? Can you really be so cruel? No, I will not believe it. I feel that my words have persuaded you. Fëdor Ivanych, God will reward you for your goodness; and now accept your wife from my hands . . .'

Lavretsky involuntarily sprang up; Maria Dmitrievna also rose and, passing swiftly behind a screen, led out Varvara Pavlovna. Pale, seeming only half alive, with downcast eyes, she seemed to have renounced all thought and will of her own and put herself entirely in Maria Dmitrievna's hands.

Lavretsky recoiled a pace.

'You were here!' he exclaimed.

'Don't blame her,' said Maria Dmitrievna, hastily, 'she would not have stayed for anything in the world, but I made her, and I put her behind the screen. She assured me that it would anger you still more; I would not even listen to her; I know you better than she does. Accept your wife, then, from my hands; go, Varya, do not be afraid, fall at his feet' (she pulled her by the arm), 'and my blessing . . .'

'Stop, Maria Dmitrievna,' Lavretsky interrupted her in a muted but frightening voice. 'You probably love sentimental scenes' (he was not mistaken: ever since her schooldays Maria Dmitrievna had cherished a passion for the dramatic); 'they entertain you, but they do harm to other people. However, I shall not talk to you: in *this* scene you are not playing the principal role. What do you want from me, madam?' he added, turning to his wife. 'Have I not done what I could for you? Don't protest that it was not you who contrived this interview; I shall not believe you – and you know that I cannot believe you. What do you want then? You are intelligent, you do not do anything without a motive. You must understand that I simply cannot live with you on the same footing as before, not because I am angry, but because I have become a different person. I told you so the day after you returned, and you yourself, at this moment, agree with me in your heart. But you wish to reinstate yourself in general esteem; it is not enough for you to live in my house, you want to live under the same roof with me, don't you?'

'I want you to forgive me,' said Varvara Pavlovna, without raising her eyes.

'She wants you to forgive her,' repeated Maria Dmitrievna.

'Not for myself, for Ada,' whispered Varvara Pavlovna.

'Not for herself, for your little Ada,' echoed Maria Dmitrievna.

'Excellent. That is what you want?' said Lavretsky with an effort. 'Very well, I agree to that, too.'

Varvara Pavlovna threw him a swift glance, but Maria Dmitrievna exclaimed, 'Well, thank God!' and again plucked Varvara Pavlovna by the arm. 'Now, from my hands . . .'

'Stop, I tell you,' interrupted Lavretsky. 'I agree to live with you, Varvara Pavlovna,' he went on; 'that is, I will take you to Lavriki and stay there with you as long as I have strength to do so, and then I shall go away – and come back occasionally. You see, I do not want to deceive you; but do not demand anything more. You yourself would laugh if I were to carry out the wish of our respected cousin and press you to my heart, assuring you that . . . that the past has never been and that the tree that was cut down will flourish again. But I see that I must submit. You will misunderstand that word . . . it doesn't matter. I repeat . . . I will live with you . . . or no, that I cannot promise . . . I will be friends with you, I will consider you my wife again . . .'

'At least give her your hand on that,' said Maria Dmitrievna, whose tears had long ceased to flow.

'I have never deceived Varvara Pavlovna,' objected Lavretsky, 'and she will believe me without that. I will take her to Lavriki – and remember, Varvara Pavlovna: our agreement must be considered broken as soon as ever you leave there. Now permit me to go.'

He bowed to both women and hurriedly left the room.

'You are not taking her with you,' Maria Dmitrievna called after him . . .

'Leave him alone,' whispered Varvara Pavlovna, and at once began to embrace and thank her, kiss her hands, and say she had saved her.

Maria Dmitrievna graciously accepted her caresses, but at heart she was pleased with neither Lavretsky nor Varvara Pavlovna, nor indeed with any of the scene she had staged. The result had not been pathetic enough; Varvara Pavlovna, in her opinion, ought to have flung herself at her husband's feet.

'How was it you didn't understand me?' she argued. 'After all, I did tell you to fall at his feet.'

'It was better as it was, dear aunt; don't worry – everything went splendidly,' Varvara Pavlovna maintained.

'Well, of course he is as cold as ice,' remarked Maria Dmitrievna. 'Even if you didn't weep, after all *I* was crying my eyes out. He wants to shut you up in Lavriki. Why, you won't even be able to come and see me! Men have no feelings,' she said in conclusion, with a portentous shake of her head.

'But women know how to value kindness and generosity,' said Varvara Pavlovna, sinking smoothly to her knees in front of Maria Dmitrievna, embracing her plump waist with both arms and hiding her face in her bosom. The face wore a surreptitious smile, but Maria Dmitrievna's tears had begun to flow again.

Lavretsky went home, shut himself into his valet's little room, flung himself on the sofa, and lay there till the morning.

XLIV

The following day was Sunday. Lavretsky was not awakened by the sound of the bell for early mass – he had not closed his eyes all night – but it recalled to him that other Sunday, when he had gone to church to please Liza. He rose hurriedly: a mysterious voice was telling him that he would find her there again today. He left the house quietly, having given orders that Varvara Pavlovna, who was still asleep, was to be told that he would return for dinner, and with long strides followed the plaintive, monotonous summons of the bells. He arrived early: hardly anybody was yet in the church; the clerk was reading prayers in the choir; his voice, broken by an occasional cough, droned along, now dying away, now swelling. Lavretsky took his place not far from the entrance. The worshippers came in one by one, stopped, crossed themselves, and bowed to all sides; their steps rang in the empty stillness and echoed back clearly from the arches. A decrepit little old woman in an ancient cloak and hood was kneeling near Lavretsky and praying fervently; her toothless, yellow, wrinkled face expressed tense emotion; her red eyes looked up fixedly at the icons on the iconostasis; her bony hands continually emerged from her cloak and with slow, firm gestures made great, sweeping signs of the cross. A moujik with a thick beard and a morose expression, tousled and dishevelled, entered the church, knelt down at once on both knees, and immediately proceeded to cross himself repeatedly and rapidly, throwing back and tossing his head after each prostration. There was such bitter sorrow in his face and his every gesture that Lavretsky made up his mind to go and ask him what was the matter. The moujik recoiled, with an expression at once grim and terrified, looked at him, rapidly pronounced the words, 'My son is dead . . .', and began once more to bow himself down to the ground . . . 'What could replace the consolations of the church for such as these?' thought Lavretsky, and himself made an effort to pray; but his heart was hard and heavy and his thoughts were far away. He was waiting all the time for Liza – but Liza did not come. The church had begun to fill; still she had not come. The mass had begun, the deacon had already read the gospel, the bell rang for the Ave. Lavretsky moved forward a little – and suddenly saw Liza. She had been there before him, but he had not noticed her; huddled into the space between the wall and the choir, she did not move or turn round. Lavretsky did not take his eyes off her until the very end of the service: he was taking his last leave of her. The people began to disperse, but still she stood there; it looked as though she were waiting for Lavretsky to go away. At last she crossed herself for the last time and went out, without turning round; she had only a maid with her. Lavretsky followed her out of the church and overtook her in the street; she was walking very quickly, with her head bent and a veil drawn over her face.

'Good morning, Lizaveta Mikhaylovna,' he said loudly, with forced easiness, 'may I walk with you?'

She said nothing; he ranged himself by her side.

'Are you pleased with me?' he asked, lowering his voice. 'Have you heard what happened yesterday?'

'Yes, yes,' she whispered, 'that was well done.'

And she walked even quicker.

'Are you pleased?'

Liza only inclined her head.

'Fëdor Ivanych,' she began in calm but faint tones, 'I wanted to ask you something: please don't come to see us again, go away as soon as possible; we may see one another again afterwards — at some time, after a year, perhaps. But now do this for me; do what I ask you, for God's sake.'

'I am ready to obey you in everything, Lizaveta Mikhaylovna; but surely we ought not to part like this? surely you will say one word to me? . . .'

'Fëdor Ivanych, here you are walking beside me now . . . And yet you are far away, far from me. And not only you, but . . .'

'Go on, I beg you!' exclaimed Lavretsky. 'What were you going to say?'

'You will hear, perhaps . . . but whatever happens, forget . . . no, do not forget me, think of me.'

'For me to forget you . . .'

'No more, goodbye. Don't follow me.'

'Liza,' Lavretsky was beginning.

'Goodbye, goodbye,' she repeated, lowering her veil still further, and almost running away.

Lavretsky followed her with his eyes, and then, with hanging head, turned back along the street. He bumped into Lemm, who was also walking with his hat pulled over his eyes, looking down at his feet.

They looked at one another in silence.

'Well, what have you to say?' said Lavretsky at last.

'What have I to say?' gloomily retorted Lemm. 'Nothing. Everything is dead, and we are dead too. (*Alles ist todt, und wir sind todt.*) I suppose you go to the right?'

'Yes.'

'And I to the left. Goodbye.'

The next morning Fëdor Ivanych and his wife set off for Lavriki. She travelled in front in the carriage, with Ada and Justine; he came behind in the tarantass. The pretty child spent the whole journey gazing out of the window; she marvelled at everything: peasant men and women, cottages, wells, horses' yokes and bells, and the multitudes of rooks; Justine shared her wonder; Varvara Pavlovna laughed at their exclamations and remarks. She was in spirits; before they left O—— she had had a talk with her husband.

'I understand your situation,' she had said to him, and he could deduce from the expression of her clever eyes that she did indeed fully understand his position, 'but you will do me this justice at least, that it is easy to live with me; I shall not intrude on you or interfere with you; I wanted to make Ada's future secure; I need nothing more.'

'Yes, you have gained all your ends,' said Fëdor Ivanych.

'I have only one dream now: to bury myself for ever in the depths of the country; I shall always remember your generosity . . .'

'Fie! that's enough,' he interrupted her.

'And I shall know how to respect your independence and your privacy,' she ended her prepared speech.

Lavretsky bowed low. Varvara Pavlovna understood that her husband was thanking her from the bottom of his heart.

The next day they reached Lavriki in the evening; a week later Lavretsky went to Moscow, leaving his wife five thousand roubles for living expenses, and the day after Lavretsky's departure, Panshin, whom Varvara Pavlovna had asked not to forget her in her solitude, appeared. He received the warmest of welcomes and until late into the night the lofty rooms of the house and the very garden resounded to the sound of music, singing, and cheerful French conversation. Panshin remained as Varvara Pavlovna's guest for three days; as he said goodbye and warmly pressed her beautiful hands, he promised to return very soon – and he kept his word.

XLV

Liza had her own little room on the first floor of her mother's house, clean and bright, with a little white bed, pots of flowers in the corners and in front of the windows, a small writing-table, a bookcase, and a crucifix on the wall. This room was called the nursery: Liza had been born in it. On her return from the church after she had seen Lavretsky, she set everything in order more carefully than usual, dusted everywhere, looked through all her music-books and her friends' letters and tied them up with ribbons, watered her flowers and caressed each one with her fingers. All this was done without haste or noise, while her face expressed a kind of quiet and tender solicitude. She stood at last in the middle of the room, looked lingeringly all round her and then, going to the table over which hung the crucifix, sank to her knees, laid her head on her clasped hands, and remained there motionless.

Martha Timofeevna came in and found her in this posture. Liza did not notice her entrance. The old lady retreated and coughed loudly several times outside the door. Liza rose swiftly to her feet and wiped her eyes, which were glittering with bright, unshed tears.

'Well, I see you have been tidying up your little cell,' said Martha Timofeevna, stooping low over a young rose-bush in a pot. 'What a wonderful scent!'

Liza looked thoughtfully at her aunt.

'How strange that you should use that word!' she whispered.

'What word was that?' the old lady caught her up. 'What are you trying to say? This is terrible,' she said, snatching off her cap and sitting down on Liza's bed, 'it is more than I have the strength for: this is the fourth day that I've been on fire with anxiety; I can't pretend any longer that I don't notice anything. I cannot watch you growing pale, pining away, and weeping, I cannot, I cannot.'

'What is the matter, auntie?' said Liza. 'I am all right . . .'

'All right?' exclaimed Martha Timofeevna. 'Tell that to other people, not to me! All right! – and who was kneeling here just now, whose eyelashes are still wet with tears? All right! Just look at yourself, what have you done to your face, what has happened to your eyes? – All right! Don't I know everything?'

'It will pass, auntie; give it time.'

'It will pass, but when? Good God, Father Almighty! Did you really love him so much? but he's an old man, Lizochka. Well, I won't deny that he's a good man, I've nothing against him; but what then, what of that? We are all good people; the world is wide, and there will always be plenty of that commodity about.'

'I tell you, all this will pass; it has passed already.'

'Listen to what I say, Lizochka,' said Martha Timofeevna abruptly, setting Liza beside her on the bed and arranging now her hair and now her neckerchief. 'It is only now, in the first passion of sorrow, that it seems to you that there is no remedy. Oh, my darling, death is the only thing for which there is no cure. Only say to yourself: "I won't give in," say, "and that's flat!", and afterwards you will think it was miraculous how quickly and easily it all passed over. Only be patient.'

'It is over already, auntie,' said Liza. 'It is all over.'

'Over! What do you mean? Why, even your little nose has got quite sharp, and you say it's over. Over, indeed!'

'Yes, it is over, auntie, if only you will help me,' said Liza with sudden animation, throwing herself on Martha Timofeevna's neck. 'Dear auntie, be kind to me, help me, don't be angry, try to understand . . .'

'But what is all this, what's all this, my girl? Please don't frighten me; I shall scream in a minute; don't look at me like that. Tell me quickly, what is it?'

'I . . . I want . . .' Liza hid her face in Martha Timofeevna's bosom. 'I want to go into a convent,' she said softly.

The old lady positively jumped where she sat.

'Heaven forbid, my darling, my Lizochka; try to be calm, think what you are saying, God help you!' she babbled at last. 'Lie down, darling, have a little nap. This is all because you haven't been sleeping, my dearest.'

Liza raised her head, her cheeks aflame.

'No, auntie,' she said, 'don't say such things. I have made up my mind; I prayed, I asked God for counsel; it is all finished, my life with you is finished. This lesson was not sent for nothing; and besides, it is not the first time I have thought of it. Happiness has not come to me; even when I had hopes of being happy, there was always a pain at my heart. I know everything, my own sins and other people's, and how papa made a fortune for us, everything; I know it all. It must all be atoned for by prayer, it must be atoned for. I am sorry for you; I am sorry for mama and Lenochka, but it can't be helped; I feel that life here is not for me; I have said goodbye to everything already, I have bowed to everything in my home for the last time. Something is calling me away; I feel sick at heart, I must shut myself up for ever. Don't try to hold me back, don't try to dissuade me; help me, or else I shall go away alone . . .'

Martha Timofeevna listened to her niece in horror.

'She is ill, she is wandering,' she thought; 'I must send for a doctor, but which? Gedeonovsky was praising one not long ago; everything he says is all lies, but perhaps this time he was telling the truth.' But when she was convinced that Liza was not ill, and not delirious, when to all her objections Liza constantly made the same reply, Martha Timofeevna grew afraid and distressed in good earnest.

'But really, you don't know, my own darling,' she began to argue, 'what life in a convent is like! My dear child, they will feed you on green-hemp oil, they will give you the coarsest of coarse linen to wear, they will make you go about in the cold; really, you won't be able to endure it all, Lizochka. All this goes back to Agasha; she led you astray. But she, after all, had lived first, and lived for her own pleasure; you must live too. At least let me die in peace; and then do what you please. Who ever heard of going into a nunnery because of a goat's beard, God forgive me, a man? Well, if you are so sick at heart, go on a pilgrimage, pray to a saint, or have masses said, but don't cover your head with the black hood, my darling, my dearest . . .'

And Martha Timofeevna began to weep bitterly.

Liza tried to console her, wiped away her tears, wept herself, but remained unyielding. In despair, Martha Timofeevna tried to use the threat of telling her mother everything . . . but even this did not help. It was only because the old lady redoubled her entreaties that Liza agreed to defer the fulfilment of her intention for six months; Martha Timofeevna, in return, had to give her word that she would help her and try to win Maria Dmitrievna's consent, if by the end of that time Liza had not changed her mind.

With the coming of the first frosts Varvara Pavlovna, in spite of her promise to bury herself in the country, provided herself with money and removed to St Petersburg, where she rented a modest but elegant little flat found for her by Panshin, who had quitted the Province of O—— even before she did. In the latter part

of his stay in O——— he had completely lost favour with Maria
Dmitrievna; he had suddenly ceased to visit her and was hardly
ever away from Lavriki. Varvara Pavlovna had enslaved him, in
the exact meaning of the word, for no other could express her
limitless, unalterable, irresistible power over him.

Lavretsky spent the winter in Moscow, and in the spring of
the following year the news reached him that Liza had become
a nun in the convent of B———, in one of the remotest parts of
Russia.

EPILOGUE

Eight years have passed. Spring has come again . . . But let us first
say a few words of the fate of Mikhalevich, Panshin, and Madame
Lavretsky – and take our leave of them. After long-continued wan-
derings, Mikhalevich has at last lighted on the very occupation for
him: he has been given the post of senior superintendent of a State
academy. He is highly pleased with his lot, and his pupils 'adore'
him, although they mimic him too. Panshin has gained considerable
promotion in the service, and is already aiming at a directorship;
he stoops a little as he walks; it must be the weight of the cross of
the Order of Vladimir, which he wears round his neck, dragging
him down. The official in him has taken definite precedence of the
artist; his still youngish face has grown yellow, his hair is sparse,
and he no longer sings, or draws, but busies himself in secret with

literature: he has written a little comedy, something in the nature of a '*proverbe*', and since all authors nowadays are obliged to offer a 'portrayal' of some particular type, he has 'portrayed' a coquette in it; he sometimes reads it privately to two or three ladies who look on him with favour. He has, however, never married, although two or three excellent opportunities have presented themselves: for this Varvara Pavlovna is to blame. As for her, she lives permanently in Paris, as she used to do: Fëdor Ivanych has settled an allowance on her and so purchased his freedom from her and from the possibility of a second unheralded descent on him. She has grown older and fatter, but she is still charming and elegant. Every man has his ideal; Varvara Pavlovna has found hers – in the dramatic productions of M. Dumas *fils*. She diligently frequents the theatres where consumptive and sentimental *Dames aux Camélias* are portrayed on the stage; to be a Madame Doche seems to her the topmost peak of human bliss: she once declared that she desired no better lot in life for her daughter. We may hope that fate will spare Mademoiselle Ada that felicity: from a chubby rosy child she has become a pale, weak-chested girl; she already suffers from disordered nerves. The number of Varvara Pavlovna's admirers has diminished, but they still exist. Recently the most ardent of them has been a certain Zakurdalo-Skubyrnikov, a bewhiskered retired guardsman some thirty-eight years old, of unusually robust physique. The French frequenters of Madame Lavretsky's salon call him *le gros taureau de l'Ukraine*; Varvara Pavlovna never invites him to her fashionable evening parties, but he enjoys her favours to the full.

And so . . . eight years have passed. Once again the radiant happiness of the spring breathes from the skies; once again it smiles on the earth and on men; again blossom and love and song respond to its caress. The town of O—— has changed very little in the course of these eight years, but Maria Dmitrievna's house seems to have renewed its youth: its newly painted walls are white and friendly, the panes of the open windows shine redly in the light of the setting sun; from those windows the bright, joyful sound of clear young voices and constant laughter echoes in the street; the whole house seems to be seething with life and overflowing with gaiety. The mistress of the house has long been in her grave: Maria Dmitrievna died some two years after Liza took the veil, and Martha Timofeevna did not long survive her niece; they sleep side by side in the cemetery of O——. Nastasya Karpovna also is no more; the faithful old woman went every week for several years to pray over the remains of her friend . . . Her hour came, and her bones also were laid in the damp ground. But Maria Dmitrievna's house has not passed into the hands of strangers or gone out of her family, the nest has not been destroyed: Lenochka, grown into a graceful young beauty; her fiancé, a fair-haired young officer of Hussars; Maria Dmitrievna's son, recently married in St Petersburg and now spending the spring in O—— with his wife; his wife's sister, a sixteen-year-old schoolgirl with glowing cheeks and bright eyes; Shurochka, also grown up and grown prettier – these are the young people whose chatter and laughter proclaim their presence within the walls of the Kalitin house. Everything in it has changed;

everything is in keeping with its new masters. Beardless house-serfs, cheerful grinning young fellows, have replaced the staid old retainers; where once fat old Roska trotted importantly about, two retrievers rush madly round and jump on the sofas; the stables are full of lean trotting-horses, spirited shaft-horses, fiery out-runners with plaited manes, Cossack saddle-horses; the hours of luncheon, dinner, and supper have all been thrown into confusion; as the neighbours say, 'unheard-of arrangements' have been introduced.

On the evening of which we are speaking, the members of the Kalitin household (the oldest of them, Lenochka's fiancé, was only twenty-four) were occupied in a not very complicated but, judging by their frequent laughter, thoroughly amusing game; the dogs, too, were dashing about, barking wildly, and the canaries in the cages hanging in the windows were bursting their throats, vying with each other and reinforcing the general din with the clear trilling of their passion of song. At the height of the deafening merriment a mud-spattered tarantass drove up to the gates and a man of about forty-five, in travelling-dress, descended from it and paused in amazement. He stood still for some time, his attentive gaze fixed on the house, then entered the courtyard by the wicket-gate and slowly climbed the steps. He met nobody in the hall; but suddenly the door of the large drawing-room swung open and Shurochka, crimson-faced, bounded in, and a moment later the whole troop of young people ran shouting in after her. They stopped short and fell silent at the sight of the stranger; but the bright eyes fixed on him remained just as friendly and the fresh faces did not cease to smile. Maria Dmitrievna's son went up to the visitor and courteously asked what he could do for him.

'I am Lavretsky,' answered the visitor.

A shout of welcome answered him from all their throats – not because all the young people were delighted at the arrival of a distant and almost forgotten relative but simply because they were ready to be pleased and to make a noise at any favourable opportunity. Lavretsky was immediately surrounded: Lenochka, as an old acquaintance, named herself first, assured him that given a little more time she would certainly have recognized him, and then introduced the rest of the company to him, naming each, even her fiancé, by the diminutives of their names. The whole group moved through the dining-room to the drawing-room. The wallpapers in both rooms were different, but all the furniture was unchanged; Lavretsky recognized the piano; there was even the same embroidery-frame standing in the same position near the window – and holding what might almost have been the same piece of unfinished embroidery as eight years ago. He was placed in a comfortable arm-chair; the others ranged themselves decorously round him. Questions, exclamations, stories, came thick and fast.

'It is a long time since we saw you,' remarked Lenochka naïvely, 'and we haven't seen Varvara Pavlovna either.'

'Of course not,' hastily interrupted her brother. 'I took you away to St Petersburg, and Fëdor Ivanych has been living in the country all the time.'

'Yes, and of course mama has died since then.'

'And Martha Timofeevna,' said Shurochka.

'And Nastasya Karpovna,' went on Lenochka, 'and M. Lemm . . .'

'What, is Lemm dead too?' asked Lavretsky.

'Yes,' answered young Kalitin. 'He went away from here, to Odessa; they say somebody lured him away; and then he died there.'

'Do you know whether he left any music behind?'

'I don't know; it is hardly likely.'

They were all silent, looking at one another. The shadow of sorrow fell across all the young faces.

'But Matroska's alive,' said Lenochka suddenly.

'And so is Gedeonovsky,' added her brother.

At Gedeonovsky's name a laugh burst from all of them at once.

'Yes, he's alive, and he still tells as many lies as ever,' went on Maria Dmitrievna's son. 'And what do you think? this madcap here' (he pointed to the schoolgirl, his wife's sister) 'put pepper in his snuff-box yesterday.'

'How he sneezed!' exclaimed Lenochka, and the irrepressible laughter rang out again.

'We had news of Liza not long ago,' said young Kalitin – and again a hush fell over everything. 'She is all right, her health is improving a little now.'

'Is she still in the same cloister?' asked Lavretsky, not without an effort.

'Yes.'

'Does she write to you?'

'No, never; news reaches us through other people.'

A sudden profound silence fell and everybody thought, 'An angel is flying overhead.'

'Wouldn't you like to go into the garden?' Kalitin said, addressing Lavretsky. 'It is very nice just now, although we have let it go a little.'

Lavretsky went into the garden, and the first thing that met his eyes was that same bench on which he had once passed with Liza a few happy, never-repeated moments; it was warped and blackened but he recognized it, and his heart was filled with a feeling which has no equal for sweetness or sadness – the feeling of intense regret for lost youth and a happiness once possessed. He walked along the avenues with the young people: the limes had grown only a little older and taller in the past eight years, their shade a little thicker; but all the bushes had shot up, the raspberry canes were thick and strong, the hazels were quite choked, and everything smelt of fresh growth, of wood and grass and lilac.

'This would be a good place to play Puss-in-the-Corner,' exclaimed Lenochka, as she came out into a grassy space surrounded by lime-trees, 'and it just happens there are five of us.'

'Have you forgotten Fëdor Ivanych?' asked her brother, 'or weren't you counting yourself?'

Lenochka blushed slightly.

'But, at his age, could Fëdor Ivanych . . . ?' she began.

'Please do play,' Lavretsky hastily interposed, 'never mind

about me. I shall be better pleased if I know I am not in your way. And there is no need to try to entertain me; old men like me have things to occupy us that you know nothing about yet, and that no amusements could replace: memories.'

The young people listened to Lavretsky with friendly and very faintly ironical deference, as though he were a teacher giving a lesson, and then suddenly scattered away from him and ran on to the grass; four of them stood close to the trees, and one in the middle, and the fun began.

Lavretsky returned to the house and went into the dining-room; he walked up to the piano and touched one of the keys: it gave out a faint but pure note that vibrated in his secret heart: it was the first note of that inspired melody with which, so long ago, on that night of happiness, Lemm, poor Lemm, had raised him to such rapturous heights. Then Lavretsky crossed into the drawing-room, and stayed there for a long time: there, where he had so often seen Liza, her image rose more clearly before him; he seemed to feel all round him the traces of her presence; but his grief for her was oppressive and not easy to bear: it had none of the tranquillity brought by death. Liza's life still continued somewhere, muted and far away; he thought of her as living, and did not recognize the girl he had once loved in that dim, pale phantom dressed in the habits of a nun and enveloped in clouds of incense. Lavretsky would not have recognized himself if he could have looked at himself as now, in his thoughts, he looked at Liza. In the course of those eight years he had finally passed a turning-point in his life, a turning-point which many men never reach, but without which no man can retain his integrity to the end; he had really ceased to think of his own happiness and of selfish ends. He had found peace and – why conceal the truth? – grown old not only in face and body, but also in spirit; to preserve, as some say, a young heart into one's old age is both difficult and almost ridiculous; a man may well be content if he does not lose his faith in goodness, the constancy of his will, and his desire for activity. Lavretsky had every right to be content: he had made himself into a good landlord and really learned to till the soil, and his labours were not for himself alone; he had done what he could to make the existence of his peasants prosperous and secure.

Lavretsky went out into the garden, sat down on the familiar seat – and in that dear place, in front of the house where he had for the last time vainly stretched out his hands to grasp the magic cup, frothing and sparkling with the golden wine of pleasure – there, a solitary, homeless wanderer, with the glad cries of the new generation that had already supplanted him ringing in his ears, he looked back on his life. Sorrow filled his heart, but it was not painful or crushing: he had cause for regret but not for shame. 'Play, young creatures, be happy, grow in strength,' he thought, and there was no bitterness in his thoughts, 'life is before you, and for you life will be easier: you will not, like us, have to search for your path, struggling, stumbling in the darkness and rising again; we had to strive to escape destruction – and how many of us failed! – but you must act, you must work, and our blessing, the blessing of all of us old men, go with you. For me, after today with all its emotions, it remains to take my last leave of you and sadly, but without envy or any dark feelings, say, in sight of the end and of the God who waits for me, "Welcome, lonely old age! Burn out, useless life!"'

Lavretsky rose quietly, and quietly slipped away; nobody noticed him, nobody tried to detain him; the cheerful shouts came louder than ever from behind the high, thick, green wall of the lime-trees. He got into the tarantass and ordered the coachman to drive home, letting the horses go at their own pace.

'And what was the end?' the dissatisfied reader will perhaps ask. 'What happened afterwards to Lavretsky? And to Liza?' But what is there to say of people who, though they are still living, have already left this world behind? Why should we return to them? Lavretsky is said to have visited that remote convent where Liza had hidden herself – and seen her there. Crossing from choir to choir, she passed close to him, passed with the smooth, meek, hurried gait of the nun – and did not look at him; only the eyelashes on the side nearer to him trembled ever so slightly, only her wasted face was bent still lower, and the fingers of her clasped hands, entwined with the rosary, pressed together still more closely. What were their thoughts, what their feelings? Who knows? Who can say? There are such moments in life, such feelings . . . We can only point to them – and pass by.

1858

A QUIET BACKWATER

Characters

ASTÁKHOV, Vladímir Sergéich (Sergéevich)
IPÁTOV, Mikhaíl Nikoláich (Nikoláevich)
Nástya *and*
Kátya, *his daughters*
Márya Pávlovna: Másha, *his sister-in-law*
BODRYAKÓV, Iván Ilyich
    "   Sergéy Sergéich (Sergéevich)
VERÉTYEV, Peter Alexéich (Alexéevich)
VERÉTYEVA, Nadézhda Alexéevna: Nádya
AKÍLIN, Gavríla Stepánych (Stepánovich)
STELCHÍNSKY
EVSYUKÓV, Stepán Stepánych (Stepánovich)
TSÉNTELER, Antón Kárlych (Kárlovich)
Agéy Fomích
Egór Kapitónych (Kapitónovich)
Matrëna Márkovna

Mítka

Yakhím

Efím

For a Note on Pronunciation, *see p. 5 above.*

246

A Quiet Backwater

I

IN A FAIRLY LARGE, recently whitewashed room in the owner's small lodge in the village of Sasovo, in the Province of T——, a young man in an overcoat was sitting on a narrow wooden chair at a little warped old table, looking over some accounts. Two stearine candles burned in travelling silver candlesticks set in front of him; in one corner of the room, on a bench, stood an open hamper, in another a servant was setting up an iron bedstead. Behind a low partition a samovar hissed and grumbled; a dog was turning round and round on a freshly strewn bed of hay. In the doorway, intently watching the seated young man, stood a peasant with a big beard and a clever face, wearing a new long overcoat belted with a red sash, to all appearances the bailiff. Against one wall of the room was a tiny and very ancient piano, and beside it a chest of drawers of equal antiquity, with holes instead of locks; between the windows glimmered a dark looking-glass; on the partition hung an old portrait, from which much of the paint had peeled away, of a woman with powdered hair, wearing a hooped skirt and with a black ribbon round her slender neck. Judging by the noticeable crookedness of the ceiling and the slope of the crannied floor, the little house into which we have introduced the reader had existed for a very long time; nobody lived permanently in it, it merely served to house the owner of the estate on his visits. The young man sitting at the table was in fact the owner of the village of Sasovo. He had arrived only the day before from his principal estate, some hundred versts away, and intended to leave on the following day, when he had completed his inspection of the management of this estate, heard the peasants' requests, and scrutinized all the accounts.

'Well, that's enough,' he said, raising his head; 'I'm tired. You may go now,' he added to the bailiff, 'and tomorrow come as early as you can and tell the peasants to come here in the morning for a meeting. Do you hear?'

'Yes, sir.'

'And tell the constable to submit his report for the last month. You did well, though,' the gentleman went on, looking round, 'to whitewash the walls. It seems cleaner, at all events.'

The bailiff also looked round at the walls.

'Well, now go.'

The bailiff bowed and went out.

The gentleman stretched.

'Hey!' he shouted. 'Bring me some tea. It's time for bed.'

The servant went behind the partition and soon returned with a glass of tea, a handful of rusks bought in the town, and a cream-jug, all on an iron tray. The gentleman began to drink his tea, but he had hardly taken two sips when there was the sound of people coming into the next room, and a squeaky voice asked:

'Is Vladimir Sergeich Astakhov at home? May we see him?'

Vladimir Sergeich (for this was the name of the young man in the overcoat) looked at his servant in perplexity and said in a hurried whisper:

'Go and see who it is.'

The man went out, slamming behind him the door which had not been properly shut.

'Tell Vladimir Sergeich,' came the same squeaky voice again, 'that his neighbour Ipatov would like to see him, if it is quite convenient; and another neighbour, Ivan Ilyich Bodryakov, has come with me and also wishes to pay his respects.'

An involuntary gesture of annoyance escaped Vladimir Sergeich, but when the servant came into the room he said:

'Ask them in.'

And he stood up to receive his visitors.

The door opened and they appeared. One of them, a stout, grey-haired little old man with a round little head and bright little eyes, led the way; the other, bringing up the rear, was a tall, lean man of about thirty-five, with a long, swarthy face

249

and untidy hair. The little old man wore a neat grey frock-coat with big pearl buttons; a pink cravat, half-hidden by the turn-down collar of his white shirt, loosely encircled his neck; gaiters adorned his legs; the pattern of his plaid trousers was agreeably bright, and altogether he produced a pleasant impression. His companion, on the other hand, aroused a less favourable feeling in the spectator: he wore an old black swallow-tail, closely buttoned up; his trousers, of thick winter tricot, resembled it in colour; neither round his neck nor at his wrists was any linen visible. The old man approached Vladimir Sergeich first and, with a polite bow, began in the same thin voice:

'I have the honour to introduce myself: your nearest neigh-bour, and indeed a relative, Mikhail Nikolaich Ipatov. I have long desired the pleasure of making your acquaintance. I hope I do not disturb you.'

Vladimir Sergeich answered that he was very pleased . . . and had himself been desirous . . . and that he was not in the least disturbed, and would they not please sit down . . . and have some tea?

'And this gentleman,' the little old man, having heard Vladimir Sergeich's fragmentary phrases with an indulgent smile, went on, indicating with his arm the gentleman in the swallow-tailed coat, 'also a neighbour of yours . . . and my very good friend, Ivan Ilyich Bodryakov, was most desirous of making your acquaintance.'

The gentleman in the swallow-tail, from whose face nobody

could have supposed that he had ever been 'most desirous' of anything in his life – the gentleman in the swallow-tail bowed limply and awkwardly. Vladimir Sergeich bowed in return and again begged his guests to be seated.

The visitors sat down.

'I am very pleased, very pleased indeed,' began the old man, agreeably waving his arms, while his companion applied himself with half-open mouth to a contemplation of the ceiling, 'very pleased to have the honour at last of seeing you in person. Although, indeed, you have your permanent residence in a district somewhat removed from these parts, yet we count you also among our local landowners.'

'I find that very flattering,' replied Vladimir Sergeich.

'Flattering or not, it is so. You must excuse me, Vladimir Sergeich, we are plain, blunt folk here, we live simply and say what we think without beating about the bush. Even when we pay our name-day visits to one another, I must confess we wear our frock-coats. Truly! It is quite the accepted custom here. In the other districts round about they call us the "frock-coats" for it, and even accuse us of bad form, but we don't take any notice! What, live in the country and stand on ceremony?'

'Of course, what could be better . . . in the country . . . than such easy informality?' remarked Vladimir Sergeich.

'However,' rejoined the old gentleman, 'there are people living even in our district who are, one might say, of the highest intellectual type, people of European education, even though they do not wear dress coats. Take, for example, our historian, Stepan Stepanych Evsyukov; he studies Russian history from the earliest times and is known in St Petersburg, a most scholarly person! In our town, you know, we have an ancient Swedish cannon-ball . . . it has been set up in the centre of the square . . . well, it was he who discovered it. Truly! Anton Karlych Tsenteler . . . he is learned in natural history; however, they say science comes natural to all Germans. When an escaped hyena was killed here, about ten years ago, you know it was Anton Karlych who discovered that it really was a hyena, on account of the peculiar structure of its tail. Then we have a landed proprietor, Kaburdin: he writes articles, mostly in a light vein; he has a very clever pen and his articles appear in *Galatea*. Bodryakov . . . not Ivan Ilyich, no, Ivan Ilyich looks down on that kind of thing, but another Bodryakov, Sergey . . . now what the deuce is his patronymic, Ivan Ilyich? . . . what the devil is it?'

'Sergeich,' put in Ivan Ilyich.

'Yes, Sergey Sergeich, – he goes in for verse. Well, of course he's no Pushkin, but sometimes he can polish someone off as neatly as anybody in the capital. Do you know his epigram on Agey Fomich?'

'What Agey Fomich?'

'Oh, excuse me; I am always forgetting that, after all, you don't live here. He is our captain of police. The epigram turned out very amusing. I think you will remember it, Ivan Ilyich.'

'*Our noblemen all,*' began Bodryakov indifferently,

'. . . *will agree when we state,*

There's none better to fill a position of weight . . .'

'I must tell you,' Ipatov interrupted, 'that our Noblemen's Assembly elected him almost without one blackball, for he is a most worthy man.'

'*Our noblemen all,*' repeated Bodryakov,

'. . . *will agree when we state,*

There's none better to fill a position of weight,

For Agey Fomich sure will never grow thinner,

So long as he eats such a very good dinner!'

The old gentleman laughed.

'He-he-he! Not bad, is it? From that time, if you'll believe me, every one of us will say, for example, "Good morning, Agey Fomich," and be certain to add, "none better to fill a position of weight." And do you imagine it makes Agey Fomich cross? Not at all! No, that's not our way. Ask Ivan Ilyich here!'

Ivan Ilyich only rolled his eyes.

'Lose your temper over a joke, no, you can't do that! Take Ivan Ilyich here: our nickname for him is Mr Pliable, because he's always ready to agree to anything at once. Well, does Ivan Ilyich take offence? Never!'

Ivan Ilyich, blinking slowly, looked first at the old gentleman and then at Vladimir Sergeich.

The title of Mr Pliable really did suit Ivan Ilyich very well. There was not a trace in him of anything that could be called will or character. Anybody who wanted could take him anywhere he liked; it sufficed to say, 'Come on, Ivan Ilyich,' and he took his hat and went; but let somebody else turn up and say, 'Stay where you are, Ivan Ilyich,' and he put his hat down again and stayed. He was of a quiet and peace-loving disposition, had been a bachelor all his life, and though he did not play cards, liked to sit near the players and look from one face to another in turn. He could not live without society, solitude was unbearable to him; his own company depressed him, but he very seldom had to suffer it. He had one other peculiarity: he got out of bed very early in the morning and began to hum softly the old drawing-room ballad:

'On his estate a baron once
Lived in his simple rustic way . . .'

In consequence of this peculiarity, Ivan Ilyich had another nickname: 'The Siskin'; a caged siskin is known to sing only once during the day, in the early morning. Such was Ivan Ilyich Bodryakov.

The conversation between Ipatov and Vladimir Sergeich continued for some time, but no longer on what might be called the same intellectual and speculative level as before. The old gentleman cross-questioned Vladimir Sergeich about his estates, about the condition of his forest-lands and other properties, and about the improvements he had already introduced or merely intended to introduce, into the management of his land; communicated to him some of his own observations; advised him, among other things, to destroy the hummocks in his meadows by scattering oats round them, which would induce the pigs to root them up with their snouts; and so forth. At last, however, noticing that Vladimir Sergeich could not keep his eyes open, and that his words showed a certain sluggishness and incoherence, the old gentleman rose, bowed politely, and declared that he had no intention of causing further inconvenience by his presence, but that he hoped to have the pleasure of receiving him as an honoured guest not later than the next day at dinner.

'In my village,' he added, 'I won't say the smallest child, but I *will* venture to say the first hen or peasant woman you come across, will show you the way; you need only ask for Ipatovka. The horses will find their own way.'

Vladimir Sergeich answered, but in the slightly hesitant fashion that was characteristic of him, that he would try . . . that if nothing hindered him . . .

'No, we shall expect you without fail,' interrupted the old gentleman warmly, shook his hand vigorously and went swiftly out, half-turning in the doorway to exclaim: 'Quite informally!'

Mr Pliable Bodryakov bowed silently and disappeared in the wake of his companion, after a preliminary stumble on the threshold.

When he had seen his unexpected visitors out, Vladimir Sergeich at once undressed, lay down, and fell asleep.

Vladimir Sergeich Astakhov belonged to that class of people who, having cautiously tested their powers in two or three different fields, say of themselves that they have finally decided to take a severely practical view of life and devote their leisure to the increasing of their incomes. He was intelligent, rather careful with money and very sensible, liked reading, society, and music, but all in moderation . . . and always behaved with great propriety. He was twenty-seven years old. We have bred many young men like him in recent times. He was of medium height and well built, and had pleasant, if small, features; their expression hardly ever changed, and his eyes always had the same hard, bright look; only very rarely were they softened by a faint veil of something that partook of both sadness and boredom; the polite smile hardly ever left his lips. His hair was really beautiful, fair and silky, lying in long waves. Vladimir Sergeich's excellent estate was reckoned to be of about six hundred souls, and he was thinking of marriage, a marriage of inclination – but advantageous as well. He particularly wanted to find a wife with good connexions. He found that he himself had not enough connexions. In short, he deserved the title, which had recently become fashionable, of a 'gentleman' in the English style.

Rising the next morning very early, as was his habit, our 'gentleman' occupied himself with business matters and, to give him his due, did so very capably, something which cannot always be said for our practical young people in Russia. He listened patiently to his peasants' muddled requests and complaints, satisfied them as far as he could, sorted out the quarrels and arguments that had cropped up between relatives, appealing to the better feelings of some and lecturing others, examined the constable's report, brought to light two or three of the bailiff's sharp practices, and, in short, dealt with things so efficiently that he felt pleased with himself, and his peasants spoke well of him as they returned to their homes. Vladimir Sergeich had decided to dine at home and even ordered, from the cook he had brought with him, his favourite giblet soup with rice, when suddenly, perhaps in consequence of the feeling of satisfaction that had filled him ever since the morning, he clapped his hand to his forehead and exclaimed aloud, not without consciousness that he was taking a risk, 'I believe I *will* go to that old chatter-box's!' No sooner said than done; half an hour later, seated in his small new tarantass, behind four sturdy peasant horses, he was on his way to Ipatovka, which was not more than twelve versts away, on good roads.

II

Mikhail Nikolaich Ipatov's home consisted of two separate small houses built facing one another on opposite sides of a pond of running water. A long dam, planted with silver poplars, bounded this pond; almost on a level with it the roof of a little water-mill was visible. Built exactly alike, and both painted the same lilac colour, the houses seemed to look at one another across the smooth expanse of water through the shining panes of their clean little windows. From the middle of the front of each little house projected a semi-circular terrace, above which rose a pointed pediment supported on four close-set white columns. A very old garden surrounded the whole pond: it had avenues and thick clumps of lime-trees; here and there ancient pines with pale yellow trunks, dark oaks, magnificent ashes, reared high their solitary crests; the thick foliage of overgrown lilacs and acacias crowded up to the very walls of both little houses, leaving uncovered only their fronts, from which little winding paths paved with brick ran down the slope. In separate flotillas, bright-coloured ducks and grey and white geese sailed over the clear water of the pond: it always remained free from weeds, thanks to the abundant springs flowing into its head from the bottom of a steep-sided ravine. It was a good site for a house: inviting, secluded, and beautiful.

In one of the two little houses lived Mikhail Nikolaich himself; his mother, an infirm old lady of seventy, lived in the other. Driving on to the dam, Vladimir Sergeich did not know at which house to apply. He looked about him; a little boy was fishing, standing bare-foot on a half-rotten log which lay in the water. Vladimir Sergeich called out to him.

'Which do you want, the old mistress or the young master?' rejoined the boy, without taking his eyes from his float.

'What mistress?' answered Vladimir Sergeich; 'I've come to see Mikhail Nikolaich.'

'Oh, the young master? Well then, go to the right.'

And the boy tugged at his line and pulled out of the still

water a small, silvery crucian carp. Vladimir Sergeich turned to the right.

Mikhail Nikolaich was playing draughts with Mr Pliable when Vladimir Sergeich was announced. He was delighted, jumped up from his arm-chair and ran into the hall, where he kissed his visitor three times.

'You find me with my constant companion, Vladimir Sergeich,' began the garrulous old man, 'with Ivan Ilyich, who, let me say in passing, is quite charmed by your amiability.' (Ivan Ilyich looked silently into a corner.) 'He was good enough to stay in and play draughts with me; all my family are walking in the garden, but I will send for them at once . . .'

'But why should you trouble . . ?' Vladimir Sergeich was beginning.

'Nonsense, no trouble at all. Hi, Vanka, run after the young ladies, quickly now . . . and tell them a visitor has come. And how do you like this place? not bad, is it? Kaburdin has written a poem about it; it begins, "*Ipatovka, that blest retreat,*" and it goes on very well too, only I can't remember it all. The garden is very big, that's the trouble: it's too much to keep up. These two houses which, as you may have noticed, are so very much alike, were built by two brothers, my father and my uncle Sergey; it was they who laid out the gardens, too; they were very great friends . . . Damon and . . . there now, I've forgotten what the other one was called . . .'

'Python,' remarked Ivan Ilyich.

'Really, was it? Well, it doesn't matter.' (At home the old gentleman talked much less ceremoniously than in other people's houses.) 'It is probably not unknown to you, Vladimir Sergeich, that I am a widower; I have lost my wife; the older children are at boarding-schools, and I have only my two younger daughters with me, and my sister-in-law, my wife's sister, you will see her presently. But come, I haven't offered you anything. Ivan Ilyich, my dear chap, see about some refreshment . . . What kind of vodka do you prefer?'

'I don't drink anything before dinner.'

'Good heavens, you don't say! However, just as you choose. A guest must be allowed to do as he pleases. We live very simply here, you know. But it is not so much a dreary provincial hole as, if I may venture to express it so, a peaceful backwater, a real peaceful backwater, a quiet nook – that's it! But why don't you sit down?'

Vladimir Sergeich sat down, but without relinquishing his hat.

'Allow me to relieve you of that,' said Ipatov, and considerately taking his hat out of his hands he carried it into a corner, returned, looked into his guest's face with an amiable smile and, not knowing what to say to please him, asked in the heartiest manner whether he liked playing draughts.

'I am bad at all games,' answered Vladimir Sergeich.

'And quite right, too,' rejoined Ipatov; 'but draughts isn't a game, it's more of an amusement, a pastime for one's leisure hours, isn't it, Ivan Ilyich?'

Ivan Ilyich looked at Ipatov apathetically, as though thinking, 'Who's to tell whether it's a game or a pastime?', but after a short pause he brought out:

'Yes; draughts doesn't count.'

'Now chess, they say, is another matter,' went on Ipatov; 'it's said to be a very difficult game. But in my opinion . . . ah, here come my family!' he interrupted himself, glancing through the half-open french window leading into the garden.

Vladimir Sergeich rose and turned round, and saw, first two little girls about ten years old, in pink cotton dresses and big hats, skipping up the steps of the terrace, and on their heels a tall, plump, graceful girl of about twenty, in a dark-coloured dress. They all came into the room and the little girls curtseyed sedately to the visitor.

'Now let me introduce my little daughters,' said the host. 'This one is called Katya, and this is Nastya; and here is my sister-in-law, Marya Pavlovna, whom I have had the pleasure of mentioning to you already. I am sure you will get on very well together.'

Vladimir Sergeich bowed to Marya Pavlovna; she answered with an almost imperceptible inclination of the head.

Marya Pavlovna was holding a large, open knife in her hand; her thick fair hair was a little ruffled, a small green leaf clung to it and a plait was escaping from under the comb, her brown cheeks were flushed and her red lips parted; her dress seemed a little rumpled. She was breathing quickly and her eyes were shining; she had evidently been working in the garden. She went out of the room again at once; the little girls ran after her.

'They must tidy up a little,' remarked the old man to Vladimir Sergeich; 'they always have to do that.'

Vladimir Sergeich smiled widely in reply, and grew a shade thoughtful. He had been struck by Marya Pavlovna. It was a long time since he had seen such a true beauty of the Russian steppes. She soon returned, sat down on the sofa, and remained there motionless. She had straightened her hair but not changed her dress, nor even put on cuffs. Her features expressed not so much pride as austerity, almost harshness; her forehead was low and broad, her nose short and straight; occasionally a slow, indolent smile curved her lips; her straight brows frowned disdainfully. She almost always kept her large dark eyes cast down. 'I know,' her ungracious young face seemed to say, 'I know you are all looking at me; look, then! I am sick of it!' When she did raise her eyes, there was in them something wild, beautiful, and unseeing, that recalled the look of a fallow deer. She had a magnificent figure; a classical poet would have compared her to Ceres or Juno.

'What were you doing in the garden?' Ipatov asked, trying to draw her into the conversation.

'I was cutting off dead branches and digging the flower-beds,' she replied in a rather low-pitched but clear and agreeable voice.

'And are you tired, then?'

'The children are; I am not.'

'I know,' the old man rejoined; 'you are a regular Bobelina! Have you been in to see grandmother?'

'Yes; she is having a sleep.'

'Do you like flowers?' Vladimir Sergeich asked her.

'Yes.'

'Why don't you put a hat on when you go out?' asked Ipatov. 'Look how red and sunburnt you are.'

She silently passed her hand over her face. Her hands were not large, but they were a trifle broad and somewhat red. She did not wear gloves.

'And do you like gardening?' Vladimir Sergeich asked again.

'Yes.'

Vladimir Sergeich began to tell them about the beautiful garden of a rich landowner in his neighbourhood. 'The head gardener alone gets two thousand silver roubles; he's a German,' he said.

'What's the gardener's name?' asked Ivan Ilyich suddenly.

'I don't remember; Meyer, I think, or Müller. Why?'

'Oh, nothing. I just wanted to know,' answered Ivan Ilyich.

Vladimir Sergeich went on with what he was saying. The little girls, Mikhail Nikolaich's daughters, came in, quietly sat down and quietly listened . . .

A servant appeared in the doorway and announced that Egor Kapitonych had come.

'Ah, show him in, show him in!' exclaimed Ipatov.

A short, fat little gentleman, the kind of person who always gets called 'Shorty' or 'Tubby', with a face that was both puffy and wrinkled, like a baked apple, came into the room. He wore a grey Hussar jacket with black frogs and a stand-up collar; his wide coffee-coloured velveteen trousers ended far above his ankles.

'How do you do, my dear Egor Kapitonych?' exclaimed Ipatov, advancing to meet him. 'We have not seen anything of you for quite a long time.'

'Oh but, after all, Mikhail Nikolaich,' returned Egor Kapitonych in a plaintive, burring voice, when he had first bowed to everybody present, 'I'm not a free agent, am I?'

'Oh, and why aren't you free, Egor Kapitonych?'

'Why, Mikhail Nikolaich, my family, business . . . And besides there's Matrëna Markovna.'

And he waved his arm.

'What about Matrëna Markovna?'

Here Ipatov winked at Vladimir Sergeich, as though he wanted to draw his attention to what would follow.

'No secret about it,' retorted Egor Kapitonych, sitting down; 'she's always annoyed with me, surely you must know! Whatever I say, it's always wrong, it's not delicate, it's not nice. And why it isn't nice, God only knows. And the young ladies, I mean my daughters, take their cue from their mother. I say nothing against her: Matrëna Markovna is a fine woman, but she really is very strict about manners.'

'But surely there is nothing wrong with your manners, Egor Kapitonych?'

'That's the way I look at it myself, but, you see, she's hard to please. For example, yesterday at dinner I said, "Matrëna Markovna", I said' (and Egor Kapitonych gave his voice a most ingratiating tone), '"Matrëna Markovna, why is it Aldoshka won't look after the horses? and he can't drive," I said; "the black stallion is badly knocked up." Ee-ee, Matrëna Markovna simply flared up! said I ought to be ashamed. "You don't know," says she, "how to express yourself decently in the presence of ladies." Well, the young ladies left the table at once, and the very next day the Biryulëv young ladies, my wife's nieces, already knew all about it. And what had I said? – judge for yourself. And whatever I say – sometimes I'm a little careless, certainly, but who isn't, especially at home? – by the very next day the Biryulëv young ladies know all about it. I simply don't know what to do. Sometimes when I'm sitting and thinking, I have a trick – perhaps you know this? – of breathing rather heavily, and Matrëna Markovna begins to tell me I ought to be ashamed again: "Don't wheeze like that," she says, "you never hear anyone else wheezing!" "Why do you scold me, Matrëna Markovna," say I; "you ought to be kind and sympathetic to me," I say, "and instead you scold me." Well, I've stopped thinking when I'm at home. I just sit and look at the floor all the time. Honestly, that's all I do! Then not long ago we were going to bed and I said, "Matrëna Markovna," I said, "Why do you spoil your page so badly? You know," I said, "he's a filthy little pig. He might at least wash his face, if it's only on Sunday." Well, you'd have thought, wouldn't you? that was delicate enough, but even that didn't please her; Matrëna Markovna starts crying shame on me again: "You don't know how to behave in the presence of ladies," she says – and the very next day the Biryulëv young ladies knew all about it. Well, how can I think of going out, Mikhail Nikolaich?'

'What you tell me is very surprising,' rejoined Ipatov. 'I shouldn't have expected it of Matrëna Markovna; I should think she . . .'

'She's a fine woman,' put in Egor Kapitonych, 'and a model wife and mother, you might say, but she's a bit strict about questions of manners. She says there ought to be *ensemble* in everything, and it seems I haven't any. I don't speak French, you know, I only just understand it. But what is this *ensemble* I haven't got?'

Ipatov, who was not terribly good at French himself, merely shrugged his shoulders.

'And how are your children, the boys, I mean?' he asked Egor Kapitonych a little later.

Egor Kapitonych looked at him out of the corner of his eye.

'Oh, the boys are all right. I'm pleased with them. The girls have got out of hand, but I'm pleased with my sons. Lëlya is doing well in the service and his superiors think well of him; my Lëlya's a clever boy. But Mikhets – it's different with him: he's turned out a kind of philanthropist.'

'Why a philanthropist?'

'God knows, he never talks to anybody, he's too shy. Matrëna Markovna makes him worse. "Why do you have to follow your father's example?" says she. "Honour him, but when it comes to manners, copy your mother." But he'll catch up when he's old enough.'

Vladimir Sergeich requested Ipatov to introduce him to Egor Kapitonych, and they began to talk. Marya Pavlovna took no part in the conversation; Ivan Ilyich, who had sat down near her, exchanged only a word or two with her; the little girls went up to him and began to tell him something in a whisper . . . The housekeeper, a thin old woman with a dark-coloured handkerchief bound round her head, entered and announced that dinner was ready. They all went into the dining-room.

Dinner lasted rather a long time. Ipatov kept a good chef and imported wine of decent quality, if not from Moscow, at any rate from the capital of the province. Ipatov did himself, as the saying goes, very well. His property did not comprise more than three hundred souls, but he had no debts and the estate was in good order. At table it was the host who did most of the talking. Egor Kapitonych seconded his efforts, but did not forget to look after himself; he ate and drank his full share. Marya Pavlovna was still silent, only occasionally answering with a half-smile the torrential speeches of the little girls who sat on either side of her; they were obviously very fond of her. Vladimir Sergeich tried several times to get into conversation with her, but without any marked success. Bodryakov, Mr

Pliable, was languid and indifferent even in his eating. After dinner they all went on to the terrace for coffee. The weather was glorious; the faint scent of the lime-trees, just then in full bloom, drifted from the garden; the summer air, slightly cooled by the thick shade of the trees and the moisture of the pond, had a caressing warmth. Suddenly the quick drumming of hoofs came from beyond the poplars by the dam, and a moment later a horsewoman in a long habit and a round grey hat, on a bay horse, appeared; she rode at a gallop, and a page bounced along behind her on a small white pony.

'Ah!' exclaimed Ipatov, 'Nadezhda Alexeevna is coming – this is a pleasant surprise.'

'Alone?' asked Marya Pavlovna, who had been standing quite still near the door.

'Yes . . . evidently Peter Alexeich has been detained.'

Marya Pavlovna looked up from under lowered brows; colour flooded her face and she turned away.

Meanwhile the rider had come through the garden gate, galloped up to the terrace, and leapt lightly to the ground, without waiting either for her page or for Ipatov, who had started in her direction. Nimbly picking up the skirts of her habit, she ran up the steps, exclaiming gaily as she reached the terrace:

'Here I am!'

'Please come in!' said Ipatov. 'This is unexpected, this is nice! Allow me to kiss your hand . . .'

'If you wish,' returned the visitor, 'only you must take off my glove yourself. I can't.' And as she held out her hand to him, she gestured with her head towards Marya Pavlovna. 'Masha, what do you think? my brother isn't coming today,' she said with a small sigh.

'I can see that he is not here,' answered Marya Pavlovna in an undertone.

'He told me to tell you that he is busy. Don't be angry. How do you do, Egor Kapitonych? how do you do, Ivan Ilyich? Good afternoon, children ... Vasya,' added the visitor, turning to her page, 'tell them to walk Krasavchik carefully, do you hear? Masha, please give me a pin to fasten up my train ... Mikhail Nikolaich, come here a moment.'

Ipatov went a little closer to her.

'Who is the new-comer?' she asked, fairly loudly.

'A neighbour, Vladimir Sergeich Astakhov; you know, Sasovo is his. Would you like me to introduce him to you?'

'Very well, later. Ah, what glorious weather!' she went on. 'Tell me, Egor Kapitonych, can Matrëna Markovna grumble even in such weather?'

'Matrëna Markovna never grumbles, whatever the weather is like, madam; she is only a little strict about manners ...'

'And what are the Biryulëv young ladies doing? It's true, isn't it, that the very next day they know all about everything? ...'

And she laughed a clear, silvery laugh.

'You are always ready to laugh,' protested Egor Kapitonych. 'However, when should one laugh, if not at your age?'

'Egor Kapitonych, don't be angry, my dear! Oh, I'm tired, let me sit down . . .'

Nadezhda Alexeevna sank into a chair and playfully pulled her hat down over her eyes.

Ipatov led Vladimir Sergeich to her.

'Nadezhda Alexeevna, allow me to introduce our neighbour, Mr Astakhov, of whom you have probably often heard.'

Vladimir Sergeich bowed, and Nadezhda Alexeevna looked at him from under the brim of her round hat.

'Nadezhda Alexeevna Veretyeva, our neighbour,' Ipatov continued, addressing Vladimir Sergeich, 'lives here with her brother Peter Alexeich, formerly a lieutenant in the Guards. She is a great friend of my sister-in-law's, and generally favourably disposed towards our household.'

'A complete dossier,' said Nadezhda Alexeevna with a mocking smile, glancing at Vladimir Sergeich as before from under her hat.

Meanwhile Vladimir Sergeich was saying to himself, 'This one is very pretty, too.' And indeed, Nadezhda Alexeevna was a very charming young lady. Slender and graceful, she seemed much younger than she really was: she was already twenty-seven. She had a round face, a little head, fluffy golden hair, a sharp, almost impertinently turned-up little nose, and gay, somewhat sly eyes. A mocking spirit flashed in them, kindling showers of sparks. Her extraordinarily lively and mobile features sometimes assumed an almost comical expression; humour shone through them. Occasionally, usually with great suddenness, a pensive shade fell over her face, and then it became meek and gentle, but she could not give herself up to thoughtfulness for long. She easily seized on the funny side of people and was rather good at drawing caricatures. From the day she was born everybody had spoilt her, and this was instantly noticeable: people who have been spoiled as children carry the special stamp of it until the end of their lives. Her brother was very fond of her, although he used to assert that her sting was like a wasp's, not a bee's, because the bee stings and dies, but a sting costs the wasp nothing. The comparison always made her angry.

'Are you here for long?' she asked Vladimir Sergeich, dropping her eyes and twisting her riding-crop in her hands.

'No, I intend to leave tomorrow.'

'Where for?'

'Home.'

'Home? Why, if I may ask?'

'Why? I have business at home that does not allow of delay.' Nadezhda Alexeevna looked at him.

'Are you so . . . punctilious?'

'I try to be,' retorted Vladimir Sergeich. 'In this practical age every decent man *ought* to be practical and businesslike.'

'That's absolutely right,' remarked Ipatov. 'Isn't it, Ivan Ilyich?'

Ivan Ilyich only looked at Ipatov, but Egor Kapitonych said: 'Yes, that's true.'

'A pity,' said Nadezhda Alexeevna. 'We happen to need a *jeune premier* just now. I suppose you can play comedy, can't you?'

'I have never tried my hand in that line.'

'I am sure you could act well. You have such a . . . dignified manner, and that is essential for present-day *jeunes premiers*. My brother and I mean to get up an amateur dramatic society here. But we shan't play only comedies, we shall produce everything – dramas, ballets, even tragedies. Masha would be absolutely right for Cleopatra or Phèdre. Just look at her.'

Vladimir Sergeich turned . . . Leaning her head against the door, Marya Pavlovna, with folded arms, was gazing thoughtfully into the distance . . . At that moment her regular features really were reminiscent of the faces of antique sculptures. She had not heard Nadezhda Alexeevna's last words; but when she noticed that all eyes were suddenly turned on her, she immediately guessed what they were talking about, blushed, and would have retreated into the drawing-room . . . Nadezhda Alexeevna swiftly seized her hand and with a kitten's coquettish tenderness drew her towards herself and kissed that almost masculine hand. Marya Pavlovna blushed even more fiercely.

'You are always up to mischief, Nadya,' she said.

'Did I say anything about you that wasn't true? I am ready to call everybody to witness . . . Well, all right, all right, I won't. But I will say again,' Nadezhda Alexeevna continued, turning to Vladimir Sergeich, 'that it's a pity you are going. It is true we have one *jeune premier*, self-appointed, but he's very bad.'

'Who is that, may I ask?'

'The poet Bodryakov. How can a poet be a *jeune premier*? To begin with, the way he dresses is awful; secondly, he writes epigrams, but in the presence of any woman, even me, imagine! he's overcome with shyness; and then he lisps, and he's always flinging one arm above his head, and I don't know what besides. Please tell me, Monsieur Astakhov, are all poets like that?'

Vladimir Sergeich drew himself up slightly.

'I have never known one personally, and I confess I have never sought their acquaintance.'

'Oh, yes, to be sure, you are a practical man. We shall have to take Bodryakov, there is no help for it. The other *jeunes premiers* are even worse. He at any rate will learn his lines by heart. Masha, besides playing the tragic parts, will fill the role of our prima donna . . . Have you heard her sing, Monsieur Astakhov?'

'No,' rejoined Vladimir Sergeich, smirking, 'I didn't even know . . .'

'What is the matter with you today, Nadya?' said Marya Pavlovna with a look of displeasure.

Nadezhda Alexeevna sprang up.

'Please, Masha, sing something for us, please do . . . I won't leave you alone until you sing us something, Masha darling. I would sing myself, to amuse your visitor, but really, you know what a bad voice I have. But on the other hand, you shall see how marvellously I will accompany you.'

Marya Pavlovna was silent for a time.

'There is no escaping you,' she said at last. 'You are like a spoilt child, used to having all your whims obeyed. Very well, I will sing.'

'Bravo, bravo,' exclaimed Nadezhda Alexeevna, clapping her hands. 'Gentlemen, let us go into the drawing-room. But as for whims,' she added laughing, 'I shall remember that. How could you expose my weaknesses before strangers? Egor Kapitonych, is *that* how Matrëna Markovna shames you in front of people?'

'Matrëna Markovna,' muttered Egor Kapitonych, 'is a very estimable woman; only on the subject of manners . . .'

'Well, come along, come along,' interrupted Nadezhda Alexeevna, going into the drawing-room.

Everybody followed her. She flung off her hat and sat down at the piano. Marya Pavlovna stood by the wall, some distance away from her.

'Masha,' said Nadezhda Alexeevna, after thinking for a moment, 'sing us "The Lad is Sowing Corn".'

Marya Pavlovna began to sing. Her voice was pure and strong, and she sang well, simply and without affectation. Everybody listened intently, and Vladimir Sergeich could not conceal his astonishment. When Marya Pavlovna finished, he went up to her and began to assure her that he had never expected . . .

'Wait, there is more yet!' interrupted Nadezhda Alexeevna. 'Masha, I will please your Little Russian heart; sing us "Down in the Forest Merry Noises" now . . .'

'You are not Little Russian, are you?' asked Vladimir Sergeich.

'Yes, I was born in the Ukraine,' she answered, and she began to sing 'Down in the Forest'.

At first she uttered the words indifferently, but the plaintive passion of her native melody began little by little to arouse her emotions, her cheeks grew flushed, her eyes sparkled, and her voice rang out warmly. She came to the end of the song.

'Good God, how well you sang that!' said Nadezhda Alexeevna, bending over the keyboard. 'What a pity my brother was not here!'

Marya Pavlovna lowered her eyes at once, and smiled her usual poignant smile.

'We must have something more,' remarked Ipatov.

'Yes, if you will be so kind,' added Vladimir Sergeich.

'You must excuse me; I shan't sing any more today,' said Marya Pavlovna, walking out of the room.

Nadezhda Alexeevna followed her with her eyes, and at first she looked thoughtful, but then she smiled and began to pick out 'The Lad is Sowing Corn' with one finger, then suddenly broke into a brilliant polka and, without finishing it, struck a loud chord, slammed down the piano lid, and stood up.

'What a pity there is nobody to dance with,' she exclaimed. 'That is just what I feel like!'

Vladimir Sergeich went up to her.

'What a marvellous voice Marya Pavlovna has,' he remarked, 'and what feeling she puts into her singing!'

'Do you like music?'

'Yes . . . very much.'

'Such a learned man, and you like music!'

'But what makes you think that I am learned?'

'Oh, yes; excuse me, I am always forgetting, you are a practical man. Where can Masha have got to? Wait, I will go and fetch her.'

And Nadezhda Alexeevna fluttered out of the drawing-room.

'A weather-cock, as you see,' said Ipatov, approaching Vladimir Sergeich, 'but the kindest of hearts. And the education she has had, you wouldn't credit it. She can speak all languages. Well, they are people of substance, it is understandable.'

'Yes,' said Vladimir Sergeich absently, 'a very nice girl. But allow me to inquire whether your late wife came from Little Russia, too.'

'Quite right, sir. My late wife was Ukrainian, just like her sister, Marya Pavlovna. My wife, to tell the truth, even had some trace of the accent; although she had a perfect command of Russian, all the same she did not pronounce it quite correctly; you know, she said *i* for *y* and things like that. Marya Pavlovna, though, left her native country while she was still very young. But you know, her Little Russian blood still shows, doesn't it?'

'Marya Pavlovna sings wonderfully well,' remarked Vladimir Sergeich.

'Not at all badly. But how is it they don't bring tea? And where have the young ladies gone? It's time for tea.'

The young ladies did not soon return. Meanwhile the samovar

was brought and the table laid for tea. Ipatov sent for them. They arrived together. Marya Pavlovna sat down at the table to pour out tea, and Nadezhda Alexeevna went to the door on to the terrace and began looking out into the garden. The bright summer day had been followed by a clear, quiet evening: the sunset flamed in the sky; half flooded with its crimson, the broad pond lay a motionless mirror, majestically reflecting in the nebulous silver of its deep bosom all the unfathomable, airy vault of the sky, and the upside-down trees that seemed dyed black, and the house. A hush had fallen over everything; there was not a sound anywhere.

'Look how lovely,' said Nadezhda Alexeevna to Vladimir Sergeich, who had gone up to her. 'Over there, down in the pond, a star has been kindled next to a light in the house; one is red, the other golden. And here comes grandmother,' she added aloud.

From behind a lilac-bush had appeared a small carriage drawn by two men. In it sat an old woman, all muffled up and huddled together, with her head bent down to her breast. The fringe of her white cap almost entirely covered her shrivelled and shrunken little face. The little carriage stopped in front of the terrace. Ipatov went out of the room and his daughters ran out after him. During the whole evening they had been scurrying like little mice from one room to another.

'I wish you good evening, mother dear,' said Ipatov, as he reached the old woman, raising his voice. 'How are you feeling?'

'I have come to have a look at you,' the old lady said in a thin voice, with an effort. 'See what a wonderful evening. I have been asleep all day, and now my legs have begun to ache dreadfully. Oh, these legs of mine! They are no good to me, and they ache.'

'Mother dear, let me introduce our neighbour, Mr Vladimir Sergeich Astakhov.'

'Very pleased,' replied the old lady, looking at him with her large black eyes, now grown dim. 'I hope you will make friends with my boy. He is a good man; I gave him such education as I could; of course, a woman is not much good. He is still a youngster, but with God's grace he'll cut his wisdom teeth yet, and not before time; it's high time I handed over to him. Is that you, Nadya?' added the old woman, looking at Nadezhda Alexeevna.

'Yes, grandmother.'

'Is Masha pouring out tea?'

'Yes, she is, grandmother.'

'And who is here besides?'

'Ivan Ilyich and Egor Kapitonych.'

'Matrëna Markovna's husband?'

'Yes, grandmother.'

The old lady mumbled her lips.

'Very well. Now, Misha, I can't get hold of the bailiff; tell him to come and see me tomorrow morning early, I shall have a lot of business to discuss with him. Without me all your affairs go wrong, I see. Well, that's enough, I'm tired; take me home, you ... Goodbye, my dear sir, I don't remember your name and patronymic,' she added, turning to Vladimir Sergeich; 'you must excuse an old woman. And you, grand-daughters, don't come with me. No need for that. You'd like to do nothing but run about. Sit still, sit still and learn your lessons, do you hear? Masha spoils you. Well, get along.'

The old lady's head, lifted with such difficulty, fell back on her bosom ...

The little carriage quietly bowled away.

'How old is your mother?' asked Vladimir Sergeich.

'She is only seventy-three: but it is twenty-six years since she lost the use of her legs; it happened soon after my father's death. She used to be a beauty.'

For a time nobody spoke.

Suddenly Nadezhda Alexeevna gave a start.

'What was that? I am sure I saw a bat fly past. Ugh, how horrid!'

And she hurriedly returned to the drawing-room.

'It is time I went home. Mikhail Nikolaich, tell them to saddle my horse.'

'Time for me to go, too,' remarked Vladimir Sergeich.

'But where will you go?' said Ipatov. 'Spend the night here. Nadezhda Alexeevna has only two versts to go, but you have quite twelve. And you, too, Nadezhda Alexeevna, why in such a hurry? Wait for the moon, it will soon rise now. Then it will be lighter for your ride.'

'Perhaps I will,' said Nadezhda Alexeevna. 'I have not ridden by moonlight for a long time.'

'And will you stay the night?' Ipatov asked Vladimir Sergeich.

'Well, I really don't know . . . However, if I shall not be a nuisance . . .'

'Why, not at all. I will have a room got ready for you at once.'

'You know, it is very nice riding by moonlight,' Nadezhda Alexeevna began, as soon as candles and tea had been brought in, and Ipatov had sat down to play two-handed preference with Egor Kapitonych, while Mr Pliable silently settled himself near them, 'especially in the forest, among the hazel-bushes. It is both frightening and agreeable, and what a strange play of light and shade! – it always seems as though somebody were hiding behind you, or in front . . . !'

Vladimir Sergeich smirked condescendingly.

'Or else,' she went on, 'have you ever sat near a wood on a warm, dark, quiet night? – it always seems to me that just behind you, close to your ear, two voices are arguing violently in a whisper almost too faint to hear.'

'That is your blood in your ears,' said Ipatov.

'You describe things very poetically,' remarked Vladimir Sergeich.

Nadezhda Alexeevna looked at him.

'Do you think so? . . . In that case my descriptions would not please Masha.'

'Why? Doesn't Marya Pavlovna like poetry?'

'No; she thinks it is all invented, all false, and she doesn't like that.'

'What an odd objection to raise!' exclaimed Vladimir Sergeich. 'Invented! What else could it be? And what else are poets for?'

'Well, I dare say; however, you ought not to like poetry either.'

'On the contrary, I like good verse, when it is really good and melodious and, how shall I put it? presents thoughts and ideas . . .'

Marya Pavlovna got up.

Nadezhda Alexeevna turned swiftly to her.

'Where are you going, Masha?'

'To put the children to bed. It will soon be nine o'clock.'

'But can't they go to bed without you?'

But Marya Pavlovna took the children's hands and went off with them.

'She is not in spirits today,' remarked Nadezhda Alexeevna; 'and I know why,' she added softly. 'But it will pass.'

'May I ask,' began Vladimir Sergeich, 'where you intend to spend the winter?'

'Perhaps here, perhaps in St Petersburg. But I think I should be bored in St Petersburg.'

'In St Petersburg, surely not! How could you?'

And Vladimir Sergeich began to describe all the conveniences, all the advantages and charms of life in the capital. Nadezhda

Alexeevna listened closely, without taking her eyes off him. She seemed to be studying his features, and once or twice she smiled to herself.

'I see you are very eloquent,' she said at last; 'I shall have to spend the winter in St Petersburg.'

'You won't regret it,' observed Vladimir Sergeich.

'I never regret anything: it is not worth while. If you've done something silly, try to forget it as soon as possible, that's all.'

'May I ask,' Vladimir Sergeich asked in French, after a short pause, 'whether you have known Marya Pavlovna long?'

'May I ask,' Nadezhda Alexeevna retorted with a flashing smile, 'why you chose to ask just that question in French?'

'I just happened . . . there was no special reason . . .'

Nadezhda Alexeevna smiled again.

'No, I have not known her very long. But she is a remarkable girl, isn't she?'

'She is a very original character,' said Vladimir Sergeich through his teeth.

'Oh? – on your lips, the lips of a practical man, is that praise? I don't think so. Perhaps you think I am original too? But,' she added, rising and looking out of the open window, 'the moon must have risen, that is its reflection over the poplars. It is time I went . . . I will go and order Krasavchik to be saddled.'

'He's saddled already,' said Nadezhda Alexeevna's page, stepping out of the shadows of the garden into the band of light falling on the terrace.

'Oh? Splendid! Masha, where are you? Come and say goodbye to me.'

Marya Pavlovna appeared from the next room. The men got up from the card-table.

'Are you going already?' asked Ipatov.

'Yes, it's quite time.'

She approached the garden door.

'What a night!' she exclaimed. 'Come here, hold up your face to it! can you feel how it seems to breathe? And what scent! all the flowers are awake now. They are awake – and we are preparing to go to sleep . . . Yes, by the way, Masha,' she added, 'I have told Vladimir Sergeich you don't like poetry. Now goodbye . . . here comes my horse . . .'

And she ran swiftly down the steps of the terrace, sprang lightly into the saddle, called 'Till tomorrow!' and, striking the horse's neck with her crop, galloped towards the dam; the page set off after her at a trot.

They followed her with their eyes . . .

'Till tomorrow,' came her voice once more from beyond the poplars.

The sound of hoofs was audible for a long time in the stillness of the summer night. At length Ipatov proposed a return to the house.

'It is very nice in the open,' he said, 'but we must finish our game.'

They fell in with his suggestion. Vladimir Sergeich began

to question Marya Pavlovna about why she did not like poetry.

'I don't care for it,' she rejoined, as if reluctantly.

'But perhaps you have not read much poetry?'

'I haven't read it myself, but I have had it read to me.'

'And didn't you like any of it?'

'No.'

'Not even Pushkin?'

'Not even Pushkin.'

'Why not?'

Marya Pavlovna did not answer, and Ipatov, turning round, remarked over the back of his chair, with a good-humoured laugh, that it was not only poetry she did not like, but sugar as well, and that she could not bear anything sweet at all.

'But, after all, there is some verse that is not sweet,' objected Vladimir Sergeich.

'What, for example?' asked Marya Pavlovna.

Vladimir Sergeich scratched his head. He himself knew very little poetry by heart, especially any that was not sweet.

'Yes, here you are!' he exclaimed at last. Do you know Pushkin's "Upas-tree"? No? Well, nobody could call that poem sweet.'

'Say it,' said Marya Pavlovna, dropping her eyes.

Vladimir Sergeich first looked up at the ceiling, then frowned, muttered a little to himself, and finally recited 'The Upas-tree'.

After the first four lines, Marya Pavlovna slowly raised her eyes, and when Vladimir Sergeich came to the end, said just as slowly:

'Will you say it again, please?'

'So you liked this poem?' asked Vladimir Sergeich.

'Say it again.'

Vladimir Sergeich repeated 'The Upas-tree'. Marya Pavlovna got up, went into the next room, and returned with a sheet of paper and a pen.

'Would you please write it out for me?' she asked Vladimir Sergeich.

'Certainly, with pleasure,' he replied, beginning to write, 'but I confess I wonder why you liked this particular poem so much. I only said it for you to prove that not all poetry is sweet.'

'I'm convinced!' exclaimed Ipatov. 'What do you think of the poem, Ivan Ilyich?'

Ivan Ilyich, as usual, simply looked at Ipatov, and said not a word.

'There, it's done,' said Vladimir Sergeich, putting an exclamation mark at the end of the last line.

Marya Pavlovna thanked him and took the page of writing to her room.

Half an hour later, supper was served, and an hour afterwards all the guests had gone to their rooms. Vladimir Sergeich had tried to talk to Marya Pavlovna more than once, but it was difficult to conduct a conversation with her, and she did not seem very interested in what he had to say. As he went to bed, he

thought a great deal about her and about Nedezhda Alexeevna.
He would probably, however, have fallen asleep at once if his
neighbour, Egor Kapitonych, had not prevented him. Matrёna
Markovna's husband, already undressed and in bed, talked at
very great length to his servant, scolding and lecturing him all
the time. Every word was clearly audible to Vladimir Sergeich;
only a thin partition separated them.

'Hold the candle in front of you,' said Egor Kapitonych
peevishly; 'hold it so that I can see your face. You are turning
my hair white, completely white, you godless creature, you've
made me old before my time.'

'But, Egor Kapitonych, how am I turning your hair white?'
came the toneless and sleepy voice of the servant.

'How? I'll tell you how. How many times have I told you?
"Mitka," I've said, "when you go anywhere with me on a visit,
always take two of everything, especially . . ." – hold the candle
in front of you – "especially underclothes." And now what have
you done today?'

'What, sir?'

'What, sir? What am I to put on tomorrow?'

'The same as today, sir.'

'You've made me old before my time, you wretch! Even
today I didn't know what to do for the heat. Hold the candle in
front of you when I tell you, and don't go to sleep when your
master is talking to you.'

'And Matrёna Markovna said it was enough, sir; she said

why always take such a terrible lot with you. It only wears them out.'

'Matrëna Markovna . . . Is it a woman's business to meddle with such things? You're turning my hair white. Oh dear, quite white!'

'And Yakhim said so too, sir.'

'Yakhim, Yakhim!' reproachfully repeated Egor Kapitonych. 'Eh, they'll drive me mad, the damned fools, they don't even know how to speak Russian properly. Yakhim! what's Yakhim? Efim – well, at any rate it's possible to say that; because the real Greek name is Euthymius, do you understand? – hold the candle in front of you – so for shortness one may perhaps say Efim, but not on any account Yakhim. Yakhim!' added Egor Kapitonych, emphasizing the *ya*. 'You're driving me crazy, wretched creatures that you are. Hold the candle in front of you!'

And for a good deal longer Egor Kapitonych went on giving his servant the benefit of his wisdom, in spite of Vladimir Sergeich's sighs, coughs, and other signs of impatience . . .

At last he let his Mitka go, and fell asleep; but this made things no better for Vladimir Sergeich: Egor Kapitonych's snores were so frequent and powerful, skipped so playfully from the top notes to the very bottom, were punctuated with such whistles and even snorts, that the very partition-wall seemed to vibrate in response; poor Vladimir Sergeich was on the verge of tears. The room assigned to him was very stuffy, and the feather-bed on which he lay enveloped his whole body in a kind of crawling heat.

In despair, Vladimir Sergeich got up at last, opened his

window and avidly began to inhale the sweet-scented freshness of the night. The window looked on to the garden; the sky was bright, the round face of the full moon was now clearly reflected in the pond, now drawn out into a long golden sheaf of slowly wavering spangles. On one of the garden paths, Vladimir Sergeich caught sight of a figure in women's clothes; he peered at it: it was Marya Pavlovna; her face looked pale in the moonbeams. She was standing quite still, and suddenly she began to speak . . . Vladimir Sergeich cautiously put out his head . . .

'*Yet to the upas-tree a man . . . His fellow-man with tyrant's glance has sent*,' was what reached his ears.

'What an impression,' he thought, 'the poem must have made . . .'

And he listened with redoubled attention . . . But Marya Pavlovna had ceased speaking and turned her face even more directly towards him; he was able to distinguish her great dark eyes and her austere brow and lips . . .

Suddenly she started, turned, entered the shadow thrown by a thick wall of tall acacias, and disappeared. Vladimir Sergeich stood for a considerable time longer at his window, but then lay down again, although he did not at once fall asleep.

'A strange person,' he thought, as he turned from side to side, 'and yet they say there is nothing remarkable in the provinces . . . How wrong they are! A strange person! Tomorrow I will ask her what she was doing in the garden.'

Egor Kapitonych still snored as loudly as ever.

III

Vladimir Sergeich woke rather late the next morning, and immediately after breakfasting with the others in the dining-room left for home to finish his business, although old Ipatov tried to keep him. Marya Pavlovna was also present in the dining-room, but Vladimir Sergeich did not think it necessary to question her about her walk of the previous night; he was one of those people who find it difficult to concentrate for two days together on any unaccustomed ideas or theories. He would have had to talk about poetry, and the so-called 'poetic vein' soon wearied him. All that day until dinner-time he spent in the open fields, then dined with a hearty appetite, had a nap, and when he woke up began to deal with the constable's reports; but before he had finished the first page he ordered his tarantass and set off for Ipatovka. Evidently not even practical people have a heart of stone in their bosoms, and they are no fonder of being bored than other simple mortals.

As he drove on to the dam he heard the sound of voices and music. In the Ipatovs' house they were singing Russian popular songs in chorus. He found the whole company he had left in the morning assembled on the terrace; all of them, and Nadezhda Alexeevna besides, were sitting in a semicircle round a man of about thirty-two, a swarthy, black-haired, black-eyed man in a velvet jacket, with a carelessly tied red kerchief round his neck and a guitar in his hands. This was Peter Alexeevich Veretyev, Nadezhda Alexeevna's brother. When he saw Vladimir Sergeich, old Ipatov with a delighted exclamation went forward to meet him, then led him up to Veretyev and introduced them to one another. Astakhov exchanged the usual greetings with his new acquaintance and bowed politely to his sister.

'We were singing in the country fashion, Vladimir Sergeich,' began Ipatov, and added, indicating Veretyev, 'Peter Alexeich here has been singing the solos – and very well! you must hear him!'

'This is very pleasant,' rejoined Vladimir Sergeich.

'Wouldn't you like to make one of the chorus?' Nadezhda Alexeevna asked him.

'I should be delighted, but I have no voice.'

'You need not let that worry you! Look, even Egor Kapitonych is singing, and so am I. All you need do is join us. Sit down; and you, brother, begin.'

'What should we sing now?' said Veretyev, plucking the strings of his guitar, then suddenly ceasing and glancing at Marya Pavlovna, who was sitting beside him. 'I think it is your turn now,' he said to her.

'No, you sing,' replied Marya Pavlovna.

'There's a song called "Down Mother Volga",' announced Vladimir Sergeich solemnly.

'No, we'll save that till the end,' answered Veretyev, and he struck a chord and began to drawl out 'The Setting Sun'.

He sang remarkably well, with dash and gaiety. His manly face, expressive enough at all times, grew even more animated when he sang; occasionally he shrugged his shoulders, laid the palm of his hand suddenly on the guitar-strings, raised his arm, shook his curly hair and gazed round like a falcon. He had more than once seen the celebrated gipsy Ilya in Moscow, and he modelled himself on him. The chorus joined harmoniously in. Marya Pavlovna's ringing voice flowed distinct from all the others, seeming to lead them after it; but she refused to sing alone and Veretyev remained the only soloist.

They sang many more songs . . .

Meanwhile, with the evening, a storm was approaching. Even at midday it had been sultry, with mutterings of thunder, but now a low bank of cloud that had long been lying in a leaden pall on the very edge of the horizon began to grow and loom over the tops of the trees, the stifling air vibrated more distinctly, shaken more and more violently by the approaching thunder; the wind rose, rustled gustily among the leaves, died down, rustled again, more lengthily, began to howl; a sullen twilight fell, abruptly banishing the last gleams of sunset; a layer of cloud sailed up as though suddenly released and spread in an instant over the sky; drops of rain began to fall, lightning flashed in a red flame, there was a heavy, angry crash of thunder.

'Let us go in,' said old Ipatov, 'or we may perhaps get wet.'

They all got up.

'Presently!' exclaimed Veretyev; 'one last song. Listen:

"*Ha! my porch-oh, my new porch-oh . . . Oh, my lovely porch so new . . .*",' he began to sing in a loud voice, rapidly strumming with his whole hand the strings of the guitar. The chorus, as though carried away in spite of themselves, took up the refrain, 'My new porch-oh, built of maple'. At almost the same moment the rain became torrential, but Veretyev sang 'My New Porch' through to the end. The bold gaiety of the song, occasionally drowned in peals of thunder, seemed intensified by the noisy drumming and rustling of the rain. At last they reached the last resounding chorus, and the whole company ran laughing into the drawing-room. Ipatov's little daughters laughed loudest of all as they shook the raindrops from their dresses. Ipatov, however, as a precaution, shut the window and the door and Egor Kapitonych expressed his approval, remarking that Matrëna Markovna, too, always had everything closed during a thunderstorm, for the reason that electricity plays more freely in an empty space. Bodryakov looked into his face, then, as he moved aside, knocked over a chair; little accidents of this kind were always happening to him.

The storm passed very quickly. The doors and windows were opened again and a damp fragrance filled the rooms. Tea was brought in and after tea the old men sat down again to cards. Ivan Ilyich, as usual, joined them. Vladimir Sergeich would have gone up to Marya Pavlovna, who was sitting in the window with Veretyev, but Nadezhda Alexeevna called him to her and immediately entered into a lively conversation on St

Petersburg and the life of the capital. She attacked it; Vladimir Sergeich began to defend it. Nadezhda Alexeevna seemed to be trying to keep him by her side.

'What are you arguing about?' asked Veretyev, rising and coming over to them.

His walk had a lazy sort of roll; all his movements revealed something between negligence and lassitude.

'About St Petersburg,' answered Nadezhda Alexeevna. 'Vladimir Sergeich can't praise it enough.'

'It's a nice town,' remarked Veretyev, 'but then I think everywhere is nice. I really do. Given a few women, and, if you will excuse my frankness, wine, nobody has the right to demand more.'

'That surprises me,' retorted Vladimir Sergeich; 'are you really of the opinion that for an educated man nothing exists . . . ?'

'Perhaps . . . exactly . . . I quite agree with you,' interrupted Veretyev who, with all his politeness, had a habit of not listening to objections to his remarks, 'but that is not in my line; I'm no philosopher.'

'Neither am I,' answered Vladimir Sergeich, 'and I have not the slightest wish to be one; but we are talking of something quite different.'

Veretyev glanced rather vacantly at his sister and she, with a faintly mocking smile, leaned towards him and half whispered:

'Petrusha darling, do act Egor Kapitonych for us, there's a dear.'

Veretyev's face changed in a flash and, by God knows what miracle, became extraordinarily like Egor Kapitonych's, although there was not the slightest resemblance between the features of one and those of the other, and although all Veretyev did was to wrinkle his nose slightly and turn down the corners of his mouth.

'Of course,' he began to whisper in a voice exactly resembling Egor Kapitonych's, 'Matrёna Markovna is a lady who is very strict in the matter of manners; but nevertheless she is a model wife. It is true that whatever I say . . .'

'Is all known to the Biryulёv young ladies,' put in Nadezhda Alexeevna, hardly able to suppress her laughter.

'Is all known the very next day,' answered Veretyev, with such a funny grimace and sidelong look of embarrassment that even Vladimir Sergeich laughed.

'I see you have a great talent for mimicry,' he remarked.

Veretyev passed his hand over his face, his features resumed their normal expression, and Nadezhda Alexeevna exclaimed:

'Oh, yes! he can take off anybody he likes . . . He is very good at it.'

'Could he do me, for example?' asked Vladimir Sergeich.

'Certainly he could,' replied Nadezhda Alexeevna. 'Of course!'

'Oh, do please imitate me,' said Astakhov, turning to Veretyev. 'Don't stand on ceremony, I beg you.'

'You didn't believe her, did you?' answered Veretyev, very slightly narrowing one eye and giving his voice the sound of

Astakhov's, but so cautiously and delicately that only Nadezhda Alexeevna noticed and bit her lip. 'Please don't believe her; she will tell you other untruths about me.'

'And what an actor he is, if you only knew,' went on Nadezhda Alexeevna; 'he can play any kind of part. Simply marvellous. He is our producer and prompter and everything else you can think of. It is a pity you are going away soon.'

'Sister, your partiality makes you blind,' Veretyev pronounced pompously, still giving the same sound to his voice. 'What will Mr Astakhov think of you? He will set you down as an ignorant provincial.'

'Oh, really . . .' Vladimir Sergeich was beginning.

'Petrusha, I'll tell you what,' put in Nadezhda Alexeevna. 'Please do the drunken man who can't manage to get his handkerchief out of his pocket; or no, better still, do the boy catching a fly on the window and the fly buzzing under his fingers.'

'You're an absolute child,' answered Veretyev.

Nevertheless he got up, went to the window where Marya Pavlovna was sitting, and began passing his hand over the pane and imitating a boy catching a fly. The realism with which he reproduced its plaintive whine was astonishing. It really seemed as though a real fly were struggling in his hand. Nadezhda Alexeevna laughed, and one by one everybody in the room laughed too. Only Marya Pavlovna's face did not change, and her lips did not even quiver. She sat with downcast eyes, but raised them at last, looked seriously at Veretyev and said through her teeth:

'How can you make such a fool of yourself?'

Veretyev instantly turned away from the window and, after standing for a time in the middle of the room, went out on to the terrace and thence into the garden, where it was already quite dark.

'An amusing fellow, that Peter Alexeich!' exclaimed Egor Kapitonych, bringing down the seven of trumps with a flourish on his opponent's ace. 'Really amusing.'

Nadezhda Alexeevna rose, hurriedly crossed to Marya Pavlovna and asked her in an undertone:

'What did you say to my brother?'

'Nothing,' she answered.

'Nothing? Impossible!'

And after a short pause, Nadezhda Alexeevna said, 'Let us go!', took Marya Pavlovna's arm and made her get up and go into the garden with her.

Vladimir Sergeich, at a loss, followed the young women with his eyes. Their absence, however, was not prolonged; within a quarter of an hour they returned, and Peter Alexeich came in with them.

'What a glorious night!' exclaimed Nadezhda Alexeevna as she entered. 'It is wonderful in the garden.'

'Ah, yes, by the way,' said Vladimir Sergeich, 'may I ask, Marya Pavlovna, whether it was you I saw in the garden last night?'

Marya Pavlovna glanced quickly into his eyes.

'And what's more, as far as I could make out, you were reciting Pushkin's "Upas-tree".'

Veretyev frowned slightly and also began to look at Astakhov.

'Yes, it was me,' said Marya Pavlovna, 'but I was not reciting anything: I never recite.'

'Perhaps I only imagined it,' began Vladimir Sergeich, 'but . . .'

'You imagined it,' said Marya Pavlovna coldly.

'What is this about a upas-tree?' asked Nadezhda Alexeevna.

'Don't you know it?' replied Astakhov. 'Pushkin's poem: "In grudging, barren soil" – surely you must remember it.'

'I don't seem to . . . This upas – is it the poisonous tree?'

'Yes.'

'Like the datura . . . Do you remember, Masha, how lovely the daturas on our balcony looked in the moonlight, with their long white flowers? Do you remember the scent pouring out of them, so sweet and so insidious and deceitful?'

'Deceitful scent!' exclaimed Vladimir Sergeich.

'Yes, deceitful. What are you surprised at? They say it is dangerous, but it is alluring. Why should evil be attractive? Evil ought not to be beautiful.'

'Oho! what speculations!' remarked Peter Alexeich. 'What a long way we've got from poetry!'

'I recited the poem to Marya Pavlovna yesterday,' put in Vladimir Sergeich, 'and she liked it extremely.'

'Oh, please repeat it now,' said Nadezhda Alexeevna.

'If you like.'

And Astakhov repeated 'The Upas-tree'.

'Too high-flown,' pronounced Veretyev, it seemed involuntarily, as soon as Vladimir Sergeich had finished.

'The poem is too high-flown?'

'No, not the poem . . . Excuse me, I don't think you say it simply enough. It speaks for itself; however, I may be wrong.'

'No, you're not wrong,' said Nadezhda Alexeevna deliberately.

'Oh, no, of course not! We all know I'm a genius in your eyes, the most gifted of men, who knows everything and could do anything, except that unfortunately he is completely ruled by laziness: isn't that it?'

Nadezhda Alexeevna only nodded her head.

'I won't argue with you, you ought to know best,' remarked Vladimir Sergeich, turning a little sulky. 'It is not my line.'

'I was wrong, forgive me,' Veretyev hastened to say.

Meanwhile the card-game had ended.

'Oh, by the way, Vladimir Sergeich,' began Ipatov, rising, 'one of our local landowners, Gavrila Stepanych Akilin, a delightful and most respectable man, has commissioned me to ask you if you will not do him the honour of attending a ball at his house, at least I call it that, because it sounds well, but really it's simply a social evening with dancing, quite informal. He would have called on you himself, without fail, but he was afraid of disturbing you.'

'I am very grateful to the gentleman,' replied Vladimir Sergeich, 'but I simply must go home . . .'

'But when do you think the ball is to be, then? The ball is tomorrow, you know. It is Gavrila Stepanych's name-day tomorrow. One day can make no difference, and you don't know how delighted he will be! And it is only ten versts from here. We will take you with us, if you will allow us.'

'I really don't know,' began Vladimir Sergeich. 'Are you going?'

'The whole family! And Nadezhda Alexeevna, and Peter Alexeich, everybody is going!'

'You may ask me for the fifth quadrille now, if you wish,' remarked Nadezhda Alexeevna. 'The first four are already booked.'

'You are very kind; and are you already engaged for the mazurka?'

'Am I? Let me think . . . no, I don't think I am.'

'In that case, if you will be so kind, I should like to have the honour . . .'

'Does that mean you are going? Splendid! Very well, then.'

'Bravo!' exclaimed Ipatov. 'Well, Vladimir Sergeich, we are obliged to you. Gavrila Stepanych will be simply delighted. Won't he, Ivan Ilyich?'

Ivan Ilyich was going to remain silent, as was his invariable custom, but he thought better of it and made an affirmative sound.

'What on earth made you,' Peter Alexeich said an hour later to his sister, who was sitting beside him in a light gig which he drove himself, 'what on earth made you thrust yourself on that milksop for the mazurka?'

'I have a scheme of my own,' retorted Nadezhda Alexeevna.

'And what is it, may I ask?'

'That is my secret.'

'Aha!'

And he struck the horse, which had begun pricking up its ears and trying to snort and shy, lightly with his whip. The animal had been frightened by the shadow of a great clump of willows, which fell across the road in the dim moonlight.

'And are you dancing with Masha?' asked Nadezhda Alexeevna in her turn.

'Yes,' said her brother indifferently.

'Yes! yes!' repeated Nadezhda Alexeevna reproachfully. 'You men,' she added after a pause, 'really do not deserve to be loved by decent women.'

'You think not? Well, and that St Petersburg milksop, does he deserve it?'

'More than you!'

'Indeed!'

And Peter Alexeich recited with a sigh: '*Oh what a burden 'tis, good Lord . . . To be a grown-up . . . sister's brother!*'

Nadezhda Alexeevna laughed.

'I cause you a lot of trouble, I must say. I'm the one who bears the burden, with you.'

'Really? I never suspected it.'

'I am not talking about Masha.'

'What then?'

Nadezhda Alexeevna's face looked a little distressed.

'You know yourself,' she said quietly.

'Ah, I understand! What would you have, Nadezhda Alexeevna? – I like to take a drink with a good friend, sinner that I am, I like it.'

'Stop, brother, please, don't talk like that . . . It's no laughing matter.'

'Tra-la-la-pom-pom,' muttered Peter Alexeich through his teeth.

'It will be your ruin, and you joke about it . . .'

'The lad is sowing corn, but poppy-seed his wife,' Peter Alexeich began to sing loudly, and he struck the horse with the reins, so that it broke into a swift trot.

IV

When they arrived home, Veretyev did not undress, and two hours later, when the sky had only just begun to show signs of dawn, he had already left the house.

Halfway between his estate and Ipatovka, on the steep slope of a broad ravine, there was a small birch-wood. The young trees grew very thickly, no axe had yet touched their slender trunks, the thin but almost unbroken shadow of their small leaves lay on the fine soft grass, all freckled with the golden heads of the buttercups, the white spots of the bell-flowers and the little red crosses of the wild pinks. The newly risen sun flooded the whole grove with its strong but not yet dazzling light; dewdrops sparkled everywhere, and here and there a big drop would suddenly flash crimson; everything breathed freshness and life and the triumphant innocence of the earliest moments of the morning, when everything is already so bright, but still so silent. Nothing could be heard but the scattering song of skylarks over the distant fields and a few birds in the wood itself, unhurriedly trying over two or three short bars and seeming to listen afterwards to the result. A strong, healthy scent rose from the damp earth, cool currents ran through the pure, light air. The morning, the glorious summer morning, filled everything, everything shone and smiled with the morning, like the rosy, newly washed face of an awakened child.

Not far from the edge of the ravine Veretyev was sitting on a cloak thrown down in a grassy clearing. Marya Pavlovna stood near him, leaning against a birch-tree with her hands behind her.

Both were silent. Marya Pavlovna looked unmoving into the distance; a white scarf had slipped down from her head to her shoulders and the breeze stirred and lifted the ends of her hastily arranged hair. Veretyev stooped as he sat, flicking the grass with a twig.

'Well,' he began at last, 'are you angry with me?'

Marya Pavlovna did not answer.

Veretyev glanced up at her.

'Masha, are you angry?' he repeated.

Marya Pavlovna threw him a rapid glance, turned a little away and said:

'Yes.'

'What about?' asked Veretyev, throwing away the twig.

Again Marya Pavlovna did not answer.

'You certainly have the right, however, to be angry with me,' began Veretyev, after a short silence. 'You must consider me not only frivolous, but even . . .'

'You do not understand me,' interrupted Marya Pavlovna. 'I am not angry with you on my own account at all.'

'On whose, then?'

'On yours.'

Veretyev raised his head and smiled.

'Ah! I understand!' he said. 'Again! the question is beginning to bother you again: why don't I make something of myself? You know, Masha, you are an astonishing creature, really you are. You worry so much about other people and so little about yourself. There is no egoism in you whatever, really. There isn't another girl like you in the world. There's only one thing wrong: I certainly am not worth your concern; I say this quite seriously.'

'So much the worse for you. You feel, but you do nothing.'

Veretyev smiled again.

'Masha, take your hand from behind your back and give it to me,' he said, with an insinuating tenderness in his voice.

Marya Pavlovna only shrugged her shoulders.

'Give me your beautiful, honest hand, I want to kiss it, respectfully and tenderly. Just as an empty-headed pupil kisses the hand of his indulgent teacher.'

And Veretyev leaned towards Marya Pavlovna.

'Stop it!' she said. 'You are always laughing and joking, you will joke your life away.'

'Hm! joke my life away! A new expression! I hope, Marya Pavlovna, you used the verb "joke" in an active sense.'

'Stop, Veretyev,' she repeated.

'Joke my life away,' went on Veretyev, raising himself, 'but you will manage things worse than I shall; you will gloom your life away. You know, Masha, you remind me of a scene from Pushkin's *Don Juan*. Have you read Pushkin's *Don Juan*?'

'No.'

'Oh, no, I had forgotten, you don't read poetry. Well, in this, guests come to see a certain Laura and she drives them all away except one, Carlos. They both go out on the balcony; it is a wonderful night, Laura admires it, and suddenly Carlos begins to prove to her that as time passes she will grow old. "What then?" answers Laura; "perhaps in Paris it is cold and wet at this moment, but here with us 'the night is scented with laurel and with lemon-trees'." Why try to read the riddle of the future? Look round you, Masha, isn't it beautiful here? Look how everything glories in life, everything is young. And aren't we young ourselves?'

Veretyev drew nearer to Marya Pavlovna; she did not move away, but she did not turn her head towards him.

'Smile, Masha,' he went on, 'but smile your kind smile, not your usual mocking one. I love your kind smile. Raise your proud, stern eyes. What are you doing? Turning away? At least stretch out your hand to me.'

'Ah, Veretyev,' began Masha, 'you know I don't know how to talk. You have told me about this Laura. But after all she was a woman . . . It is forgivable if a woman does not think about the future.'

'While you are speaking, Masha,' rejoined Veretyev, 'you are blushing all the time with self-consciousness and shyness, and the blood simply floods your cheeks with crimson. I adore that in you.'

Marya Pavlovna looked straight into his eyes.

'Goodbye,' she said, throwing the scarf over her head. Veretyev held her back.

'Stop, stop, wait a moment!' he exclaimed. 'What do you want? Give me your orders! Would you like me to become a civil servant or an agricultural expert? Do you want me to publish songs with guitar accompaniment, on print my collected verses, or my drawings, or take up painting or sculpture or tight-rope walking? I will do anything, anything you tell me, if only you will be pleased with me! Really and truly, Masha, believe me.'

Marya Pavlovna looked at him again.

'All this is only a matter of words with you, not deeds. You say you obey me . . .'

'Of course I do.'

'You obey me, but how many times have I asked you . . . ?'

'What?'

Marya Pavlovna hesitated.

'Not to drink,' she said at last.

Veretyev laughed.

'Oh, Masha, Masha! You, too! My sister is distressed about that, too. But first, I am no drunkard, and secondly, do you know why I drink? Look over there at that swallow . . . See how daringly it manages its little body, flinging it in any direction it wants. There it has spiralled up, now it plunges down, and even screams with joy, do you hear it? So that is why I drink, Masha, to experience the same feeling as that swallow knows . . . Fling yourself where you want to go, fly wherever the fancy takes you . . .'

'But what is it all for?' interrupted Masha.

'What for? – But why live at all, then?'

'But is it really impossible without drinking?'

'Yes, it is: we are all corrupted, all vitiated. Passion now . . . that produces the same effect. That is why I love you.'

'Like vodka . . . I humbly thank you.'

'No, Masha; I don't love you in the way I love vodka. Wait, I will prove it to you some day, when we are married and go abroad together. Do you know, I am already looking forward to leading you up to the Venus de Milo? That will be the right time to say:

> "*If with proud eyes she stood beside*
> *The Cyprian who from Melos came,*
> *She'd outmatch Venus in her pride*
> *And make the marble blush for shame . . .*"

How is it I keep on repeating poetry today? It must be the effect of the morning on me. What air! like drinking wine!'

'Drinking again,' remarked Marya Pavlovna.

'Well, why not? A morning like this, and you with me, and not feel drunk! "With proud eyes" . . . Yes,' continued Veretyev, gazing intently at Marya Pavlovna, 'that is right . . . But yet I remember I have seen, rarely, but I *have* seen those magnificent dark eyes, I have seen them look tender! And how beautiful they are then! Come, Masha, don't turn away, come, at least laugh . . . let me see your eyes look merry, even if they will not spare a tender glance for me.'

'Stop, Veretyev,' said Marya Pavlovna. 'Let me go; it is time I went home.'

'But I will make you laugh yet,' said Veretyev, 'I swear I'll make you laugh. And talking of that, look, there's a hare running . . .'

'Where?' asked Marya Pavlovna.

'Over there, on the other side of the hollow, in the oat-field. Somebody must have frightened it; they don't run in the morning. If you like, I will make it stop at once.'

And Veretyev whistled loudly. The hare instantly squatted, pricked up its ears, tucked in its front paws, stretched itself up, making nibbling movements with its lips, sniffed the air and nibbled again. Swiftly Veretyev squatted on his haunches like the hare, and began to twitch his nose and sniff and nibble like it. The hare passed its paws once or twice over its face, shook itself – they must have been wet with the dew – dropped its ears and hopped away. Veretyev rubbed his hands over his cheeks and shook himself too . . . Marya Pavlovna was compelled to laugh.

'Bravo!' exclaimed Veretyev, jumping up, 'bravo! I'll tell you what it is, you're no coquette. Do you know that if a fashionable young lady had teeth like yours she would never stop laughing? But that's why I love you, Masha, because you're not a fashionable young lady, you don't laugh without a cause, you don't wear gloves on your hands, which are so pleasant to kiss because they are sunburnt and because you can feel the strength in them . . . I love you because you don't try to be clever, and because you are proud and silent and don't read books or like poetry . . .'

'Would you like me to say a poem for you?' Marya Pavlovna interrupted, with a somewhat peculiar expression on her face.

'A poem?' asked Veretyev, astonished.

'Yes, a poem, the one the gentleman from St Petersburg recited yesterday.'

'The Upas-tree again! . . . So you really were reciting it in the garden in the night? It suits you . . . But did you really like it so much?'

'Yes, very much.'

'Say it.'

But Marya Pavlovna turned shy . . .

'Say it, say it,' repeated Veretyev.

Marya Pavlovna began to recite it. Veretyev stood in front of her with his arms crossed on his breast, and listened. At the first line Marya Pavlovna slowly raised her eyes to the sky: she did not want to meet Veretyev's. She spoke in her soft, level voice, like the note of a violoncello; but when she came to the lines

'*So at the feet of his Almighty Lord*
The poor slave died . . .'

– her voice trembled, her steady, imperious brows were raised as naïvely as a little girl's and her eyes rested with involuntary devotion on Veretyev . . .

Suddenly he flung himself at her feet and embraced her knees.

'*I* am your slave,' he exclaimed, '*I* am at your feet, you are my sovereign, my goddess, my ox-eyed Hera, my Medea . . .'

Marya Pavlovna tried to push him away, but her hands stayed quite still on his thick curls and with a confused smile she let her head fall on her breast . . .

V

Gavrila Stepanych Akilin, at whose house the ball was to be held, was one of those gentlemen who arouse the astonishment of their neighbours by their ability to live well and keep open house on insignificant means. With no more than four hundred serfs, he received the whole province in an enormous stone mansion he had built himself, with columns, and a tower, and a flagstaff on the tower. His estate, which had come to him from his father, had never been conspicuously well-managed; Gavrila Stepanych had been absent from it for many years while he was in St Petersburg in the government service; finally, fifteen years earlier, he had returned to his native place with a moderate rank in the service and with a wife and three daughters, and set about both reorganizing the estate and building at the same time, quickly acquired an orchestra and begun to give dinners and parties. At first everybody prophesied his early and inevitable ruin; more than once there were rumours that Gavrila Stepanych's estate had come under the hammer; but the years passed, the dinners, balls, suppers, concerts, succeeded one another as usual, new buildings sprang up like mushrooms, and still Gavrila Stepanych's estate was not put up for auction and he continued to live as before, and had even begun recently to put on weight. Then his neighbours' talk took a different turn; they began to hint at some secret hoard of wealth or talk of hidden treasure ... 'If he was even a good manager,' so the gentlemen argued among themselves, 'but no! not a bit of it! That's what is so astonishing and so impossible to understand.' However that may have been, everybody was very willing to go to Gavrila Stepanych's house: he made his guests heartily welcome and played cards for any stakes. He was a little grey-haired man with a pointed head, a yellow face and yellow eyes; he was always carefully shaved and scented with eau-de-cologne; weekdays and Sundays alike he

310

wore a capacious blue swallow-tail coat, buttoned up to the top, a large cravat in which he had the habit of burying his chin, and foppish linen; he screwed up his eyes and pursed his lips when he took snuff, and his speech was always soft and affable and full of expressions of politeness. Gavrila Stepanych's appearance did not suggest that he was distinguished for liveliness, his exterior, indeed, was not very prepossessing and although from time to time his eyes had a cunning gleam, he did not look clever. He had settled his two elder daughters well, but the youngest still remained at home unmarried. Gavrila Stepanych had a wife as well, an insignificant creature who never said anything.

Vladimir Sergeich presented himself at the Ipatovs' at seven o'clock in the evening, wearing a dress coat and white gloves. He found everybody already dressed, the little girls sitting very primly for fear of crumpling their starched white dresses. When he saw Vladimir Sergeich's dress coat, old Ipatov scolded him playfully, indicating his own frock-coat. Marya Pavlovna wore a dark-pink muslin dress which suited her very well. Vladimir Sergeich paid her a few compliments. He found Marya Pavlovna's beauty attractive, although she was evidently shy of him; he liked Nadezhda Alexeevna also, but her unconstrained manner embarrassed him a little. Besides, her speech, her eyes, her very smile, often expressed a mockery that disturbed his well-bred St Petersburg soul. He would not have been averse from joining her in mockery of other people, but it made him uncomfortable to think that she might perhaps be capable of laughing at him.

The ball had already begun; a fair number of guests had assembled and the home-grown orchestra was scraping, blaring, and squealing away in the gallery when the Ipatovs and Vladimir Sergeich entered the Akilin ball-room. Their host met them at the door and thanked Vladimir Sergeich for his consideration in giving them this pleasant surprise – so he expressed himself – then took Ipatov's arm and led him to the card-tables in the drawing-room. Gavrila Stepanych's education had been poor and nothing in the house, neither the music, nor the furniture, nor the food nor the wine, could have been called even second class, not to mention first. On the other hand there was abundance of everything, and he himself was unpretentious and unaffected . . . ; the local gentry demanded no more of him and remained quite content with the entertainment he provided. At supper, for example, the caviare was served in pieces cut from a block, and was over-salted; but there was nothing to prevent one from taking it with the fingers and there was something to drink with it, wine of the cheapest quality, it is true, but still wine made from grapes, not some other kind of drink. The springs of Gavrila Stepanych's furniture were really a little uncomfortable by reason of their unyielding stiffness; but, not to mention that in many of the sofas and arm-chairs there were no springs at all, anybody might put a wool-work cushion underneath himself, and similar cushions, worked by the hands of Gavrila Stepanych's wife herself, lay about everywhere in large numbers – and this solution left nothing to be desired.

In short, Gavrila Stepanych's house was ideally suited to the taste for society and the informal manners of the inhabitants of the district, and Mr Akilin's own modesty was the only reason why the Marshal elected by the nobility at their annual meetings was not he but a retired Major Podpekin, a very respectable and worthy man, even though he did comb his hair right across from his left ear to his right temple, dyed his whiskers lavender, and, being a victim of asthma, was liable to fits of melancholy after dinner.

And so the ball had already begun. They were dancing a quadrille of ten couples. The gentlemen were officers of a regiment stationed in the neighbourhood, young and not so young, landowners and two or three officials from the town. Everything was as it should be, everything was going smoothly. The Marshal of the Nobility was playing cards with a retired official of high rank and a rich gentleman who owned three thousand souls. The official wore a diamond ring on his index finger, spoke very quietly, never moved his feet, planted with the heels together in the position adopted by dancers of an earlier age, and did not turn his head, which was half concealed by his very distinguished-looking velvet collar; the rich gentleman, on the contrary, laughed incessantly, raising his eyebrows and rolling his eyes. The poet Bodryakov, an odd and clumsy-looking man, was talking in a corner to the learned historian Evsyukov; each held the other by one of his buttons. Beside them one gentleman with an extraordinarily long waist was expounding some daring opinion or other to another whose gaze was timidly fixed on his forehead. Along the wall sat the mamas in their bright-coloured caps, round the door clustered gentlemen of a simpler cut, the younger with bashful, the older with subdued faces. But it is impossible to describe everything; let us repeat, everything was as it should be.

Nadezhda Alexeevna had arrived even before the Ipatovs: Vladimir Sergeich saw her dancing with a young man of handsome appearance, in a smart dress coat, with expressive eyes, a small black moustache and dazzling teeth; a gold chain hung in a semicircle on his stomach. Nadezhda Alexeevna wore a light-blue dress with white flowers; a small wreath of the same flowers encircled her curly head; she was smiling, playing with her fan, and glancing gaily round; she felt she was the queen of the ball. Vladimir Sergeich went up to her, bowed, and looking at her amiably asked her whether she remembered her promise of the previous day.

'What promise?'

'Surely you are dancing the mazurka with me?'

'Yes, certainly.'

The young man standing beside Nadezhda Alexeevna reddened suddenly.

'You have probably forgotten, *mademoiselle*,' he began, 'that you had already promised me today's mazurka earlier.'

Nadezhda Alexeevna was embarrassed.

'Oh, good heavens, what shall I do?' she said. 'Please

forgive me, Monsieur Stelchinsky, I am so forgetful: really, I am ashamed . . .'

Monsieur Stelchinsky said nothing but only lowered his eyes; Vladimir Sergeich took on a dignified air.

'Please be good enough, Monsieur Stelchinsky,' continued Nadezhda Alexeevna,'– after all, you and I are old friends, and Monsieur Astakhov is a stranger here: don't put me in a difficult position, let me dance with him.'

'As you will,' returned the young man. 'But now you are to begin.'

'I am obliged to you,' said Nadezhda Alexeevna, and fluttered away to her partner.

Stelchinsky glanced after her and then looked at Vladimir Sergeich. Vladimir Sergeich in his turn looked at him and walked away.

The quadrille was soon over. Vladimir Sergeich walked around the ball-room a little, then went into the drawing-room and stopped by one of the card-tables. Suddenly he felt some-body touch his arm from behind; he turned round – Stelchinsky stood before him.

'I should like a couple of words with you in the next room, with your permission,' he said in French, very politely and without any Russian accent.

Vladimir Sergeich followed him.

Stelchinsky stopped by the window.

'In the presence of a lady,' he began in the same language,

'I could not say anything but what I did say; but I hope you do not think that I am really prepared to yield to you my right to the mazurka with Mademoiselle Verétieff.'

Vladimir Sergeich was astounded.

'What do you mean?' he asked.

'What I say,' answered Stelchinsky calmly, thrusting his hand into his bosom and expanding his nostrils. 'I am not prepared to do it, that's all.'

Vladimir Sergeich also put his hand inside his coat, but he did not expand his nostrils.

'Allow me to remark, my dear sir,' he began, 'that you may involve Mlle Verétieff in unpleasantness by this, and I do not suppose . . .'

'I should myself find that extremely unpleasant, but there is nothing to prevent your backing out, announcing that you are unwell, or leaving . . .'

'I shall not do that. Whom do you take me for?'

'In that case I shall be obliged to demand satisfaction from you.'

'But! . . . in what sense? . . . satisfaction!'

'You know very well in what sense.'

'Are you challenging me to a duel?'

'Exactly, sir, unless you renounce the mazurka.'

Stelchinsky tried to utter these words as calmly as possible. Vladimir Sergeich's heart leapt violently. He looked his unexpected, unsuspected adversary in the face. 'Pah! Good God, what stupidity!' he thought.

'Are you joking?' he said aloud.

'I am not in the habit of joking,' answered Stelchinsky with solemn dignity, 'especially with people with whom I am not acquainted. You will not give up the mazurka?' he added after a pause.

'No, I will not give it up,' retorted Vladimir Sergeich, as if after deliberation.

'Excellent! We fight tomorrow.'

'Very good.'

'Tomorrow morning my second will call on you.'

And with a polite bow Stelchinsky retreated, evidently pleased with himself.

Vladimir Sergeich remained a few moments longer by the window.

'Well, that's a fine thing!' he thought. 'That's new acquaintances for you! I had to come here! Fine! Splendid!'

But at length he turned away and went into the ball-room.

There they were already dancing the polka. Marya Pavlovna passed swiftly before Vladimir Sergeich's eyes with Peter Alexeich, whom he had not noticed until now; she looked pale and even sad. Then Nadezhda Alexeevna flashed past, full of joyful radiance, with a little bow-legged but fiery cavalry officer; on the second round of the room she was with Stelchinsky. Stelchinsky kept violently tossing back his hair as he danced.

'Well, my dear sir?' Ipatov's voice said suddenly behind Vladimir Sergeich, 'are you only watching, not dancing? But confess, although this is, so to speak, a backwater, it is not bad here, is it?'

'A fine backwater, devil take it,' thought Vladimir Sergeich, and muttering something in reply to Ipatov he walked away to another corner of the room.

'I shall have to look for a second,' he continued his deliberations, 'and where the devil shall I find one? I can't ask Veretyev, and I don't know anybody else; it's the devil of a ridiculous situation!'

Vladimir Sergeich, when he was angry, was fond of referring to the devil.

At this moment Vladimir Sergeich's eyes fell on Mr Pliable, Ivan Ilyich, who was standing idly by the window.

'What about him?' he thought, and with a shrug of the shoulders added almost aloud, 'it will have to be him.'

Vladimir Sergeich approached him.

'Something very odd has just happened to me,' our hero began with a strained smile; 'imagine, an unknown young man has challenged me to a duel; there is no possibility of refusing and it is absolutely necessary for me to have a second. Would you care to do it?'

Although Ivan Ilyich was distinguished, as the reader knows, for his undisturbable impassivity, this unusual request surprised even him. He stared thunderstruck at Vladimir Sergeich.

'Yes,' repeated Vladimir Sergeich, 'I should be much obliged to you: I know nobody here. Only you . . .'

'I can't,' said Ivan Ilyich, as if he had just waked up, 'I absolutely can't.'

'But why not? You are afraid of unpleasantness; but I hope it will all remain secret . . .'

As he said this, Vladimir Sergeich himself felt that he was blushing and becoming confused.

'How stupid! How terribly stupid all this is!' he was repeating to himself at the same time.

'Excuse me, I cannot possibly,' repeated Ivan Ilyich, shaking his head and backing away, once again overturning a chair as he did so.

For the first time in his life he had been obliged to answer a request with a refusal; but after all, what a request this was!

'At least,' went on Vladimir Sergeich in an agitated voice, seizing him by the hand, 'you will do me the favour of not mentioning what I have told you to anybody; I most humbly beg this of you.'

'That I can do, that I can do,' hastily rejoined Ivan Ilyich, 'but the other, I'm sorry, I can't, I am decidedly not able to.'

'Very well, very well,' said Vladimir Sergeich, 'but don't forget, I count on your discretion . . . Tomorrow I shall inform the gentleman,' he muttered to himself angrily, 'that I could not find a second, and he must make what arrangements he can, I am a stranger here. And it was the devil himself who induced me to ask this gentleman! But what was I to do?'

Vladimir Sergeich felt extremely out of sorts.

Meanwhile the ball continued. Vladimir Sergeich would have liked nothing better than to leave at once, but there could be no thought of leaving until after the mazurka. How could he let his adversary triumph over him? Unfortunately for Vladimir Sergeich, the master of ceremonies was an easy-mannered young man with long hair and a hollow chest down which his black satin cravat cascaded like a small waterfall. This young gentleman passed all over the province for a man who knew to a nicety all the customs and usages of the best society, although he had never spent more than six months in St Petersburg and had not succeeded in penetrating any higher than the houses of Collegiate Councillor Sandaraki and his son-in-law, State Councillor Kostandaraki. He acted as master of ceremonies at all the balls, giving signals to the musicians by clapping his hands, calling above the blaring of the trumpets and the squeaking of the violins, '*En avant deux*', or '*Grande chaîne*', or '*À vous, mademoiselle*', and occasionally, pale and perspiring, dashing violently about the floor, sliding and scraping his feet. He never began the mazurka before midnight. 'And that is a kindness,' he would say; 'in St Petersburg I should keep you waiting until two o'clock.' How long this ball seemed to Vladimir Sergeich! He wandered like a shadow from ball-room to drawing-room, occasionally exchanging a cold glance with his rival, who did not miss a single dance; he would have asked Marya Pavlovna for the quadrille, but she was already engaged; and once or twice he exchanged a few words with his solicitous host, who seemed worried by the expression of boredom on his new guest's face. At last the long-desired mazurka was struck up. Vladimir Sergeich sought out his lady, brought two chairs, and sat down with her among the last couples, almost opposite Stelchinsky.

As might have been expected, the young master of ceremonies was in the first couple. The air with which he began the mazurka, the way he pulled his lady along behind him and stamped his foot and tossed his head – all this is perhaps beyond the power of human pen to describe.

'It seems to me, Monsieur Astakhov, that you are bored,' began Nadezhda Alexeevna, abruptly addressing Vladimir Sergeich.

'I? Not in the least. Why should you think so?'

'Oh, simply from the expression on your face . . . You have not smiled once since you arrived. I did not expect this of you. It does not suit you practical people to be scowling and unsociable à la Byron. Leave that to the artists.'

'I notice that you frequently call me a practical man, Nadezhda Alexeevna, as though to make fun of me. You must consider me a very cold and cautious creature, not capable of anything . . . But let me tell you something: a practical person may often feel very heavy-hearted, but he does not consider it necessary to show others what is going on inside himself; he prefers to keep silent.'

'What do you mean by that?' asked Nadezhda Alexeevna, throwing him a glance.

'Nothing,' replied Vladimir Sergeich with feigned indifference, adopting an air of mystery.

'But?'

'Nothing, really . . . You will know one day, afterwards.'

Nadezhda Alexeevna was continuing her interrogation, but at that moment a young lady, the host's daughter, led up to her Stelchinsky and another gentleman in dark-blue spectacles.

'Life or death?' she asked in French.

'Life!' exclaimed Nadezhda Alexeevna, 'I don't want death yet.'

Stelchinsky bowed; she went off with him.

The gentleman in dark spectacles who went by the name of death led away the host's daughter. Both names had been devised by Stelchinsky.

'Please tell me, who is this Mr Stelchinsky?' Vladimir Sergeich asked Nadezhda Alexeevna, as soon as she returned to her place.

'He is the Governor's assistant, a very amiable young man. He is not from these parts. He is perhaps a little foppish, but then that comes naturally to all of them. I hope you didn't have any discussion with him about the mazurka?'

'None at all, of course,' replied Vladimir Sergeich with slight hesitation.

'I am so forgetful, you can't imagine!'

'I ought to be glad of your forgetfulness; it procured me the pleasure of dancing with you today.'

Nadezhda Alexeevna looked at him with a slight narrowing of the eyes.

'Really? Do you like dancing with me?'

Vladimir Sergeich answered with a compliment, and little by little began to talk. Nadezhda Alexeevna was always charming, and that evening more so than ever; Vladimir Sergeich found her delightful. The thought of the next day's duel, stimulating his nerves, gave added brilliance and liveliness to his talk; under its influence he allowed himself a little exaggeration in the expression of his feelings . . . 'Come what may!' he thought. In all his words, in his stifled sighs, in his suddenly clouded glances, there was half revealed something mysterious and involuntarily mournful, something elegantly despairing. He talked himself at last into a mood for discussing love, women, his future, his conception of happiness and what he demanded of life . . . He expressed himself in hints and allusions. On the eve of his possible death, Vladimir Sergeich was flirting with Nadezhda Alexeevna.

She listened intently, laughed, shook her head, now argued with him, now pretended to be incredulous . . . The conversation, often interrupted by the approach of other dancers, took towards the end a rather strange turn . . . Vladimir Sergeich had begun to ask Nadezhda Alexeevna questions about herself, her character and her tastes . . . At first she laughed them off, then suddenly, and quite unexpectedly to Vladimir Sergeich, she asked him when he was going.

'Where?' he asked in astonishment.

'Home.'

'To Sasovo?'

'No, to your estate a hundred versts from here.'

'I should like it to be very soon,' he said with a troubled look. 'I think tomorrow . . . if I live. After all, I have plenty of things to attend to! But what put it into your head to ask about that?'

'Oh, nothing!' replied Nadezhda Alexeevna.

'But what was your reason?'

'Oh, nothing,' she repeated. 'I am surprised that a man who is leaving tomorrow should be so curious to find out my character today . . .'

'But really . . .' began Vladimir Sergeich.

'Oh, apropos . . . read this,' Nadezhda Alexeevna interrupted him, laughing, and she held out to him the motto from the bon-bon she had just taken from a little table near them, and rose to meet Marya Pavlovna, who had stopped in front of her with another lady.

Marya Pavlovna was dancing with Peter Alexeich. Her face was flushed and heated, but no happier.

Vladimir Sergeich looked at the paper – on it was printed in bad type: '*Qui me néglige me perd.*'

He raised his eyes and met Stelchinsky's, looking straight at him. Vladimir Sergeich, with a forced smile, leaned his elbow on the back of his chair and crossed his legs.

'That for you!' he thought.

The fiery artillery officer whirled Nadezhda Alexeevna to

her chair, slowly circled in front of it with her, bowed, clinked his spurs and went off. She sat down.

'May I know,' began Vladimir Sergeich slowly, 'how I am to understand that motto . . . ?'

'Now, what did it say?' said Nadezhda Alexeevna. 'Oh yes! *Qui me néglige me perd.* Well! It is excellent worldly advice, which may come in useful at any time. In order to succeed in anything whatever, you must neglect nothing . . . You ought to grasp at everything and perhaps you will get something at least. But this is funny: I . . . I to talk to you, the practical man, about worldly wisdom!' Nadezhda Alexeevna laughed, and it was in vain that Vladimir Sergeich tried, until the very end of the mazurka, to renew the previous conversation. Nadezhda Alexeevna evaded his efforts with the wilfulness of a capricious child. Vladimir Sergeich talked to her of his feelings and she either did not answer at all or drew his attention to the ladies' dresses, the comical faces of some of the men, the skill of her brother's dancing, or the beauty of Marya Pavlovna; she talked of the music, of the events of the previous day, of Egor Kapitonych and his wife Matrëna Markovna . . . and it was only at the very end of the mazurka, when Vladimir Sergeich had begun to make his bows, that she said, with an ironical smile on her lips and in her eyes:

'So you really are going tomorrow?'

'Yes; and, perhaps, going a very long way,' said Vladimir Sergeich significantly.

'I wish you a pleasant journey.'

And Nadezhda Alexeevna went quickly up to her brother, gaily whispered something in his ear, then asked aloud:

'Are you grateful to me? Yes? You are, aren't you? Or else he would have asked *her* for the mazurka.'

He shrugged his shoulders and said:

'All the same nothing will come of it . . .'

She led him away into the drawing-room.

'Coquette!' thought Vladimir Sergeich and, with his hat in his hand, slipped unnoticed from the ball-room, sought out his footman, whom he had previously ordered to be in readiness, and was already putting on his overcoat when suddenly, to his extreme astonishment, the servant announced that he could not go, as the coachman had somehow contrived to drink himself into a stupor and there was no possibility of rousing him. Having cursed the coachman with unaccustomed brevity but extraordinary vigour (this happened in the hall and other people were present), and informed his servant that if the coachman was not in a fit state by the first light next morning there was no telling what the consequences would be, Vladimir Sergeich returned to the ball-room and asked the butler to provide him with a bedroom, without waiting for the supper which was already being laid in the drawing-room. The master of the house seemed to spring up suddenly out of the ground at Vladimir Sergeich's elbow (Gavrila Stepanych wore boots without heels and consequently moved noiselessly) and tried to detain him, assuring him that there would be caviare of the best quality at supper; but

Vladimir Sergeich excused himself on the ground of a headache. Half an hour later he was already lying on a small bed, under a short blanket, and trying hard to go to sleep.

But he could not sleep. However often he turned from side to side, however much he strove to think of something else, the figure of Stelchinsky persistently loomed before him . . . Now he took aim . . . now he fired . . . 'Astakhov is killed,' said a voice. Vladimir Sergeich could not call himself a hero, though he was no coward either, but the very idea of a duel with anybody whatever had never entered his head . . . Fight! . . . with his good sense, his peaceful propensities, his respect for the proprieties, his dreams of future prosperity and a good marriage! If his own person had not been involved in the matter he would have laughed aloud, so absurd and ridiculous did the whole business seem to him. Fight! with whom and for what?

'Ugh! The devil! What nonsense!' he involuntarily exclaimed aloud. 'Well, but if he really does kill me,' he pursued his deliberations, 'I must take steps to put my affairs in order . . . Will anybody regret me?'

Then, annoyed, he shut his wide-open eyes and drew the blanket up to his neck . . . but all the same he could not fall asleep . . .

Dawn had already broken and Vladimir Sergeich, exhausted by feverish wakefulness, was beginning to fall into a doze, when suddenly he felt a weight on his legs. He opened his eyes . . . Veretyev was sitting on his bed . . .

'Allow me to ask . . .' he began, throwing out his arms . . .

'I have come,' said Veretyev thickly; 'excuse me for being in such a state . . . We have had a little to drink . . . I wanted to reassure you. I said to myself, "There is that gentleman, probably lying awake. Let's help him." Listen carefully; you are not fighting tomorrow, you can go to sleep . . .'

Vladimir Sergeich was even more astonished.

'What did you say?' he muttered.

'Yes, it is all settled,' went on Veretyev; 'the gentleman from the banks of the Vistula . . . Stelchinsky apologizes to you . . . you will receive a letter tomorrow . . . I tell you again: it's all over . . . You can sleep soundly.'

And with these words Veretyev rose and walked unsteadily towards the door.

'But wait, wait,' began Vladimir Sergeich, 'How could you know, and why should I trust . . . ?'

'Ah! You think . . . that I . . .' (and he swayed forward a little) 'I tell you . . . he will send you a letter tomorrow . . . I don't feel particularly sympathetic towards you, but generosity is my great weakness. But what is the use of talking? . . . All this is such nonsense . . . But confess,' he added, winking, 'you were scared all the same, eh?'

Vladimir Sergeich lost his temper.

'Excuse me, my dear sir,' he said . . .

'All right, all right,' interrupted Veretyev with a good-natured smile. 'Don't get annoyed. After all, you don't know that we

328

never have a single ball without something of the sort . . . It's an old custom. There are never any consequences. Who wants to risk his skin? Well, but why not put on a bit of a show, eh? in front of a new-comer, for instance? *In vino veritas.* However, neither you nor I understand Latin. However, I can tell by your face that you want to sleep. I wish you a good night, Mr Practical Man, you well-meaning mortal. Accept the good wishes of a fellow mortal who is not worth a copper copeck himself. *Addio, mio caro.'*

And Veretyev departed.

'The devil knows what it is all about!' exclaimed Vladimir Sergeich a little later, thumping his pillow. 'There is neither rhyme not reason in it! . . . It will have to be explained! I shall not put up with it!'

In spite of all this, five minutes later he was sleeping quietly and soundly. A weight had been lifted from his heart . . . A danger past fills the heart of a man with sweetness and light . . .

This is what had happened before Vladimir Sergeich's unexpected nocturnal interview with Veretyev:

Gavrila Stepanych's second cousin lived in his house, occupying bachelor quarters on the ground floor. When there was a ball, the young men dropped in on him in the intervals between dances for a hasty smoke (of tobacco from Zhukov's) and after supper assembled in his rooms for a friendly drink. On this night there were a fair number of guests there. Stelchinsky and Veretyev were among them; Ivan Ilyich, Mr Pliable, had also wandered along after the others. They made punch. Although Ivan Ilyich had promised Astakhov not to tell anybody of the forthcoming duel, when Veretyev happened to ask him what he had been discussing with that milksop (Veretyev never called Astakhov anything else), Mr Pliable could not forbear repeating all his conversation with Vladimir Sergeich word for word.

Veretyev laughed, then grew thoughtful.

'But who is he going to fight?' he asked.

'That I cannot say,' replied Ivan Ilyich.

'Who did he talk to, at any rate?'

'Various people ... Egor Kapitonych. Surely he is not fighting him?'

Veretyev walked away from Ivan Ilyich.

So the punch was made and they began to drink it. Veretyev sat in the most prominent position; gay and dissipated, he excelled at gatherings of young men. He had thrown off his coat and cravat. He was asked to sing, and he took a guitar and sang several songs. Heads got a little heated; the young men began proposing toasts. Suddenly Stelchinsky, with a red face, sprang up on the table and, raising his glass high above his head, exclaimed loudly:

'To the health of ... I know whom,' he hurriedly substituted, drained his glass, dashed it to the ground and added, 'May my enemy be reduced to the same smithereens tomorrow.'

Veretyev, who had been observing him for some time, raised his head sharply ...

'Stelchinsky,' he said, 'to begin with, get off the table: it's disgraceful, and besides your boots are pretty awful. In the second place, come here, I have something to say to you.'

He led him apart.

'Listen, my friend, I know you are going to fight the gentleman from St Petersburg tomorrow, aren't you?'

Stelchinsky started.

'How . . . who told you?'

'I am telling you. And I know who it is you are fighting for, besides.'

'Who is it then? I'm curious to know.'

'Oh you, trying to be a Talleyrand of cunning! My sister, of course. Well, well, don't pretend to be surprised. It makes you look like a goose. I can't tell you how it happened, but it is true enough. Stop it, my dear chap,' Veretyev continued; 'what's the use of pretending? After all, I know you've been running after her for a long time.'

'All the same, that doesn't prove . . .'

'Stop it, please. And just listen to what I say now. I will not on any account allow this duel. Do you understand? The whole silly business will recoil on my sister. Excuse me: while I live . . . it shall not happen. You and I will go to ruin – that's what we're heading for, but she must have a long life still, and a happy one. Yes, I swear,' he added, with sudden heat, 'I will betray everybody else, even those who are ready to sacrifice everything for me, before I will allow a hair of her head to be touched.'

Stelchinsky uttered a forced laugh.

'You are drunk, old man, and raving . . . that's all.'

'And you aren't, I suppose? But whether I'm drunk or not, it makes no difference. I'm talking sense. You are not going to fight the gentleman, I'll answer for that. And what induced you to get involved with him? Jealous, were you? Well, they speak the truth when they say people in love are idiots! And she was only dancing with him so that he shouldn't take it into his head to ask . . . Well, but that's not the point. But this duel shall not take place.'

'Hm! I should like to know how you are going to stop me.'

'Like this: if you don't give me your word immediately to withdraw from this duel, I shall fight you myself.'

'Indeed?'

'Never doubt it, my dear chap. I will insult you immediately, in the most elaborate manner, in front of everybody, and then it will be shooting – even over a handkerchief, if need be. And I think you would find that unpleasant for many reasons, eh?'

Stelchinsky flushed, began to say that this was intimidation, that he would allow nobody to meddle in his concerns, that he would not consider anything . . . and ended by reconciling himself and renouncing any attempt on Vladimir Sergeich's life. Veretyev embraced him, and before another half-hour had passed they had drunk *Bruderschaft* (that is, with the arms that held their glasses interlaced) for the tenth time . . . The young master of ceremonies also drank *Bruderschaft* with them, keeping pace with them to begin with, until at last he fell asleep in the most innocent fashion and lay for a long time on his back in a condition of complete unconsciousness . . . The expression of his pale little face was both comic and pathetic . . . Good God! what would any fashionable ladies of his acquaintance have said if they had seen him in such a humiliating state? But fortunately for him he did not know a single fashionable lady.

Ivan Ilyich also distinguished himself that night. First he astonished the guests by suddenly striking up 'A baron in the country once'.

'The Siskin! The Siskin has sung his song!' everybody shouted. 'When was a siskin ever known to sing at night?'

'As though I only knew one song!' retorted Ivan Ilyich, heated by the drink. 'I know others besides.'

'Well, well, well, show us your skill.'

Ivan Ilyich was silent for a time and then suddenly, in a bass voice, burst into 'Krambambuli, legacy of my fathers', but so oddly and out of tune that his voice was immediately drowned in a general burst of laughter, and he stopped.

When the party dispersed, Veretyev went off to Vladimir Sergeich, and the short conversation already described took place between them.

Next day Vladimir Sergeich left for Sasovo very early. He spent the whole morning in a state of excitement, almost took a merchant who called for the second, and relaxed only when the footman brought him a letter from Stelchinsky. Vladimir Sergeich read the letter several times; it was very adroitly written . . .

Stelchinsky began with the words: '*La nuit porte conseil, monsieur,*' and made no apologies, since, in his opinion, he had not in any way offended his opponent; he admitted, however, that he had been a little too heated on the previous evening, and finished by declaring that he remained entirely at the disposal of Mr Astakhov (*de M——r Astakhof*) but that he himself no longer desired satisfaction. Having composed and dispatched a reply, full at one and the same time of civility that became positively playful and a sense of dignity in which there was, however, no vanity, Vladimir Sergeich sat down to dinner, rubbing his hands, ate with great enjoyment, and immediately afterwards left for home, without even sending a relay of horses ahead. The road along which he travelled passed within about four versts of Ipatov's house. Vladimir Sergeich looked towards it . . .

'Goodbye, quiet backwater!' he said with an ironic smile.

The image of Nadezhda Alexeevna and that of Marya Pavlovna rose for a moment before the eyes of his mind; he made a gesture of his arm, turned away, and fell into a doze.

VI

More than three months had passed. The autumn had long set in; the yellowing forests were stripping off their leaves, the blue-tits had flown in and, sign of the nearness of winter, the wind had begun to howl and wail. But there had been no heavy rains as yet, and the surface of the roads had not dissolved into mud. Taking advantage of this circumstance, Vladimir Sergeich had gone into the chief town of the province to finish off certain business. The morning he spent in various calls, and in the evening he went to the club. In the huge, gloomy room he found several acquaintances, among them an old retired captain of cavalry, Flich, a business man, wit, card-player, and gossip known to everybody. Vladimir Sergeich entered into conversation with him.

'Oh, by the way,' exclaimed the captain suddenly, 'a lady you know passed through here recently and asked to be remembered to you.'

'What lady was this?'

'Madame Stelchinskaya.'

'I don't know any Madame Stelchinskaya.'

'You knew her before she was married . . . Her maiden name was Veretyeva . . . Nadezhda Alexeevna. Her husband was one of our Governor's assistants. You must have seen him, too . . . A lively young man with moustaches . . . He's hooked a fine little piece, and with a fortune, too.'

'Really!' said Vladimir Sergeich. 'So she has married him . . . Hm! And where have they gone?'

'To St Petersburg. She said we were to remind you of some motto from a bon-bon . . . What was it, may I ask?'

And the old gossip fairly poked his sharp nose forward.

'Really, I don't remember — some sort of joke,' rejoined Vladimir Sergeich. 'May I ask where her brother is now?'

'Peter? Well, he's gone to the bad.'

Mr Flich raised his foxy little eyes to the heavens and sighed.

'How is that?' asked Vladimir Sergeich.

'He's taken to drink. He's done for.'

'And where is he now?'

'Nobody knows. He went off somewhere, after the gipsies, that's the most likely. He's not in the province, that I'll swear.'

'And old Ipatov, is he still living there?'

'Mikhail Nikolaich? That quaint old man? Yes, he's still there.'

'And everything in his house . . . is the same as before?'

'Of course, of course. What about your marrying his sister-in-law? You know, she's not a woman, she's an absolute monument, really. He-he! We used to say . . . we said . . .'

'Really!' said Vladimir Sergeich, frowning.

At this moment Flich was offered a game of cards and the conversation ended.

Vladimir Sergeich had proposed to return home at once, but he received a report by courier from his bailiff that six houses in Sasovo had burned down, and resolved to go there himself. From the town to Sasovo was reckoned about sixty versts. By evening Vladimir Sergeich had arrived at the little house already known to the reader, and he at once sent for the bailiff and the constable and gave them a thorough dressing-down; in the morning he inspected the scene of the fire, took the necessary steps and then, after dinner, set off to visit Ipatov. Vladimir Sergeich would have stayed at home if he had not heard from Flich of Nadezhda Alexeevna's departure: he had no wish to meet her; but he was not averse from seeing Marya Pavlovna once more.

As on his first visit, Vladimir Sergeich found Ipatov at draughts with Mr Pliable. The old man was delighted to see him, but to Vladimir Sergeich his face seemed troubled and his talk did not flow as freely and easily as before.

Ivan Ilyich and Vladimir Sergeich exchanged glances without speaking. Both felt a little uncomfortable; they were soon, however, more at ease.

'Are all your household well?' asked Vladimir Sergeich, sitting down.

'Yes, God be praised, I thank you kindly,' answered Ipatov. 'Only Marya Pavlovna is not quite . . . at her best; she keeps to her room a good deal.'

'Has she caught a chill?'

'No . . . yes. She will come in for tea.'

'And Egor Kapitonych? What is he doing with himself?'

'Ah, poor Egor Kapitonych is a broken man! His wife is dead.'

'She can't be!'

'She died in twenty-four hours, of cholera. You would not know him now, he's been quite unlike his old self. "Without Matrëna Markovna," he says, "my life is a burden to me. I shall die," he says, "and thank God for it," he says; "I've no wish to go on living," he says. Yes, poor man, he's done for.'

'Good God, how distressing this is!' exclaimed Vladimir Sergeich. 'Poor Egor Kapitonych!'

They were all silent for a time.

'Your neighbour, I hear, is married,' began Vladimir Sergeich, blushing slightly.

'Nadezhda Alexeevna? Yes, she's married.'

Ipatov cast a sidelong look at Vladimir Sergeich.

'Yes indeed . . . yes indeed, married and gone away already.'

'To St Petersburg?'

'Yes.'

'Marya Pavlovna, I suppose, misses her? They were great friends, I think.'

'She misses her, of course. She could not do otherwise. But as for friendship, let me tell you, girls' friendship is worse even than men's. It's all right while you are together, but out of sight out of mind.'

'Do you think so?'

'I'm quite sure of it. Take Nadezhda Alexeevna, for example. Since she left, she has not written to us once, and she promised, you know, she even swore she would. Of course, she has something better to do now.'

'But has she been gone long?'

'Yes, it will be about six weeks. She was off and away the day after the wedding, in the foreign fashion.'

'They say her brother is not here either,' said Vladimir Sergeich a little later.

'No, he's not. But after all, they were used to living in the city; they were not likely to stay in the country very long!'

'And does nobody know where he went?'

'No, nobody.'

'Here today and gone tomorrow,' remarked Ivan Ilyich.

'Here today and gone tomorrow,' repeated Ipatov. 'Well now, what about you, Vladimir Sergeich? How have you been getting along?' he added, turning round in his chair.

Vladimir Sergeich began to tell him about himself and Ipatov listened, listened and at last exclaimed:

'Why doesn't Masha come? Ivan Ilyich, you might go and fetch her.'

Ivan Ilyich left the room and returned with the announcement that Marya Pavlovna was coming at once.

'What is it, has she a headache?' asked Ipatov in an undertone.

'Yes,' answered Ivan Ilyich.

The door opened and Marya Pavlovna came in. Vladimir Sergeich stood up and bowed, but could not utter a word for astonishment: Marya Pavlovna had so greatly changed since the last time he had seen her. The colour had disappeared from her wasted cheeks; great black rings encircled her eyes; her lips were bitterly compressed; her whole face, dark and set, might have been turned to stone.

She raised her eyes, and there was no lustre in them.

'How do you feel?' asked Ipatov.

'I am quite well,' she answered, sitting down at the table where the samovar was already hissing.

For Vladimir Sergeich it was a thoroughly melancholy

evening. Nobody, indeed, was in good spirits. The conversation was always taking a far from cheerful turn.

'Do you hear that?' said Ipatov, among other things, as he listened to the wailing of the wind; 'what strange music! The summer is past, long past; now autumn is going too, and winter is just ahead. We shall have the snowdrifts all round us again. If the snow would only fall soon! As it is, you go into the garden, and it makes you miserable . . . It's like some sort of tumble-down old ruin. The branches of the trees creak . . . Yes, the good days are gone!'

'Yes, gone,' repeated Ivan Ilyich.

Marya Pavlovna stared silently out of the window.

'Please God, they will return,' remarked Ipatov.

He drew no response.

'Do you remember how nice it was then, singing songs?' said Vladimir Sergeich.

'Indeed I do,' sighed the old man.

'But perhaps you could sing now,' continued Vladimir Sergeich, turning to Marya Pavlovna. 'You have such a lovely voice.'

She did not answer.

'How is your mother?' Vladimir Sergeich asked Ipatov, not knowing what to talk about.

'Thank God, she struggles through pretty well. She was out in her little carriage again today. I tell you what, she is like a broken tree, creaking away, yet you see one that is young and strong fall, while it goes on standing. Eh dear, dear!'

Marya Pavlovna dropped her hands on her knees and bent her head.

'All the same, it's a poor sort of life,' Ipatov began again. 'They are right to say age is no joy.'

'Youth is not joyful either,' said Marya Pavlovna as though to herself.

Vladimir Sergeich wanted to return home for the night, but it was so dark out of doors that he decided not to go. He was given the same upstairs room in which, thanks to Egor Kapitonych, he had spent so disturbed a night three months earlier . . .

'I wonder if he is snoring now,' thought Vladimir Sergeich, remembering the lecture he had given his servant and remembering Marya Pavlovna's unexpected appearance in the garden.

Vladimir Sergeich went to the window and leaned his forehead against the cold pane. His own face looked dimly at him from outside, his eyes seemed to be gazing into a black curtain, and only after some time could he distinguish, against the starless sky, the branches fitfully tossing in the darkness, harassed by the restless wind.

Suddenly Vladimir Sergeich thought he glimpsed something white passing swiftly along the ground . . . He peered, smiled, shrugged his shoulders and, exclaiming under his breath, 'What a thing it is to have an imagination!' went to bed.

He fell asleep very quickly, but he was not destined to have a peaceful night this time either. He was awakened by a commotion in the house . . . He raised his head from the pillow . . . He could hear agitated voices, exclamations, hurrying footsteps, doors banging; now there came the sound of a woman crying, shouts were raised in the garden, other shouts answered them from further away . . . The disturbance in the house grew and became noisier with every moment . . . 'Fire!' flashed into Vladimir Sergeich's mind. He sprang out of bed in panic and rushed to the window; but there was no glow of fire, only red points of light moving rapidly along the garden paths – men running with lanterns. Vladimir Sergeich went swiftly to the door, opened it and almost fell over Ivan Ilyich. Pale and dishevelled, only half dressed, he was rushing along without knowing where he was going.

'What is it? what has happened?' asked Vladimir Sergeich in agitation, clutching his arm.

'She's gone, she's drowned, she threw herself in the water,' answered Ivan Ilyich in a stifled voice.

'Who jumped into the water, who's gone?'

'Marya Pavlovna! Who else could it be, if not Marya Pavlovna? He has destroyed that loving heart! Help! Run, everybody, quick! Hurry, friends!'

And Ivan Ilyich plunged down the stairs.

Vladimir Sergeich struggled somehow into his boots, threw his overcoat over his shoulders and went down after him.

He found nobody left in the house, they had all run out into the garden; he came across nobody but the two little girls, Ipatov's daughters, in the passage, near the hall; half-dead with fright, they stood in their little white petticoats, their hands clasped and their little feet bare, by a night-light placed on the floor. Through the drawing-room, past an overturned table, Vladimir Sergeich ran out on the terrace. Through the trees, towards the dam, there were glimpses of lights and shadows . . .

'Boat-hooks! Boat-hooks, quick!' came Ipatov's voice.

'A net, a net, the boat!' other voices shouted.

Vladimir Sergeich ran towards the shouting. He found Ipatov at the edge of the pond; a lantern hung on a branch lit the old man's grey head clearly. He was wringing his hands and staggering like a drunken man; near him a woman lay on the grass writhing and sobbing; there was a bustle of people all round them. Ivan Ilyich was in the water up to his knees, groping along the bottom with a pole; the coachman was undressing, his whole body shivering; two men were dragging a boat along the bank; there was a sharp clatter of hoofs along the village street . . . The wind shrieked past, as though straining to blow out the lanterns, and the pond, black and threatening, splashed noisily.

'What do I hear?' exclaimed Vladimir Sergeich. 'Can it be true?'

'Boat-hooks, bring boat-hooks,' the old man groaned in answer . . .

'But perhaps you are making a mistake, really now, Mikhail Nikolaich . . .'

'No! No chance of a mistake!' wailed the tearful voice of the woman lying on the ground, Marya Pavlovna's maid. 'I

343

heard her myself, my darling, jump into the water, I heard her struggling in the water and shouting "Help!" and then just once more, "Help!"'

'Why didn't you stop her, for heaven's sake?'

'How could I, sir, how could I, my dear? Why, when it came to me all at once, she wasn't in her room, and I knew, it was because I knew in my heart . . . All these last days she has been so sad and she never said a word, and so I knew at once and I ran straight into the garden, it was like someone was telling me to come here. All of a sudden something went splash in the water: "Help!" she shouted, I heard her . . . "help!" . . . Oh, oh, oh, my dears! Oh, oh, good people!'

'But perhaps you dreamed it.'

'How could I have? Besides, where is she? where could she have got to?'

'So that was what the white thing was that I saw in the darkness,' thought Vladimir Sergeich.

Meanwhile men had come running with the boat-hooks and dragging a net, which they began to spread on the grass; a large number of people had gathered and there was a good deal of crowding and scrambling about . . . the coachman seized one boat-hook, the bailiff another, and both jumped into the boat, pushed off and began dragging the water with the hooks; others lighted them from the bank. It was strange and terrible to see their movements and their shadowy figures in the haze above the disturbed waters of the pond, by the dim and uncertain light of the lanterns.

'Hey! . . . something's caught,' shouted the coachman suddenly.

The whole crowd froze in their places.

The coachman drew the hook towards him and stooped down . . . Something horned and dark rose slowly towards the surface . . .

'A log,' said the coachman, tugging out the hook.

'Come back, come back,' they shouted from the bank; 'you won't do anything with the hooks, you need the net.'

'Yes, yes, the net,' repeated others.

'Wait,' said the bailiff, 'I have caught on to something, too . . . It's soft, I think,' he added, after a short pause.

Something white showed near the boat.

'The young lady!' shouted the bailiff suddenly. 'It's her!'

He was not mistaken . . . The boat-hook had caught in the sleeve of Marya Pavlovna's dress. The coachman seized her at once and pulled her out of the water . . . with two mighty pushes the boat was at the bank . . . Ipatov, Ivan Ilyich, Vladimir Sergeich, all plunged towards Marya Pavlovna; they raised her and carried her home in their arms, undressed her at once and began to warm and try to revive her . . . But all their striving and effort was in vain . . . Marya Pavlovna did not revive . . . The life had left her body.

Early the next morning Vladimir Sergeich left Ipatovka; before he left he went to take his leave of the dead girl. She lay on the table in the drawing-room in a white dress . . . Her thick hair was not quite dry, her pale face, as yet unchanged, had an expression of sad perplexity; her parted lips seemed trying to speak, to ask a question . . . her crossed hands seemed to cling in anguish to her breast . . . But whatever the griefs which had driven the poor girl to her end, death had laid on her its stamp of eternal silence and submission . . . and who can understand, who can describe, the dead face in those few moments when for the last time it meets the gaze of the living, before it disappears for ever and moulders in the grave?

Vladimir Sergeich stood for a short time in seemly thoughtfulness before the corpse of Marya Pavlovna, crossed himself three times and went out without noticing Ivan Ilyich weeping quietly in a corner . . . And he was not the only one who wept that day, all the servants in the house shed tears of sorrow; Marya Pavlovna left gentle memories behind her.

Here is what old Ipatov wrote a week later in answer to the letter from Nadezhda Alexeevna which had come at last:

Dear Madam, Nadezhda Alexeevna,

A week ago my unhappy sister-in-law and your friend, Marya Pavlovna, wilfully ended her own life, throwing herself into the pond at night, and we have already consigned her body to the earth. She resolved on this sad and terrible step without taking leave of me or leaving behind a letter or so much as a note to explain her last wishes . . . But you, Nadezhda Alexeevna, know better than anybody on whose soul this great and mortal sin ought to be laid! Let God judge your brother, but my sister-in-law could neither cease to love him nor survive the separation . . .

Nadezhda Alexeevna received this letter when she was in Italy, where she had gone with her husband, Count de Stelchinsky, as he was called in all the hotels. But it was not only hotels he frequented: he was known in gambling-houses and in Kursaals at watering-places . . . At first he lost a great deal of money, but then he ceased to lose and his face acquired the peculiar expression, half-suspicious, half-insolent, of a man who is always unexpectedly finding himself involved in scandalous proceedings . . . He did not see his wife very often. Nadezhda Alexeevna, however, was not bored in his absence. She had developed a passion for the arts. She came to know more and more artists and she liked discussing beauty with young men. Ipatov's letter distressed her extremely, but did not prevent her from going that very day to the Cave of Dogs to watch the poor animals, plunged into its sulphurous vapours, suffocate.

She had not gone there alone. She was escorted by several cavaliers. The most charming among them was considered to be a certain Mr Popelin, an unsuccessful French painter with a beard and a check jacket. He sang the latest drawing-room ballads in a thin little tenor voice, made very free with his witticisms, and although of somewhat lean and hungry build ate a great deal.

VII

It was a sunny, frosty January day; the Nevsky Prospect was thronged. The clock on the Duma tower pointed to three. Along the broad pavement, strewn with yellow sand, our old friend Vladimir Sergeich Astakhov was walking. He had matured considerably since the time when we parted from him, grown luxuriant whiskers, and filled out everywhere, but was still in the prime of his manhood. He moved among the crowd without haste, stopping occasionally to look about him: he was waiting for his wife, who had preferred to ride in the carriage with her mother. Vladimir Sergeich had been married for five years, and married exactly as he had always wished: his wife was rich and extremely well-connected. Courteously raising his beautifully polished hat to the numerous acquaintances he met, Vladimir Sergeich was continuing to stroll along with the easy gait of a man who is content with his lot when suddenly, near the Arcade, he was almost bumped into by a gentleman in a Spanish cloak and a cap, with a face that showed considerable signs of wear and tear, a dyed moustache and large, rather puffy eyes. Vladimir Sergeich moved to one side with dignity, but the gentleman in the cap looked at him and exclaimed suddenly:

'Ah! Good morning, Mr Astakhov!'

Vladimir Sergeich did not answer but stopped in amazement, unable to understand how a man who was capable of walking along the Nevsky Prospect in a cap could know his name.

'You don't recognize me,' went on the gentleman in the cap. 'I met you about eight years ago in the country, in the province of T——, at the Ipatovs'. My name is Veretyev.'

'Oh! Good God! Excuse me,' exclaimed Vladimir Sergeich, 'but you have changed so much since those days . . .'

'Yes, I am older,' replied Peter Alexeich, passing his ungloved hand over his face. 'But you have not altered.'

Veretyev had not so much aged as grown thin and run to seed. Small fine wrinkles covered his face and when he spoke his lips and cheeks twitched slightly. It was clear in every way that he was a man who had lived hard.

'Where did you get to all this time, that nobody has seen anything of you?' asked Vladimir Sergeich.

'Oh, I've wandered about here and there. And have you been in St Petersburg all the time?'

'Mostly in St Petersburg.'

'Are you married?'

'Yes.'

And Vladimir Sergeich adopted a rather severe expression, as though to say to Veretyev, 'Don't think, my dear sir, of asking me to present you to my wife.'

Veretyev seemed to understand him. A smile of mocking indifference just touched his lips.

'And how is your sister?' asked Vladimir Sergeich. 'Where is she?'

'I cannot tell you for certain. Probably in Moscow. I have not had any letters from her for a long time.'

'Is her husband alive?'

'Yes.'

'And Mr Ipatov?'

'I don't know; he's still alive, too, probably; but he may be dead.'

'And that other gentleman, what was his name? – Bodryakov – what about him?'

'The one you asked to be your second, if you remember, when you were in such a funk? God only knows!'

Vladimir Sergeich, with a self-important expression, said nothing for a short time.

'I have always,' he went on, 'been happy to remember those evenings when I had the pleasure' (he had been almost on the point of saying 'the honour') 'of meeting your sister and yourself. She is a very charming person. And do you still sing as well as ever?'

'No, my voice has gone . . . Yes, those were good days.'

'I visited Ipatovka once afterwards,' added Vladimir Sergeich, with a mournful raising of his brows, '– that, I think, was what they called the village – on the very day a dreadful thing happened . . .'

'Yes, yes, terrible, terrible,' hurriedly interrupted Veretyev. 'Yes, yes. And do you remember very nearly fighting a duel with my present brother-in-law?'

'Hm! I remember!' retorted Vladimir Sergeich with deliberation. 'However, I must confess that so much time has gone by since then that sometimes it all seems like a dream . . .'

'Like a dream,' repeated Veretyev, and his pale cheeks flushed, 'like a dream . . . No, it wasn't a dream, at least not for me. Those were the days of youth and gaiety and happiness, days of boundless hope and invincible strength, and if it was a dream, it was a wonderful dream. But this, that you and I have grown old and stupid, and dye our whiskers, and loiter along the Nevsky Prospect, and are not much good for anything, like broken-down old crocks, that we're a little played out, a little faded, and either put on airs and pretend to be somebody, or shuffle about in a slipshod kind of fashion and, I'm afraid, try to drown our sorrows in drink – it is this that is more like a dream, and a hideous dream at that. We have lived our lives, and lived them emptily, ridiculously, vulgarly – that is what is bitter! If we could only shake this off like a dream, if we could only wake up from this! . . . And then, everywhere and always, one horrible memory, one ghost . . . However, goodbye.'

Veretyev walked rapidly away, but when he drew level with one of the principal cafes in the Nevsky Prospect, he stopped, went in, drank a glass of orange vodka at the bar, crossed the billiard-room, all dim and hazy with tobacco-smoke, and entered the back room. There he found some acquaintances and former boon companions: Petya Lazurin, Kostya Kovrovsky, Prince Serdyukov, and two others who were referred to simply as

Vasyuk and Philet. They were all men who were getting on in years, though unmarried; some were losing their hair, others turning grey, their faces were covered with wrinkles, they had double chins – in short, all these gentlemen had, as they say, begun going downhill. They all, however, continued to regard Veretyev as somebody unusual, destined to astonish the world, and he was wiser than they only in that he was very well aware of his own utter and fundamental worthlessness. Even outside his own circle there were people who thought that, if he had not been his own worst enemy, there was no telling what he might not have made of himself . . . They were mistaken; the Veretyevs never make anything of themselves.

Peter Alexeich's friends welcomed him as usual. They were puzzled at first by his gloomy looks and jaundiced remarks, but he soon grew calmer and more cheerful, and the time passed as usual.

Vladimir Sergeich, as soon as Veretyev left him, frowned and drew himself up. He had been extremely perplexed and even offended by Peter Alexeich's unexpected outburst.

'Grown old and stupid, drown our sorrows, dye our whiskers . . . *parlez pour vous*, *mon cher*,' he said at last, almost aloud, and, snorting once or twice from an access of involuntary indignation, prepared to continue his stroll.

'Who was that talking to you?' asked a loud and self-satisfied voice behind him.

Vladimir Sergeich turned and saw one of his closest friends, a certain Mr Pomponsky. This Mr Pomponsky was a tall, heavy man who occupied a fairly important position and had never once felt any misgivings about himself since his earliest youth.

'Oh, nobody; an odd specimen,' said Vladimir Sergeich, taking Mr Pomponsky's arm.

'Really, Vladimir Sergeich, is it permissible for a respectable man to talk in the street to an individual who wears a cap? It is most improper. I was amazed! Where can you have met such a person?'

'In the country.'

'In the country ... One should not know one's country neighbours in the city ... *ce n'est pas comme il faut*. A gentleman ought always to conduct himself as a gentleman if he wishes ...'

'There is my wife,' Vladimir Sergeich hastened to interrupt him. 'Let us go to her.'

And both gentlemen turned their steps towards a smart little low carriage, from the window of which looked the pale, weary, irritable, supercilious face of a woman still young but past her first bloom.

Behind her could be seen another lady, also apparently out of humour, her mother. Vladimir Sergeich opened the carriage door and offered his wife his arm. Pomponsky walked with the mother-in-law and the couples turned along the Nevsky Prospect, escorted by a tall, black-haired footman in pea-green gaiters, with a big cockade in his hat.

1854

353

FIRST LOVE

Characters

Sergéy Nikoláich (Nikoláevich)

Vladímir Petróvich: Volódya, Woldemar, *the narrator*

ZASÉKINA, *Princess*

"   Zinaída Alexándrovna (later DÓLSKAYA): Zína, Zínochka

Peter Vasílyevich, *and*

Maria Nikoláevna, *the narrator's parents*

BELOVZÓROV, Victor Egórych (Egórovich)

Count MALÉVSKY

Doctor LÚSHIN

MAYDÁNOV

Captain NIRMÁTSKY

TONKOSHÉEV

Dunyáshka

Fëdor

Másha

For a Note on Pronunciation, *see p. 5 above.*

First Love

(*Dedicated to P. V. Annenkov*)

THE GUESTS HAD LONG since dispersed. The clock had struck half-past twelve. There remained in the room only the host, Sergey Nikolaich and Vladimir Petrovich.

The host rang the bell and gave orders for the remains of supper to be removed.

'Well, that's agreed, then,' he said, settling himself deeper into his arm-chair and lighting a cigar. 'Each of us is to tell the story of his first love. It is your turn first, Sergey Nikolaich.'

Sergey Nikolaich, a chubby little man with a plump, fair-skinned face, looked at his host and then raised his eyes to the ceiling.

'I never had a first love,' he said at last; 'I began straight away with the second.'

359

'How was that?'

'It was quite simple. I was eighteen when I first began to pay court to a very nice young lady; but I courted her as if the business was not new to me at all, exactly as I used to court other young ladies afterwards. Strictly speaking, I fell in love for the first and last time at the age of six or so – with my nurse; but that is a very long time ago, the details of our association have faded from my memory, and even if I could remember them, who could be interested in them?'

'Well, then, what are we to do?' began the host. 'My first love affair isn't very entertaining, either: I had never fallen in love with anybody before I met Anna Ivanovna, who is now my wife – and everything went smoothly for us: our fathers had arranged the marriage, we very soon fell in love with each other, and we got married without delay. My story can be told very shortly. I confess, gentlemen, that when I raised the topic of first love, I was pinning my hopes on you – I won't say old, but still not very young – bachelors; will *you* amuse us with something, Vladimir Petrovich?'

'My first love really was not entirely commonplace,' answered Vladimir Petrovich, with a slight stammer. He was about forty, and his black hair was beginning to turn grey.

'Ah!' exclaimed the host and Sergey Nikolaich with one voice. 'So much the better . . . Fire away!'

'As you please . . . or no: I won't tell it: I am no expert at story-telling; it always comes out dry and too short or long-winded and unconvincing. But if you like I will write it all down in a notebook and read it to you.'

His friends would not agree to this at first, but Vladimir Petrovich stood his ground. Two weeks later they met again, and Vladimir Petrovich proved as good as his word.

This is what was set down in his notebook.

I

I was sixteen years old at the time. All this happened in the summer of 1833.

I was living in Moscow with my parents. They had rented a suburban summer villa near the Kaluga Gate, opposite Neskuchny Gardens. I was preparing for the university, but I was in no hurry and did very little work.

Nobody interfered with my freedom. I did as I pleased, especially after I parted with my last tutor, a Frenchman who could never get used to the idea of having dropped 'like a bomb' (*comme une bombe*) into Russia, and would lie on his bed all day with an embittered expression. My father treated me with amiable indifference; my mother paid hardly any attention to me, although she had no other children: she was engrossed by other cares. My father, a man still young and very handsome, had married her for her money; she was ten years older than he. My mother led a sad life: she was in a perpetual state of agitation, jealousy and anger – but not in my father's presence; she was very much afraid of him, and he was always stern, cold and distant . . . I never saw a man more consummately composed, self-assured, and despotic.

I shall never forget the first weeks I spent in the villa. It was glorious, settled weather; we had removed from the town on St Nicholas's Day, the 9th of May. I went for walks, now in the garden of our house, now in Neskuchny Gardens, now outside the Gate; I would take a book with me – Kaydanov's *Ancient History*, perhaps – but I rarely opened it; more often I would recite poetry, of which I knew an immense amount by heart; the blood fermented in my veins, and my heart ached – so sweetly and absurdly; I was all expectancy and diffidence and wonder and eagerness; my fancies played and darted, always round the same images, like martins at daybreak round a bell-tower; I was pensive, melancholy, even tearful; but even through the tears and the melancholy induced now by a melodious line of verse, now by the beauty of evening, there pushed up, like spring grass, a joyful sense of youthful, effervescent life.

I had a horse of my own. I would saddle it myself and ride off, break into a gallop and imagine I was a knight at a tournament (how cheerfully the wind whistled round my ears!), or, turning my face to the sky, receive its radiant light and colour into my expanded soul.

I remember that at that time the image of womanhood, the shadowy vision of woman's love, almost never took definite shape in my mind; but in everything I thought and everything I felt lurked the shy, half-conscious presentiment of something new, ineffably sweet, feminine . . .

This presentiment, this expectation, permeated my whole being; I breathed it, it ran through my veins in every drop of blood . . . it was destined soon to become reality.

The place we had rented consisted of a wooden house with columns, flanked by two small, low annexes; that on the left housed a minute manufactory of cheap wall-paper; more than once I had been there to watch a dozen thin, tousled little boys, with hollow cheeks and dirty overalls, jumping on the wooden levers that pressed down the rectangular blocks, and thus stamping out the bright-coloured patterns on the wall-papers with the weight of their puny bodies. The building on the right stood empty and was to let. One day, some three weeks after the 9th of May, its shutters were flung open and women's faces appeared at the windows: somebody was living there. I remember that that same day at dinner my mother inquired of the butler who our new neighbours were and, somewhat impressed on hearing the name Princess Zasekina, first said: 'Ah, a princess . . .', and then added: 'She must be poor.'

'They came in three cabs, ma'am,' remarked the butler, respectfully handing a dish; 'they have no carriage, and the furniture is very poor stuff.'

'Yes,' replied my mother. 'All the same, it's a good thing.'

My father glanced coldly at her: she said no more.

Princess Zasekina really could not have been a rich woman: the cottage she had rented was so ramshackle and small and low that nobody in even fairly comfortable circumstances would have consented to live in it. However, all this went over my head at the time. The title of princess made little impression on me: I had recently read Schiller's *Robbers*.

II

I had a habit of wandering in the garden every evening with a gun to watch for crows. I nursed a long-standing hatred of those wary, greedy, cunning birds. On the day of which I am speaking I had gone into the garden as usual, and after I had patrolled all the avenues without success (the crows knew me and kept up a spasmodic cawing from a safe distance), I found myself by chance close to the low fence that separated what was properly *our* domain from the narrow strip of garden stretching behind the building on the right and belonging to it. I was walking with bent head; suddenly the sound of voices reached my ears. I looked up across the fence, and stopped dead . . . A strange sight met my eyes.

A few steps away from me, on a lawn among the green raspberry-bushes, stood a tall, shapely young girl in a striped pink dress, with a white handkerchief on her head; round her crowded four young men, and she was tapping them in turn on the forehead with some of those smallish grey-blue flowers – I do not know their name, but children are familiar with them: the flowers are in the form of small sacks or pouches and burst open with a pop when you strike them on a firm surface. The young men so eagerly tendered their foreheads, and in the movements of the girl (I was seeing her in profile) there was something so bewitching, imperious, caressing, bantering, and charming, that I all but exclaimed aloud in wonder and pleasure and, I think, would have given everything in the world on the spot if only those pretty little fingers had tapped my forehead too. My gun slid into the grass and I forgot everything while my eyes feasted on the shapely waist, the little neck, the beautiful hands, the slightly dishevelled fair hair under the white handkerchief, that half-closed intelligent eye, those eyelashes, and the soft cheek below them . . .

'Young man! Young man!' suddenly said a voice close to me. 'Is it permissible to stare like that at strange young ladies?'

I started violently and stood thunderstruck. Beside me on the other side of the fence stood a man with close-cropped black hair, looking at me quizzically. At that moment the young girl also turned towards me . . . I saw the enormous grey eyes in the expressive, animated face – and the face suddenly quivered into laughter, the white teeth flashed, the brows were comically raised . . . I blushed fiercely, snatched my gun up from the ground and, followed by the ringing, but not unfriendly, laughter, fled into my own room, flung myself down on the bed and covered my face with my hands. My heart was leaping wildly; I was very much ashamed and very happy: I felt an unprecedented excitement.

When I was rested, I combed my hair, washed my hands, and went downstairs for tea. The young girl's image floated in front of me; my heart had ceased to leap, but had a kind of pleasant tension.

'What is the matter with you?' asked my father suddenly. 'Have you shot a crow?'

I would have liked to tell him everything, but I refrained and only smiled to myself. When I went to bed, I twirled round three times on one leg, without in the least knowing why, then put pomade on my hair, lay down – and slept all night like the dead. Just before morning I awoke for a moment, raised my head, gazed round with delight – and fell asleep again.

III

'How can I get to know them?' was my first thought when I awoke in the morning. I went out into the garden before breakfast, but did not go too close to the fence, and saw nobody. After breakfast I walked several times up and down the street in front of the house – and glanced into the windows from a distance . . . All at once I thought I saw *her* face behind the curtain and retreated in panic as quickly as possible. 'But I simply must get to know them,' I thought, aimlessly wandering about the sandy stretch of ground in front of Neskuchny Gardens. 'But how? That is the question.' I remembered the smallest details of the previous day's encounter; somehow my clearest recollection was of how she had laughed at me . . . But even while I was anxiously constructing plan after plan, fate was already taking a hand on my behalf.

In my absence my mother had received from her new neighbour a letter on grey paper, sealed with the sort of brown wax that is used only on post-office bundles and the corks of cheap wine. In this letter, ungrammatically written in an unpractised hand, the princess asked my mother to exert her influence on her behalf: my mother, said the princess, was well acquainted with certain important people on whom her fortunes and the fortunes of her children depended, since she was involved in some very momentous legal business: 'I adress myself to you,' she wrote, 'as one Noblewoman to another, and allso I am very Happy to avale myself of this Oportunity.' She ended by asking my mother's permission to call on her. I found my mother in an uncomfortable state of mind: my father was out, and she had nobody to consult. Not to answer a 'noblewoman', and a princess besides, was impossible, but how to answer? – that my mother could not decide. It would be unsuitable, she thought, to write a note in French, but she herself was not very strong on Russian spelling, and she knew it, and did not wish to give herself away. She was very glad I had come in, and at once commanded me to go to the princess and tell her by word of mouth that my mother was always ready to do her Excellency any service that lay in her power, and ask her to be kind enough to call between twelve and one. This unexpectedly speedy fulfilment of my secret wishes both delighted and terrified me; I did not, however, betray my confusion – and as a preliminary went to my room to put on my new tie and frock-coat: at home I still wore a short jacket and turn-down collar, although I disliked having to do so.

IV

In the overcrowded and untidy entrance-passage of the cottage, which I entered with an involuntary tremor of my whole body, I was met by an old, grey-haired servant with a dark, copper-coloured face and the deepest wrinkles in his forehead and temples I had ever seen in my life. He was carrying a plate containing the backbone of a herring. Closing with his foot the door leading to the next room, he said abruptly:

'Yes?'

'Is Princess Zasekina at home?' I asked.

'Boniface!' called a woman's grating voice from the other side of the door.

The servant, without a word, turned his back on me, revealing the threadbare back of his livery, with its one solitary crested button, and went out, depositing the plate on the floor.

'Have you been to the police-station?' went on the feminine voice. The servant murmured something. 'What? . . . Somebody has come?' I heard next. 'The young gentleman from next door? Well, show him in.'

'Please go into the drawing-room,' said the servant, returning and picking up the plate from the floor.

I straightened my coat and tie and entered the 'drawing-room'.

I found myself in a small and not particularly tidy room, with shabby furniture set about in a hasty, haphazard way. By the window, in a chair with a broken arm, sat a plain woman of fifty. She was without a cap and wore an old green dress with a bright-coloured woollen shawl round her neck. Her small black eyes absolutely bored into me.

I went up to her and bowed.

'Have I the honour of addressing Princess Zasekina?'

'I am Princess Zasekina. And are you Mr V.'s son?'

'Yes, ma'am. I have brought you a message from my mother.'

'Please sit down. Boniface! Where are my keys? Have you seen them?'

I gave Princess Zasekina my mother's reply to her letter. As she listened to me, she drummed with her thick, red fingers on the window-sill, and when I had finished she fixed her eyes on me again.

'Very well; I will certainly be there,' she said at last. 'But how young you are! May I ask your age?'

'Sixteen,' I replied, with an involuntary stammer.

The princess took from her pocket some dirty scraps of

paper covered with writing, brought them close to the end of her nose, and began to look through them.

'A good age,' she pronounced abruptly, fidgeting in her chair. 'Now, please don't stand on ceremony. We are simple people.'

'Too simple,' I thought, studying her unprepossessing figure with involuntary disgust.

At this moment the other door of the drawing-room swung open, and on the threshold stood the girl I had seen in the garden. She raised her hand, and a mocking smile flashed across her face.

'And here is my daughter,' said the princess, motioning with her elbow towards her. 'Zinochka, this is the son of our neighbour, Mr V. May I ask your name?'

'Vladimir,' I answered, rising and stammering in my agitation.

'And your patronymic?'

'Petrovich.'

'Well! I used to know a chief of police, and his name was Vladimir Petrovich, too. Boniface! Don't go on looking for my keys; they are in my pocket.'

The young girl continued to look at me with the same smile as before, slightly narrowing her eyes and putting her head a little on one side.

'I have seen M. Woldemar before,' she began. (The silvery sound of her voice sent a shiver of pleasure through me.) 'Will you allow me to call you that?'

'Please do,' I murmured.

'Where was that?' asked the princess.

Her daughter did not answer.

'Are you busy just now?' she asked, still not taking her eyes off me.

'Not in the least.'

'Would you like to help me wind some wool? Come into my room.'

She nodded to me and went out; I followed her.

In the room we went into, the furniture was a little better, and more tastefully arranged. I was not, however, in a state to notice anything much at that moment: I was moving in a dream and filled with a sensation of quite idiotic bliss.

The young princess sat down, took a skein of red wool and, indicating a chair opposite her, carefully untwisted it and put it on my hands. She did all this silently, in a droll, dawdling kind of way, with the same bright, sly smile on her parted lips. She began to wind the wool on a folded card, and suddenly flashed at me a smile so swift and dazzling that I involuntarily dropped my eyes. When her eyes, usually somewhat narrowed, opened to their full extent, her face was transformed: it seemed to be flooded with light.

'What did you think of me yesterday, M. Woldemar?' she asked after a pause. 'You probably disapproved.'

'I . . . Princess . . . I didn't think . . . how could I?' I answered in confusion.

'Listen,' she retorted. 'You don't know me yet: I am a very odd person, I always want to be told the truth. I hear you are sixteen, and I am twenty-one: you see, I am much older than you, so you must always speak the truth to me . . . and do what I tell you,' she added. 'Look at me – why don't you look at me?'

I was even more confused; but I raised my eyes to her. She smiled, not as before, but with a different, approving smile.

'Look at me,' she said, lowering her voice caressingly. 'I do not mind. I like your face; I feel that we are going to be friends. Do you like me?' she added archly.

'Princess . . .' I was beginning.

'To begin with, call me Zinaida Alexandrovna; next, why should children' (she corrected herself), 'young people, never say straight out what they feel? That is all very well for grown-ups. Surely you do like me?'

Although I was pleased that she should talk so frankly to me, I was a little offended also. I wanted to show her that she was not dealing with a child and, adopting as serious and confident an air as I could, I said:

'Of course I like you very much, Zinaida Alexandrovna; I am not trying to conceal it.'

She shook her head with slow deliberation.

'Have you a tutor?' she asked abruptly.

'No, I haven't had one for a long time.'

I was lying: I had parted from my Frenchman not a month before.

'Oh! I see you are quite grown up.'

She struck my fingers lightly. 'Hold your arms straight!' And she applied herself diligently to winding her ball.

I took advantage of the fact that her eyes were lowered to study her, at first stealthily, then more and more openly. Her face seemed to me still more delightful than it had the day before: everything about it was so delicate, intelligent, and charming. She was sitting with her back to the window, with its white blind; a ray of sunlight, passing through the blind, flooded with tender light her fluffy, golden hair, her innocent neck, sloping shoulders and soft, placid breast. I watched her – and how near and dear she had become! It seemed to me that I had known her for a long time, that I had known nothing, had not lived, until she came . . . She was wearing a dark, rather shabby dress and an apron; I think I would gladly have stroked every fold of that dress and that apron. The tips of her little boots peeped out beneath her skirts: I could have prostrated myself in worship before them . . . 'Here I am, sitting with her,' I thought. 'I have got to know her . . . oh, God, what happiness!' I could have leapt up from my chair in rapture, but I only shuffled my feet like a child eating sweets.

I felt in my element, and I could have stayed in that room and on that spot for ever.

Her eyelids lifted quietly, and again her bright eyes shone warmly on me, again she smiled with a hint of mockery.

'How you look at me!' she said slowly, shaking her finger at me.

I blushed . . . 'She knows everything, she sees everything,' flashed through my mind. 'Indeed, how can she help it?'

Suddenly there was a noise in the next room, the clatter of a sabre.

'Zina!' called the princess from the drawing-room. 'Belovzorov has brought you a kitten.'

'A kitten!' exclaimed Zinaida, jumping from her chair and throwing the ball of wool on my knees as she ran out.

I stood up also, laid the skein of wool and the ball on the window-sill, went into the drawing-room, and stopped uncertainly: in the middle of the room sprawled a striped kitten; Zinaida was kneeling in front of it and carefully supporting its little face. Near the princess, filling almost the whole space between the windows, loomed a dashing young hussar officer, with fair, curly hair, a red face, and goggle eyes.

'What a comical little thing!' Zinaida kept repeating. 'And its eyes are not grey, but green, and what big ears! Thank you, Victor Egorych! It was very nice of you.'

The hussar, in whom I had recognized one of the young men I had seen the previous day, smiled and bowed, with a clinking of spurs and a rattle of sabre-rings.

'Yesterday you were pleased to say you wanted a striped kitten with big ears . . . so I've got one. Your word is law.' And he bowed again.

The kitten squeaked faintly and began to sniff the floor.

'It's hungry,' exclaimed Zinaida. 'Boniface! Sonya! Bring some milk.'

A housemaid in an old yellow dress, with a faded kerchief

round her neck, came in with a saucer of milk in her hand and set it down in front of the kitten. The kitten quivered, closed its eyes and began to lap.

'What a pink little tongue it has,' remarked Zinaida, putting her head almost on the floor and watching the kitten from close by its head.

The kitten drank its fill and began to purr, daintily kneading with its paws. Zinaida stood up and said indifferently to the servant:

'Take it away!'

'In return for the kitten, may I kiss your hand?' said the hussar, simpering, while his whole muscular body, tightly encased in a new uniform, twitched.

'Both,' replied Zinaida, and held out her hands to him. While he kissed them, she watched me over her shoulder.

I stood motionless on the same spot, not knowing whether I ought to laugh, find something to say, or just be silent. Suddenly, through the open door of the passage, the figure of our manservant Fëdor caught my eye. He was making signs to me. I went out to him mechanically.

'What do you want?' I asked.

'Your mother sent me for you,' he said in a whisper. 'She is angry because you have not come back with the answer.'

'Why, have I been long?'

'More than an hour.'

'More than an hour!' I involuntarily repeated and, returning to the drawing-room, I began to take my leave, with elaborate bows.

'Where are you going?' asked the young princess, looking up at me over the hussar's shoulder.

'I must go home. So,' I added, turning to the older woman, 'I will say you will call between one and two o'clock.'

'Yes, do, young man.'

The princess swiftly took out her snuff-box and inhaled so noisily that I positively jumped.

'Yes, do,' she repeated, tearfully blinking and wheezing.

I bowed once more, turned and left the room with that uncomfortable feeling in my back that a young man experiences when he knows that people's eyes are following him.

'Remember, you must come and see us again, M. Woldemar,' called Zinaida, and once more began to laugh.

'Why is she always laughing?' I wondered, returning home in the company of Fëdor, who said nothing but stalked disapprovingly behind me. My mother scolded me and wondered what I could have been doing for so long at that princess's. Without answering, I went off to my own room. I felt suddenly very sad . . . I held back the tears with an effort . . . I was jealous of the hussar!

V

The princess called on my mother, as she had promised – and did not make a good impression. I was not present at their interview, but at table my mother told my father that the Princess Zasekina seemed to be *une femme très vulgaire*, that she had been very tiresome with her requests that my mother should intercede with Prince Sergey on her behalf, that she seemed to have a great deal of legal and financial business in hand – *des vilaines affaires d'argent* – and that she must be very litigious. My mother added, however, that she had invited her and her daughter to dinner the next day (I bent low over my plate when I heard the word 'daughter'), since after all she was a neighbour – and titled. On this, my father declared that he now remembered who the lady was; that when he was a young man he had known the deceased Prince Zasekin, a highly educated but empty and stupid man; that society had called him *le Parisien* on account of his long residence in Paris; that he had been very rich, but had gambled away all his property – and that for some unknown reason, though it could hardly have been for anything but money – he might, however, have made a better choice, my father added, smiling coldly – he had married the daughter of some minor official, taken to speculating – and completed his ruin.

'If only she does not attempt to borrow money,' remarked my mother.

'It's quite possible she will,' said my father calmly. 'Does she speak French?'

'Very badly.'

'Hm. However, it doesn't matter. I think you said you had invited her daughter; somebody or other told me she is a very nice girl, and well educated.'

'Oh! That means she does not take after her mother.'

'Nor her father,' retorted mine. 'He was well educated, too, but he was stupid.'

My mother sighed and pondered. My father said no more. I had felt very uncomfortable during the conversation.

After dinner I went into the garden, but without my gun. I had promised myself I would not go near the 'Zasekin garden', but I was irresistibly drawn towards it – and not in vain. I had no sooner approached the fence than I saw Zinaida. This time she was alone. She was holding a book in her hands and walking slowly along the path. She did not notice me.

I had almost let her pass, but all at once I pulled myself together and coughed.

She turned round, but did not stop; she pushed aside the wide blue ribbon of her round straw hat, looked at me, smiled quietly, and again fixed her eyes on her book.

I took off my cap, lingered uncertainly for a time, and then walked away with a heavy heart. '*Que suis-je pour elle?*' I said to myself (God knows why) in French.

Familiar footsteps sounded behind me: I looked round – my father was walking towards me with his light rapid step.

'Was that the younger princess?' he asked me.

'Yes.'

'Do you know her?'

'I saw her this morning at the princess's.'

My father stopped, turned on his heel, and went back. As he drew level with Zinaida, he bowed courteously. She returned his bow, not without some surprise in her expression, and lowered her book. I saw her eyes following him. My father always dressed very elegantly, with characteristic simplicity; but his figure had never seemed to me more handsome, and his grey hat had never sat more becomingly on his scarcely thinning curls.

I would have gone towards Zinaida but, without so much as a glance at me, she raised her book again and walked on.

VI

I passed all that evening and the next morning in a kind of dreary stupor. I remember that I made an effort to work, and took up Kaydanov, but the famous textbook's lines and pages of large print passed in vain under my eyes. I read the words 'Julius Caesar was distinguished for military audacity' at least ten times without understanding a word. I discarded the book. Before dinner I once again pomaded my hair and put on my frock-coat and tie.

'What is that for?' asked my mother. 'You are not a student

yet, and God knows whether you will pass your examinations. And besides, it is not long since your jacket was made. You can't just give up wearing it.'

'We are having guests,' I whispered almost desperately.

'Nonsense! Fine guests, indeed!'

I had to give in. I changed my frock-coat for the jacket, but I did not take off my tie. The princess and her daughter appeared half an hour before dinner; over the green dress I had seen before the older woman had thrown a yellow shawl, and she had put on an old-fashioned cap with flame-coloured ribbons. She at once began to talk of money matters, sighed, bemoaned her poverty, pestered us with complaints about her lot and requests for assistance, and did not in any way stand on ceremony: she inhaled her snuff just as noisily and fidgeted in her chair just as freely as at home. It seemed not to enter her head that she was a princess. Zinaida, on the other hand, was stern, almost haughty – a true princess. Her face showed cold impassivity and consequence – and I could hardly recognize her, hardly recognize her looks or her smile, although even in this new aspect I thought her beautiful. She was wearing a light barège dress with a pale blue pattern; her hair fell in long ringlets beside her cheeks, in the English fashion: this coiffure suited the cold expression of her face. My father sat beside her at dinner and entertained his partner with his own elegant and sober courtesy. He glanced at her from time to time, and from time to time she glanced at him, but very strangely, almost with hostility. Their conversation was conducted in French; I remember that I was astonished at the purity of Zinaida's accent. At table the princess was as unconstrained as ever, ate a great deal, and praised the cooking. My mother plainly found her burdensome and answered her with a kind of melancholy negligence; from time to time my father just perceptibly knitted his brows. My mother did not care for Zinaida either.

'What a proud thing she is!' she said the next day. 'And if you think of it, what has she to be proud of? — *avec sa mine de grisette*!'

'Obviously you have never seen any grisettes,' remarked my father.

'No, thank God!'

'Thank God, certainly . . . but how can you tell what they are like?'

Zinaida paid not the slightest attention to me. Soon after dinner the princess began to take her leave.

'I shall hope for your protection, Maria Nikolaevna and Peter Vasilyevich,' she drawled in a sing-song voice. 'What can one do? There was a time — but those days are gone. Here am I, her Excellency,' she added with a disagreeable smile, 'but honour buys no beef in the market.'

My father bowed politely and escorted her to the door. I stood there in my short-tailed jacket and looked at the floor, like a man condemned to death. Zinaida's treatment of me had annihilated me. How great, then, was my surprise when, as she passed me, she whispered rapidly and with the same caressing light in her eyes as before:

'Come over at eight o'clock without fail, do you hear?'

I could only fling out my hands but she had already thrown her white scarf over her head and was gone.

VII

At exactly eight o'clock, wearing my frock-coat and with my hair brushed into a quiff, I entered the passage of the princess's house. The old manservant looked at me sullenly and got up unwillingly from his bench. There was a sound of voices in the drawing-room. I opened the door – and stopped dead in amazement. In the middle of the room, on a chair, stood the young princess, holding a man's hat in front of her; round the chair crowded five men. They were trying to get their hands into the hat and she was holding it high and shaking it vigorously. At sight of me she called out:

'Wait, wait! Here's a new visitor, we must give him a ticket too.' And jumping lightly down from the chair, she laid her hand on my cuff. 'Come along,' she said, 'why are you standing there? *Messieurs*, allow me to introduce you: this is M. Woldemar, the son of our neighbour. And these,' she added, turning to me and pointing out each of her guests in turn, 'are Count Malevsky, Doctor Lushin, the poet Maydanov, Captain Nirmatsky, retired, and our hussar, Belovzorov, whom you know already. Please all be friends.'

I was so embarrassed that I did not even bow to anybody; in Doctor Lushin I recognized the swarthy man who had so pitilessly put me to the blush in the garden; the others were unknown to me.

'Count!' continued Zinaida, 'write out a ticket for M. Woldemar.'

'That's not fair,' objected the count, in a slight Polish accent. He was a very good-looking, foppish, dark-haired young man with expressive brown eyes, a thin white nose, and a wisp of moustache over his tiny mouth. 'He wasn't playing forfeits with us.'

'It isn't fair,' repeated Belovzorov and the gentleman who had been described as a retired captain, a man some forty years old, disfigured with pock-marks, as curly-headed as a negro, round-shouldered, bow-legged, and dressed in a military coat without epaulettes, which he wore unbuttoned.

'Do as you are told, write out a ticket,' repeated the princess. 'This is mutiny! M. Woldemar is with us for the first time, and as far as he is concerned there are no rules today. No use grumbling; do it because I want you to.'

The count shrugged his shoulders but, with an obedient inclination of the head, took up the pen in a white hand adorned with rings and, tearing off a scrap of paper, began to write on it.

'At least let me tell M. Woldemar what it is all about,' began

Lushin in an ironic tone of voice; 'as it is, he is quite lost . . . You see, young man, we are playing forfeits; the princess has had to pay a forfeit and the one who draws the lucky ticket will have the right to kiss her hand. Do you understand?'

I simply glanced at him and continued to stand there like a man in a daze, while the princess again jumped on the chair and again began to shake the hat. Everybody stretched out his arm, and I followed their example.

'Maydanov,' said the princess to a tall young man with a thin face, short-sighted small eyes, and extraordinarily long black hair, 'as a poet you ought to be generous and give up your ticket to M. Woldemar, so that he can have two chances instead of one.'

But Maydanov shook his head and tossed back his hair. I was the last to put my hand in the hat, take out a ticket and unfold it . . . I could hardly believe my eyes when I saw on it the word 'Kiss'.

'Kiss!' I cried involuntarily.

'Bravo, he's won!' the princess chimed in. 'I'm so glad!' She came down from the chair and looked me in the face with a glance so bright and sweet that my heart began to race. 'Are you glad?' she asked me.

'I? . . .' I stammered.

'Sell me your ticket,' boomed Belovzorov suddenly in my very ear. 'I will give you a hundred roubles.'

I answered the hussar with so indignant a shake of the head

that Zinaida clapped her hands and Lushin exclaimed: 'Good for you!'

'But,' he continued, 'as master of ceremonies, I am obliged to see that all the rules are kept. M. Woldemar, go down on one knee! That is the way we do things here.'

Zinaida stood in front of me, with her head a little inclined to one side, as though to see me better, and extended her hand with solemn dignity. There was a mist in front of my eyes; I started to go down on one knee, landed on both, and approached Zinaida's hand with my lips so clumsily that I grazed the end of my nose with her fingernail.

'Good!' cried Lushin, helping me to rise.

The game of forfeits continued. Zinaida set me beside her. What forfeits she invented! There was one time when she had to be a 'statue', and she chose the ugly Nirmatsky as her pedestal, making him lie face downwards and with his face pressed against his shoulder. The laughter never died down for a moment. As for me, a solitary boy, soberly brought up in a gentleman's sedate household, all this uproarious noise, this unceremonious, almost riotous, gaiety, this unwonted contact with strangers, simply went to my head. I was intoxicated, as if I had been drinking. I began to laugh and chatter louder than anybody, so that even the old princess, sitting in the next room with a petty legal official who had been called in for consultation, came out to look at me. But I felt so blessedly happy that I didn't care a twopenny damn, as they say, and I did not give a rap for anybody's sneers or sidelong glances. Zinaida continued to show me special favour and would not let me leave her side. For one forfeit I was made to sit beside her, both our heads covered with one silk handkerchief: I was to tell her *my secret*. I remember how we found ourselves suddenly in a stifling, half-translucent, fragrant haze, how her eyes shone soft and near, how the warm breath came from between her parted lips, and her teeth showed, and the ends of her hair tickled and burned. I was silent. She smiled mysteriously and tenderly, and at last whispered, 'Well, what is it?' but I only blushed, and laughed, and turned away my head, hardly able to draw breath. The game of forfeits grew tedious and we began to play at passing the ring. Heavens, what transports I felt when, having let my attention wander, I was recalled by a sharp and stinging rap on the knuckles from her, and afterwards how I tried on purpose to look as though I were not attending, but she teased me by not touching the hands I thrust forward so prominently!

What did we not do in the course of that evening? We played the piano, and sang, and danced, and acted a gipsy camp – we dressed Nirmatsky like a bear and gave him salt and water to drink. Count Malevsky showed us card-tricks, ending by shuffling the pack and dealing himself a whist-hand containing all the trumps, on which Lushin 'had the honour of congratulating him'. Maydanov recited passages from his poem, 'The Assassin' (this was when the Romantic movement was at its height), which he intended to publish in a black binding, with blood-red capitals; we stole away the cap the legal official was holding on his knee and made him do a Cossack dance to redeem it; we dressed old Boniface up in a woman's cap, and Zinaida put on a man's hat . . . There is no telling the things we did. Belovzorov alone retreated farther and farther into a corner, scowling and angry . . . Sometimes his eyes became bloodshot, he flushed crimson, and it seemed that at any moment he would round upon us and scatter us like shavings; but the young princess would look at him and admonish him with her finger, and he would retreat into his corner.

We were exhausted at last. The old princess was, as she put it, game for anything – no amount of shrieking could disturb her – but even she had grown weary and wanted a rest. It was nearly twelve o'clock when supper was served; it consisted of a piece of ancient, dry cheese and some cold patties filled with chopped ham, that tasted better to me than any dainties; there was only one bottle of wine, and that a strange one: it was dark-coloured, with a swollen neck, and the wine in it looked and tasted like pink paint. Nobody drank it, however. Tired out and blissfully exhausted, I left the house; when we said goodbye, Zinaida pressed my hand and again smiled an enigmatic smile.

The night air blowing against my heated cheeks was heavy and damp; a storm seemed to be brewing; black clouds grew and mounted in the sky, their smoky outlines changing as I watched. A breeze restlessly shivered in the dark trees, and somewhere far below the horizon the thunder muttered faintly and angrily to itself.

I reached my room by way of the back door. My old servant was sleeping on the floor, and I had to step over him; he woke up, saw me, and announced that my mother was angry with me again and had wished to send for me once more, but my father had restrained her. (I never went to bed without saying good-night and asking for her blessing.) That could not be helped!

I told my man that I would undress and go to bed by myself . . . and extinguished the candle. But I did not undress or lie down.

I crouched on a chair, and sat there for a long time, like one under a spell . . . What I felt was so new to me, and so sweet – I sat, hardly looking at anything, without moving, breathing slowly, and at moments laughing silently at some remembrance of the evening or growing inwardly cold at the thought that I was in love, that this was she, that this was love. Zinaida's face floated silently before me in the darkness, floated always in the same spot; her lips smiled just as enigmatically, her eyes looked a little sidelong at me, with a questioning, thoughtful, tender look . . . as at that moment when I parted from her. At last I rose, tiptoed to the bed and, without undressing, cautiously laid my head on the pillow, as if afraid that a sudden movement would scare away the thoughts with which I was filled . . .

I lay down, but I did not even close my eyes. Soon I noticed that faint, intermittent lights were constantly reflected into the room . . . I raised myself and glanced through the window. The frame was sharply distinct against the vague and mysterious paleness of the glass. 'The storm,' I thought; and it was indeed a storm, but passing in the remote distance, so that the thunder was not audible; but long, forked-looking, indistinct streaks of lightning flickered incessantly in the sky; they did not so much flash as flutter and twitch like the wing of a dying bird. I got up and went to the window, and stood there till morning . . . The lightning never ceased for a moment; it was what the people call a 'sparrow's' night. I looked at the silent, sandy, open ground, the dark mass of Neskuchny Gardens, the yellowish façades of the distant buildings, which also seemed to flicker with every faint pulsation . . . I looked – and could not tear myself away: those mute lightnings, those subdued flashes, seemed to respond to the voiceless, secret impulses which had flared up also in me . . . The morning was breaking; pale-red streaks of dawn appeared. With the approach of the sun the lightning-flashes grew steadily paler and shorter: they flickered more and more rarely and disappeared at last, extinguished by the sober and confident light of the risen day.

My lightnings, too, had vanished. I felt a great weariness and peace . . . but Zinaida's image still rode triumphant over my soul. But now this image seemed itself at peace: like a swan in flight above the marshy reeds, it had left behind the other, uncomely figures that had surrounded it, and as I fell asleep, I knelt for the last time before it in farewell and trusting adoration . . .

Oh, gentle emotions, soft sounds, blessed renewed tranquillity of a soul stirred to its depths, fleeting joy of the first tenderness of love – where are you, where are you now?

VIII

The next morning, when I went down for tea, my mother scolded me – less, however, than I had expected – and made me tell her how I had spent the previous evening. I answered her in few words, omitting many of the details, and trying to give everything the most innocent appearance.

'All the same, they are not people *comme il faut*,' remarked my mother, 'and you have no business to be dancing attendance on them instead of getting on with your work and preparing for your examinations!'

Since I knew my mother's concern for my work would be limited to those few words, I did not think it necessary to argue; but after morning tea my father took my arm and, proceeding into the garden with me, made me tell him everything I had seen at the Zasekins'.

My father's influence on me was a strange one, and the relationship between us was strange. He took hardly any interest in my education, but he took care never to hurt my feelings; he respected my freedom, he was even, if I may so express myself, polite to me . . . but he would never let me get near him . . . I loved him, I admired him, he seemed to me a model of what a man should be – and heavens, how passionately I would have attached myself to him, if I had not always felt his hand warding me off! On the other hand, he could, when he wished, arouse in me almost instantaneously, with one word, one gesture, a boundless trust in him. My heart opened, I chattered to him as to an intelligent friend or an indulgent teacher . . . and then, just as abruptly, he dropped me, and again I was held at arm's length – gently and affectionately, but definitely.

He sometimes had fits of gaiety – and then he was ready to romp and play with me like a boy (he liked all kinds of strenuous physical exercise); once – but only once! – he caressed me so tenderly that I could have wept . . . But his merriment and his tenderness alike disappeared without trace, and what had passed between us left me with no more hope for the future than if I had dreamed it all. Sometimes I would scrutinize his clear, handsome, clever face, and my heart would quiver and my whole being yearn towards him . . . and he would seem to feel what was going on inside me and tap my cheek in passing – then walk away, or busy himself with something, or suddenly freeze, as only he was capable of freezing, and I would shrink on the instant and grow cold in my turn. His infrequent fits of favour to me were never evoked by my wordless but unmistakable entreaties; they came quite unexpectedly. Pondering subsequently over my father's character, I have come to the conclusion that he had no time to spare for me – or for family life; his liking lay elsewhere, and he indulged his liking to the full. 'Take what you can, and don't put yourself in anybody's power; to belong to yourself alone is the whole secret of life,' he once said to me. On another occasion I, as a young democrat, allowed myself to argue on the subject of freedom in his presence (that day his mood was what I called 'good'; at such times you could talk to him of anything you pleased).

'Freedom,' he repeated. 'And do you know what it is that can give a man freedom?'

'What?'

'Will, his own will, and it gives power, too, which is better than freedom. Learn to use your will – and you will both be free yourself and command others.'

What my father desired, before all and above all, was life . . . and he lived to the full; perhaps he had a foreboding that he would not have long to profit by the 'whole secret' of life: he died when he was forty-two.

I told my father all the details of my visit to the Zasekins. He listened to me, half attentive, half abstracted, sitting on a garden-bench and drawing in the sand with the end of his riding-whip. From time to time he chuckled, throwing me a bright amused glance, and prompted me with a few words of question or comment. At first I could not make myself even utter Zinaida's name, but I could not long refrain from singing her praises. My father went on chuckling. Then he became thoughtful, stretched himself, and rose.

I remembered that as we left the house he had ordered a horse to be saddled. He was an excellent horseman, and, long before M. Reri, he could break in the wildest horses.

'May I ride with you, father?' I asked him.

'No,' he answered, and his face took on its usual expression of amiable indifference. 'Go by yourself, if you like; and tell the coachman I shall not be riding.'

He turned his back on me and walked rapidly away. I followed him with my eyes until he disappeared beyond the gates. I saw his hat moving along the fence: he turned in at the Zasekins'.

He stayed there no more than an hour, but immediately left for town and did not return home until evening.

After dinner I went to the Zasekins' myself. In the drawing-room I found only the old princess. When she saw me, she scratched her head under her cap with the point of a knitting-needle, and abruptly asked if I could copy out an application for her.

'With pleasure,' I answered, sitting down on the edge of a chair.

'Only see that you write it as big as possible,' said the princess, handing me a dirty piece of paper, 'and could you do it today, my dear young man?'

'Certainly, I will do it today.'

The door of the next room opened the merest crack, and in the opening appeared Zinaida's face – pale and pensive, with hair carelessly flung back; she looked at me with great cold eyes and quietly closed the door.

'Zina, Zina!' said the old woman.

Zinaida did not answer. I took away the old woman's application and sat over it all the evening.

IX

My 'passion' dated from that day. I think, looking back, that my feelings then were like those that a man must have when he embarks on his career: I had already ceased to be merely a young boy; I was a lover. I have said that my passion dated from that day; I might have added that my suffering began with that same day. I languished in Zinaida's absence: I could not concentrate, I could not work, my hands were idle, my over-tense thoughts revolved round her all day long . . . I languished . . . but I was no better off in her presence. I was jealous, I was conscious of my insignificance, I was stupidly rebellious – and stupidly servile; nevertheless, an irresistible force drew me to her, and I crossed the threshold of her room each time with an involuntary thrill of happiness. Zinaida instantly divined that I had fallen in love with her, and indeed I had no thought of hiding it; she laughed at my passion, teased and tormented me. It is sweet to be the sole cause, the despotic and absolute source, of another's heights of bliss or depths of despair – and in Zinaida's hands I was wax. I was not, however, the only one in love with her: all the men who visited the house were beside themselves about her, and she kept them all on a leash – at her feet. It amused her to arouse now their hopes, now their fears, and to spin them about in the wind of her caprices (she called this 'playing people off against one another'), and they never thought of resisting, but submitted willingly. In her whole being, so beautiful and vital, there reigned a peculiarly fascinating blend of cunning and carelessness, artificiality and simplicity, tranquillity and high spirits; over everything she did or said, over every gesture, there was diffused a subtle and delicate charm, in everything there spoke a singular and playful strength. Her face, too, was constantly changing, it too seemed playful: it expressed, almost at one and the same time, mockery, pensiveness and passion. From time to time the most varied moods, as light and swift as the cloud-shadows on a day of sun and wind, chased one another over her lips and eyes.

Each one of her admirers was necessary to her. Belovzorov, whom she sometimes called 'my bear' and sometimes simply 'mine', would willingly have thrown himself in the fire for her; unable to rely on intellectual capacity or other merits, he was always offering her marriage and insinuating that the others' talk was only talk. Maydanov answered to the poetic chords in her soul: a rather cold man, like almost all creative artists, he strenuously assured her, and perhaps himself also, that he adored her, hymned her praises in endless verses, and read them to her in an ecstasy that was at once artificial and sincere. She both sympathized with him and laughed at him a trifle; she had very little faith in him and, when she had listened to his outpourings, would make him read Pushkin in order, as she said, to clear the air. Lushin, the sardonic, cynical-tongued doctor, knew her better than anybody else – and loved her more, although he abused her to her face and behind her back. She respected him, but did not spare him, and from time to time, with special, malicious pleasure, made him feel that he, too, was in her power. 'I am a flirt, I have no heart, I have an actor's nature,' she said to him once in my presence; 'very well, give me your hand, and I will stick a pin in it. You will feel humiliated before this young man, and it will be painful, but all the same, Mr Truthful, you will please laugh.' Lushin blushed and turned away, biting his lips, but ended by submitting his hand. She pricked him, and he did indeed begin to laugh . . . and she laughed, driving the pin deep and looking into his eyes, which he tried in vain to turn away . . .

What I least understood was the relationship existing between Zinaida and Count Malevsky. He was good-looking, shrewd and intelligent, but there seemed, even to me, a sixteen-year-old boy, to be something dubious, something false, about him, and I marvelled that Zinaida did not notice it. But perhaps she did notice the falsity and was not repelled by it. An incorrect upbringing, strange friends and strange habits, the constant presence of her mother, the poverty and disorder of the household – all, beginning with the very freedom the young girl enjoyed and the consciousness of her ascendancy over the people around her, developed in her a kind of half-scornful carelessness and relaxation of standards. Whatever happened – whether Boniface came to announce that there was no sugar, or some wretched scandal came to light, or her guests quarrelled, she used only to shake her curls and say: 'It doesn't matter' – and remain unmoved.

My blood, on the other hand, used to boil when Malevsky went up to her, slinking slyly along like a fox, leaned elegantly over the back of her chair, and began to whisper in her ear with a smug, ingratiating little smile – and she folded her arms on her breast, watched him attentively and herself smiled and shook her head.

'Why on earth are you willing to receive Count Malevsky?' I asked her once.

'He has such a dear, charming little moustache,' she answered. 'And it is no business of yours.'

'You don't think I love him, do you?' she said to me another time. 'No; I cannot love people I am obliged to look down on. I need somebody who could break me . . . And I shan't run into anybody like that, thank God. I shan't fall into anybody's clutches, never fear!'

'Does that mean you will never love anybody?'

'And what about you? Don't I love you?' said she, flicking my nose with the end of her glove.

Yes, Zinaida found me very amusing. For three weeks I saw her every day – and what a dance, what a terrible dance she led me! She came to us only rarely, and I was not sorry for it: in our house she changed into a young lady, a princess – and I fought shy of her. I was afraid of giving myself away before my mother; she did not look on Zinaida with any favour and watched us with unfriendly eyes. I was not so much afraid of my father: he seemed not to notice me, and to her he spoke little, but with particular cleverness and significance. I had ceased to work or read – I had even given up my country walks and my rides. Like a beetle tied by the leg, I revolved ceaselessly round the beloved little house: I think I could have remained there for ever ... but that was impossible; my mother grumbled, and sometimes Zinaida herself turned me away. Then I shut myself up in my room, or walked down to the very bottom of the garden, clambered up on what remained of the ruins of a high stone orangery and, with my legs dangling from the top of the wall which faced the road, sat for hours staring in front of me and seeing nothing. Beside me white butterflies fluttered lazily among the dusty nettles; a bold sparrow perched not far away on a broken fragment of red brick and chirped maddeningly, turning its whole body endlessly from side to side and flirting its tail; occasionally the still mistrustful crows cawed from where they sat high, high up in the bare top of a birch-tree; the sun and wind played softly among its thin, drooping branches; the sound of the bells of the Donskoy monastery came floating to me at intervals, melancholy and subdued, and I sat on, staring and listening, and filled with a nameless emotion that included everything: sadness, and joy, and foreboding of the future, and desire for life, and fear of life. But I understood nothing of this then, and I could not have named any of the feelings that fermented within me – or would have called them all by the same name, the name of Zinaida.

And Zinaida continued to play with me, like a cat playing

with a mouse. Now she would flirt with me – and I grew warm and excited, now she abruptly repulsed me – and I dared not approach her, I dared not even look at her.

I remember that once she was very cold to me for several days together; I lost all self-confidence and, when I slipped over to the cottage to see them, timidly tried to stay near the old princess, although just at that time she did nothing but scold and shout: her monetary affairs were going badly and she had already been twice interviewed by the local policeman.

One day in the garden, as I walked past the familiar fence, I saw Zinaida sitting motionless on the grass, propping herself on both arms. I would have gone cautiously away, but suddenly she raised her head and beckoned imperiously. I stood stock still, not at first understanding what she wanted. She repeated her gesture: I hurriedly leapt across the fence, and was running joyfully up to her, but she stopped me with a look and pointed to the path a few paces from her. Confused and uncertain what to do, I knelt at the side of the path. She was so pale, and every feature expressed such bitter sorrow and such profound weariness that my heart contracted, and I mumbled involuntarily:

'What is the matter?'

Zinaida stretched out her hand, plucked a piece of grass, bit it and threw it as far from her as possible.

'You love me very much, don't you?' she asked at last. 'Do you?'

I did not answer – and indeed, what was I to answer?

'Yes,' she repeated, looking at me as before. 'You do. The eyes are the same,' she added thoughtfully, covering her face with her hands. 'I am sick of everything,' she whispered; 'if only I could go to the ends of the earth! I cannot bear it, it is too much for me . . . And what lies ahead for me? . . . Oh, I am so wretched . . . my God, how wretched!'

'Why?' I asked timidly.

Zinaida did not answer me, but only shrugged her shoulders. I continued to kneel and watch her, filled with the deepest depression. Every word she spoke cut into my heart. At that moment I think I would gladly have given my life, if only she would not grieve. I looked at her, and, although I did not understand what had made her sad, I vividly imagined how, in a burst of unendurable sorrow, she had rushed into the garden and sunk, overwhelmed, to the ground. All around was green and bright; the wind rustled in the leaves and from time to time rocked a long raspberry branch above Zinaida's head. Somewhere doves were cooing, and bees hummed, flying low over the scanty grasses. The sky overhead was tenderly blue – and I felt so melancholy . . .

'Say some poetry,' said Zinaida in a low tone, leaning on her elbow. 'I like you to recite poetry. You sing it, but that doesn't matter, it is your youth. Say Pushkin's "Hills of Georgia". But sit down first.'

I sat down and recited 'The Hills of Georgia'.

'"And it cannot choose but love",' repeated Zinaida, as I

came to the end. 'That is what is good about poetry: it tells us something that isn't true, and yet is not only better than the truth, but even comes nearer to reality . . . "And it cannot choose but love" – it may not want to, but it must!' She was silent again, and then abruptly shook herself and stood up. 'Come along. Maydanov is sitting with my mother; he brought me his poem, and I left him. Now he's upset, too . . . but it can't be helped! Some day you will know . . . only don't be angry with me!'

Zinaida hastily pressed my hand and ran on ahead. We returned to the house. Maydanov at once began to read us his newly printed 'Assassin', but I did not listen. He chanted out his iambic octosyllables in a sing-song voice, the rhymes chimed monotonously, like sleigh-bells, loud and empty, and I went on watching Zinaida and trying to understand the meaning of her last words.

'*Or did a secret rival lurk . . . And overcome you unaware?*' intoned Maydanov – and my eyes met Zinaida's. She lowered hers and blushed slightly. I saw the blush and turned cold with fear. I had been jealous of her before, but it was only at that instant that the idea that she was in love flashed into my mind: 'My God! She has fallen in love!'

X

My real torments began with that moment. I racked my brains, wavered, changed my mind – and ceaselessly, although as far as possible secretly, watched Zinaida. There had been a change in her – that was evident. She went walking alone, and stayed out a long time. Sometimes she would not come near her visitors; she would sit for hours in her own room. She had not been given to that before. All at once I had become, or thought I had, extraordinarily clear-sighted. 'Is he the one? or is *he*?' I asked myself, my thoughts turning anxiously from one of her admirers to another. Privately (although having to admit as much made me ashamed for Zinaida) I thought Count Malevsky the most dangerous.

My watchful eyes did not see beyond the end of my own nose, and my attempts at secrecy probably deceived nobody; at least, Doctor Lushin quickly saw through me. He too, however, had recently changed: he was thinner and, although he laughed just as often, his laughter was hollower, briefer, more ill-natured – an involuntary nervous irritability had replaced his former light irony and assumed cynicism.

'Why are you always trailing over here like this, young man?' he said to me once when we were left together in the Zasekins' drawing-room. (Zinaida had not yet returned from her walk, and we could hear from the attic floor the princess's voice noisily scolding the housemaid.) 'You ought to be studying, you ought to work while you are young, and what are you doing?'

'How can you know whether I work or not at home?' I retorted, not without haughtiness, but also not without embarrassment.

'Work, indeed! No, you have other things on your mind. But I will not argue . . . at your age it is in the nature of things. But you have not made a very happy choice. Don't you see what sort of house this is?'

'I don't understand you,' I observed.

'You don't? So much the worse for you. I consider it my duty to put you on your guard. Old bachelors like me can afford to come here: what could happen to us? We are hardened, nothing can get through our hides, but yours is still soft. The air here is bad for you – believe me; you can be infected.'

'What do you mean?'

'What I say. Are you healthy now? Are you really in a normal condition? Is what you feel really – good for you, or right?'

'And what do I feel?' I said, knowing in my heart that the doctor was right.

'Oh, young man, young man,' went on the doctor with an expression that seemed to say that those two words contained a meaning thoroughly offensive to me, 'what is the use of pretending? Your face still, thank God, shows everything that is in your heart. But who am I to talk? I should not come here myself, if I –' the doctor clenched his teeth – 'if I were not the same kind of fool. Only this is what surprises me: how is it that you, with your brain, can't see what is going on around you?'

'And what *is* going on?' I took up, thoroughly on the alert.

The doctor looked at me with a kind of mocking sympathy.

'I'm a fine one, too,' he said, as if to himself; 'what need was

403

there to tell him? In one word,' he added, raising his voice, 'I repeat: the atmosphere here is not good for you. You may like it here, but it leaves much to be desired. An orangery smells nice, too, but you can't live in it. You do what I tell you, go back to your Kaydanov!'

The old princess came in and began to complain to the doctor that she had toothache. Then Zinaida appeared.

'Now,' added the princess, 'please scold her, doctor. She drinks iced water all day long. Can that be good for her health, with her weak chest?'

'Why do you do that?' asked Lushin.

'What could it do?'

'What could it do? You might catch cold and die.'

'Really? Is that true? Well, what then? – it would serve me right.'

'Really!' grumbled the doctor.

The old princess went out.

'Really!' repeated Zinaida. 'Is life so wonderful? Just look round you . . . Well, do you find it good? Or do you think that I don't understand, that I don't feel it? It gives me pleasure to drink iced water, and you can seriously assert that such a life is sufficiently worth while not to risk it for a moment's pleasure – not to mention happiness!'

'Well,' remarked Lushin, 'whims and independence – those two words sum you up completely: your whole nature is in them.'

'You are behind the times, my dear doctor. You don't use

your eyes, you are getting out of date. Put your spectacles on. I have no use for whims now; making fools of you, making a fool of myself – too amusing for words! But as for independence . . . M. Woldemar,' added Zinaida suddenly, stamping her little foot, 'don't make melancholy faces. I can't bear people to be sorry for me.' She went out swiftly.

'It is bad, this atmosphere is bad for you, young man,' said Lushin to me once more.

XI

That evening the usual guests had gathered at the Zasekins'. I was one of the number.

We were talking about Maydanov's poem; Zinaida praised it whole-heartedly.

'But I tell you what,' she said to him, 'if I were a poet, I should choose different subjects. Perhaps it is all nonsense – but sometimes strange thoughts come into my head, especially when I can't sleep, just before morning, when the sky is beginning to turn grey and pink at the same time. For example, I . . . You won't laugh at me?'

'No! No!' we all exclaimed with one voice.

'I should depict,' she went on, folding her arms on her breast and straining her eyes past us, 'a whole company of young girls, at night, in a big boat, on a calm river. The moon is shining and they are all in white, with wreaths of white flowers, and they are singing, you know, something like a hymn.'

'I understand, I understand. Go on,' said Maydanov, dreamily and significantly.

'Suddenly – noise, laughter, torches, tambourines, on the bank . . . A rout of Bacchanals running along, singing and shouting. But it is your business to paint the picture, Mr Poet . . . only I should like the torches to be red and the smoke thick and the Bacchanals' eyes glittering under their garlands, and the garlands ought to be dark. Don't forget the leopard-skins, too, and goblets – and gold, lots of gold.'

'But where ought the gold to be?' asked Maydanov, tossing back his smooth hair, his nostrils flaring.

'Where? – on shoulders, arms, legs, everywhere. They say the women of antiquity wore golden rings round their ankles. The Bacchanals call the young girls in the boat to them. The girls have ceased their hymn – they cannot continue it – but they do not stir: the river carries them towards the bank. And now suddenly one of them rises quietly . . . This must be well described: how she rises quietly in the moonlight, and her friends are terrified . . . She steps over the side of the boat, the Bacchanals have surrounded her and whirled her away into the night, into the dark . . . Here you must present swirling clouds of smoke, and everything is blurred. But their cries can be heard, and her wreath is left lying on the bank.'

Zinaida was silent. ('Oh, she is in love!' I thought again.)

'And is that all?' asked Maydanov.

'That is all,' she answered.

'That cannot be the subject of a whole long poem,' he commented solemnly, 'but I will use your idea for a lyric.'

'In the romantic manner?' asked Malevsky.

'Of course; romantic, Byronic.'

'In my opinion, Hugo is better than Byron,' said the young count carelessly, 'more interesting.'

'Hugo is a writer of the first class,' said Maydanov, 'and my friend Tonkosheev, in his Spanish novel, *El Trovador* . . .'

'Oh, is that the book with the question-marks upside-down?' Zinaida broke in.

'That is the way the Spaniards do it. I was going to say that Tonkosheev . . .'

'Well, you are going to argue about classicism and romanticism again,' Zinaida interrupted once more. 'We had better have a game . . .'

'At forfeits?' put in Lushin.

'No, forfeits are boring; at similes.' (This was a game Zinaida herself had invented: some object was named and everybody tried to find something to compare it with; the winner was the one who found the best simile.)

She went to the window. The sun had just set; long red clouds stood motionless high in the sky.

'What are those clouds like?' asked Zinaida and, without waiting for us to answer, said: 'I think they are like the purple sails of Cleopatra's golden barge, when she went to meet Antony. Do you remember, Maydanov, you were telling me about it not long ago?'

All of us, like Polonius in *Hamlet*, declared that the clouds were very like those purple sails, and that not one of us would find a better simile.

'How old was Antony then?' asked Zinaida.

'Probably he was a very young man,' remarked Malevsky.

'Yes, he was young,' Maydanov asserted confidently.

'Excuse me,' exclaimed Lushin, 'he was over forty.'

'Over forty,' repeated Zinaida, casting him a quick glance.

I soon left for home. 'She is in love,' my lips whispered of their own accord. 'But with whom?'

XII

The days passed. Zinaida became steadily stranger and harder to understand. Once I went into her room and saw her sitting on a straw-seated chair, with her head pressed against the sharp edge of the table. She straightened herself . . . her whole face was bathed in tears.

'Oh! You!' she said, with a cruelly mocking smile. 'Come here.'

I went up to her; she put her hand on my head and, suddenly seizing a lock of my hair, began to twist it.

'That hurts,' I said at last.

'Ah! It hurts! And do you think I'm not being hurt? Do you?' she repeated.

'Oh!' she exclaimed suddenly, when she saw that she had pulled out a small quantity of hair. 'What have I done? Poor M. Woldemar!'

She carefully smoothed out the tuft of hair, wound it round her finger and twisted it into a ring.

'I will put your hair in a locket of mine and wear it,' she said, and her eyes still glittered with tears. 'Perhaps that will comfort you a little . . . and now goodbye.'

I returned home and found trouble there. My mother was making a scene with my father: she was reproaching him with something or other while he, according to his custom, remained coldly and politely silent – and soon he left. I had not been able to hear what my mother was talking about and, indeed, I was not concerned with it; but I remember that as soon as the interview came to an end she sent for me to her room, and spoke with great displeasure of my frequent visits to the princess, whom she spoke of as *une femme capable de tout*. I kissed her hand (as I always did when I wished to cut a conversation short) and went to my own room. Zinaida's tears had quite distracted me: I absolutely did not know what to think, and was myself near to tears: in spite of my sixteen years, I was still only a child. I no longer thought of Malevsky, although Belovzorov was growing more and more menacing every day and glaring at the shifty count like a wolf at a lamb; but then I did not think of anything or anybody whatever. I lost myself in musing and constantly sought out solitary places. I especially liked the ruins of the orangery. I used to clamber up the high wall and sit there, such an unhappy, lonely and melancholy youth that I felt sorry for myself – and how much satisfaction these sad emotions gave me, how I wallowed in them! . . .

Once, then, I was sitting on the wall, gazing into the distance and listening to the sound of bells . . . when suddenly something passed over me – not exactly a breeze, and not a shiver, but something like a breath, a feeling that somebody was near . . . I lowered my eyes. Below, in the road, Zinaida in a light, pale-grey dress, with an open pink sunshade resting on her shoulder, was walking rapidly towards me. She saw me, stopped, and, pushing back the brim of her straw hat, raised her velvety eyes to me.

'What are you doing there, so high up?' she asked, with a rather odd smile. 'See,' she went on, 'you are always saying that you love me – jump down to me in the road, if you really do love me.'

Almost before she had had time to utter the words, I was flying down, as though I had been pushed from behind. The wall was about fourteen feet high. I landed on my feet, but the impact was so violent that I could not check myself: I fell to the ground and momentarily lost consciousness. When I came to myself, without opening my eyes, I could feel Zinaida close to me.

'My dear boy,' she was saying, as she bent over me – and there was anxious tenderness in her voice, 'how could you do it, how could you listen . . . ? I do love you . . . please get up.'

Her breast rose and fell beside me, her hands touched my head, and suddenly – what were my feelings then? – her soft cool lips began to cover my face with kisses . . . they brushed my lips . . . But here Zinaida must have guessed from the expression of my face that I had come to my senses, although I still had not opened my eyes – and, swiftly raising herself, said:

'Get up, you naughty, crazy boy; why are you lying in the dust?'

I raised myself.

'Give me my sunshade,' said Zinaida, 'you can see I dropped it over there; and don't look at me like that . . . What a stupid trick! Are you bruised? I suppose you stung yourself on the net-tles? I tell you, don't look at me . . . But he doesn't understand, he doesn't answer me,' she added, as though to herself. 'Go home, M. Woldemar, and clean yourself up – and don't follow me, or else I shall be angry, and never again . . .'

She did not finish her sentence, but hurried away, and I sat down in the road . . . my legs would not bear me. The nettles had stung my hands, my back ached, and my head was spinning, – but the sensation of bliss I experienced then has never come to me again in my life. It was like a sweet ache in all my limbs, and it found expression at last in ecstatic leaps and exclamations. Truly, I was still a child.

XIII

I was so proud and happy all that day, I so vividly preserved the sensation of Zinaida's kisses on my face, I remembered every word she had spoken with such a thrill of ecstasy, I so cherished my unexpected happiness, that I was even afraid, I did not even want to see her, the cause of these new emotions. It seemed to me that there was nothing more I could ask of fate, that now it only remained for me 'to take, to breathe one last sigh, and then to die'. But next day, going to the cottage, I felt great embarrassment, which I strove in vain to conceal under the mask of modest ease of a man who wishes it to be known that he can keep a secret. Zinaida received me very simply, without any agitation; she only shook her finger at me and asked if I had any bruises. All my modest ease and discretion vanished on the instant, and my embarrassment with them. Of course, I had expected nothing special, but Zinaida's calmness was like a cold douche: I understood that I was a child in her eyes – and I was very much depressed. Zinaida walked up and down the room, throwing me a swift smile whenever she looked at me; but her thoughts were far away, as I could clearly see . . . 'I ought to bring up the subject of yesterday's events myself,' I thought, 'and ask her where she was hurrying to, so as to know at last . . .' but I renounced the idea and sat down in a corner.

Belovzorov came in; I was delighted to see him.

'I haven't been able to find you a horse for riding, not a quiet enough one,' he said in a severe tone. 'Freitag has one he is willing to vouch for, but I am not convinced. I am afraid.'

'What are you afraid of,' asked Zinaida, 'if I may ask?'

'What am I afraid of? After all, you don't know how to ride. God forbid, but anything might happen! What a wild idea to take into your head all at once!'

'Well, it's my business, my M'sieur Bear. In that case, I will ask Peter Vasilyich . . .' (My father's name was Peter Vasilyich. I was surprised that she should mention his name so lightly and freely, as though she was sure of his readiness to do her a service.)

'So that's it,' retorted Belovzorov. 'You want to ride with *him*?'

'With him or with somebody else, it makes no difference to you. But not with you.'

'Not with me,' repeated Belovzorov. 'As you please. Well, I will get you a horse.'

'And take care that it isn't a cow. I warn you that I want to gallop.'

'Do, by all means. And who is it you intend to ride with, Malevsky?'

'And why not, soldier? Well, calm down,' she added, 'and don't glare at me. I will take you too. You know what Malevsky means to me now – pah!' She shook her head.

'You are only saying that to console me,' muttered Belovzorov. Zinaida frowned.

'It consoles you, does it? . . . Oh . . . oh . . . oh . . . you

413

soldier!' she said at last, as if she could not find another word. 'And you, M. Woldemar, would you like to go with us?'

'I don't like . . . too many people . . .' I muttered, without raising my eyes.

'You prefer a tête-à-tête? . . . Well, each to his taste,' she said with a sigh. 'Run along then, Belovzorov, set about it. I need the horse for tomorrow.'

'Yes, and where shall we get the money?' the princess put in.

Zinaida knitted her brows.

'I shall not ask you for it; Belovzorov will trust me.'

'Trust you, trust you . . .' grumbled the princess, and suddenly shouted at the top of her voice, 'Dunyashka!'

'*Maman*, I gave you a bell,' remarked her daughter.

'Dunyashka!' repeated the old woman.

Belovzorov took his leave; I went out with him . . . Zinaida did not try to keep me.

XIV

The next morning I got up early, cut myself a stick, and set out past the Kaluga Gate. I told myself I would walk to shake off my gloom. It was a fine, clear day, not too warm: a cool, cheerful breeze wandered over the ground, softly rustling and playing, stirring everything and disturbing nothing. For a long time I wandered over the hills and through the woods; I did not feel happy – I had left the house with the intention of giving myself up to melancholy; but youth, fine weather, fresh air, the diversion of brisk walking, the pleasure of lying alone in the thick grass – all had their effect: the recollections of those unforgettable words, and those kisses, came crowding again into my heart. It was gratifying to think that Zinaida could not but recognize my resolution and heroism . . . 'She may think others preferable to me,' I thought; 'let her! They only talk about what they will do, but I did it . . . And I could do the same again, for her! . . .' My imagination was aroused. I saw myself saving her from the hands of enemies, or, streaming with blood, wresting her from a dungeon, or dying at her feet. I remembered a picture hanging in our drawing-room: 'Malec-Adel carrying off Mathilde' – and then my attention was caught by a Greater Spotted woodpecker, busily working its way up the slender trunk of a birch-tree and glancing anxiously from behind it, first on one side, then on the other, like a musician from behind the neck of his double bass.

Then I began to sing 'Is not the white snow', and went on to the well-known ballad of the day, 'I wait for thee when sportive breezes'; then I began to declaim aloud Ermak's address to the stars in Khomyakov's tragedy; I even tried to compose something myself in a sentimental vein, and got as far as thinking of the line which should end the whole poem: 'Oh, Zinaida, Zinaida!' but nothing further emerged. Meanwhile the dinner-hour was approaching. I had come down into a valley; a narrow sandy path wound through it and led to the town. I followed this path . . .

The muffled sound of horses' hoofs came from behind me. I looked round, and involuntarily stopped dead, taking off my cap: I had seen my father and Zinaida. They were riding side by side. My father was saying something to her, his whole body leaning towards her, while he supported himself with a hand on the horse's neck; he was smiling; Zinaida listened silently, her eyes sternly cast down and her lips compressed. At first I saw only the two of them; it was only after some moments that Belovzorov emerged from beyond a turning in the valley, in his hussar uniform and short furred cape, on a black, foam-flecked horse. The spirited animal was tossing its head, snorting and prancing: the rider was both holding it back and at the same time applying the spurs. I stood aside. My father lifted the reins and leaned away from Zinaida, she slowly raised her eyes to his – and both broke into a gallop . . . Belovzorov pounded along in pursuit, his sabre rattling . . . 'He is as red as a lobster,' I thought, 'and she . . . why is she so pale? She has been riding all the morning – and still pale?'

I hastened my steps – and reached home only just in time for dinner. My father, washed, changed, and cool, was already sitting beside my mother's chair and reading to her in his deep, even voice an article in the *Journal des Débats*; but my mother was not attending and, when she saw me, asked where I had got to all day, and added that she objected to people hanging about God knows where with God knows whom. 'But I went for a walk by myself,' I was on the point of answering, then I looked at my father and for some reason said nothing.

XV

During the next five or six days I hardly saw Zinaida: she was said to be unwell, but this did not prevent the usual visitors to the cottage from coming – as they put it – on duty, all except Maydanov, who lost heart and grew despondent as soon as he lacked an excuse for being ecstatic. Belovzorov sat glumly in a corner, buttoned up and scarlet; an unkind smile played constantly on Count Malevsky's thin face; he really had fallen into disfavour with Zinaida, was now making special efforts to get into the old princess's good graces, and had even gone with her in a hired carriage to call on the Governor-General; this excursion, however, proved unsuccessful and even caused trouble for Malevsky: he was reminded of an incident involving certain Transport officers, and was obliged to excuse himself on the ground that at the time he had lacked experience. Lushin came twice a day, but did not remain long; I was a little afraid of him after our last conversation – and felt at the same time genuinely attracted to him. Once he went for a walk in Neskuchny Gardens with me; he was very good-natured and amiable, told me the names and properties of various herbs and flowers, and then suddenly, without either rhyme or reason, as they say, he exclaimed, striking himself on the forehead: 'And I, like a fool, thought she was a flirt! Self-sacrifice is evidently sweet – to some people.'

'What do you mean by that?' I asked.

'Nothing for *your* ears,' rejoined Lushin abruptly.

Zinaida avoided *me:* my appearance – and I could not help but see it – had an unpleasant effect on her. She involuntarily turned away from me . . . involuntarily: that was what hurt, that was what crushed me; but it could not be helped – and I endeavoured not to come into her sight, watching her only from a distance, but I was not always successful in this. As before, something incomprehensible was happening to her: her face had altered, the whole of her was different. I was especially struck by the change taking place in her one calm, warm evening. I was sitting on a low bench under a spreading elder-bush; I was fond of this little corner: from it I could see the window of Zinaida's room. I was sitting there; over my head, in the darkening foliage, a little bird fluttered busily; a grey cat, its spine extended to its fullest extent, was cautiously slinking into the garden, and the first cockchafers buzzed heavily in air still translucent, although no longer bright. I sat and watched the window, waiting in the hope that it would open: it did indeed open, and Zinaida appeared at it. She was wearing a white dress and she herself – her face, shoulders, and arms – was so pale that she too seemed white. She stood there for a long time motionless, and for a long time gazed fixedly straight before her from under knitted brows. I did not even know she was capable of such a look. Then she clenched her hands together, tight, tight, raised them to her lips, her forehead – and suddenly, stretching wide her fingers, shook her hair away from her ears and tossed it back — then with an air of decision nodded her head once and clapped the window shut.

Three days later she met me in the garden. I was turning aside, but she stopped me.

'Give me your hand,' she said in her old affectionate tone; 'it is a long time since you and I had a talk.'

I looked at her: her eyes shone softly and her face seemed to smile through a mist.

'Are you still ill?' I asked her.

'No, I am quite better now,' she answered, plucking a small red rose. 'I am a little tired, but that will pass, too.'

'And will you be the same as before?' I asked.

Zinaida raised the rose to her face, and I thought the reflection of its bright petals fell on her cheek.

'Have I changed then?' she asked me.

'Yes, you have changed,' I said in a low voice.

'I have been cold to you, I know,' Zinaida began, 'but you should not have taken any notice . . . I could not do otherwise . . . But it is no use talking about it.'

'You don't want me to love you, that's it,' I exclaimed glumly, with an involuntary gust of feeling.

'Yes, I do; love me, but not the way you did before.'

'How, then?'

'Let's be friends, that is how.' Zinaida offered me the rose to smell. 'Listen: after all, I am much older than you — I might be your aunt, really; well, not your aunt, but your elder sister. But you . . .'

'You think I'm a child,' I interrupted.

'Well, but a nice, good, clever child I am very fond of. Do you know what? This very day I appoint you my page; and don't forget that pages are not supposed to leave their mistresses. Here is a token of your new dignity,' she added, putting the rose in my button-hole, 'a token of my favour to you.'

'I had another kind of favour from you before,' I muttered.

'Ah!' said Zinaida, with a sidelong look at me. 'What a memory he has! Well, I am still prepared . . .'

And she leaned towards me and impressed a chaste, un-troubled kiss on my forehead.

I could only look at her and, turning away, she said, 'Follow me, my page,' and walked towards the cottage. I followed her, quite bewildered. 'Can this meek, sensible girl,' thought I, 'really be the Zinaida I knew?' Even her walk seemed calmer and her whole figure more stately and graceful . . .

And, God! with what new ardour hope burned within me!

XVI

After dinner the usual visitors gathered at the cottage – and the young princess came out to them. The whole company was present in full force, as on that first unforgettable evening. Even

Nirmatsky had dragged himself along, and Maydanov arrived this time before anybody else – he had brought some new verses. We began another game of forfeits, but no longer with the same wild tricks as before, or the noise and fooling – the gipsyish element had disappeared. Zinaida introduced a new mood into the gathering. I sat near her, as was the right of a page. Among other things, she suggested that anybody who had to pay a forfeit should describe a dream. But it was not a success. The dreams proved either uninteresting (Belovzorov had dreamed that he was feeding his horse on fish, and that it had a wooden head), or unnatural, invented . . . Maydanov treated us to a whole story: it contained tombs, and angels with harps, and talking flowers . . . and voices from nowhere . . . Zinaida would not let him finish.

'If it has come to making things up,' she said, 'let's all tell something that has to be imaginary.'

It was again Belovzorov who had to speak first. The young hussar was embarrassed.

'I can't make anything up!' he exclaimed.

'What nonsense!' retorted Zinaida. 'Imagine, for example, that you were married, and tell us how you would spend the time with your wife. Would you keep her locked up?'

'Yes, I should.'

'And would you remain with her yourself?'

'Certainly I should.'

'Very good. Well, what if that bored her and she betrayed you?'

'I should kill her.'

'And if she ran away?'

'I should catch up with her and still kill her.'

'All right. But suppose I were your wife, what would you do then?'

Belovzorov paused.

'I should kill myself.'

Zinaida laughed.

'I see you can only sing a short song.'

The next forfeit was Zinaida's. She raised her eyes to the ceiling and pondered.

'Listen,' she began at last, 'this is what I have made up. Imagine a magnificent ball-room, a summer night, and a wonderful ball. The ball is given by a young queen. Gold everywhere, and marble, crystal, silk, lights, diamonds, flowers, incense, all the refinements of luxury . . .'

'Do you love luxury?' Lushin interrupted her.

'Luxury is splendid,' she replied, 'and I love everything splendid.'

'More than the beautiful?' he asked.

'Now you are being clever — I don't understand you. Don't interrupt. Well, the ball is magnificent. A multitude of guests, all young, handsome, brave, and all madly in love with the queen.'

'Are there no women among the guests?' asked Malevsky.

'No . . . or wait a moment — yes, there are.'

'All plain?'

'Charming . . . but the men are all in love with the queen. She is tall and shapely . . . and she has a little gold crown on her black hair.'

I looked at Zinaida – and in that moment she seemed to me so far above the rest of us, and there shone from her white forehead and level brows such clear intelligence and such authority, that I thought: 'You yourself are that queen.'

'They are all crowding round her,' went on Zinaida, 'and all lavishing the most flattering speeches on her.'

'And does she like flattery?' asked Lushin.

'What a tiresome man – always interrupting . . . Who doesn't like flattery?'

'One last question,' put in Malevsky: 'has the queen a husband?'

'I hadn't thought about that. No, why a husband?'

'Oh, of course,' Malevsky took up, 'why a husband?'

'*Silence!*' exclaimed Maydanov, who spoke French badly.

'*Merci,*' said Zinaida. 'Well, then, the queen listens to the speeches, she listens to the music, but she does not look at any of the guests. Six windows stand open from top to bottom, from the ceiling to the floor, and beyond them is the dark sky with its great stars and a dark garden with its great trees. The queen is gazing into the garden. There, near the trees, is a fountain; it glimmers white in the darkness, and tall, tall, like a ghost. The queen can hear, through the music and the sound of voices, the quiet plashing of the fountain, and she is thinking: 'You,

423

gentlemen, are all noble, rich, and clever, you are all round me, you treasure every word I speak, you are all ready to die at my feet, I rule you . . . but there, by the fountain, by that splashing water, there stands waiting for me the one I love, the one who rules me. He wears neither rich clothes nor precious jewels, nobody knows him, but he is waiting for me and is sure that I shall come – and I will go, there is no power that can stop me, when I wish to go to him, and be with him, and lose myself with him, there in the darkness of the garden, hearing the rustling of the trees and the splashing of the fountain . . .'

Zinaida was silent.

'And that is . . . all made up?' asked Malevsky slyly.

Zinaida did not even glance at him.

'And what should we do, gentlemen,' said Lushin suddenly, 'if we were among the guests and knew of the happy man by the fountain?'

'Wait, wait,' interrupted Zinaida, 'I will tell you myself what you would each do. You, Belovzorov, would challenge him to a duel; you, Maydanov, would compose an epigram on him – no, stop – you can't write epigrams: you would write a long iambic poem, in the style of Barbier, on him, and publish your work in the *Moscow Telegraph*. You, Nirmatsky, would borrow from him . . . no, you would lend him money on interest; you, doctor . . .' She stopped. 'Well, I don't know what you would do.'

'In my capacity as court physician,' answered Lushin, 'I

should advise the queen not to give balls when she did not want to be troubled with guests.'

'Perhaps you would be right. And you, count . . .'

'And I?' repeated Malevsky, with his evil smile.

'You would give him a poisoned sweetmeat.'

For an instant Malevsky's distorted features gave him a Jewish look, but almost immediately he began to laugh.

'As for you, Woldemar . . .' continued Zinaida; 'however, that's enough. Let's play another game.'

'M. Woldemar, in his capacity as the queen's page, would hold her train when she ran into the garden,' remarked Malevsky venomously.

I flushed, but Zinaida swiftly laid her hand on my shoulder and, rising, said in a voice that trembled slightly:

'I have never given your Excellency any right to be insolent, and therefore I ask you to leave.' She pointed to the door.

'Really, princess,' muttered Malevsky, turning pale.

'The princess is right,' exclaimed Belovzorov, also rising.

'I honestly didn't expect . . .' went on Malevsky, 'I don't think there was anything in my words . . . I had no idea of being offensive . . . Forgive me.'

Zinaida threw him a cold glance and laughed as coldly.

'Stay if you please,' she said with a careless wave of her hand. 'M. Woldemar and I did wrong to be angry. If it amuses you to sting people . . . do, by all means.'

'Forgive me,' said Malevsky again, and I, remembering

Zinaida's gesture, thought that a real queen could not have dismissed a presumptuous person with greater dignity.

The game of forfeits did not last long after this little scene; everybody was somewhat uncomfortable, not so much because of the scene itself as because of another feeling, not altogether definite, but unpleasant. Nobody spoke of it, but everybody was conscious of it in himself and in his neighbours. Maydanov read us his verses – and Malevsky praised them with exaggerated warmth. 'Now he feels he must show us how nice he is,' whispered Lushin to me. We soon dispersed. Zinaida had suddenly lapsed into a fit of brooding; the princess sent out to say that her head ached; Nirmatsky began to complain of his rheumatism.

For a long time I could not sleep: Zinaida's 'story' had made a vivid impression on me.

'Did it contain a hint?' I asked myself. 'And who, or what, was she hinting at? And if there really is something to hint at – how could she venture . . . ? No, no, it can't be,' I whispered, tossing from one feverish cheek to the other . . . But I remembered Zinaida's expression while she talked . . . I remembered the exclamation that had escaped from Lushin in Neskuchny Garden, the abrupt changes in her manner to me – and lost myself in speculation. 'Who is he?' Those three words seemed to hang before my eyes, written in the darkness; it was as though a low, ominous cloud hung over me – and I felt its oppression, and waited for it to burst at any moment. I had grown used to many things lately, I had seen many things at the Zasekins': the disorder, the tallow candle-ends, the broken knives and forks, the gloomy Boniface, the shabby maids, the princess's own manners – all that strange way of life no longer struck me . . . On the other hand, I could not grow used to what I vaguely sensed now in Zinaida . . . 'An adventuress' my mother had called her once. An adventuress – she, my idol, my divinity! The name stung me, I tried to bury myself away from it in my pillow, I grew indignant . . . and yet, what would I not have consented to, what would I not have given, to be that fortunate being by the fountain?

My blood boiled and seethed. 'The garden . . . the fountain,' I thought. 'I will go into the garden.' I dressed swiftly and slipped out of the house. The night was dark; the trees hardly rustled; a peaceful coolness was falling from the sky, the scent of fennel reached me from the kitchen-garden. I walked along all the paths; the light sound of my footsteps both disturbed and emboldened me; many times I stopped, waited, and listened to my heart beating – quick and hard. At last I came near the fence, and leaned against a slender post. Suddenly – or was it only imagination? – a woman's figure slipped past a few paces from me . . . I strained my eyes into the darkness – I held my breath . . . What was that? – could I hear footsteps, or was it the beating of my heart again? 'Who is there?' I murmured almost inaudibly. What was that again? – stifled laughter . . . or a rustling among the leaves . . . or a sigh close to my ear? Terror seized me . . . 'Who is there?' I said again, more softly still.

The air stirred for a moment; a bright streak flashed across the sky: a star had fallen. 'Zinaida?' I tried to ask, but the sound died on my lips. And suddenly everything became still and silent all around, as so often in the middle of the night . . . Even the crickets ceased to chirp among the trees – but somewhere a window was clapped shut. I stood for some time and then returned to my room and my cold bed. I felt a strange agitation, as though I had been to a rendezvous – but found myself remaining solitary, and passing close to the happiness of another.

XVII

The next day I caught only a glimpse of Zinaida, going somewhere in a cab with the princess. But I saw Lushin, who, however, hardly vouchsafed me a greeting, and Malevsky. The young count simpered and began to talk to me amicably. Of all the princess's visitors, he was the only one who had managed to insinuate himself into our house, and my mother had taken to him. My father did not care for him and treated him with almost offensive politeness.

'*Ah, monsieur le page*,' began Malevsky. 'I am very pleased to see you. What is your beautiful queen doing?'

His fresh handsome face was so distasteful to me at that moment, and he looked at me with such contemptuous jocularity, that I made no answer.

'Are you still angry?' he went on. 'You needn't be. After all, I wasn't the one who called you a page, and it is mainly queens who have pages. But allow me to remark that you are not performing your duties properly.'

'Why not?'

'Pages ought to be inseparable from their mistresses; pages ought to know everything they do; indeed, they ought to watch over them,' he added, lowering his voice, 'day – and night.'

'What do you mean?'

'What do I mean? I think I express myself quite clearly. Day – and night. By day it is not so bad; it is light and there are people about; but at night – you can expect trouble at any moment. I advise you to stay awake at night and watch, watch with all your might. Remember – in the garden, at night, by the fountain . . . that is where you must be on your guard. You will thank me afterwards for this.'

Malevsky laughed and turned his back on me. He probably attached no particular importance to what he said; he had the reputation of a hoaxer and prided himself on his ability to baffle people at masquerades, in which he was greatly assisted by the almost unconscious mendacity with which his whole being was imbued . . . He had only wanted to tease me; but every word spread like poison through all my veins. The blood rushed to my head. 'Ah! That's it!' I said to myself. 'Good! So it was not for nothing I felt drawn into the garden! But it must not be!' I exclaimed aloud, striking my breast with my fist, although I really did not know in the least *what* must not be. 'Whether Malevsky himself visits the garden,' I thought (he had perhaps loitered about there: he had enough impudence for it), 'or somebody else' (the garden-fence was very low and it would be no trouble to climb over it), 'it will be the worse for anyone I come across. I don't advise anybody to fall in with me! . . . I will show the whole world, including her, the traitress' (I actually called her traitress), 'that I know how to revenge myself.'

I returned to my room, took out of the desk a recently purchased English knife, felt its sharp edge and, scowling, thrust it with cold and concentrated resolution into my pocket, just as though I found nothing out of the way in such an action and as though it were not for the first time. My heart swelled with bitter malice and seemed turned to stone; all the rest of the day my forehead kept its scowl and my lips remained compressed, and every now and then I paced backwards and forwards, my fingers clutching the hot dagger in my pocket, steeling myself in anticipation of some terrible deed. This new, unfamiliar emotion so occupied and even cheered me that I gave little thought to Zinaida herself. Aleko and the young gipsy in Pushkin's poem were constantly before my eyes: 'Whither, handsome youth? – Lie still . . .' and then: 'You, all blood-bespattered! . . . Ah, what have you done? – Nothing!' How cruel was the smile with which I repeated that 'Nothing!' My father was not at home, but my mother, who had been for some time in a state of almost unremitting dull irritation, noticed my face of doom and said to me at supper: 'Why are you so surly, like a dog with a bone?' In answer, I only smiled in a superior manner, and thought: 'If they only knew!' Eleven o'clock struck; I went to my room, but did not undress: I was waiting for midnight; at length it struck, too. 'It is time!' I whispered through my teeth and, buttoning myself up to the chin, and even tucking up my sleeves, I went into the garden.

I had already picked out a place to keep watch from: at the end of the garden, where the fence separating our part from the Zasekins' joined the boundary wall, grew a solitary fir-tree; standing beneath its dense, low branches, I could see everything happening around me as well as the darkness would allow; past the place wound a path which always seemed mysterious to me: it meandered sinuously by the fence, which at this point showed traces of having been climbed over, and led to a round arbour of close-set acacias. I made my way to the fir-tree, leaned against its trunk, and began my vigil.

The night was as calm as the previous one had been, but there were fewer clouds in the sky, and the outlines of the bushes, and even of the taller flowers, were more plainly visible. The first moments of waiting were trying, even frightening. I had made up my mind to anything! I only wondered how I should proceed. Should I thunder out: 'Where are you going? Halt! Give an account of yourself – or die!' or simply strike? . . . Every sound, every rustle and murmur, seemed to me significant and unusual . . . I prepared myself . . . I leaned forward . . . But half an hour passed, and then an hour: the fever in my veins abated and died away; the realization that this was all in vain, that I had made myself rather ridiculous, that Malevsky had been making fun of me, began to steal into my mind. I abandoned my lying in wait and made a tour of the whole garden. As if to spite me, there was not a sound anywhere; everything was at rest; even the dog was asleep, curled into a ball by the garden gate. I climbed up on the orangery ruins – saw before me the distant open country, remembered my meeting with Zinaida, and plunged into thought . . .

I started . . . I thought I had heard the squeak of a door opening, then the slight crack of a broken branch . . . I came down from the ruins in two bounds – and froze to the spot. Quick, light, but cautious steps sounded in the garden . . . They were approaching. 'Here he is . . . here he is at last!' – the thought darted through my mind. With convulsive movements I pulled the knife from my pocket and opened it – red sparks whirled before my eyes, the hair rose on my head with terror and malice . . . The steps were advancing straight towards me – I stopped, straining towards them . . . A man appeared . . . good God! it was my father!

I knew him at once, although he was wrapped in a dark cloak, with his hat pulled forward over his face. He did not see me, although there was nothing to hide me, but I was so crouched and huddled that I seemed part of the ground itself. The jealous Othello, prepared to commit murder, became a schoolboy on the instant ... I was so terrified by my father's unexpected appearance that at first I did not even notice where he was coming from or in which direction he had disappeared. It was only when everything was silent once more, that I straightened myself and wondered: 'What is my father doing in the garden at night?' In my fright I had dropped my knife in the grass, but I did not even look for it: I felt dreadfully ashamed. I had sobered down in a moment. As I returned home, however, I went to my seat beneath the elder-bush and looked at Zinaida's bedroom window. The small, slightly uneven panes had a dim, bluish glimmer in the pale light of the night sky. Suddenly their light began to change ... Behind them ... I could see this, see it clearly – a white blind was being carefully and quietly lowered; it came down to the window-sill – and remained there.

'What could it have been?' I said aloud, almost involuntarily, when I found myself once more in my room. 'A dream, chance, or ... ?' The conjectures that had come into my head were so new and strange that I simply dared not entertain them.

XVIII

I got up next morning with a headache. The previous day's excitement had vanished. It had been replaced by a gloomy bewilderment and a hitherto unexperienced sadness, as though something within me had died.

'Why do you look like a rabbit with half its brain removed?' said Lushin when he chanced to meet me.

At breakfast I cast stealthy glances now at my father, now at my mother: he was calm, as usual, while she, as usual, was full of secret irritation. I waited to see whether my father would start a friendly conversation with me, as he sometimes did . . . But he did not even give me his usual cold embrace. 'Shall I tell Zinaida everything?' I wondered. 'After all, it makes no difference – all is over between us.' I went to see her, but not only did I not tell her anything, I did not even have an opportunity to talk to her as I wanted. The princess's son, a boy some twelve years old, had arrived from his cadet school in St Petersburg for the holidays: Zinaida immediately put her brother in my charge.

'Here, my dear Volodya,' she said – it was the first time she had called me that – 'is a companion for you. He is called Volodya too. I do hope you will like him; he is a little shy yet, but he has a good heart. Show him Neskuchny Gardens, go for walks with him, take him under your wing. You will do it, won't you? you are so good-hearted, too.'

She placed both her hands caressingly on my shoulders, and I was lost. The arrival of this boy had reduced me also to the status of a child. I looked silently at the cadet, whose gaze was fixed just as silently on me. Zinaida laughed and pushed us towards each other.

'Put your arms round one another, then, children!'

We did so.

'Shall I take you into the garden?' I asked.

'Yes please,' he answered huskily, in a real cadet's voice.

Zinaida laughed again . . . I had time to observe that the colour in her face had never been so lovely. The cadet and I went off. There was a very old swing in our garden. I set him on the thin plank seat and began to swing him. He sat quite still, in his thick, new, cloth uniform with its wide gold lace, and clutched the ropes tight.

'You ought to undo your collar,' I told him.

'It's all right, we are used to it,' he said, clearing his throat.

He was like his sister: his eyes especially recalled hers. It was pleasant to do things for him, and yet all the time a nagging ache gnawed quietly at my heart. 'Today I'm nothing more than a child,' I thought, 'while yesterday . . .' I remembered where I had dropped my knife the day before, and found it. The cadet borrowed it from me, plucked a thick, hollow stalk, cut a whistle from it, and began to blow. The jealous Othello did some whistling too.

But in the evening, how he wept, that same Othello, in Zinaida's arms, when she sought him out in a corner of the garden and asked him why he was so sad. My tears flowed with such violence that she was frightened.

'What is the matter, Volodya, what is the matter with you?' she insisted, and seeing that I did not answer her or stop crying, she took it into her head to kiss my damp cheek. But I turned away and whispered through my sobs:

'I know everything; why have you been playing with me? . . . What did you need my love for?'

'I have done you a great wrong, Volodya . . .' said Zinaida. 'Oh, I am very much to blame . . .' she said, clenching her fists. 'How much bad and dark and sinful I have in me . . . But I am not playing with you now, I love you . . . you do not even suspect why or how much . . . Only . . . what do you know?'

What could I say? She stood before me, looking at me, and I belonged wholly to her, from head to foot, the moment she looked at me . . . A quarter of an hour later, I was running races with Zinaida and her brother; I was not crying, I was laughing, although laughing made tears run from my swollen eyes; round my neck, instead of a tie, was Zinaida's ribbon, and I shrieked with joy when I succeeded in catching her round the waist. She could do as she liked with me.

XIX

I should be in some difficulty if I were obliged to relate in detail how things went with me during the week after my unsuccessful nocturnal expedition. It was a strange, feverish time, a sort of chaos, in which the most contradictory emotions, ideas, suspicions, hopes, joys and suffering whirled like a tornado; I dreaded to look into my own heart, if indeed a sixteen-year-old boy can ever look into his own heart, I dreaded a clear realization of anything whatever – I simply tried to get through the day as quickly as possible; at night, on the other hand, I could sleep . . . helped by a child's irresponsibility. I did not wish to know whether I was loved, and I refused to admit to myself that I was not loved; I avoided my father . . . but Zinaida I could not avoid . . . In her presence I burned as with fire . . . and why should I seek to know what kind of fire it was that melted and consumed me? – it was bliss to be so sweetly melted and consumed. I gave myself up to every passing impression and practised a cunning self-deception, turning away from memories of what was past and shutting my eyes to all forebodings of the future . . . This exhausted state would probably not have endured for very long . . . but a thunderbolt put a sudden end to it and turned my life in a new direction.

When I returned for dinner one day after a rather prolonged walk, I learned to my amazement that I was to dine alone; my father had gone out and my mother was unwell, refused to eat, and had shut herself up in her bedroom. I guessed from the faces of the servants that something extraordinary had been going on. I dared not question them, but I had a friend among them, the young butler Philip, a passionate lover of poetry and an artist on the guitar – I had recourse to him. From him I learned that a terrible scene had taken place between my mother and father (and every word had been audible in the maids' quarters; a great deal of what was said was in French – but the housemaid, Masha, had lived five years with a sempstress from Paris and understood all of it); my mother was reproaching my father for infidelity and for his friendship with the young lady next door, while my father, who began by making excuses, flared up afterwards and in his turn said something cruel 'about madam's age, like', which made my mother cry; my mother had also mentioned a promissory note which had apparently been given to the old princess, and called her many bad names, and the young lady too, and at this my father had been very angry.

'And all the trouble,' went on Philip, 'started with a 'nomynous letter, and nobody knows who wrote it; and if it wasn't for that, there wouldn't have been no reason for any of this business to come out.'

'But was there really anything?' I brought out with difficulty, while my hands and feet grew cold and something fluttered deep in my breast.

Philip winked significantly.

'Yes, there was. You can't hide that sort of thing; your dad was ever so careful this time – but after all you've got to hire a carriage, for instance, and all that . . . and you can't get on without servants, neither.'

I sent Philip away, and threw myself on the bed. I did not burst into sobs or give myself up to despair; I did not ask myself when and how this had all come about; I did not wonder why I had not guessed it before, not guessed it long since – I did not even murmur against my father . . . What I had learned was too much for my strength: the sudden revelation had crushed me . . .

All was over. All my flowers had been torn up in one instant, and they lay around me, scattered and trampled.

XX

My mother declared on the following day that she was moving back into the town. During the morning my father went to her bedroom and stayed there alone with her for a long time. Nobody heard what he said to her, but my mother did not cry any more; she grew calmer and demanded something to eat – but she did not appear or change her mind. I remember that I wandered about all day, but I did not go into the garden and never once looked at the cottage – and in the evening I was a witness of a surprising happening: my father led Count Malevsky by the arm out of the large drawing-room into the hall and, in the presence of the manservant, told him coldly: 'A few days ago your Excellency was shown the door in one house; now I do not propose to enter into explanations with you, but I have the honour to inform you that if you call upon me again, I shall throw you out of the window. I do not care for your handwriting.' The count hung his head, clenching his teeth and cringing, and disappeared.

Preparations began for our removal to town, to our own house in the Arbat. My father himself had probably no desire to stay in the villa any longer; but he had evidently persuaded my mother not to make a scandal; everything was done quietly and without haste, and my mother even sent a polite message to the princess expressing her regret that, on account of her indisposition, she could not see her again before leaving. I wandered about like one crazy, wanting only one thing, the speediest possible end to all this. One idea would not leave my mind: how could she, a young girl – and, after all, a princess – bring herself to take such a step, knowing that my father was not a free man, and having a chance of marriage, even if it was only to Belovzorov, for example? What could she have hoped for? How could she not have been afraid of ruining her whole future? 'Yes,' thought I, 'this is love, this is passion, this is devotion . . .' and I remembered Lushin's words: 'Self-sacrifice is sweet – to some people.' Once I chanced to see a pale blotch in one of the windows of their house . . . 'Can that be Zinaida's face?' I wondered. It was indeed her face. I could endure no longer. I could not part from her without one last word of fare-well. I watched for a favourable moment, and went to the house.

In the drawing-room the older princess received me with her usual slipshod, negligent greeting.

'Why is it, young man, that your people are taking flight so early?' she said, cramming snuff into her nostrils.

I looked at her, and a load was lifted from my heart. What Philip had said about a promissory note had been tormenting me. She suspected nothing, or at least so it seemed to me then. Zinaida appeared from the next room, wearing a black dress, pale and with her hair uncurled; without saying anything she took my hand and led me away with her.

'I heard your voice,' she began, 'and came out at once. Was it so easy for you to desert us, bad boy?'

'I have come to say goodbye to you, princess,' I answered, 'probably for ever. You have perhaps heard – we are leaving.'

Zinaida's eyes were fixed on me.

'Yes, I have heard. Thank you for coming. I was beginning to think I should not see you. Remember me kindly. I treated you cruelly sometimes; but all the same, I am not what you think me.'

She turned away and leaned against the window.

'Really, I am not. I know you think ill of me.'

'I?'

'Yes, you . . . you.'

'I?' said I again, sadly, and my heart began to quiver under the influence of the old irresistible, inexpressible fascination. 'I? Believe me, Zinaida Alexandrovna, whatever you may have done, however cruelly you may have treated me, I shall love and worship you to the end of my days.'

She turned swiftly towards me, opened her arms wide, embraced my head and kissed me hard and fervently. God knows for whom that long, farewell kiss was meant, but I greedily drank in its sweetness – I knew it could never again be repeated.

'Goodbye, goodbye!' I said again and again . . .

She tore herself away and went out. I, too, left. I am not capable of expressing the feeling with which I went away. I should not wish it ever to be repeated; but I should count myself unhappy if I had never experienced it.

We removed to the town. It was long before I cut myself off from the past, long before I could apply myself to work. My wound healed slowly, but I felt no bitterness towards my father. On the contrary, he seemed to have increased in stature in my eyes . . . let psychologists explain the contradiction as they can. Once, walking along one of the boulevards, to my indescribable joy I bumped into Lushin. I liked him for his straightforward and unhypocritical nature, and besides, he was dear to me because of the memories he recalled for me. I rushed up to him.

'Aha!' he said, wrinkling his brow. 'It is you, young man. Let me look at you. You are still yellow, but all the same there is not the same wretched look about your eyes. You look like a man, not a lap-dog. That's good. Well, what are you doing? working?'

I sighed. I did not want to lie, but I was ashamed to tell the truth.

'Well, it doesn't matter,' went on Lushin; 'don't lose faith in yourself. The important thing is to live a normal life and not be carried away by enthusiasms. Otherwise, what's the use? Wherever you allow yourself to drift with the wave, it's bad; a man must stand up, if it's only on a stone – but on his own feet. I'm coughing, you see . . . and Belovzorov – have you heard?'

'Heard what? No.'

'Sunk without trace; they say he's gone to the Caucasus. A lesson for you, young man. The whole point is that some people can't cut loose in time, can't break out of the net. Now you, it seems, have got away safe and sound. See you don't get caught again. Goodbye.'

'I shan't be caught . . .' I thought. 'I shall not see her again.' But I was fated to see Zinaida once more.

XXI

My father went out riding every day; he had a marvellous English horse, a red roan, with a long thin neck and long legs, a tireless and bad-tempered brute called Electric. Nobody but my father could ride him. One day he came to me in a very good mood, such as he had not known for a long time; he was ready to go out and had already put on his spurs. I asked him to take me with him.

'We'd better play leapfrog instead,' answered my father, 'you will never keep up with me on your German pony.'

'Yes, I shall; I'll put on my spurs, too.'

'Very well, then.'

We set out. I had a shaggy, black pony, strong on his legs and fairly mettlesome; it is true that he had to gallop at top speed when Electric was going at a full trot, but nevertheless I was not left behind. I have never seen a rider like my father; his seat was so elegant and carelessly skilful that it seemed as though the very horse under him felt it and showed him off. We rode right along the boulevards, turned on to the Maidens' Field, jumped a few fences (at first I had been afraid of jumping, but my father despised timid people – and so I stopped being afraid), crossed the River Moskva twice, and I was beginning to think we were going back home, especially as my father had noticed that my horse was tired, when suddenly he turned away from me towards the Crimean Ford and galloped off along the bank. I followed him. As he came up to a high pile of old logs, he leapt nimbly down from his horse, told me to dismount, handed me Electric's reins, bade me wait for him there, by the logs, turned into a narrow side-street and vanished. I began to walk backwards and forwards along the bank, leading the horses behind me, and swearing at Electric, who every now and then as we walked would toss his head, shake himself, snort, or whinny, and when I stopped, by turns pawed up the ground with his hoof and, squealing, nipped my pony's neck – who, in short, behaved like a spoilt darling *pur sang*. My father did not return. An unpleasant dampness crept up from the river; a fine rain began to fall softly, making dark little streaks on the stupid, grey logs round which I wandered, and of which I was heartily sick. Utter boredom seized me, and still my father did not come. A Finnish policeman, himself as grey as the logs, with an immense old round hat like a pot on his head and carrying a halberd (what, I wonder, could a policeman have been doing on the bank of the Moskva?), approached me and, turning his wrinkled, old-woman's face towards me, said:

'What are you doing here with those horses, young gentleman? Give them here, I'll hold them.'

I did not answer him; he asked me for tobacco. In order to get away from him (and besides, I was in a fever of impatience), I took a few steps in the direction in which my father had disappeared; then I walked to the end of the cross-street, turned the corner, and stopped. In the street, forty paces away, before the open window of a little wooden house, my father was standing with his back to me; he was leaning his breast against the window-sill, and in the house, half-hidden by the curtains, a woman in a dark dress sat talking to him; the woman was Zinaida.

I was stunned. This, I confess, I had not in the least expected. My first impulse was to flee. 'If my father looks round,' I thought, 'I am lost . . .' but a strange feeling, a feeling stronger than curiosity, stronger even than jealousy, stronger than fear, stopped me. I began to watch, I strained my ears. My father seemed to be insisting on something, and Zinaida refusing to agree. As if it were now I can see her face – sad, serious, beautiful, bearing the inexpressible stamp of devotion, sorrow, love, and something like despair – I can find no other word. She spoke in monosyllables, without raising her eyes, but smiling – meekly and obstinately. From nothing but that smile I could have recognized my old Zinaida. My father shrugged his shoulders and straightened his hat on his head – always a sign of impatience with him. Then I heard the words: '*Vous devez vous séparer de cette . . .*' Zinaida sat up straight and stretched out her arm . . . Then something unbelievable happened before my eyes: my father suddenly raised the riding-whip with which he had been gently beating

445

the dust from the skirts of his coat – and I heard a sharp blow on that arm, bare to the elbow. I could hardly refrain from crying out, and Zinaida started violently, looked at my father in silence and, slowly raising her arm to her lips, kissed the crimsoning weal. My father flung down his whip, rushed up the steps of the little porch, and burst into the house . . . Zinaida turned round – and, with outflung arms and head thrown back, she, too, moved away from the window . . .

In a passion of fear and bewilderment, I fled through the cross-street, where I almost let Electric get away from me, and back to the river-bank. I could not think coherently. I knew that my cold, self-controlled father was sometimes subject to fits of blind fury – nevertheless, I could not grasp what it was I had seen . . . but I felt at that moment that however long I lived it was for ever impossible for me to forget Zinaida's gesture, her look, her smile, that her image, this new image that had so suddenly confronted me, was for ever imprinted in my memory. I gazed unseeingly at the river and did not notice that my tears were pouring down. 'She is beaten,' I thought, 'beaten . . . beaten . . .'

'Well, what are you doing? – give me my horse!' came my father's voice from behind.

Mechanically I handed him the reins. He leapt into the saddle . . . ; the horse, chilled with standing, reared and plunged forward a full ten feet . . . but my father soon mastered him, thrusting the spurs into his sides and striking him on the neck with his fist . . . 'Ha! no whip!' he muttered.

I remembered the recent whistle and slash of that whip – and shuddered.

'What did you do with it?' I asked after a pause.

My father did not answer, but galloped on ahead. I overtook him. I felt I must see his face.

'Did you get tired of waiting for me?' he said through his teeth.

'A little. Where did you drop your whip, though?' I asked him again.

He glanced swiftly at me.

'I didn't drop it,' he said, 'I threw it away.'

He galloped on once more, and I could not overtake him again; I arrived home a quarter of an hour after him.

'So that is love,' I said to myself again that night, sitting at my desk, which had already begun to be strewn with books and papers, 'that is passion. How, I wonder, could anyone not be resentful, how could anyone submit to a blow, from whatever hand . . . even the dearest? But evidently it is possible, if you love . . . And I . . . I imagined . . .'

The past month had greatly matured me – and my love, with all its agitations and sufferings, seemed even to myself something small, and childish and paltry, compared with that other, unknown passion, at which I could hardly even guess, and which frightened me like an unfamiliar, beautiful, but cruel face, which you strive in vain to make out in the half-light . . .

I had a strange and terrible dream that night. I dreamed I went into a small, low, dark room . . . My father stood there with a whip in his hand, stamping his foot; Zinaida crouched in a corner and on her forehead, not her arm, there was a red mark . . . and behind them both rose the blood-dabbled figure of Belovzorov, opening its pale lips and wrathfully menacing my father.

Two months later I entered the university, and six months afterwards my father died of a stroke in St Petersburg, where he had just removed with my mother and myself. A few days before his death he received a letter from Moscow which agitated him extremely . . . He went to my mother with some request and, they say, even wept – my father! On the morning of the day of his stroke, he had just begun a letter to me in French: 'My son,' he wrote, 'fear the love of woman, fear that bliss, that poison . . .' After his death, my mother sent a considerable sum of money to Moscow.

XXII

Four years passed. I had just left the university and was not yet quite sure what to begin to make of myself, or at which door to knock; meanwhile, I was idling the time away. One fine evening I met Maydanov at the theatre. He had by this time married and become a government official, but I could find no change in him. He was still as liable to be enraptured without cause or depressed without warning.

'You know,' he said casually, 'Madame Dolskaya is here.'

'What Madame Dolskaya?'

'Surely you haven't forgotten? The former Princess Zasekina, whom we were all in love with, you included. Don't you remember, in the country, near Neskuchny Garden?'

'She has married some Dolsky?'

'Yes.'

'And she is here, in the theatre?'

'No, here in St Petersburg; she arrived a few days ago. She is going abroad.'

'What sort of man is her husband?' I asked.

'A splendid young fellow, and very well off. He's a colleague of mine, he comes from Moscow. You understand – after that business . . . you must know all about that . . .' Maydanov smiled significantly. 'It was not easy for her to make a good match; there were consequences . . . but with a mind like hers anything can be done. Go and see her: she will be very pleased. She is even prettier than she was.'

Maydanov gave me Zinaida's address. She was staying in the Demuth Hotel. Old memories began to stir in me . . . I promised myself that I would visit my old 'flame' the very next day. But some business turned up: one week passed, and then another, and when at last I made my way to the Demuth Hotel and asked for Madame Dolskaya, I learned that she had died three days earlier – rather suddenly – in childbirth.

It was like a thrust into my heart. The idea that I might have seen her, and had not seen her, and should never see her again – this bitter thought pierced me with all the force of unescapable reproach. 'Dead!' I repeated, staring stupidly at the hall-porter, quietly left the hotel and walked blindly and aimlessly away. All the past rose on the instant and confronted me. This then was the end, it was towards this that the young, ardent, brilliant life had hastened with such eager striving! Thinking such thoughts, I imagined those loved features, those eyes, that hair – in a narrow coffin, in damp subterranean darkness, – there, not far from me, and perhaps only a few steps away from my father . . . I thought of all this, I strained my imagination – and yet, and yet, the words echoed in my inmost heart:

'Tidings of death, by lips uncaring spoken,

My ears uncaring heard . . .'

Oh, youth, youth! you care for nothing, you possess all the treasures of the universe, even sorrow rejoices you, even grief becomes you, you are self-confident and foolhardy, you proclaim: 'Behold, I alone live' . . . and your days speed past and disappear without trace, unnumbered, and everything about you melts away, like wax in the sun, like snow . . . And perhaps the whole secret of your enchantment is, not that you can do everything, but that you can think you will do everything – it is that you scatter to the winds powers that you do not know how to use in any other way, it is that each one of us in all seriousness accounts himself a spendthrift, in all seriousness supposes he has the right to say: 'Ah, what could I not have done, if I had not wasted my time!'

And myself . . . what were my hopes, my expectations, what rich future did I look forward to, when I could spare hardly one sigh, hardly one pang of grief, for the fleeting ghost of my first love?

And what came of all those hopes of mine? Even now, when the shadows of evening begin to fall across my life, what is left to me that is fresher or dearer than the memories of that short-lived storm of a morning in spring?

Yet I malign myself unjustly. Even then, in those youthful, frivolous days, I was not deaf to the sorrowful voice that called to me, the solemn sound that reached me from beyond the grave. I remember being present, by my own irresistible impulse, a few days after I learned of Zinaida's death, at the death of a poor old woman, living in the same house with us. Covered with rags, and lying on bare boards with a sack under her head, she had a hard and grievous end. Her whole life had passed in a bitter struggle against perpetual want, she had never known joy, never tasted the honey of happiness, and it seemed impossible that she should not welcome death, its freedom, its rest. Yet, while her decrepit body still refused to give in, while her breast heaved painfully under the icy hand that had been laid upon it, until her last strength abandoned her, the old woman still crossed herself, still whispered: 'Lord, absolve my sins . . .' – and the expression of terror and of horror of the end in her eyes disappeared only with the last spark of consciousness . . . And I remember that there, at that old woman's death-bed, I was stricken with anguish for Zinaida, and filled with the desire to pray for her, for my father – and for myself.

1860

A LEAR OF THE STEPPES

Characters

Dmítrí Semënych (Semënovich): Mítenka, *the narrator*

Natálya Nikoláevna, *his mother*

KHÁRLOV, Martýn Petróvich

KHÁRLOVA, Evlámpia Martýnovna: Evlámpiyushka, *his younger daughter*

SLËTKIN, Vladímir Vasílyich (Vasílyevich): Volódya, Volódka, *his son-in-law*

SLËTKINA, Ánna Martýnovna, *his elder daughter*

BYCHKÓV: Souvenir, *his brother-in-law*

ZHITKÓV, Gavríla Fedúlych (Fedúlovich)

KVITSÍNSKY, Vikénty Ósipycli (Ósipovich)

Maxímka, Maxímushka

Alexéich

Ereméich

Prokófy

VIKÚLOV

For a Note on Pronunciation, *see p. 5 above.*

A Lear of the Steppes

T HERE WERE SIX OF us gathered together one winter
evening at the house of a very old university friend. The
talk had turned on Shakespeare and his characters, and on the
depth and faithfulness with which they had been drawn, from
the very heart of human nature. We wondered especially at their
truth to life and their universality; each of us could name Hamlets,
Othellos, Falstaffs, even Richard IIIs or Macbeths (these last, of
course, only potentially) with whom he had come into contact.

'And I, gentlemen,' exclaimed our host, a man no longer
young, 'I have known a King Lear!'

'What do you mean?' we asked him.

'Just that. Would you like me to tell you about it?'

'Please do.'

And our friend at once proceeded to tell us the story.

I

All my childhood (he began) and my early youth, until I was fifteen years old, was spent in the country, on the estate of my mother, who was a rich landowner in the Province of ———. Almost the most vivid impression which has remained in my memory of these already distant days is the figure of our nearest neighbour, a certain Martyn Petrovich Kharlov. It would indeed be difficult to efface that impression: I have never met anybody like Kharlov in all my life since. Imagine a man of gigantic stature. On the huge trunk rested, slightly askew, and without any trace of a neck between, a monstrous head; a shock of tousled yellowish-grey hair rose above it, springing almost from the tangled eyebrows. On the wide area of the face, bluish-grey in colour as though it had been skinned, projected a robust knob of a nose, the tiny blue eyes protruded haughtily – and the equally tiny mouth, crooked and pouched, was the same colour as the rest of the face. The voice that issued from this mouth, although husky, was extraordinarily strong and loud ... The sound of it reminded one of iron bars clanking in a cart over a rough road – and Kharlov talked as though he were shouting to somebody on the other side of a wide ravine through a high wind. Kharlov's face was such a vast expanse that it was difficult to say exactly what it expressed ... It was too large to be taken in at one glance. But it was not an unpleasant face, it even showed some majesty, although of a very singular and remarkable kind. And what hands he had – as huge as pillows! What fingers, and what legs! I know I could never look at Martyn Petrovich's back, as broad as a barn-door, or his shoulders like millstones, without a feeling of respectful awe; but what most impressed me were his ears! They were positive jug-handles, full of twists and convolutions; his full cheeks made them stand out high on each side of his head.

Summer and winter alike Martyn Petrovich wore a high-necked wide-skirted coat of green cloth, fastening up one side, with a narrow leather belt, and greased boots. I never saw him wear a cravat and, indeed, I do not know where he could have tied it. His breathing was slow and heavy, like a bull's, but he moved noiselessly. One could suppose that, when he found himself in a room, he was in constant dread of breaking or overturning something and consequently moved from place to place cautiously, usually sideways, and as it were stealthily. His strength was truly Herculean, and he was greatly respected for it in the neighbouring district: in our parts to this day the simple people have a high regard for the warrior-heroes of the legendary past. He was even the subject of legends himself: there was a story that once, meeting a bear in the forest, he had wrestled with and all but vanquished it; another that he had found a peasant, a stranger, trying to rob his bee-hives, and thrown him, horse, cart, and all, bodily over the fence; and so on. Kharlov himself never boasted of his strength. 'If my right hand is blessed,' he used to say, 'it is because it is God's will.' He was proud, but his pride was not in his strength, but in his name and lineage, and in his good sense.

'Our family is descended from a Shwede —' this was his pronunciation of the word 'Swede' — 'a Shwede called Carolus,' he would assert, 'who came to Russia in the reign of Ivan the Blind (that's a long time ago!); and this Shwede Carolus did not want to be a count in the Finnish marches, but he wanted to be a nobleman at the Russian court, and entered his name in the Golden Book. That's where we Kharlovs came from! . . . And for the same reason all we Kharlovs are born with fair hair and blue eyes and white skins: we come from the snowy north!'

'But, Martyn Petrovich,' I would try to argue with him, 'there never was an Ivan the Blind; there was Ivan the Terrible. It was Grand Prince Basil who was called the Blind!'

'You can just go on telling your lies,' Kharlov tranquilly answered. 'If I say something it is so.'

On one occasion, my mother took it into her head to praise him to his face for his really remarkable disinterestedness.

'Oh, Natalya Nikolaevna!' he said, almost vexed. 'What a thing to think of praising a man for! We masters can't do anything else; no serf, no peasant, no underling ought to dare even to think ill of us! I am Kharlov, I derive my name from yonder . . .' (here he pointed his finger to some spot very high above him in the ceiling), 'and *I* to be without honour? How could that be?'

On another occasion a high official, one of my mother's guests, took it into his head to tease Martyn Petrovich, who had again begun to talk about the Shwede Carolus, who came to Russia . . .

'In King Solomon's days?' interrupted the official.

'No, not King Solomon's; Grand Prince Ivan the Blind's.'

'But I fancy your family is much more ancient than that, and even goes back before the flood, when mastodons and megatheria still existed . . .'

These learned terms were quite unfamiliar to Martyn Petrovich, but he knew that he was being laughed at.

'Perhaps so,' he retorted. 'Our family is certainly very ancient: they say that when my great-great-great-grandfather arrived in Moscow, there was a fool there who could match your Excellency, and only one fool like that occurs in a thousand years.'

The official was furiously angry, but Kharlov tossed back his head, thrust out his chin, snorted with laughter, and took himself off. Two days later he turned up again. My mother began to scold him.

'Let it be a lesson to him, ma'am,' Kharlov interrupted, 'not to jump on anybody without finding out who he has to deal with. He's still young and green, he needs schooling.'

The official was almost the same age as Kharlov; but the giant habitually thought of everybody else as not fully grown. He was sturdily confident in himself.

'What can anybody do to me? I should like to see the man

who would try!' he would say, and laugh his abrupt, short, but deafening laugh.

II

My mother was very particular in her acquaintances; but she always made Kharlov especially welcome and forgave him much: twenty-five years earlier he had saved her life by holding back her carriage on the brink of a deep ravine into which the horses had already plunged. The traces and breech-straps broke, but Martyn Petrovich did not loose his hold on the wheel he had seized, although the blood spurted from under his fingernails. My mother found a wife for him, too: a seventeen-year-old orphan whom she had brought up in her own house; he, at that time, was turned forty. Martyn Petrovich's wife was frail – they say he lifted her over his threshold with one hand – and she had not long to live with him; but she bore him two daughters. After her death, my mother continued to take a benevolent interest in Martyn Petrovich; she got his elder daughter accepted at an Imperial boarding-school and later found a husband for her – and she already had another in mind for the younger daughter. Kharlov managed his estate – he had nearly nine hundred acres of land – pretty well; little by little he was doing some building, and his peasants did as he told them, no question of that! Because of his weight, Kharlov went hardly anywhere on foot:

462

the ground would not bear him. He went everywhere in a low racing droshky, himself driving the horse, a lean thirty-year-old mare with the scar of an old wound on her shoulder: she had received the wound at the battle of Borodino, where she carried the sergeant-major of a regiment of heavy cavalry. This horse always seemed to be lame in all four legs at once; it could not go at a walk, but only at a bouncing shaky jog-trot; it used to eat the wormwood and other coarse weeds growing between the fields, a thing I never saw any other horse do. I remember that I used to wonder how this half-dead, broken-down old crock could pull such a terrific load. I dare not even tell you how many poods our neighbour weighed. His swarthy page-boy, Maximka, was always stationed behind Martyn Petrovich's back in the droshky. With his whole body and face pressed against his master, and his bare feet supported by the back axle, he looked like a leaf or a caterpillar accidentally caught on the gigantic carcass towering in front of him. This boy used to shave Martyn Petrovich once a week. To perform this operation, they say, he had to stand on a table; some facetious persons averred that he was obliged to run round his master's chin. Kharlov did not like to stay at home for long, and therefore was very often to be seen driving about in his invariable turnout, the reins gathered into one hand (the other, with the elbow well turned out, rested on his knee), with a minute old cap perched on the very top of his head. His little, bearish eyes gazed briskly round, his thunderous voice hailed all the peasants, tradesmen, and merchants they met; the village priests, whom he much disliked, he showered with blessings, and once, drawing level with me (I was out with a gun), he raised such a hullaballoo over a hare crouching by the roadside that my ears were still ringing with the noise that evening.

III

My mother, as I have said, was always glad to welcome Martyn Petrovich; she knew the deep respect he felt for her. 'Madam! my lady! Flower of our countryside!' That was how he addressed her. He praised her beneficence, and she saw in him her devoted giant, who would not hesitate to come to her rescue alone against a horde of moujiks; and although even the possibility of such an encounter was not to be anticipated, yet my mother held that, in the absence of a husband (she was widowed early in life), she ought not to despise a protector like Martyn Petrovich. Besides, he was an upright man, subservient to nobody, he never borrowed money, he did not drink, and he was no fool, either, although he had never had any education. My mother trusted Martyn Petrovich. When she wanted to make her will, she asked him to witness it, and he went home on purpose for his round steel spectacles, without which he could not write; even with the spectacles on his nose it took him a full quarter of an hour, panting and puffing, to inscribe his rank, Christian name, patronymic, and surname in huge square letters with flourishes and long tails; when he had finished his labours he remarked that he was tired and that, for his part, he would as soon catch a flea as write. Yes, my mother esteemed him . . . but he was never invited farther into our house than the dining-room. A really very strong odour proceeded from him: he smelt of the soil, of wind-fallen trees, of swamp mud. 'A regular wood-goblin!' declared my old nurse. At dinner, a special table was laid for Martyn Petrovich in a corner, and he was not offended by this; he knew that it was uncomfortable for other people to sit beside him, and he himself felt freer to eat: and he ate as I suppose nobody else has eaten since Polyphemus. He was always supplied, as a precaution, with a bowl of some six pounds of *kasha* at the very beginning of dinner. 'Otherwise, you know, you will eat me up,' my mother used to say. 'Even as it is, I shall eat you up, ma'am, my lady!' Martyn Petrovich would reply, grinning.

My mother liked to listen to his opinions on any subject connected with estate management; but she could not endure his voice for long at a time.

'Really, my dear man!' she would exclaim, 'Surely you could at least take something for it! You've absolutely deafened me. What a trumpet!'

'Natalya Nikolaevna! Benefactress!' Martyn Petrovich used to answer. 'I am not responsible for my throat. Besides, what sort of medicine could I take – can you tell me that? I had better not talk for a bit.'

I really do not think that any medicine could have affected Martyn Petrovich. He had never been ill in his life.

He was no good at telling a story, and did not like to try. 'Talking a long time makes me out of breath,' he would say reproachfully. But when he was led on to the subject of 1812 (he served in the militia and received a bronze medal which he wore on special occasions on the ribbon of his Order of Vladimir), and asked about the Frenchies, he would produce some stories of a sort, although at the same time he constantly asserted that no Frenchman had arrived in Russia, not real ones, only free-booters, marauding from hunger, and that he had thrashed a lot of that riff-raff in the forests.

IV

And yet even this sturdily self-reliant, indestructible giant was visited by moments of doubt and melancholy. He would suddenly fall into despondency without any visible cause; then he shut himself up alone in his room and buzzed — literally buzzed, like a whole swarm of bees; or else he called his boy, Maximka, and ordered him to read aloud from the only book that had ever strayed into his house, an old volume of Novikov's *Gentle Labourer* — or else to sing. And Maximka, who was just able, by some freak of chance, to spell out elementary words, would begin chanting, with breaks between the syllables and misplaced accents, sentences like:

'But the sen-sú-al man dé-duces, from this void which he finds in cre-á-tures, quite con-tra-dic-tory con-clu-sions. No cre-á-ture, he says, is ca-pa-ble of bestowing hap-pi-ness,' and so on. Or he would intone in the squeakiest little voice imaginable a mournful ditty of which nothing was distinguishable but 'Ee . . . i . . . eh . . . ee . . . eh . . . ee . . . ah . . . oh . . . oo . . . ee . . .' And Martyn Petrovich would shake his head and talk of how everything is transitory, everything is dust and ashes, fading like the grass of the field, passing away to return no more. He had somehow got hold of a little picture which showed a lighted candle and winds, with puffed out cheeks, blowing on it from all sides; underneath was an inscription, 'Such is the life of man!' He took a great fancy to it and hung it up in his own room; but at ordinary times, when he was not melancholy, he used to turn its face to the wall so that it should not disturb him. Kharlov the colossus was afraid of death. He very seldom had recourse to the assistance of religion or to prayer, even in his fits of melancholia; even then he trusted more in his own good sense. He had no great bent towards piety; he was not often seen in church; it is true that he used to say he didn't go there for the reason that he was afraid his bulk would squeeze everybody else out. Martyn Petrovich's fits of gloom usually ended by his beginning to whistle – and suddenly he would thunder out an order for his droshky to be harnessed and drive off somewhere, flourishing his free hand over the brim of his cap, not without bravado, as though to say, 'Now everything is as right as rain!' He was a true Russian.

V

Enormously powerful men like Martyn Petrovich are usually of phlegmatic disposition; he, on the contrary, was rather easily irritated. He lost patience especially readily with his dead wife's brother, who was given asylum in our house in the capacity half of clown, half of hanger-on – a certain Bychkov, who had been nicknamed Souvenir almost as a baby, and remained Souvenir to everybody, even the servants, who, I assure you, called him Souvenir Timofeich. I don't think even he himself knew his real name. He was a pitiful creature, whom everybody looked down on: in one word, a dependant. All the teeth were missing from one side of his mouth, which gave his little wrinkled face a distorted look. He was always restless and on the move, creeping into the maids' workroom or the estate office, off to the town to see the priests, or else to the bailiff's house; everywhere he was driven away, but he only cowered and screwed up his squinting little eyes, and laughed in a nasty, gurgling way, like somebody rinsing out a bottle. I always thought that if Souvenir had had any money, he would have developed into the worst of men, immoral, wicked, even cruel. Poverty 'docked' him willy-nilly. He was allowed drink only on holidays. He was decently dressed, by my mother's orders, since he had to play piquet or boston with her in the evenings. Souvenir was always saying 'Immejitly, if you please, immejitly . . .' 'And what is *immejitly*?' my mother would ask severely. He would instantly draw back his wildly waving arms, and murmur in a subdued way, 'As you will, madam.' Listening at keyholes, carrying tales, and, above all, teasing and 'prodding' people, were his only occupations, and he 'prodded' as though it were his right, as though he were taking his revenge for something. He called Martyn Petrovich dear brother, and hated him worse than poison. 'Why did you drive my sister Margarita Timofeevna to her death?' he would nag away, revolving before him, with a titter. On one occasion Martyn Petrovich was sitting in the billiard-room, where it was cool, and where nobody had ever seen a single fly; our neighbour, who shunned heat and sun, greatly favoured it on that account. He was sitting between the wall and the billiard-table. Souvenir slipped past his 'belly', grimacing and planting his verbal darts . . . Martin Petrovich, wishing to thrust him away, moved both his arms forward. Luckily for Souvenir, he managed to dodge, and his dear brother had to steady his hands on the edge of the billiard-table – and the heavy wooden table jumped off all six of the screws that held it . . . How flat Souvenir would have been crushed if those powerful hands had touched him.

VI

I had long been curious to see the home Martyn Petrovich had built for himself; what sort of house was it? Once I volunteered to ride with him to Eskovo (that was the name of his estate). 'There now! You want to see my territory,' said Martyn Petrovich. 'All right! I'll show you the garden, and the house, and the threshing-floor, and everything else. I have lots of everything!' We set out. It was only three versts from our village to Eskov. 'There it is, that's my territory!' Martyn Petrovich suddenly thundered out, trying to turn his immovable head and waving his arm to right and left. 'This is all mine!' Kharlov's house, with its outbuildings, was on the crest of a slope, on which a few miserable little peasants' huts clung round a small pond. At the edge of the pond, on a raft, an old woman in a checked home-spun skirt was thrashing her tightly wrung linen with a paddle.

'Axinya!' roared Martyn Petrovich, so loud that the rooks rose in a flock from the near-by oat-field. 'Washing your husband's britches?'

'That's right, my dear,' her voice came faintly.

'Good, good! Now look,' Martyn Petrovich went on, trotting past the rotting hurdle fence, 'this is my hemp, and that over there is the peasants'; do you see the difference? And here is my garden; I planted the apple-trees, and the willows, too. Otherwise there wouldn't be any trees here at all. Yes, that's right; there's a lesson here for you.'

We turned into a courtyard, surrounded by a fence; directly opposite the gates stood an ancient, ramshackle little structure with a thatched roof and a minute porch supported by thin posts; beside it was another, rather newer, and with a tiny upper floor, but it also stood on spindly legs. 'Here's something else for you to learn', said Kharlov; 'you can see the kind of little houses our fathers lived in; and now look what a mansion I have built for myself.' The mansion looked like a house of cards. Five or six dogs, each shaggier and uglier than the last, barked a welcome to us. 'Sheep dogs,' remarked Martyn Petrovich. 'Real Crimeans! Shut up, you noisy brutes! I'll hang the lot of you if you don't look out!' On the porch of the new house appeared a young man in a long nankeen overall, the husband of Martyn Petrovich's elder daughter. Hurrying swiftly to the droshky, he respectfully supported his father-in-law by the elbow as he got down, and even made a gesture with one hand as though he would take hold of the giant leg that Martyn Petrovich, leaning his body forward, was bringing with a great swing over the driving-seat; then he helped me off my horse.

'Anna!' shouted Kharlov. 'Natalya Nikolaevna's boy has come to see us; we must give him something to eat. And where is Evlampiyushka?' (Anna was the name of his elder daughter, Evlampia of the younger.)

'She is not at home; she had gone to pick cornflowers in the fields,' replied Anna, appearing at the little window by the door.

'Have we some curds?' asked Kharlov.

'Yes.'

'And cream?'

'Yes.'

'Well, put it on the table, and meanwhile I will show him my room. Please come in, come this way,' he added, turning to me and beckoning with his forefinger. In his own house he did not call me 'thou': a host must be courteous. He led me along a passage. 'This is my part of the house,' he said, stepping sideways across the threshold of a wide door. 'And here is my room. Please come in.'

The room proved to be large, unplastered and almost empty; on nails unsymmetrically driven into the walls there hung two whips, a rusty three-cornered hat, a single-barrelled gun, a sabre, an odd-looking horse-yoke decorated with metal plates, and the picture showing a burning candle with the winds blowing on it; in one corner stood a wooden sofa, covered with a bright-coloured carpet. Hundreds of flies buzzed on the ceiling; the room, however, was cool, but it smelt very strongly of the peculiar forest odour which accompanied Martyn Petrovich everywhere.

'Well, do you like my room?' asked Kharlov.

'Very much.'

'Have a look at my Dutch yoke over there,' Kharlov went on, slipping into the habit of 'thouing' me again. 'It's a marvellous yoke. I swapped something with a Jew for it. Look at it!'

'It's a very good yoke.'

'It's meant for use – no fancy stuff. And just smell it . . . what leather!'

I sniffed at the yoke. It smelt of musty train-oil, nothing more.

'Well, sit down – there on that nice little chair. Make yourself comfortable,' said Kharlov, lowering himself on to the sofa, where he closed his eyes and seemed to doze off, even emitting a gentle snore.

I watched him in silence, and could not contain my wonder: a mountain, that was what he was! Suddenly he started up.

'Anna!' he shouted, and his huge belly rose and fell like the waves of the sea. 'What are you doing? Hurry up! Didn't you hear me?'

'It's all ready, father; come along,' answered his daughter's voice.

I marvelled inwardly at the speed with which Martyn Petrovich's commands had been carried out, as I followed him into the drawing-room, where the food already waited on a table covered with a red cloth, embroidered with white arabesques: there were curds, cream, wheaten bread, even powdered sugar and ginger. While I dealt with the curds, Martyn Petrovich, amicably grumbling, 'Eat, my young friend, eat, my dear; don't despise our country fare,' once more sat down in a corner and again seemed to doze off. In front of me, with downcast eyes, Anna Martynovna stood motionless, and through the window I could see her husband walking my pony up and down the yard and wiping the chain of the snaffle with his own hands.

VII

My mother did not care for Kharlov's elder daughter; she thought her stuck-up. Anna Martynovna hardly ever called on us, and she behaved in my mother's presence with cold formality, although she was indebted to her for her boarding-school education and her marriage, and on her wedding day had received from her a thousand paper roubles and a yellow Turkish shawl, admittedly a little worn. She was a spare woman of medium height, very quick and lively in her movements, with masses of red hair and a beautiful, dark-skinned face in which the narrow, pale-grey eyes had a strange but attractive appearance; she had a straight, thin nose, lips that were also thin and a pointed chin. Anybody looking at her would probably have thought, 'Well, you've got a sharp mind – and a sharp temper, too!' With all this, there was something very attractive about her; even the dark moles, scattered like buckwheat over her face, suited her and enhanced the impression she created. With her hands thrust under the ends of her kerchief, she stood looking stealthily down on me (I was seated, she remained standing); an unkind smile strayed about her lips and cheeks and in the shadow of her long lashes. 'Oh, you're a spoilt young gentleman,' the smile seemed to say. With every breath she drew her nostrils dilated slightly, and this also was a little strange; but even so, it seemed to me that if Anna Martynovna were to love me, or even feel a desire to kiss me with those thin harsh lips, I should leap as high as the ceiling with rapture. I knew she was very stern and exacting, and that the peasant women and girls feared her like fire, but what did that matter? Anna Martynovna secretly excited my imagination . . . However, I was only fifteen then, and at that age . . . !

Martyn Petrovich started awake again.

'Anna!' he shouted, 'you might give us a tune on the piano-forte . . . Young gentlemen like that.'

474

I looked round: there was a pitiful semblance of a pianoforte in the room.

'Certainly, father,' answered Anna Martynovna. 'Only what shall I play for him? It won't amuse him very much.'

'Well, what did they teach you in your *boor*ding-school?'

'I've forgotten it all . . . and besides, the strings are broken.'

Anna Martynovna's voice was very pleasant; clear and plaintive, like the note of a bird of prey.

'Well,' said Martyn Petrovich, beginning to ponder. 'Well,' he began again, 'wouldn't you like to see the threshing-floor, and look round a little? Volodka will take you. Hi, Volodka,' he shouted to his son-in-law, who was still walking up and down the yard with my horse. 'Just take this young man to the threshing-floor . . . and generally . . . show him my farm. I must have a nap. That's right! Goodbye to you, my dear boy!'

He went out, and I followed him. Anna Martynovna at once began to clear the table, briskly, as though she was annoyed with it. On the threshold I turned round and bowed to her; but she seemed not to notice my bow, and only smiled again, even more nastily than before.

I took my horse from Kharlov's son-in-law and led it by the bridle. We went together to the threshing-floor, but since we discovered nothing particularly interesting there, and since he could not expect to find a passion for farming in a young boy like me, we returned through the garden to the road.

VIII

I knew Kharlov's son-in-law well: he was called Vladimir Vasilyevich Slëtkin; he was the orphaned son of a petty official, my
mother's agent in money matters, and she had brought the boy
up. He was first placed in the district school, then he entered
the 'patrimonial' office, later became a clerk in a government
warehouse, and finally married Martyn Petrovich's daughter. My
mother called him the little Jew, and certainly he reminded one
of the Jewish type, with his curly hair, his black eyes, always
moist-looking, like boiled prunes, his hawk-like nose and wide
red mouth, but his skin was white and he was altogether quite
good-looking. He had an obliging disposition, except when his
personal advantage was concerned. Then he was beside himself
with anxious greed even to the point of weeping; he was ready to
whine and beg all day over a bit of rag; if he had been promised
anything he would mention it a hundred times, and be offended
and whimper if the promise were not immediately carried out.
He was fond of wandering about the countryside with a gun;
and when he succeeded in bagging a hare or a duck he would
put his booty in his knapsack with immense satisfaction, saying
'There, now play what tricks you like, you won't get away! Now
you are *mine*!'

'Yours is a nice pony,' he said in his lisping voice, helping me
into the saddle, 'I wish I had a little horse like that! But where

should I get one? It's not my luck. If you were just to ask your mother . . . remind her!'

'Did she promise you one?'

'Promise? No; but I thought, out of the great kindness of her heart . . .'

'You ought to try Martyn Petrovich.'

'Martyn Petrovich!' repeated Slëtkin, with long-drawn-out emphasis, 'as far as he is concerned I mean no more than any nobody of a boy like Maximka. He treats us like dirt, and no mistake, and we've nothing from him to show for all our hard work!'

'Really?'

'As true as I'm standing here. When he says, "My word is sacred!" – well, it's like an axe coming down. You can ask as much as you want, it makes no difference. And besides, Anna Martynovna, my wife, isn't a favourite with him, like Evlampia Martynovna.'

'Oh, my God, oh, heaven protect us!' he suddenly interrupted himself, wringing his hands in despair. 'Look! what's happened? Some rogue has cut down half a rod of oats, our oats. There's a fine thing! . . . What a life! Thieves, robbers! It's true what they say, I tell you: never trust Eskovo, Beskovo, Erino, Belino!' (these were the names of four neighbouring villages). 'Oh, oh, this is terrible! Just think, a rouble and a half, or even two, lost!'

There was almost the sound of sobbing in Slëtkin's voice. I nudged my horse's ribs and left him.

I was still within range of Slëtkin's outcries when suddenly, at a turn in the road, I came upon Kharlov's second daughter, Evlampia, who, according to Anna Martynovna, had been looking for cornflowers in the fields. A thick crown of the flowers encircled her head. We silently exchanged bows. Evlampia was also very good-looking, as much so as her sister, but in a different way. She was tall and heavily built; everything about her was on a large scale: head, and hands, and feet, and snow-white teeth and especially the prominent languishing eyes, darkest blue like glass bugles; everything about her was positively monumental (it was not for nothing that she was Martyn Petrovich's daughter), but beautiful. She plainly did not know what to do with her thick braid of fair hair, and wore it wound three times round her head. Her mouth was charming, as fresh as a rose, and as red as raspberries, and when she talked, the centre of her upper lip lifted in a delightful way. But there was something wild and almost fierce in the glance of her enormous eyes. 'A wild, free creature – Cossack blood,' Martyn Petrovich said of her. I was a little afraid of her . . . This stately beauty reminded me of her father.

As I rode a little farther, I heard her singing in a strong, even rather harsh voice, a regular peasant's voice; then she stopped suddenly. I looked round and from the top of the hill saw her standing with Kharlov's son-in-law by the plot where the oats had been cut. He was waving his arms and pointing, but she stood motionless. The sun lighted up her tall figure and the crown of cornflowers on her head was clear bright blue.

IX

I think I have already told you, gentlemen, that my mother had a husband in view for Kharlov's second daughter also. He was one of our poorest neighbours, a retired army major, Gavrila Fedulych Zhitkov, a man no longer young and, as he himself put it, not without some smugness, as though it were a recommendation, 'battered and broken'. He could barely read or write and was very stupid, but he secretly hoped to become my mother's steward, for he felt himself to be an 'executive'. 'If nothing else, smashing in the teeth of the peasants is something I understand down to the ground,' he would say, almost clashing his own teeth, 'because I got used to it,' he explained, 'in my former employment, I mean.' If Zhitkov had been less stupid, he would have known that the position of my mother's steward was precisely what he had not the least chance of obtaining, since to do so he would have had to supersede her present steward, one Kvitsinsky, a self-willed and capable Pole, whom my mother trusted completely. Zhitkov had a long horsy face, completely overgrown with dust-coloured hair, even to his cheeks just under the eyes, and in the very coldest weather it was bathed in abundant sweat, like dew-drops. When he saw my mother he would instantly spring to attention, his head beginning to quiver with zeal, his great hands lightly clapping his thighs, and his whole figure seeming to clamour, 'Command me! . . . I will leap to obey!' My mother had no illusions about his capabilities, but this did not prevent her from making his marriage to Evlampia her concern.

'Only will you be able to manage her, my friend?' she asked him once.

Zhitkov smiled complacently.

'Come, Natalya Nikolaevna! I have kept a whole company in order, I made them toe the line, and what is this? Child's-play!'

'That was a company of soldiers, my friend, and this is a girl of good family, and a wife,' remarked my mother with displeasure.

'Really, Natalya Nikolaevna, madame!' exclaimed Zhitkov again. 'We can understand all that very well. In short, a young lady, a tender plant!'

'Well,' my mother decided at last, 'Evlampia won't take anything lying down.'

X

Once – towards evening of a day in June – a manservant announced Martyn Petrovich. My mother was astonished: we had not seen him for more than a week, and he never came to see us so late. 'Something has happened!' she exclaimed in an undertone. Martyn Petrovich's face, when he blundered into the room and immediately sank into a chair near the door, had such a singular expression and looked so abstracted and even pale that my mother involuntarily repeated her exclamation aloud. Martyn Petrovich fixed his little eyes on her, remained silent for a moment, sighed heavily, was silent again, and at last declared that he had come about a certain matter . . . which . . . of such a kind, that because of . . .

With these disjointed phrases he rose abruptly and went out.

My mother rang and ordered the footman who answered the bell to follow Martyn Petrovich immediately and bring him back without fail, but he had by then had time to get into his droshky and drive away.

The next morning my mother, who was surprised and indeed troubled, alike by Martyn Petrovich's strange behaviour and by his extraordinary expression, was on the point of sending a messenger to him when he again made his appearance. This time he seemed calmer.

'Tell me, my dear friend,' exclaimed my mother as soon as she saw him, 'tell me, what on earth is the matter with you? Yesterday I really thought, "Good heavens!" I thought, "has our old friend suddenly gone clean out of his mind?"'

'No, ma'am, I have not gone out of my mind,' answered Martyn Petrovich; 'I am not that sort of man. But I need your advice.'

'What about?'

'But I am in doubt whether what I have to communicate will be pleasing to you . . .'

'Speak, speak, my good man, but a little more simply. Don't alarm me so! What is the point of it? Speak more simply. Have you got another attack of melancholia?'

Kharlov frowned.

'No, it's not my melancholia – I have that when the moon is new; but allow me to ask you, ma'am, what you think about death?'

My mother was startled.

'About what?'

'About death. Is it possible for death to spare anybody whatever on this earth?'

'What notion have you taken into your head now, my dear sir? Which of us is immortal? Even you, giant though you may be – your end will come too.'

'It will come, oh, it will come!' Kharlov chimed in, casting down his eyes. 'I have been sent a dream . . .' he said slowly, at last.

'What did you say?' my mother interrupted.

'A dream,' he repeated. 'I have the gift of seeing things in dreams, you know!'

'You?'

'Yes, I. Didn't you know?' Kharlov sighed. 'Well, then . . . I was having a nap, ma'am, a week ago and more, right on the eve of St Peter's fast; I lay down after dinner for a little rest, and I fell asleep; and I dreamed that a black foal came running into my room. And this same foal began kicking up its heels and showing its teeth. A foal as black as a beetle.'

Kharlov stopped speaking.

'Well?' said my mother.

'And all of a sudden this foal turned round and gave me a kick on the left elbow, right on the point! I woke up: and I really couldn't move my arm, or my left leg either. Well, I thought it was paralysis; but I massaged it a bit, and then I could move it again; but I had pins and needles in my joints for a long time, and I still have them. When I open my hand they begin again.'

'Why, Martyn Petrovich, you must have been lying on your arm somehow.'

'No, ma'am, you are mistaken! It was a warning to me . . . Of my death, I mean.'

'Well, really!' my mother was beginning.

'A warning! Man, it said, prepare yourself! And so, ma'am, this is what I have to tell you, without any delay. Not being desirous,' Kharlov suddenly began to shout, 'that death should find me, God's servant, unprepared, I have resolved in my mind that now, while I am alive, I should divide my estate between my two daughters, Anna and Evlampia, as the Lord God guides my heart.' Martyn Petrovich stopped, sighed, and added, 'Without any delay.'

'Why not? It is a good thing to do,' remarked my mother, 'only I think there is no need to be in such a hurry.'

'And since I wish,' went on Kharlov, raising his voice still more, 'to observe due order and legality in this matter, I humbly request your son, Dmitri Semënovich – you, ma'am, I do not venture to trouble – I request your said son, Dmitri Semënovich, and I require my kinsman, Bychkov, as a matter of plain duty, to be present at the conclusion of the formal deed and the entering into possession of my two daughters, Anna, married, and Evlampia, spinster: which deed is appointed to be put into operation the day after tomorrow, at twelve o'clock in the forenoon, at my estate of Eskovo, alias Kozyulkino, in the presence of the duly constituted authorities and the officials concerned, who are already invited to the said ceremony.'

Martyn Petrovich could hardly get to the end of his speech, evidently learned by heart and interrupted by frequent sighs . . . It was as though he could not get enough air into his lungs: his pale face grew crimson again, and several times he wiped away the sweat from it.

'And have you already drawn up the deed dividing the property?' asked my mother. 'When did you find time for that?'

'Time . . . oh, dear! Neither drinking nor eating . . .'

'Did you write it yourself?'

'Volodya . . . oh, dear! helped me.'

'And have you applied for permission?'

'Yes, and the High Court has sanctioned it, and the District Court has been given directions, and the Court of Petty Sessions . . . oh, dear! . . . has been appointed to attend.'

My mother laughed.

'I see, Martyn Petrovich, you have already arranged everything in the proper manner – and how quickly! I take it money was no object?'

'No, ma'am, it was not!'

'Exactly! And you say you want my advice . . . Well, Mitenka may go; I will let Souvenir go with him as well, and I will speak to Kvitsinsky . . . And have you invited Gavrila Fedulych?'

'Gavrila Fedulych . . . Mr Zhitkov . . . has likewise had an . . . announcement . . . from me. That was only proper to a promised husband!'

Martyn Petrovich had evidently exhausted all his store of eloquence. Besides, I always thought that he seemed not altogether well-disposed towards the husband my mother had found for his daughter; perhaps he had expected a better match for his Evlampia.

He rose from his chair and made his bow.

'I thank you for your consent.'

'Where are you going?' asked my mother. 'Sit a little longer; I will order some refreshment for you.'

'I am much obliged,' answered Kharlov, 'but I cannot . . . Oh, dear! I must go home.'

He took a step backward, and would have gone out of the door, in his usual manner, sideways.

'Stop, stop,' my mother went on, 'Are you really to give your daughters your property without keeping anything back?'

'Certainly.'

'Well, but you yourself . . . where will you live?'

Kharlov could only wave his arms.

'Where? How do you mean? Just as heretofore . . . so in future, in my own house. Why should there be any change?'

'Do you trust your daughters and your son-in-law so much?'

485

'Is it Volodka you are referring to? That spineless creature? Why, I push him here and push him there, wherever I please . . . What authority has he? And they, my daughters, I mean, why, to provide me with meat and drink, clothes and shoes – that is their first duty. And I shall not be a burden to them for long. My death is not far away over the hills, but close on my heels.'

'As for death, that is in God's hands,' remarked my mother, 'and it is their duty, certainly. But, forgive me, Martyn Petrovich, that elder daughter of yours is known to be a proud creature, and, well, the other looks fierce . . .'

'Natalya Nikolaevna!' interrupted Kharlov, 'What do you mean? That they would . . . My daughters . . . That I should . . . Forget their obedience? But even in their wildest dream . . . Disobey? Whom? Their father? . . . They to dare? But I could so easily lay my curse on them! They have lived in fear and trembling all their lives – and then all at once . . . ! Good God!'

Kharlov broke into a fit of coughing and wheezing.

'Well, all right, all right!' my mother hastened to pacify him; 'but all the same, I don't understand why you have taken it into your head to do the dividing *now*. It makes no difference: they will get it all anyhow after you are gone. I suppose your melancholia is the cause of all this.'

'Oh, my dear madam,' Kharlov retorted, not without annoyance, 'you work that melancholia to death! Here, perhaps, we have a higher power at work, and you say "melancholia"! I took this into my head, madam, because, still alive, I want to decide personally, while I am still here, who is to own what, and who is to be rewarded with what, and that one is to possess it, and feel grateful for it, and carry out my wishes, and whatever their parent and benefactor has decided on, then for his great kindness . . .'

Kharlov's voice failed him again.

'Well, now, that's enough, say no more, my dear friend,' my mother interrupted, 'or else your black colt really will appear.'

'Oh, Natalya Nikolaevna, don't talk about it!' groaned Kharlov. 'It was my death coming for me. I will bid you goodbye. And you, young master, we shall have the honour to expect you the day after tomorrow!'

Martyn Petrovich went out; my mother followed him with her eyes and shook her head significantly.

'No good will come of this,' she whispered, 'no good. Did you notice,' she went on, addressing me, 'that while he talked, he was blinking his eyes all the time as though the sun was in them; now that's a bad sign. When you see a man like that, something is weighing heavily on his heart and misfortune threatens him. Well, go with Vikenty Osipovich and Souvenir the day after tomorrow.'

XI

On the appointed day our big family coach with four places, harnessed behind six chestnut horses, and with the head coachman, stout, grey-bearded Alexeich, on the box, rolled smoothly up to the steps of our house. The seriousness of the step which Kharlov intended to take, and the solemnity with which he had invited our presence, had had their effect on my mother. She herself had expressly ordered this unusual vehicle to be used, and told Souvenir and me to put on our best clothes: she evidently wished to do honour to her protégé. Kvitsinsky always wore a frock-coat and white cravat. All the way Souvenir chattered like a magpie, giggling and discussing whether his brother would leave him anything, and calling him at the same moment a heathen image and a bogyman. Kvitsinsky, a morose and splenetic man, finally could endure it no longer. 'What makes you,' he said in his marked Polish accent, 'keep chattering such absurd nonsense all the time? Can't you possibly sit quiet, without all these "totally unnecessary" –' his favourite expression – 'trivialities?' 'Well, all right,' muttered Souvenir discontentedly, turning his squinting eyes out of the window. Before a quarter of an hour had passed, or the smoothly running horses had more than just begun to sweat under the narrow straps of the new harness, the Kharlov homestead had already come into sight. Through the wide-open gates our coach rolled into the courtyard; the tiny postilion, whose legs came hardly halfway down the horse's sides, for the last time, with his childish cry, bounced in the soft saddle, old Alexeich's elbows spread wide apart as he raised them – and with a soft 'whoa!', we stopped. There were no dogs this time to greet us with their barking, and the servant-boys with their long shirts gaping slightly over their big bellies had also disappeared somewhere. Kharlov's son-in-law was waiting for us on the threshold. I remember that I was greatly impressed by the birch-branches fixed on both sides of the steps, as though it were Trinity Sunday. 'Glory on glory!' Souvenir, alighting first from the coach, twanged through his nose. There was, indeed, an air of celebration everywhere. Kharlov's son-in-law was wearing a velveteen cravat with a satin bow and an extraordinarily tight black frock-coat, and Maximka, emerging from behind him, had damped down his hair with kvass so liberally that drops were trickling from it. We entered the drawing-room and saw Martyn Petrovich's motionless figure towering – absolutely towering – in the middle of the room. I do not know what Souvenir and Kvitsinsky felt at the sight of that gigantic form, but I experienced a feeling of something like awe. Martyn Petrovich was arrayed in a grey coat, which must have belonged to his uniform of 1812, with a black stand-up collar, his bronze medal hung on his breast and his sabre by his side; his left hand rested on the hilt and his right leaned on a table covered with a red cloth. Two sheets of paper covered with writing lay on this table. Kharlov did not stir, he did not even pant, and what dignity there was in his pose, what confidence in himself and his boundless and unquestioned authority! He barely greeted us, with a nod of the head, and with a hoarse murmur of 'Please!' motioned with his left forefinger in the direction of a row of chairs. Against the right-hand wall of the room stood Kharlov's daughters, in their Sunday clothes: Anna in a dress of green shot with lilac, with a yellow silk belt, Evlampia in pink, with dark-red ribbons. Beside them was Zhitkov, in a new uniform, with the usual expression of dull but greedy anticipation in his eyes and with a more than usual quantity of perspiration on his hairy face. A priest in a threadbare snuff-coloured cassock, an old man with stiff brown hair, sat against the left-hand wall. His hair, his sad, lack-lustre eyes, his large heavy hands, which seemed to be a burden to himself and lay like two piles of stones on his knees, and the greased boots visible beneath his cassock, all testified to a laborious, joyless life: his parish was a very poor one. Next to him was the district police captain, a pale, fat, slovenly little gentleman, with short plump little hands and feet, black eyes, black clipped moustache and a perpetual little smile, shallow if cheerful, on his face; he was reputed to be a great taker of bribes and even a despot, as they expressed it in those days; but not only the gentry, even the peasants were used to him and liked him. He was looking round him with a very detached and rather amused air: evidently he found all these 'proceedings' highly entertaining. In fact, he was interested only in the refreshments and vodka that would follow. The clerk of the local court sitting next to him, on the other hand, a lanky man with a long face and the sort of narrow strips of whisker from ear to nose that were worn in the time of Alexander I, was whole-heartedly absorbed in Martyn Petrovich's arrangements and never took his large, serious eyes off him: in the intensity of his attention and sympathy, his lips never ceased moving and writhing, although he did not open his mouth. Souvenir joined him and began to talk to him in a whisper, having first explained to me that he was the chief freemason in the whole province. The local petty sessions court consists, it is well known, of the district police captain, the clerk, and the constable; but the constable either was not present at all, or kept himself so much in the background that I did not notice him; in our district, however, he was nicknamed the 'non-existent', just as there are 'non-remembering' tramps, who answer all questions about themselves with 'I don't remember'. I sat next to Souvenir and Kvitsinsky next to me. On the face of the practical-minded Pole was written obvious irritation at the 'totally unnecessary' journey and the useless waste of time . . . 'My lady, with her Russian fine lady's whims!' he seemed to be whispering to himself . . . 'Oh, these Russians!'

XII

When we were all seated, Martyn Petrovich raised his shoulders, grunted, surveyed us all with his little bear-like eyes, sighed noisily, and began thus:

'Gentlemen! I have invited you here on the following account. I am growing old, gentlemen, and a prey to infirmities . . . I have already had a forewarning that the hour of death, like a thief in the night, draws nigh . . . Isn't that so, father?' he asked, addressing the priest.

The good father jumped.

'Yes, yes, quite so,' he mumbled, shaking his head.

'And therefore,' went on Martyn Petrovich, abruptly raising

his voice, 'not being desirous that the said death should find me unprepared, I have resolved in my mind . . .' and Martyn Petrovich repeated word for word the sentence he had spoken to my mother two days earlier. 'In pursuance of this my resolve,' he shouted still louder, 'this deed' (he struck with his hand the papers lying on the table) 'has been drawn up by me, and the duly constituted authorities have been invited by me in the capacity of witnesses, and the paragraphs that follow disclose what my will is. I have reigned; now my reign is over!'

Martyn Petrovich fixed his round steel spectacles on his nose, took up one of the written sheets from the table, and began:

'Deed of partition of the estate of Martyn Kharlov, lieutenant of artillery, retired, and hereditary nobleman, executed by his own hand, in the full possession of his faculties and by the exercise of his own judgement and whereby is accurately determined which of his lands and appendages are assigned to his two daughters, Anna and Evlampia – bow!' – they bowed – 'and in what manner his serfs and other property and livestock are to be divided! Given under my hand!'

'This is his own document,' whispered the police captain, with his unchanging smile, to Kvitsinsky; 'he wished to read it for the beauty of the style, but the legal deed is drawn up in the correct form, without all these flowers of speech.'

Souvenir began to snigger . . .

'In conformity with my will!' put in Kharlov, whom the remark had not escaped.

'Conforming to it in all respects,' the police captain cheerfully hastened to answer, 'but you know, Martyn Petrovich, the proper forms cannot be dispensed with. And superfluous details have been removed. For the court cannot enter into questions of piebald cows and Turkish drakes.'

'Come here, you!' roared Kharlov to his son-in-law, who had followed us into the room and remained humbly by the door.

He immediately hurried to his father-in-law.

'Take it, and read it! It's hard for me. Only see you don't go too fast! I want all the gentlemen present to be able to follow it.'

Slëtkin took the paper in both hands, and began with trepidation but audibly, with taste and feeling, to read the deed of partition. In it, what was to go to Anna and what to Evlampia, and how the dividing was to be done, was set out with the minutest accuracy. From time to time Kharlov interrupted the reading with the words, 'Hark, that's for you, Anna, for all the pains you have taken!' or 'That I bestow on you, Evlampiyushka!' and both sisters bowed, Anna from the waist, Evlampia only with an inclination of the head. Kharlov watched them with morose dignity. The 'manor-house' (the little new building) was given to Evlampia, 'as the younger daughter, according to the ancient custom'. The reader's voice cracked and faltered as he uttered these words, so displeasing to himself; and Zhitkov licked his lips. Evlampia cast him a sidelong glance: had I been in Zhitkov's place I should not have relished that glance. The disdainful expression characteristic of Evlampia, as of every true

493

Russian beauty, this time bore a special shade of significance. For himself Martyn Petrovich retained the right to live in the rooms he occupied and stipulated that he should have, as what he called his 'portion', full maintenance of 'natural victuals' and ten paper roubles a month for clothes. The last sentence of the deed of partition Kharlov wanted to read himself. 'And this my paternal will,' it ran, 'is for my daughters to fulfil and hold sacred and inviolate, like a commandment; for I, after God, am their father and master, and I am not bound to account to anybody, nor have I done so; and if they carry out my will, then my paternal blessing shall be with them; but if they do not carry out my will, which God forbid, they shall be stricken by my inexorable paternal curse, now and for ever, amen!' Kharlov raised the paper high above his head, and Anna immediately and swiftly knelt down and bowed her forehead to the ground; her husband flopped down after her. 'Well, and what about you?' Kharlov asked Evlampia. She coloured and also bowed down to the ground; Zhitkov bent his whole body forward.

'Sign!' exclaimed Kharlov, pointing to the foot of the document with his finger. 'Here: I thank you and accept, Anna! I thank you and accept, Evlampia!'

Both daughters rose and signed one after the other. Slëtkin also stood up and was reaching for the pen, but Kharlov pushed him aside, thrusting his middle finger into his cravat so that he gulped. There was a moment's silence. Then Martyn Petrovich, with something like a whimper, muttered 'Well, now . . .

it is all yours!' and moved away. His daughters and son-in-law exchanged glances, went up to him, and began to kiss his upper arm. They could not reach his shoulder.

XIII

The police captain read the real, formal document, the deed of gift executed by Martin Petrovich. Then he went out, with the clerk of the court, to the porch and announced what had taken place to the neighbours who had gathered round the gates, the witnesses, Kharlov's peasants, and a few house-serfs. Then began the entering into possession of the two new owners, who had also appeared on the porch, and to whom the police captain had pointed when, frowningly lowering one eyebrow and for a moment lending his carefree face a threatening aspect, he exhorted the peasants to 'obedience'. He might have dispensed with these exhortations: I do not suppose there have ever existed in nature more submissive countenances than those of Kharlov's peasants. Wrapped in long, threadbare coats or torn sheepskins, but all very tightly belted, as is always the case on ceremonial occasions, they stood as still as stones, and whenever he interpolated a remark like, 'You hear that, you devils? understand me, you limbs of Satan!' they all bowed together, as though at a command; each of the 'devils and limbs of Satan' clutched his hat tightly in both hands and kept his eyes fixed on the window through which the figure of Martyn Petrovich could be seen. The witnesses themselves were hardly less overawed.

'Do you know of any obstacles,' the captain yelled at them, 'to the entry into possession of these the sole and legitimate heirs and daughters of Martyn Petrovich Kharlov?'

At once, all the witnesses seemed to cower away.

'Do you, devils?' shouted the captain again.

'No, your Honour, we don't know anything,' bravely answered one witness, a pock-marked little old man, an old soldier, with a clipped beard and moustache.

'Well, Eremeich is a bold one, though!' said the other witnesses, as they dispersed.

Although the police captain requested him to do so, Kharlov refused to show himself with his daughters on the porch. 'My subjects will obey me without that!' he answered. With the completion of the partition something like melancholy had descended on him. His face had grown pale again. This new, unprecedented expression of sorrow was so ill-suited to Martyn Petrovich's plump and expansive features that I really did not know what to think. Was he indeed suffering from an attack of melancholia? The peasants, for their part, were obviously perplexed also. And small wonder: The master was alive – there he stood; and what a master, besides: Martyn Petrovich! And all of a sudden, he was not the master any longer . . . Very strange! I do not know whether it was because Martyn Petrovich divined the thoughts that wandered uncertainly through the minds of his 'subjects', or because he wanted to make one last display of authority, but suddenly he opened the hinged pane in the window, brought his head close to the opening, and shouted in a voice of thunder, 'Obey your orders!' Then he slammed the pane shut. The peasants' bewilderment, of course, was neither dispelled nor lessened by this. They were more petrified than ever, and even seemed to stop looking at anything. The group of house-serfs (their number included two muscular wenches in short print petticoats, with calves which could hardly perhaps be matched in Michelangelo's terrible *Last Judgement*, and one quite decrepit, half-blind old man, positively hoary with age, in a rough frieze great-coat, who was rumoured to have been a 'trumpetist' under Potëmkin; Kharlov had reserved the boy Maximka for himself) – this group showed more animation than the peasants; they did at least change their positions. The new owners themselves behaved in a very dignified fashion, especially Anna. With her dry lips tightly compressed, she kept her eyes obstinately down . . . her stern figure boded little good to the house-serfs. Evlampia did not raise her eyes, either; but once she turned and slowly, as if with surprise, scanned Zhitkov, her betrothed, who had thought fit to follow Slëtkin out to the porch. 'By what right are you here?' those beautiful, prominent eyes seemed to be saying. It was Slëtkin who showed the greatest change of all. His whole being displayed a brisk jauntiness, as though he felt the stirrings of appetite; the movements of his head and legs were as fawningly servile as ever, but with what cheerful bustle he waved his arms and twitched his shoulders! 'At last,' they seemed to say, 'the goal is reached!' Having brought the formalities of the entry into possession to an end, the police captain, whose mouth was positively watering at the proximity of refreshments, rubbed his hands together in the particular manner which usually precedes the 'intake' of the first glass of vodka; but it seemed that first Martyn Petrovich wished to have a service of prayers and consecration. The priest put on an old chasuble so worn that it hardly hung together; an equally decrepit deacon emerged from the kitchen, kindling incense with some difficulty in an ancient brass burner. The service began. From time to time, Kharlov sighed; he was too stout to bow down to the ground but, as he bowed his head and made the sign of the cross with his right hand, he pointed with one finger of his left hand to the floor. Slëtkin was positively radiant, and even shed a few tears; Zhitkov, in a well-bred, soldierly fashion, made very slight motions of his fingers between the third and fourth buttons of his waistcoat; Kvitsinsky, as a Catholic, remained in the next room; the clerk, on the other hand, prayed so fervently, echoed Martyn Petrovich's sighs with so much sympathy, and whispered and moved his lips with such ardour, raising his eyes to heaven, that looking at him I felt some emotion and also began to pray earnestly. When the service was finished and the holy water blessed (and everybody present, even Potëmkin's 'trumpetist', even Kvitsinsky, touched his eyes with holy water) Anna and Evlampia once more expressed their gratitude to Martyn

Petrovich, at his command, by bowing down to the ground; and then, at last, the time for luncheon had come! There was a great deal to eat, all of it excellent; we all ate far too much. The inevitable bottle of Don wine made its appearance. The police captain, as a man better acquainted than any of us with the customs of polite society, and also as the representative of authority, was the first to propose a toast, to the health of the 'beautiful owners!' Then he suggested that we should drink the health of our most highly honoured and most generous Martyn Petrovich. At the word 'generous' Slëtkin squealed and rushed to kiss his benefactor . . . 'All right, all right, don't do that,' muttered Kharlov as if annoyed, fending him off with his elbow. But here occurred an incident that was not, as they say, altogether pleasant.

XIV

It was this: Souvenir, who had been drinking continuously ever since the beginning of the meal, suddenly got up from his chair, as red as a beetroot, and, pointing his finger at Martyn Petrovich, broke into his feeble, sniggering laugh.

'Generous! Generous!' he chattered. 'We shall see whether this generosity is to his own taste when he, the servant of God, stripped naked, is flung out into the snow!'

'What rubbish is this? Fool!' said Kharlov scornfully.

'Fool! fool!' Souvenir repeated. 'Only God Almighty knows which of us two is the real fool. Well, brother, you caused the death of my sister, and your wife – now, on the other hand, you've wiped yourself out . . . ha! ha! ha!'

'How dare you insult our honoured benefactor?' squealed Slëtkin, and, tearing himself away from Martyn Petrovich's shoulder, which he was embracing, he launched himself at Souvenir. 'And do you know that if our benefactor wishes, we can annul the deed this instant? . . .'

'All the same, it will be – naked, and out into the snow with him! . . .' Souvenir managed to get out, as he dodged behind Kvitsinsky.

'Silence!' thundered Kharlov. 'If I hit you, there'll be nothing but a damp mark left on the ground where you were. And you shut up, too, puppy-dog!' he addressed Slëtkin. 'Don't push yourself in where you're not wanted! If I, Martyn Petrovich Kharlov, want to draw up a deed of partition, who can annul it? go against my will? There is no power in the world . . .'

'Martyn Petrovich!' began the clerk of the court suddenly, in a juicy bass; he also had drunk a great deal, but the effect had only been to make him more dignified. 'What if this gentleman has spoken the truth? You have done something magnificent; but what if, God forbid! . . . instead of the gratitude they owe you, some affront to you is the result?'

I glanced stealthily at Martyn Petrovich's daughters. Anna's eyes were positively glued to the speaker, and I swear I have never seen a more wicked and poisonous face, or one more beautiful in its very evil! Evlampia had turned away and folded her hands; the scornful smile twisted her full, rosy lips more than ever. Kharlov rose from his chair and opened his mouth, but his tongue evidently refused to obey him ... Suddenly he struck the table with such force that everything in the room jumped and jingled.

'Father,' Anna hastened to say, 'they don't know us and that is why they can think such things of us; but don't let yourself be upset. You are getting angry over nothing; see, your face looks all twisted.'

Kharlov looked at Evlampia; she did not move, although Zhitkov, sitting next to her, nudged her ribs.

'Thank you, Anna, my daughter,' said Kharlov dully; 'you are a good girl; I put my trust in you, and your husband, too.' Slëtkin squealed again; Zhitkov tried to throw out his chest, and tapped his foot, but Kharlov did not notice his efforts. 'That loafer,' he went on, with a gesture of his chin towards Souvenir, 'likes to bait me; but you, my good sir,' he said to the clerk, 'must not presume to judge Martyn Kharlov; your understanding is not ripe enough yet. You may be a man of official position, but what you say is utter nonsense. However, the thing is done, and there will be no changing of my decision ... Well, good day to you! I shall leave you. I am no longer the host here, I am a guest. Anna, look after them as well as you know how, I am going to my own room. I've had enough!'

Martyn Petrovich turned his back on us and without another word slowly made his way out of the room.

Our host's sudden withdrawal could not but break up our company, especially as both our hostesses soon disappeared also. Slëtkin tried in vain to keep us. The police captain did not omit to scold the clerk for his misplaced outspokenness.

'I couldn't do anything else!' he answered. 'My conscience spoke!'

'You can see he's a mason,' Souvenir whispered to me.

'Conscience!' retorted the policeman. 'We know your conscience! No doubt you keep it in your pocket, just like us sinners!'

The priest, although he was already on his feet, was still lifting one mouthful after another to his mouth in anticipation of the imminent end of the refection.

'I see you have a healthy appetite,' remarked Slëtkin caustically.

'Stocking up,' answered the priest, with a meek grimace. That answer was a revelation of inveterate hunger.

The carriages rolled up, and we went our ways.

On the homeward journey there was nobody to hinder Souvenir's chattering and grimaces, since Kvitsinsky, declaring that he was tired of all this 'totally unnecessary' unseemly behaviour, had set off before us on foot. Zhitkov took his place in our carriage instead; the retired major looked very discontented and from time to time he twitched his moustache, like a cockroach.

'Well, your Honour,' lisped Souvenir, 'I suppose all rank and seniority has gone by the board? Just you wait, and you'll see! You'll catch it, too! Oh! poor little bridegroom, poor little bridegroom, what a bridegroom!'

Souvenir was overflowing with glee, but poor Zhitkov only twitched his moustache.

When we got home, I told my mother all I had seen. She heard me out, with sundry shakes of the head.

'No good will come of it,' she said. 'I don't like all these new departures!'

XV

Next day Martyn Petrovich came to dinner. My mother congratulated him on the successful completion of his undertaking.

'Now you are a free man,' she said, 'and you should feel easier in your mind.'

'Easier indeed, ma'am,' answered Martyn Petrovich, but there was nothing in his expression to suggest that he really felt any easier. 'Now I can think of my immortal soul, and prepare myself fittingly for the hour of death.'

'Well,' asked my mother, 'and have you pins and needles in your arm still?'

Kharlov once or twice clenched and unclenched his left hand. 'I have, ma'am; and I must tell you something else; as soon as I begin to fall asleep, I hear somebody calling in my head, "Beware, beware!"'

'That's nerves,' my mother observed, and she began to speak of the previous day and referred to certain of the circumstances which had accompanied the execution of the deed of partition.

'Yes, yes,' interrupted Kharlov, 'there was something . . . unimportant. But I must tell you this,' he added deliberately, 'it was not Souvenir's silly talk that upset me yesterday, and even the legal gentleman, sensible though he is – he didn't upset me either; but I was upset by . . .' Here Kharlov faltered.

'Who?' asked my mother.

Kharlov glanced up at her.

'Evlampia!'

'Evlampia? Your daughter? How was that?'

'Really, ma'am – she might have been made of stone! Nothing but a graven image! Hasn't she got any feelings at all? Her sister Anna – well, she did everything properly. She's clever! But Evlampia – well, after all – I won't conceal it! – I've always favoured her! Doesn't she feel for me at all? It means things are going badly with me, it means I feel I am not long for this world, if I give everything up to them; and she might be made of stone! If she'd even said a word! Bow – well, she bows all right, but never a trace of gratitude!'

'Wait a little,' remarked my mother; 'when we get her married to Gavrila Fedulych that will soften her up.'

Again Martyn Petrovich glanced up frowningly at my mother.

'Well, there is Gavrila Fedulych certainly. I suppose you trust him, ma'am?'

'Yes, I do.'

'Yes, well, you should know best. But Evlampia, I must tell you – like father, like daughter: our dispositions are just the same. Cossack blood – and a heart like a burning coal!'

'But is your heart really like that, my dear friend?'

Kharlov did not answer. There was a short silence.

'Well, Martyn Petrovich,' began my mother, 'how do you propose to save your soul now? are you going on a pilgrimage to the Mitrophan or Kiev? – or perhaps you'll go to the Optin monastery, since it's in the neighbourhood? There, they say, such a holy monk has appeared . . . they call him Father Macarius; and nobody can remember one like him! He has a very penetrating eye for sins!'

'If she really turns out to be an ungrateful daughter,' said Kharlov in his hoarse voice, 'I think it would be better for me if I killed her with my own hands!'

'Come, come! How can you say such things? God be merciful! Control yourself!' exclaimed my mother. 'What a thing to say! A fine state of affairs! you should have listened to me, when you came to ask my advice! Now, see, you'll be tormenting yourself instead of thinking of your immortal soul! You'll torment yourself, but all the same you can't achieve the impossible! Yes! Now you grumble, you're afraid . . .'

This imputation seemed to pierce Kharlov to the heart. All

his old pride came flooding back. He shook himself and thrust out his chin.

'I am not the sort of man, Natalya Nikolaevna, ma'am, to grumble or be afraid,' he growled. 'I simply wanted to tell you, as my benefactress and honoured friend, how I felt. But the Lord God knows' (here he raised his arm above his head) 'that this earthly ball shall sooner shatter to pieces than I go back on my word or . . .' (here he positively snorted), 'or be afraid or repeal what I have done! I had my reasons! And my daughters will not cease to obey me, for ever and ever, amen!'

My mother covered her ears.

'Why must you trumpet so loud, friend? If you really have such faith in your household, the Lord be praised! But you've quite split my ears!'

Martyn Petrovich apologized, sighed once or twice, and was silent. My mother again referred to Kiev, the Optin monastery, and Father Macarius . . . Kharlov agreed, said, 'I must, I must . . . I shall have to . . . my soul . . .' and that was all. Until the moment he left he was depressed; from time to time he clenched and unclenched his fist, peered into his palm, and said that for him the most terrible thing would be to die without repentance, from a stroke, and that he had promised himself not to get angry, because anger was bad for the blood and drove it into the head . . . Besides, now he had put everything aside, what cause could he have to get angry? Now let others labour, let their blood suffer.

When he said goodbye to my mother, he looked at her with a

strange expression, thoughtful and questioning . . . and suddenly dragging from his pocket with a quick movement the volume of *The Gentle Labourer*, thrust it into my mother's hands.

'What is this?' she asked.

'Read it . . . here,' he said in hurried tones, 'where the corner is turned down, what it says about death. It seems to me that it is terribly well expressed, but I can't understand it at all. Won't you explain it to me, my dear kind friend? I will come back, and you shall explain it to me.' With these words Martyn Petrovich left.

'This is bad! dear me, this is bad!' remarked my mother, as soon as the door closed behind him, and she applied herself to *The Gentle Labourer*. On the page Kharlov had marked stood the following words:

'Death is a great and significant work of nature. It is nothing other than this, that the spirit, inasmuch as it is lighter, finer and much subtler than those elements to which it has heretofore been subject, nay, than the force of electricity itself, purifies itself chemically, and strives until such time as it perceives for itself a place of equal spirituality . . .' and so on.

My mother read this lucubration once or twice, exclaimed 'Pah!' and flung the book aside.

Three days later she received news that her sister's husband had died and, taking me with her, left for her sister's estate. She intended to spend a month with her, but she remained until the late autumn, and it was not until the end of September that we returned to our own estate.

The first news with which I was greeted by my valet Prokofy (he considered it his duty to keep us supplied with game), was that countless numbers of woodcock had arrived, and that they were especially thick in the birch-copse at Eskovo (Kharlov's estate). There were still three hours to dinner; I immediately seized my gun and game-bag and, with Prokofy and a setter, hurried off to the Eskovo copse. We found that there really were many woodcock in it, and we bagged two and a half brace with about thirty shots. Hastening home with our bag, I saw a peasant ploughing near the road. His horse had stopped and he, tearfully and spitefully cursing, was mercilessly tugging at its head, held all askew, with the rope harness. I looked closely at the wretched jade, whose ribs were all but protruding through the skin, and whose sides, streaming with sweat, shuddered and heaved fitfully like ill-made blacksmith's bellows – and at once recognized the feeble old mare with the scarred shoulder, that had served Martyn Petrovich for so many years.

'Is Mr Kharlov still living?' I asked Prokofy. Our shooting had so whole-heartedly engrossed us that until that moment we had not talked of anything else.

'Yes, sir. Why?'

'But isn't that his horse? Surely he hasn't sold it?'

'Yes, sir, it's his horse all right; only as for selling, he didn't sell it, they took it from him, and gave it to that peasant.'

'How do you mean, took it? Did he agree?'

'He wasn't asked, sir. Things have been happening here while you were away,' said Prokofy with a slight grin, in answer to my look of surprise. 'More's the pity! Oh lord, yes! Now he's the boss, Slëtkin runs everything there.'

'And what about Martyn Petrovich?'

'Martyn Petrovich has come to be the very last person. He's kept on dry bread – that's all about it. They've finished him off altogether. I'm afraid they'll drive him out of the place yet.'

The idea of *driving out* such a giant was something my mind refused to grasp.

'And what does Zhitkov think of it?' I asked at last. 'He's married to the second daughter, isn't he?'

'Married?' repeated Prokofy, and this time he laughed aloud. 'They won't even let him into the house. It's "go away, go back the way you came". I tell you, Slëtkin bosses everything.'

'But what about the bride?'

'Do you mean Evlampia Martynovna? Ah, master, I could tell you . . . but you are too young, that's it. Things have got to such a pitch that ee . . . ee . . . ee! Hi, look! Dianka seems to have found something!'

Indeed, my dog was standing rigid before a spreading bushy oak that screened the end of a narrow ravine where it came out on the road. Prokofy and I hurried to the dog; a woodcock rose from the bush. We both fired and missed; the woodcock flew away and we followed it.

The soup was already on the table when I got home. My mother scolded me. 'What's this?' she said with great displeasure. 'The very first day, and you have made me wait dinner for you.' I brought her the woodcock we had killed: she did not even look at them. Souvenir, Kvitsinsky, and Zhitkov were in the room with her. The retired major had retreated into the corner, for all the world like a schoolboy in disgrace; the expression of his face was a blend of embarrassment and arrogance; his eyes were red . . . One might have thought that he had been shedding tears not long before. My mother continued to be out of humour; it did not cost me much trouble to guess that my tardiness had nothing to do with this. During dinner she had hardly anything to say: the major cast occasional piteous glances at her, but nevertheless ate a good dinner; Souvenir fidgeted endlessly; Kvitsinsky preserved his usual self-confident demeanour.

'Vikenty Osipych,' my mother addressed him, 'I must ask you to send a carriage tomorrow for Martyn Petrovich, since I learn he no longer has his own; and have him told that he must come without fail, I wish to see him.'

Kvitsinsky was going to raise some objection, but restrained himself.

'And let Slëtkin know,' continued my mother, 'that I command him to come to me . . . Do you hear? I com . . . mand . . . him!'

'That's it, exactly . . . that rogue ought to be . . .' Zhitkov began to mutter; but my mother looked at him so contemptuously that he turned away at once and said no more.

'Do you hear? I command him!' repeated my mother.

'Yes, ma'am,' said Kvitsinsky humbly but with dignity.

'Martyn Petrovich won't come,' Souvenir whispered, leaving the dining-room with me after dinner. 'You will see what has happened to him! It's incomprehensible! I don't suppose he understands anything, whatever anyone says to him. Yes, the snake's been caught by the pitchfork!'

And Souvenir laughed his tittering laugh.

XVII

Souvenir's prediction proved to be correct. Martyn Petrovich refused to come to see my mother. She was not satisfied with this and sent him a letter; he sent her back half a sheet of paper on which the following words were written in a large hand: 'Really, truly, I cannot. The shame would kill me. Leave me to die. Thank you. Don't torture me. Martynko Kharlov.' Slëtkin did come, not on the day when my mother had 'commanded' him to appear, but a full twenty-four hours later. My mother ordered him to be taken to her room. God only knows what their conversation was concerned with, but it did not last long: about a quarter of an hour, no more. Slëtkin came out of my mother's room red all over, and with such a venomous and insolent expression that, meeting him in the drawing-room, I froze to the spot, and Souvenir, who was idling about in the same room, broke off his snigger in the very middle. My mother emerged from her room, also red in the face, and declared publicly that henceforward Mr Slëtkin was not to be admitted on any pretext; and if Martyn Petrovich's daughters chose to put in an appearance – they had enough impudence for it, said she – they also were to be refused admittance. At dinner she suddenly burst out, 'That wretched little Jew! It was I who dragged him out of the gutter, and introduced him to society, he owes me everything, everything – and he dares to tell me I have no right to meddle in their business. He says Martyn Petrovich is losing his wits and that it is impossible to humour him! Humour! What does he mean? Ah, he's an ungrateful puppy! The nasty little Jew!' Major Zhitkov, who was also among those dining with us, imagined that this time God himself was bidding him take advantage of the opportunity and put in his word . . . but my mother pulled him up at once. 'A fine one you are, too, my good man!' she said. 'You couldn't manage a girl, and you an officer! You command a company! I can imagine how it obeyed you! You to want to be a steward! You'd make a fine steward!'

Kvitsinsky, sitting at the end of the table, smiled to himself, not without malice, but poor Zhitkov only twitched his moustache, raised his eyebrows, and buried his hairy face in his napkin.

After dinner he went out to the porch, as usual, to smoke a pipe, and he seemed to me so pathetic and helpless that, although I disliked him, I joined him there.

'How does it happen, Gavrila Fedulych,' I began without any beating about the bush, 'that your engagement to Evlampia Martynovna has been broken off? I supposed you were married long since.'

The retired major looked dejectedly at me.

'A viper,' he began, sadly and painstakingly pronouncing every letter of every syllable, 'poisoned me with its sting and turned all my hopes into dust and ashes! And I would tell you, Dmitri Semenovich, all his spiteful tricks, but I am afraid it would make your mother angry!' (Prokofy's words, 'You are too young', flashed across my mind.) 'As it is . . .'

Zhitkov uttered a groan.

'Patience . . . patience . . . that's all there is left!' (He struck his breast with his fist.) 'Be patient, old soldier, be patient! I served my tsar faithfully . . . irreproachably . . . yes! I did not grudge blood and sweat, and now see what has become of me! If this was the regiment, and if it rested with me,' he continued after a short silence, drawing feverishly at his cherrywood pipe, 'I would . . . I would sentence him to three doses of punishment with the flat of the sword . . . I'd give him a bellyful . . .'

Zhitkov took his pipe out of his mouth and fixed his eyes on space, as though inwardly admiring the picture he had called up.

Souvenir came hurrying up and began tormenting the major with his pin-pricks. I turned aside, and made up my mind that I must at all costs see Martyn Petrovich with my own eyes. My childish curiosity had been strongly stirred.

XVIII

The next day, again with a gun and my dog, but without Prokofy, I went off to the Eskovo copse. It was a marvellous day: I do not think there are such September days anywhere in the world but in Russia. It was so quiet that you could hear a squirrel bounding over the dry leaves from a hundred yards away or the faint sound of a broken twig as it first caught on the other branches and then fell to the soft grass, to lie there for ever: it would never stir again till it rotted away. The air, neither warm nor chilly, only aromatic and, as it were, pleasantly sharp, nipped gently and agreeably at my cheeks and eyes; a long thread of gossamer, as fine as silk, with a little white ball in the middle, drifted smoothly to the barrel of my gun and clung there, floating straight out in the air – a sign of warm settled weather. The sunshine was as mild as moonlight. I came upon woodcock fairly often, but I did not pay them much attention; I knew that the wood stretched almost up to Kharlov's house, right up to his garden fence, and I made my way in that direction, although I could not imagine how I could penetrate into the homestead itself, and was indeed doubtful whether I ought to try, since my mother was incensed with the new owners.

I thought I could hear the sound of people at a short distance, I listened ... Somebody was walking through the wood ... straight towards me.

'You should have said so,' said a woman's voice.

'Talk sense!' interrupted another voice, a man's. 'Do you think everything can be done at once?'

The voices were familiar to me. A woman's blue dress flickered between the thinning hazel-bushes; a dark-coloured caftan showed beside it. A moment longer, and into the clearing, five paces away from me, came Slëtkin and Evlampia.

They were taken aback. Evlampia stepped back at once into the bushes. Slëtkin thought a moment, and then approached me. In his face there was no longer a trace to be seen of the fawning submission with which, some four months earlier, he had wiped my horse's snaffle, as he walked up and down Kharlov's yard; but neither could I read in that face the insolent challenge which had so struck me on the previous day, at the door of my mother's room. It remained as white and as good-looking as ever; but it seemed broader and stronger.

'Well, have you killed many woodcock?' he asked me, raising his cap, smirking, and smoothing his black curls with his hand. 'You are shooting in our wood . . . You are welcome! We won't stop you . . . On the contrary!'

'I haven't killed anything today,' I said, answering his first question, 'and I will leave your wood at once.'

Slëtkin hurriedly replaced his cap.

'Come now, why? We won't drive you out – indeed, we are very glad . . . Here's Evlampia Martynovna to tell you the same. Evlampia Martynovna, please come here! Where have you got to?'

Evlampia's head appeared behind the bushes, but she did not come up to us. She had grown still prettier recently and seemed even taller and plumper.

'To tell you the truth,' went on Slëtkin, 'I really am very pleased to have "met up" with you. You may be young yet, but already you have real judgement. Your mother was pleased to be angry with me yesterday, she wouldn't listen to any arguments from me, but I swear to you, as I would to God, that I have done nothing wrong. It's impossible to act any differently with Martyn Petrovich: he's absolutely in his dotage. We simply can't humour all his fancies, believe me. But we always give him the respect that is his due. Just ask Evlampia Martynovna.'

Evlampia did not move; the habitual scornful smile strayed about her lips, and the look in her beautiful eyes was unfriendly.

'But, Vladimir Vasilyevich, why did you sell Martyn Petrovich's horse?' (The thought of that horse in the hands of a peasant was particularly disturbing to me.)

'Why did we sell his horse, sir? Oh, come now, really, what use was it? It was simply eating good hay. But it can at any rate plough for a peasant. And if Martyn Petrovich takes it into his head to go anywhere, he has only to ask us. We wouldn't refuse him a carriage. On days when the horses aren't working, with the greatest pleasure!'

'Vladimir Vasilyevich!' said Evlampia tonelessly, as though she were calling him away, still without moving from her place.

She was twisting a few stalks of plantain round her fingers, and breaking off their heads by striking them against one another.

'Then again, about the page Maximka,' Slëtkin went on. 'Martyn Petrovich complains because, he says, we have taken him away from him to make him an apprentice. But judge for yourself: with Martyn Petrovich what would he have done? Wasted his time idling about, that's all. He can't even wait on people properly, on account of being stupid and too young. But now we've apprenticed him to a saddler. He'll be made into a good workman, and he will both do himself some good and be able to pay his dues to us. For people in a small way like us that's something important, sir! People in a small way can't afford to let anything slip!'

'And this is the man Martyn Petrovich called spineless!' I thought.

'But who reads to Martyn Petrovich now?' I asked.

'What is there to read? There was one book, but luckily it's got lost somewhere . . . And what does he want with reading at his age?'

'And who shaves him?' I asked again.

Slëtkin laughed approvingly, as though I had made a good joke.

'Nobody. To begin with he singed his beard himself with a candle, but now he just lets it grow. And he gets along splendidly!'

'Vladimir Vasilyevich!' repeated Evlampia insistently, 'Vladimir Vasilyevich!'

Slëtkin made her a sign with his hand.

'Martyn Petrovich is clothed and shod, and he eats the same things as we do; what more does he want? He said himself that he wished for nothing more in this world, except to look after the good of his soul. If he would only consider that whatever you like to say, everything's ours now. Another thing: he says we don't give him his allowance; but we haven't always got the money ourselves; and what good is it to him, when he has everything he needs? And we treat him just like one of ourselves: I'm telling you the truth. Well, for example, the rooms he lives in – you don't know how much we need them! Without them, we simply haven't room to turn round; but then – it's quite all right! – we put up with it. We even think up ways of keeping him amused. Well, look, for St Peter's day I bought him some marvellous hooks in the town, real English ones; expensive hooks, so that he can fish. We've got any amount of carp in the pond. He can sit and fish, and when he's sat there for an hour or two, we'll have a nice fish-soup all ready. A nice quiet occupation for an old man.'

'Vladimir Vasilyich!' said Evlampia for the third time, in a resolute tone, throwing away the stems she had been playing with. 'I am going!' Her eyes met mine. 'I am going, Vladimir Vasilyich!' she repeated, and she disappeared behind the bush.

'I'm coming at once, Evlampia Martynovna, at once!' shouted Slëtkin. 'Martyn Petrovich himself sees we are right now,' he went on, turning to me again. 'At first he took it badly, you might say, and even grumbled, until, you know, he realized; if you remember, he used to be hot-tempered and hasty – dreadful! but now, well, he's grown very quiet. That's because he saw where his own best interests lay. Your mama – and, my God, how she came down on me! . . . Of course, the lady prizes her power, too, as much as Martyn Petrovich used to; well, but you come yourself, and see – and put in a word for us when you get a chance. I feel all Natalya Nikolaevna's kindnesses very much; but we have to live, too.'

'And how was it Zhitkov was refused?' I asked.

'Fedulych? That good-for-nothing hanger-on?' Slëtkin shrugged his shoulders. 'Come now, what use could he be? He's spent all his life as a soldier, and now he takes it into his head to go in for farming. I can keep the peasants in order, says he. That's because I'm used to punching their noses. But he can't do anything. You have to know how, even to punch people's noses. And it was Evlampia Martynovna herself who refused him. An unsuitable person. All our business would have gone to rack and ruin with him!'

'Coo-ee!' came Evlampia's ringing voice.

'I'm coming! I'm coming!' Slëtkin called back. He held out his hand to me; however unwillingly, I shook it.

'Goodbye, Dmitri Semënych,' said Slëtkin, showing all his white teeth. 'Shoot as many woodcock as you like; they're migrants and don't belong to anybody. All right, but if you come across a hare, just leave it alone; that kind of game is ours.

And one more thing! Won't you be having one of your bitch's puppies to spare? You would be doing me a favour!'

'Coo-ee!' came Evlampia's voice again.

'Coo-ee! Coo-ee!' replied Slëtkin, plunging into the bushes.

XIX

I remember that, when I was left alone, I was occupied with the question of how it was that Kharlov had not given Slëtkin such a blow that 'there was nothing but a damp mark on the ground where he had been' – and how was it that Slëtkin had not been afraid of that fate? Evidently, Martyn Petrovich had indeed turned 'quiet', I thought, and I felt a still stronger desire to penetrate into Eskovo and catch at least a glimpse of the colossus whom I simply could not imagine broken and subdued. I had reached the outskirts of the wood when suddenly, with a great clatter of wings, an enormous woodcock rose from right under my feet and whirred into the depths of the wood. I took aim; my gun misfired. I was annoyed: it was a very fine bird, and I determined to see whether I could not start it again. I went in the direction of its flight and when I had covered about two hundred yards saw, on a little patch of grass under a branching birch-tree, not a woodcock, but Mr Slëtkin again. He was lying on his back with both hands under his head, looking up with a contented smile at the sky and gently swinging his left leg, which was crossed over his right knee. He did not notice my approach. A few paces away from him, slowly, with downcast eyes, Evlampia was moving backwards and forwards over the grass; she seemed to be looking for something – mushrooms, perhaps – and occasionally she stooped, with outstretched hand; she was singing softly. I stopped at once and listened. At first I could not catch what it was she was singing, but then I clearly recognized the well-known lines of the old song:

> *Come away, come away, thunder-cloud black,*
> *Kill me, oh kill me, my father-in-law,*
> *Strike down, oh strike down my mother-in-law,*
> *But ah, my young wife – I will kill her myself!*

Evlampia sang louder and louder; the last words she lengthened out with special force. Slëtkin continued to lie on his back, chuckling, and she seemed to be circling round him all the time.

'Well, well!' he said at last. 'What things do get into people's heads, to be sure!'

'What?' asked Evlampia.

'What? What sort of words are you saying now?'

'Why, Volodya, you know yourself you can't leave words out of a song,' answered Evlampia, as she turned round – and saw me.

We cried out, both at the same time, and dashed away in different directions.

I hastened to get out of the wood and found myself, as I crossed a narrow glade, in front of Kharlov's garden.

XX

I had no time – and, indeed, it would have served no purpose
– to ponder over what I had seen. But there did come into my
mind the word 'love-spell', with which I had recently become
acquainted, and whose meaning seemed very surprising to me.
I walked along beside the garden fence and in a few moments,
from behind the spreading silvery poplars, still retaining all their
leaves and luxuriantly gleaming, I saw Martyn Petrovich's yard
and modest buildings. The whole place seemed to have been
taken in hand and tidied up; there were signs everywhere of
strict and constant supervision. Anna Martynovna appeared on
the porch and, screwing up her light-blue eyes, stood for some
time gazing in the direction of the wood.

'Have you seen the master?' she asked a peasant who was
passing across the yard.

'Vladimir Vasilyich?' he answered, taking off his cap. 'He
must have gone to the wood.'

'I know he went to the wood. Hasn't he come back? Have
you seen him?'

'Nay, I've not seen him.'

The peasant went on standing bareheaded before Anna Martynovna.

'Well, get along,' she said. 'But no . . . wait a moment . . .
Where is Martyn Petrovich? Do you know?'

'Martyn Petrovich, now,' answered the peasant in a sing-song voice, raising first his right and then his left arm as though he were pointing somewhere, 'he's over yonder, sitting by the pond, with a rod. He's sitting in the reeds, with his rod. Fishing, happen; I don't know.'

'Good . . . Get along,' repeated Anna Martynovna. 'And pick up that wheel, can't you see it lying there?'

The peasant ran to carry out her order and she stood for some minutes longer on the porch, still gazing towards the wood.

Then she made a quiet, threatening gesture with one hand and slowly turned back into the house. 'Axyutka!' came her peremptory voice from inside the door.

Anna Martynovna had an irritated look, and her already thin lips were compressed with a kind of emphatic energy. Her dress was careless, and a strand of hair had escaped from her plaits and hung on her shoulder. But in spite of her careless dress and her irritation, she seemed to me as attractive as ever, and I should have been very happy to kiss her narrow hand, which also had an almost spiteful look, as she once or twice angrily pushed back that loose lock of hair.

XXI

'Can Martyn Petrovich really have turned fisherman?' I asked myself, as I made my way towards the pond, which was on the far side of the garden. I climbed up on the dam and looked in every direction . . . Martyn Petrovich was nowhere to be seen. I walked along one of the banks of the pond and at last, close to its head, by a little bay, among the flattened and broken stalks of the rusty reeds, I saw a huge, greyish mass. I looked closely: it was Kharlov. Hatless and dishevelled, in a coarse linen caftan torn along the seams and with his legs crossed under him, he sat motionless on the bare ground, so unmoving that, as I approached, a sandpiper started up from the dried mud a couple of paces away from him and flew off over the smooth water, with a whistle and a flash of wings. Evidently nobody near the bird had moved or frightened it for a long time. Kharlov's whole figure was so extraordinary that my dog stopped short as soon as she saw him, with her tail between her legs, and began to growl. He turned his head the merest fraction and fixed his wild gaze on me and the dog. He was greatly changed by the beard which, though short, was thick and curly, all white ringlets like Persian lamb. One end of his rod lay in his right hand, the other dangled limply in the water. My heart gave an involuntary bound but I plucked up my courage, went up to him, and bade him good morning. He blinked slowly, as though half asleep.

'What are you doing here, Martyn Petrovich?' I began. 'Fishing?'

'Yes . . . fishing,' he answered hoarsely, and twitched up the end of his rod, from which dangled a yard or two of string without a hook.

'Your line is broken,' I remarked, and then I saw that there was no sign of a bait-can or worms near Martyn Petrovich . . . And what kind of fishing could one do in September?

'Broken?' he said, passing his hand over his face. 'But that makes no difference!'

He again threw out his line.

'Is it Natalya Nikolaevna's boy?' he asked, after a minute or two during which I had been watching him with a certain amount of secret consternation. In spite of being very much thinner, he still looked a giant; but what rags he was wearing, and how low he had sunk!

'Quite right,' I answered, 'I am Natalya Nikolaevna B———'s son.'

'How is she?'

'My mother is well. She was very distressed at your refusal,' I added; 'she never expected that you would refuse to come and see her.'

Martyn Petrovich looked downcast.

'And have you been . . . there?' he asked, nodding his head to one side.

'Where?'

'There . . . to the house. Haven't you? You must. What can you do here? You go there. No use trying to talk to me. I don't like it!'

He paused.

'You would like to be always playing with a gun! I used to be

inclined that way myself, in my young days. But my father . . .
and I stood in awe of him, let me tell you! not like young people
nowadays. My father thrashed me with his whip, and that was
the end of it. No more playing about! That was why I stood in
awe of him . . . Oo! . . . Yes . . .'

Kharlov paused again.

'But don't you stay here,' he began again. 'You go to the
house. Everything is run famously there now. Volodka . . .'
Here he stammered slightly. 'Our Volodka can turn his hand to
anything. A clever chap! but still, what a scoundrel!'

I did not know what to say; Martyn Petrovich spoke very
calmly.

'And have a look at my daughters. You remember, I suppose,
that I had daughters. They run things, too . . . very cleverly. But
I am getting old, my dear; I've retired. For a rest, you know.'

'A fine rest!' I thought, looking round.

'Martyn Petrovich!' I said aloud. 'You absolutely must come
and see us.'

Kharlov looked at me.

'Go away, lad; be off.'

'Don't upset mama, do come.'

'Go away, lad, go away,' Kharlov insisted. 'What have you
got to talk to me about?'

'If you have no carriage, mama will send hers for you.'

'Go away!'

'But really, Martyn Petrovich!'

Kharlov again hung his head, and I thought there was a faint flush on the leaden cheeks, which might have been encrusted with earth.

'Really, do come,' I went on. 'Why sit here eating your heart out?'

'How, eating my heart out?' he said slowly.

'Just eating it out!' I repeated.

Kharlov was silent and seemed deep in thought.

Emboldened by his silence, I decided to speak frankly and be straightforward and above-board in dealing with him. (Do not forget that I was only fifteen.)

'Martyn Petrovich,' I began, sitting down beside him. 'I know everything, you see, absolutely everything. I know how your son-in-law behaves towards you, of course with your daughters' consent. And now you are in a position . . . But why lose heart?'

Kharlov still said nothing, although he dropped his rod; but how clever and philosophical I thought myself!

'Of course,' I began again, 'you acted carelessly in giving your daughters everything. It was a most generous gesture on your part, and I am not going to reproach you with it. It is a quality too rare in our age. But if your daughters display such ingratitude, you ought to show disdain . . . yes, disdain . . . and not give way to melancholy . . .'

'Stop!' whispered Kharlov all at once, grinding his teeth, and his eyes, fixed on the pond, had a baneful glitter. 'Get out!'

'But, Martyn Petrovich . . .'

'Get out, I tell you . . . or I'll kill you!'

I had pressed quite close to him; but at these last words I involuntarily started to my feet.

'I'll kill you, I tell you; get out!' Kharlov's voice burst from his breast in a wild moan, a roar, but he did not turn his head and continued to stare angrily straight before him. 'I will take you and throw you into the water and all your silly advice with you – that will teach you not to worry old people, you young whippersnapper!'

'He's gone out of his mind,' the thought flashed through my head.

I looked more carefully at him, and was completely stunned: Martyn Petrovich was crying! Tear after tear rolled from his lashes and down his cheeks, and his face had taken on an utterly savage look . . .

'Get out!' he shouted again, 'or else I'll kill you, I swear to God! to teach other people a lesson!'

He jerked his whole body to one side and bared his teeth like a wild boar; I snatched up my gun and took to my heels. My dog followed me, howling, as scared as I was.

When I got home I of course did not breathe a word to my mother of what I had seen but, meeting Souvenir, I told him all about it, God knows why. The repulsive creature was so delighted with my story, screeching with laughter and even dancing, that I very nearly struck him.

'Oh, if only I could see that dummy, that "Shwede" Kharlov,' he repeated again and again, breathless with laughter, 'crawling into the mud and sitting there . . .'

'Go to the pond, if you are so interested.'

'Yes, but what if he kills me?'

I had had quite enough of Souvenir, and repented of my misplaced confidence . . . Zhitkov, to whom he repeated my story, saw the matter in a rather different light.

'They'll have to go to the police,' was his conclusion, 'or perhaps even send for a detachment of soldiers.'

His prophecy about the detachment of soldiers was not fulfilled; but something extraordinary did happen, nevertheless.

XXII

About the middle of October, some three weeks after my meeting with Martyn Petrovich, I was standing by the window of my room on the first floor of our house and gazing dismally at the courtyard and the road that lay beyond it, without a thought in my head. For the fifth day in succession the weather was abominable; it was impossible even to think of shooting. Every living creature had taken cover; even the sparrows were silent, and the rooks had long since disappeared. The wind now howled dully, now whistled fitfully. The low clouds, without a break anywhere, were changing from an unpleasant whitish colour to an even more ominous leaden tinge, and the rain which poured endlessly and incessantly had suddenly become heavier and more driving, streaming down the panes with a lashing sound. The battered trees had taken on a grey look: nothing more, it seemed, could be stripped from them, but at intervals the wind would pounce and worry them once more. Everywhere there were pools choked with dead leaves; huge bubbles, constantly bursting and being renewed, skimmed and bounced over them. The mire made the roads impassable; the cold penetrated into rooms and through the clothes to the very bones; involuntary shivers ran through the body, and what intolerable sickness filled the heart! Sickness, not sadness. It seemed there would never again be sun, nor light, nor colour on the earth, but this mud and slime, this sodden greyness and sour damp would remain for ever, and for ever the wind would whine and moan. So there I stood moodily by the window, and I remember that a sudden darkness fell, a blue dusk, although the clock showed it to be only twelve. All at once I seemed to see a bear lumber swiftly across the yard from the gate to the porch! Not on all fours, certainly, but looking like those drawings where it is shown on its hind legs. I could not believe my eyes. If it was not indeed a bear that I had seen, it was at any rate something huge, black, and shaggy . . . Before I had time to decide what it might have been, a frantic knocking came from below. Something startling and terrible seemed to have plunged headlong into the house. There was a sudden commotion and flurry . . .

I sped downstairs and burst into the dining-room.

Facing me, my mother stood in the drawing-room doorway

as if rooted to the spot; several frightened women's faces were visible behind her; the butler, two footmen and a page, their mouths open in consternation, crowded together near the door into the hall; and in the middle of the room, covered in mire, tousled, tattered, and wet – so wet that clouds of steam arose all round and streams of water ran over the floor, knelt, swaying ponderously and seeming on the point of exhaustion, the very monster that I had seen rushing across the yard. And who was this monster? Kharlov! I had come on him from one side and I could see, not his face, but the head he was clutching with both hands in his hair, matted with filth. His breathing was laboured and spasmodic, there was even a kind of rattling in his breast, and in all that dark, bespattered mass it was possible to distinguish clearly only the tiny whites of his wildly rolling eyes. He was terrible! I thought of the official he had once cut short so abruptly for comparing him to a mastodon. In truth, such must have been the aspect of some antediluvian beast, just escaped from another, more powerful creature which had attacked it among the eternal slime of the primeval swamps.

'Martyn Petrovich!' exclaimed my mother at last, throwing up her hands. 'Is it you? Oh, Lord! Oh, merciful God!'

'Me . . . me . . .' we heard a broken voice in which each sound seemed to be forced out with a painful effort, 'oh! It is me!'

'But, good heavens! What has happened to you?'

'Natalya Nikolaevna . . . I came . . . straight to you . . . from the house . . . on foot . . . running . . .'

'Through all that filth! You don't even look human. Get up and sit down, at least ... And you,' she went on, addressing the maids, 'run for some towels, quickly. And aren't there some dry clothes?' she asked the butler.

With a gesture of his hands the butler answered the question: how should there be any of that size?

'We could get a blanket, though,' he said 'or else – there's a new horse-cloth.'

'But do get up, get up, Martyn Petrovich, and sit down!' repeated my mother.

'They've turned me out, ma'am,' groaned Kharlov suddenly, throwing back his head and stretching out his arms. 'They've turned me out, Natalya Nikolaevna! My own daughters, from my own fireside ...'

My mother uttered an exclamation.

'What are you saying? Turned you out! How wicked, how wicked!' (She crossed herself.) 'Only do get up, Martyn Petrovich, please do.'

Two maids came in with towels and stopped in front of Martyn Petrovich. It was evident that they could not imagine how to approach such a mountain of filth. Meanwhile, Kharlov went on repeating, 'Turned me out, ma'am, turned me out.' The butler returned with a woollen blanket, and he too stopped, equally puzzled. Souvenir's head was thrust round a door and then vanished.

'Martyn Petrovich! get up! and sit down, and tell me everything as it happened,' my mother commanded, in peremptory tones.

Kharlov raised himself. The butler wanted to help him, but only dirtied his hand and, shaking his fingers, he retreated towards the door. Lurching and swaying, Kharlov managed to reach a chair and sat down. The maids again approached him with the towels, but he put them aside with a movement of his hand, and refused the blanket. My mother herself, however, ceased to insist: it was plainly impossible to get Kharlov dry; they could only hastily wipe away the traces on the floor.

XXIII

'What is this about turning you out?' asked my mother, as soon as Kharlov had 'got his breath back' a little.

'Ma'am! Natalya Nikolaevna!' he began in a voice full of strain – and I was struck once again by the restless flickering of the whites of his eyes. 'I will tell you the truth: it is more my own fault than anyone's!'

'That's true enough; you wouldn't listen to me then,' said my mother, sinking into a chair and waving a scented handkerchief gently in front of her nose: Kharlov really gave off a very powerful odour . . . a forest bog does not smell so strong.

'Oh, that was not where I was wrong, ma'am, but in being proud. It was pride that ruined me, as much as it did Nebuchadnezzar. I thought God had not withheld from me my full share of sense and reason: if I made up my mind to anything that meant it was right . . . and then the fear of death came on me . . . I must have gone out of my mind! I'll show my power and might at the last, I said. I will be bountiful, and they ought to feel it to the grave . . .' Kharlov suddenly grew very agitated. 'Kicked out of the house like a mangy dog. That's their gratitude . . . !'

'But how . . .' my mother was beginning again.

'They took my boy Maximka away from me,' Kharlov interrupted (his eyes still rolled wildly and he held both hands close to his chin, with the fingers interlaced), 'they took away my droshky, they cut down my portion, they didn't pay the money that was agreed on – they pared me down to the bone all round – and all the time I didn't say anything, I put up with it all the time! And I put up with it on account . . . alas! of my pride again. So that my enemies should not say, "Look at the old fool, he's sorry now," and you, ma'am, you remember had warned me: "You can't do the impossible!" you said – so I put up with it . . . Only, today I went to my room – and it had been taken over – and my bed had been thrown out into the store-room! "You can sleep there," they said; "It's only out of kindness," they said, "that we put up with you even there; we need your room," they said, "for running the place." And who do you think said that to me? Volodka Slëtkin, the serf, the scum . . .'

Kharlov's voice broke.

'But your daughters? What about them?' asked my mother.

'I put up with it all the time,' Kharlov went on with his story; 'but it was bitter to me, God knows how bitter, and I was

534

ashamed . . . I wished I had never seen the light of day! That's why I refused to come and see even you, my dear, because of very shame and disgrace! You know, my dear ma'am, I tried everything, kindness, and threats, and appealing to their consciences, and what's more, I bowed before them . . . like this –' and Kharlov showed how he had bowed – 'and all to no purpose! And still I went on putting up with it! At the beginning, though, in the early days, my thoughts were not like that at all: "I'll take," I said, "and kill them all, I'll throw them out, I'll make a clean sweep of the lot! . . . They'll find out!" Well, but afterwards I gave in! I've been given a cross to bear, I thought; that means I must get ready to die. And then today, all of a sudden – like a dog! And who did it? Volodka! As for what you were pleased to ask about my daughters, do you suppose they have any will of their own? They're Volodka's slaves! Yes!'

My mother was astonished.

'I can understand that about Anna,' she said, 'she is his wife . . . But why your second daughter should . . .'

'Evlampia? She's worse than Anna! She's put herself absolutely in his hands. That's the reason why she refused that soldier of yours. By his, Volodka's, orders. Obviously Anna ought to feel affronted, and she can't bear her sister – but she submits! That cursed fellow has bewitched them! But then she, Anna, you can see that she is pleased to think about Evlampia, who was always so proud, she thinks, and now look at what has become of her! Oh . . . oh . . . oh! Oh God, my God!'

My mother looked anxiously at me. I moved a little to one side, as a precaution lest I should be sent out of the room . . .

'I am very sorry, Martyn Petrovich,' she began, 'that my former protégé has brought you so much sorrow and turned out such a bad man; but I was mistaken in him too, you know . . . Who could have expected it of him?'

'Ma'am,' groaned Kharlov, striking his breast, 'I cannot bear my daughters' ingratitude! I cannot, ma'am! After all, I gave them everything, everything I had! And then my conscience has been tormenting me too. Many, oh, many things I turned over in my mind, sitting by the pond and fishing! "If only you had done good to somebody in your life," that was what I thought to myself, "given to the poor, or set your peasants free, maybe, to make up for having ruined their lives! After all, you are answerable for them before God! Now vengeance is exacted for their wrongs!" And what is their lot now? it was a deep pit even in my day – why not confess it? – but now it is bottomless! I have taken all these sins on my soul, I have sacrificed my conscience for my children, and nobody cares a rap! I am kicked out of the house like a dog!'

'Don't think about it any more, Martyn Petrovich,' said my mother.

'And when he told me, that Volodka of yours,' Kharlov went on with renewed energy, 'when he told me that I was not to live in my own room any longer, I who laid every plank in that room with my own hands – when he told me that – God knows what happened to me! My mind went blank, it was like a knife in my heart . . . Well! it was either slit his throat or get out of the house! . . . So here I have come running to you, Natalya Nikolaevna, my kind friend . . . for where could I lay my head? But then – the rain and the mud . . . I must have fallen twenty times! And now . . . in this shameful state . . .'

Kharlov looked down at himself and stirred in his chair as though preparing to get up.

'Say no more about that, Martyn Petrovich, don't say any more,' my mother hastened to say; 'what does it matter? Making the floor dirty? What a thing to worry about! But this is what I should like to suggest. Listen! They will show you now to a room you can have, and give you a clean bed – and you must undress, have a wash, and then go to bed and sleep . . .'

'Natalya Nikolaevna, my dear! I could not sleep!' said Kharlov despondently. 'It feels as though great hammers were pounding in my head! Like some unclean creature, you know, I was . . .'

'Go to bed, and go to sleep,' my mother insisted again. 'Afterwards we will give you tea, and then you and I will have a talk. Don't lose heart, old friend! If you have been turned out of *your* house, you will always find shelter in *mine* . . . After all, I have not forgotten that you saved my life.'

'Kind friend, my kind friend,' groaned Kharlov, hiding his face in his hands. 'Now *you* must save *me*!'

This appeal moved my mother almost to tears.

'I am ready and willing to help you, Martyn Petrovich, in

every way I can; but you must promise that in future you will listen to me, and drive all bad thoughts away from you.'

Kharlov removed his hands from his face. 'If I must,' he said, 'I can even forgive!'

My mother nodded her head approvingly.

'It pleases me very much to see you in such a truly Christian frame of mind, Martyn Petrovich; but we will speak of that later. Meanwhile you must set yourself to rights and, most important, sleep. Show Martyn Petrovich to your old master's room, the green one,' said my mother to the butler, 'and whatever he asks for, let him have it on the instant. Have his clothes dried and cleaned, and ask the linen-maid for everything necessary in that line. Do you understand?'

'I understand,' answered the butler.

'And when he wakes up, tell the tailor to take his measurements; and his beard will have to be shaved off. Not at once, but later.'

'I understand,' repeated the butler, 'Martyn Petrovich, this way, please.'

Kharlov rose, looked at my mother, made as though to approach her, but stopped, bowed low, crossed himself three times before the ikon, and followed the butler out of the room. I slipped out after them.

XXIV

The butler led Kharlov to the green room and at once hastened off for the linen-maid, since there was no linen on the bed. Souvenir, who had met us in the hall and skipped into the room with us, immediately began, grimacing and tittering, to circle round Kharlov, who stood absently in the middle of the room, with his legs apart and his arms slightly raised away from him. The water still continued to trickle from him.

'Shwede! Carolus the Shwede!' squealed Souvenir, bent double and holding his sides. 'Great founder of the illustrious race of Kharlovs, look upon your descendant! What does he look like? Can you recognize him? Ha, ha, ha! Your Excellency, allow me to kiss your hand! Why have you got black gloves on?'

I wanted to restrain Souvenir and try to shame him, but not a bit of it!

'He used to call me a parasite and a useless hanger-on! "You have no roof of your own!" he said. And now, I suppose, he has become just as much a parasite as this poor sinner! There's nothing to choose now between Martyn Petrovich and the rogue Souvenir! He will eat the bread of charity, too! They will take a crust of stale bread that the dog has sniffed at and left alone . . . "There you are," they will say, "eat that!" Ha, ha, ha!'

Kharlov still stood there unmoving, with hanging head and arms and legs spread out.

'Martyn Kharlov! hereditary nobleman!' Souvenir squealed on. 'What airs he gave himself! Fie, oh fie! Don't come near, says he, or I'll strike you! And when out of the greatness of his wisdom he began giving away and dividing his estate, what a tremendous cackling he made about it! "Gratitude!" he yelled, "gratitude!" And what did he slight me for? Give me nothing? Perhaps I would have shown more feeling! And this means I was speaking the truth when I said they would put him out, stark naked . . .'

'Souvenir!' I shouted.

But Souvenir would not be quieted. Kharlov still did not move, he seemed only then to be beginning to feel how very wet everything about him was, and waiting for it all to be taken off. But the butler did not return.

'And a soldier besides!' Souvenir began again. 'In 1812 he saved the fatherland! he displayed his courage! I'll tell you what it is: pinching the breeches off half-frozen freebooters – that's just the thing for us; but let a wench stamp her foot at us, and our hearts sink into our own breeches . . .'

'Souvenir!' I shouted a second time.

Kharlov looked sidelong at Souvenir; until that instant he had apparently not even noticed his presence, and it was only my shout that had aroused his attention.

'Look out, brother,' he growled expressionlessly, 'don't land yourself in trouble!'

Souvenir simply rolled with laughter.

'Oh, how you've scared me, my dear, highly respected brother! how terrible you are, really! You really ought to run a comb through your hair or else if it gets dry, which God forbid, you'll never wash it clean afterwards; you'll have to mow it with a scythe.' Suddenly Souvenir completely lost control of himself. 'Still playing the big bully! A beggar, but he still swaggers! Where's your roof now? you'd better tell me that, you were always boasting about it! "I've got a roof over my head," says he, "and you're homeless!" "My ancestral roof," says he!' (Souvenir was simply obsessed with the word.)

'Mr Bychkov!' I said. 'What are you doing? Control yourself!'

But still he went on chattering, hopping and skipping round about Kharlov . . . And still the butler and the laundry-maid did not come!

I was growing frightened. I was beginning to notice that Kharlov, who had gradually calmed down in the course of his conversation with my mother and towards the end had even apparently become reconciled to his fate, had now begun to get worked up again: his breathing was quicker, his jowls seemed suddenly to have puffed up, as it were, his fingers twitched, his eyes were flickering again in the dark mask of his mud-spattered face . . .

'Souvenir! Souvenir!' I exclaimed. 'Stop! I'll tell mama!'

But Souvenir seemed possessed of the devil.

'Yes, yes, most honoured sir!' he began to chatter again. 'What a very delicate situation you and I find ourselves in now!

And your daughters and Vladimir Vasilyevich, your son-in-law, can laugh at you to their hearts' content, under your roof! If you had only laid your curse on them as you promised! You hadn't even spirit enough for that! And besides, how could you set yourself against Vladimir Vasilyevich? You called him Volodka, he's no Volodka to you! He is Vladimir Vasilyevich, Mister Slëtkin, landowner, gentleman, and who are you?'

A frenzied roar drowned Souvenir's words . . . Kharlov was roused to fury. His fists clenched themselves and rose high, his face grew dark, there was foam on his cracked lips, he shook with rage.

'Roof! you say,' his clangorous voice thundered. 'Accursed! you say . . . No! I will not curse them . . . They care nothing for that! But their roof . . . I will destroy their roof, and they shall be without a roof over their heads, as I am! They shall learn to know Martyn Petrovich! My strength is not gone yet! They shall learn to laugh at me! . . . They shall not have a roof over their heads!'

I was stupefied: never in my life had I witnessed such boundless fury. It was not a man but a wild bull who raged before me. I was petrified . . . and Souvenir – he had crept under the table in fright.

'They shall not!' shouted Kharlov for the last time, and almost sweeping the maid and the butler off their feet as they entered, he flung himself out of the house . . . He plunged headlong across the courtyard and disappeared beyond the gates.

XXV

My mother was terribly angry when the butler, with a troubled face, came and reported Martyn Petrovich's new and unexpected absence to her. He dared not conceal the reason for it, and I was obliged to support his story. 'So it was all you!' my mother cried to Souvenir, who had darted ahead like a hare and had even gone up to kiss her hand. 'Your evil tongue is to blame for it all!' 'Excuse me, immejitly, immejitly . . .' Souvenir began to babble, stuttering and thrusting his elbows behind his back. 'Immejitly, immejitly . . . I know your "immejitly!"' my mother repeated reproachfully, and she sent him out of the room. Then she rang, had Kvitsinsky sent for, and gave him an order: to go at once to Eskovo, with a carriage, to find Martyn Petrovich at all costs and bring him to her. 'Don't show your face without him!' she concluded. The gloomy Pole silently inclined his head and went out.

I returned to my room, once more sat down near the window and, I remember, pondered for a long time over what had happened under my eyes. I felt perplexed: I was quite unable to understand why Kharlov, who had borne almost without a murmur the affronts put upon him by his family, could not steel himself to bear the jeers and taunts of so worthless a creature as Souvenir. I did not yet know what intolerable bitterness may reside in an empty taunt, even when it falls from despised lips.

The hated name of Slëtkin pronounced by Souvenir had been like a spark in gunpowder; the sore spot could not endure this last pin-prick.

About an hour went by. Our carriage drove into the yard; but the steward was alone in it. And my mother had said to him: 'Don't show your face without *him*!' Kvitsinsky jumped hastily down from the carriage and ran up the steps to the front door. His face wore an expression of perturbation – something it almost never did. I went downstairs immediately and entered the drawing-room on his heels.

'Well? did you bring him?' asked my mother.

'No, I didn't bring him,' Kvitsinsky answered. 'I could not.'

'Why not? Did you see him?'

'Yes, I saw him.'

'What has happened to him? A stroke?'

'No, no, nothing has happened.'

'Then why have you not brought him?'

'He is pulling his house down.'

'What?'

'He is standing on the roof of the new house, and tearing it down. I suppose there must be forty boards or more off already, and four or five sections of the framework besides.' (I remembered Kharlov's words: 'They shall not have a roof over their heads!')

My mother stared at Kvitsinsky.

'Alone . . . standing on the roof and tearing it down?'

'Exactly, ma'am. He is walking along the planks of the under-drawing and smashing out right and left. His strength, you know ma'am, is superhuman! and besides, the roof, to tell the truth, is a poor sort of thing – criss-crossed with cheap, gapped battens and short nails.'

My mother looked at me, as though wishing to assure herself that she had not somehow misheard.

'Gapped battens,' she repeated, clearly not understanding the meaning of either word. 'Well, and what are you going to do?' she said at last.

'I have come for instructions. Nothing can be done without somebody to help. The peasants there have all hidden themselves in a fright.'

'And his daughters? what about them?'

'The daughters aren't doing anything either. They are running about aimlessly . . . and shouting . . . Where's the sense of that?'

'And is Slëtkin there?'

'He's there as well. He's howling louder than anybody, but he can't do anything.'

'And Martyn Petrovich is standing on the roof?'

'Yes . . . or rather, in the under-drawing, and he is tearing the roof down.'

'Yes, yes,' said my mother, 'the battens . . .'

The circumstances we had to face were obviously most extraordinary.

What were we to do? Send to the town for the constable, collect the peasants? My mother was quite at a loss.

Zhitkov, who had come to dinner, was also at a loss. Certainly he made another mention of a military detachment, but he could give no advice, only look submissive and devoted. Kvitsinsky, seeing that he was not going to get any instructions, suggested to my mother, with his own particular contemptuous politeness, that if she would allow him to take several grooms, gardeners, and other house-serfs, he would try . . .

'Yes, yes,' my mother interrupted. 'Try, my dear Vikenty Osipych! Only be as quick as possible, please, and I will take all the responsibility!'

Kvitsinsky smiled coldly.

'Allow me to make one thing quite clear beforehand, madam: it is impossible to guarantee the result, for Mr Kharlov's strength is great, and so is his desperation; he considers himself to have been very much wronged.'

'Yes, yes,' my mother took him up, 'and that wicked Souvenir is entirely to blame! I will never forgive him. Go, take the men, and get away, Vikenty Osipych.'

'Take as much rope as possible, Mr Steward, and fire-hooks,' said Zhitkov in his deep voice, 'and if you had a net, it wouldn't be a bad thing to take that as well. Once, in the regiment, we had . . .'

'I will thank you not to try to instruct me, sir,' Kvitsinsky interrupted with arrogance. 'I know what is wanted without you to tell me.'

Zhitkov took offence and declared that since he would also be called upon . . .

'No, no!' my mother intervened. 'You had better stay here . . . Let Vikenty Osipych act by himself . . . Go along, Vikenty Osipych!'

Zhitkov was even more offended, but Kvitsinsky bowed and went out.

I rushed to the stable, myself hastily saddled my horse, and set off at a gallop along the road to Eskovo.

XXVI

The rain had stopped, but the wind blew with redoubled strength, straight in my face. Halfway along the road, the saddle all but slipped round under me: the girth had come loose. I got down and set about tightening the straps with my teeth . . . Suddenly I heard somebody calling my name . . . Souvenir was running towards me over the winter-corn fields.

'What, my dear chap,' he shouted when he was still some distance away, 'has your curiosity got the better of you? But then who could help it? . . . You see I'm going there too, straight across country, in Kharlov's footsteps . . . After all, you don't see things like this every day!'

'You want to gloat over your handiwork,' I said indignantly, leaping on my horse and again setting it to a gallop; but the

indefatigable Souvenir kept pace with me, laughing and grimacing even as he ran. Here at last was Eskovo, here was the
dam, and there the long fence and the willow-grove of the
homestead . . . I rode up to the gates, dismounted, tethered my
horse, and stood still in amazement.

Of the front third of the roof of the new house and of its
loft, there remained only the framework, and laths and boards
lay in untidy heaps on the ground on both sides of the house.
Admittedly the roof was, in Kvitsinsky's expression, a poor sort
of thing; but all the same it was unbelievable! Along the floor-
boards of the loft, raising clouds of dust and dirt, shambled
a shapeless, blackish-grey mass, now shaking the remaining
brick-built chimney (the other had already tumbled down), now
tearing out a roof-board and flinging it down to the ground,
now snatching at the rafters themselves. It was Kharlov. At this
moment, too, he seemed to me like nothing so much as a bear:
his head, and back, and shoulders alike were those of a bear, and
the way he set his legs, wide apart and flat-footed, was also a
bear's. The cutting wind blew on him from all sides, lifting his
matted hair; it was terrible to see his naked red body showing
here and there through the rents in his tattered clothing; it was
terrible to hear his wild, hoarse muttering. There were a fair
number of people in the yard; peasant women, little boys, and
female house-serfs were pressed together along the fence; a
few men huddled in a separate group at a little distance. The
village priest, the old man whom I knew, was standing hatless

in the porch of the other house, grasping a brass cross in both hands and from time to time silently and hopelessly raising it as though showing it to Kharlov. Beside the priest Evlampia, leaning her back against the wall, stood motionlessly watching her father; Anna now thrust her head out of the window, now disappeared again, now ran out into the yard, now returned to the house; Slëtkin, pale and jaundiced-looking, in an ancient dressing-gown and a skull-cap, with a single-barrelled gun in his hands, was running about from place to place with short little steps. All the Jew in him had, as they say, come out: he was panting, waving his fist menacingly, shaking, taking aim at Kharlov, then shouldering the gun, aiming it again, shouting, weeping . . . Seeing Souvenir and me, he plunged headlong towards us.

'Look, look what is happening here!' he yelped. 'Look! He's gone mad, he's a raving lunatic . . . and see what he's doing. I've sent for the police already – but nobody comes! Nobody comes! Why, if I shot him, the law couldn't touch me, because every man has a right to defend his own property! And I will shoot him! . . . I swear I'll shoot him!'

He hurried towards the house.

'Martyn Petrovich, look out! If you don't come down – I'll shoot you!'

'Shoot!' came the hoarse voice from the roof. 'Shoot! Meanwhile, here's a present for you!'

A long board flew down from above and, turning over once

549

or twice in the air, clattered to the ground at Slëtkin's very feet. He positively jumped a foot in the air, and Kharlov roared with laughter.

'Jesus Christ!' somebody babbled behind me.

I looked round: it was Souvenir. 'Ah!' I thought, 'he is not laughing now!'

Slëtkin seized by the collar a peasant who was standing near him.

'Climb up, climb up, man; climb up, you devils,' he howled, shaking him with all his might. 'Save my property!'

The peasant took a step or two, threw back his head, waved his arms, shouted, 'Hi! you! master!', shuffled his feet without advancing, and hastily retreated.

'A ladder! Bring a ladder!' Slëtkin turned to the other peasants.

'Where are we to get one?' came the answer.

'And even if there was a ladder,' said one voice deliberately, 'who wants to climb up? D'you think we're fools? He'd wring your neck – and quick!'

'Murder you, he would,' said a young flaxen-haired lad with a half-witted face.

'Ah, that he would!' assented the others.

It seemed to me that even if the danger had not been evident, the peasants would have been reluctant to obey the orders of the new owner. Even though they wondered at him, they were almost ready to applaud Kharlov.

'Bandits! Robbers!' groaned Slëtkin. 'I'll see the lot of you . . .'

But at this point the remaining chimney collapsed with a terrific crash, and from amid the swirling cloud of yellow dust that immediately arose, Kharlov, uttering a piercing cry, and raising his bloody hands high above his head, turned to face us. Again Slëtkin aimed his gun.

Evlampia tugged at his elbow.

'Keep out of this!' he raged furiously at her.

'And don't you dare!' she said, her blue eyes flashing menacingly under lowering brows, 'Father is destroying his own house. It's his own property.'

'That's a lie: it's ours.'

'You say it's ours, but I say it's his.'

Slëtkin hissed with rage; Evlampia's eyes stared steadily into his face.

'Ah, good morning, good morning to you, dear daughter,' thundered Kharlov from above. 'Good day, Evlampia Martynovna! How do you do, you and your dear? D'you find it good to kiss, eh, and fondle each other?'

'Father!' came Evlampia's ringing voice.

'Yes, daughter?' answered Kharlov, coming close to the very edge of the wall.

His face, as far as I could make out, wore a strange smile, bright and cheerful, and for that very reason particularly terrible, an evil smile . . . Many years later I saw exactly such a smile on the face of a man condemned to death.

'Stop, father; come down.' (Evlampia did not call him 'papa'.)

'We are in the wrong; we will give everything back to you. Come down.'

'Who told you you could make free with our property?' Slëtkin intervened.

Evlampia only frowned more deeply.

'I will give you back my share, I will give it all up. Stop, come down, father! Forgive us; forgive me.'

Kharlov was still smiling.

'Too late, darling,' he said, and every word rang like metal. 'Your heart of stone has been softened too late! The avalanche has started, there's no stopping it now! And don't look at me now! I am finished! You had better look at your Volodka instead: you see what a beauty he's turned out to be! And look at your nasty spiteful sister: there's her foxy nose over there sticking out of the window; she's egging on that husband of hers! No, sirs! you wanted to take away the roof over my head, now I won't leave you one beam on another! I set them in place with my own hands, I will tear them down with my own hands – and with nothing but my own bare hands! Look, I haven't even brought an axe!'

He blew on both his palms and again began tearing at the rafters.

'Enough, father,' said Evlampia meanwhile, and her voice had become wonderfully gentle. 'Forget about the past. Come, trust me; you always did trust me. Come down; come into my little attic, and lie down on my soft bed. I will dry you and warm you; I will bandage your hurts; see, you have torn your hands. You shall live with me, and have everything you could wish for; your food will be sweet, and your sleep even sweeter. Come, we were wrong! Well, we were puffed up with pride, we were full of sin; come, forgive us!'

Kharlov shook his head.

'Go on with your lying stories! Trust you? Never! You have killed my trust! You have killed everything in me! I was an eagle, and I made myself a worm for your sakes . . . and you, will you crush even the worm now? Enough! I loved you, you know that, but now you are not a daughter to me, and I am not a father to you . . . I am finished! Don't interfere! As for you, shoot, you coward, you pinchbeck hero!' Kharlov suddenly roared at Slëtkin. 'Why don't you do anything but point your gun all the time? Or have you suddenly remembered the law that if one who has received a gift makes an attempt on the life of the giver,' said Kharlov with slow deliberation, 'then the giver is entitled to claim the return of the whole? Ha, ha! don't be afraid, little lawyer! I will not make any claims, I'll finish it all off myself . . . Now for it!'

'Father!' implored Evlampia for the last time.

'Be quiet!'

'Martyn Petrovich! dear brother, be generous and forgive!' stammered Souvenir.

'Father, darling!'

'Be quiet, bitch!' cried Kharlov. He did not so much as glance at Souvenir, only spat in his direction.

XXVII

At that moment Kvitsinsky, with all his helpers – in three carts – appeared at the gate. The tired horses snorted, and the men jumped down one by one into the mud.

'Aha!' roared Kharlov at the top of his voice. 'An army . . . look, an army! They've brought a whole army against me. Fine! But I warn you, if anybody pays me a visit here on the roof, I'll send him down again head over heels! As a host, I'm particular, I don't like guests at the wrong time! No, I don't!'

With both arms he grasped the front pair of rafters, the so-called 'standard' of the pediment, and began to shake them with all his strength. Leaning out from the edge of the flooring, he hauled them, as it were, after him, chanting rhythmically like a Volga boatman: 'One more heave now! Yo-heave-ho!'

Slëtkin ran up to Kvitsinsky and began wailing and snivelling . . . Kvitsinsky requested him to 'keep out of the way', and proceeded to the fulfilment of the plan he had worked out. He stationed himself at the front of the house and began, by way of diversion, to explain to Kharlov that he was not acting like a gentleman.

'One more heave now!' chanted Kharlov.

That Natalya Nikolaevna was very displeased with him, and that this was not what she expected of him.

'One more heave now! Yo-heave-ho!' chanted Kharlov.

Meanwhile Kvitsinsky had directed four of the bravest and strongest of the stable-boys to the opposite side of the house, so that they could get up on the roof from behind. The plan of attack, however, did not escape Kharlov; all at once he abandoned the rafters and ran nimbly to the rear part of the loft. His aspect was so fearful that two stable-boys, who had already managed to climb up into the roof, beat a hasty retreat to the ground by way of the drain-pipe, to the great delight and even amusement of the small serf-boys. Kharlov shook his fist after them and, returning to the front of the house, once more grasped the rafters and began to tug at them, resuming once more his boatman's chanting.

Suddenly he stopped, staring . . .

'Maximushka, my dear boy! my friend!' he exclaimed. 'Is that you?'

I looked round . . . The page Maximka had indeed detached himself from the crowd of peasants and stepped forward, grinning and showing his teeth. His master, the saddler, had probably given him leave to come home for a short visit.

'Climb up to me, Maximushka, my faithful servant,' Kharlov continued, 'and together we will beat back the wicked Tartars and thieving Lithuanians!'

Maximka, still grinning, immediately began climbing up . . . But he was seized and pulled away, God knows why, unless it was as an example to others: he would not have been much help to Martyn Petrovich.

'Very well, then! Very good!' said Martyn Petrovich.

'Vikenty Osipych! Let me fire,' said Slëtkin, addressing Kvitsinsky, 'mostly to frighten him, you know; my gun is loaded with small shot.'

But before Kvitsinsky had time to answer, the foremost pair of rafters, violently shaken by Kharlov's arms of steel, heeled over, cracked, and crashed down into the yard – and together with them, unable to hold himself back, Kharlov himself came headlong down and thudded heavily to the ground. Everybody started and exclaimed . . . Kharlov lay motionless on his face, pinned down by the upper longitudinal beam, the ridge-pole, which had followed the falling gable.

XXVIII

They rushed to Kharlov, lifted away the beam and turned him on his back; his face was lifeless, there was blood near his mouth, and he did not breathe. 'It's knocked the breath out of him,' muttered the peasants who had drawn close. Somebody ran to the well for water, brought back a pailful, and threw it over his head. The dust and dirt was washed off his face, but its lifeless look remained. They dragged up a bench, set it close to the house, laboriously raised Martyn Petrovich's huge bulk and sat him on it with his head leaning against the wall. The page Maximka went up to him, fell on one knee and with his other leg stretched out in a somewhat theatrical fashion, supported his old master's arm. Evlampia, as pale as death itself, stood directly in front of her father, with her enormous eyes fixed immovably on him. Anna and Slëtkin did not come close. Everybody was silent, waiting for something. At last broken, gurgling noises could be heard coming from Kharlov's throat, as though he were choking. Then one arm, the right (Maximka was supporting the left), moved feebly, he opened one eye, the right, and turning his gaze slowly round him, as though drunk with some terrible intoxication, groaned and mumbled, 'I've . . . smashed . . . my . . . self . . .' and added, after seeming to ponder for a moment, 'Here . . . it is, the . . . black . . . colt!' Suddenly blood gushed from his mouth and his whole body shuddered.

'The end!' I thought. But again Kharlov opened the same right eye (the left eyelid was as motionless as a dead man's) and, fixing it on Evlampia, uttered the scarcely audible words, 'Well, daugh . . . ter . . . I will not p—' With an abrupt gesture of his hand Kvitsinsky summoned the priest, who still stood in the porch. The old man approached, the feeble movements of his knees hampered by his tight cassock. But suddenly a kind of convulsion seized Kharlov's legs and belly, and a nervous spasm passed upwards over his face – and exactly the same shudder distorted Evlampia's face also. Maximka began to cross himself . . . I felt obscurely frightened, ran to the gate, and pressed myself against it, without looking round. A minute later a subdued murmur rose from the lips of all the crowd behind me, and I knew that Martyn Petrovich was no more.

From the post-mortem examination it appeared that his skull had been fractured by the beam, and his chest was staved in.

XXIX

'What was he trying to say to her as he was dying?' I kept asking myself as I rode homewards: 'I will not – put my curse on you'? or 'pardon you'?

It had begun to pour with rain again, but I rode at a walk. I wanted to remain alone as long as possible, to give myself up to my thoughts unhindered. Souvenir had left on one of the carts brought by Kvitsinsky. However young and thoughtless I may have been in those days, the sudden, general (not merely partial) change that is always provoked in all hearts by the unexpected (or expected, it makes no difference!) presence of death, its majesty, solemnity and truth, could not but produce a strong impression on me. I was indeed impressed . . . but at the same time my troubled, childish eyes had at once noticed many things: they noticed how Slëtkin had swiftly and furtively flung aside the gun, as though it were stolen, how he and his wife had both instantly become the objects of a general, though silent, enmity and how an empty space had appeared all round them. This enmity did not extend to Evlampia, although her fault was probably no less than her sister's. She even aroused some sympathy when she fell at her dead father's feet. But that she too was guilty – this everybody felt, nevertheless.

'You wronged an old man,' said one grey-haired, large-headed peasant, propping both hands and his beard on his long stick like some antique judge; 'it is a sin that lies on your soul! You wronged him!' The word 'wronged' was at once accepted by everybody as an inexorable judgement. The people's justice had spoken. I understood that at once. I noticed also that at first Slëtkin *did not dare* to give any orders. The body was lifted and carried into the house without him; without asking him, the priest went off to the church for the things he needed and the village elder ran to the village to get a horse and cart which would go to the town. Even Anna Martynovna, ordering the samovar to be put on 'so that there should be hot water for washing the body', forbore to use her usual imperious tone. Her order sounded like a request – and the answer she received was off-hand . . .

But the question that preoccupied me all the time was this: what exactly had he been trying to say to his daughter? Did he want to forgive her or to curse her? Finally I decided it was to forgive her.

Three days later Martyn Petrovich's funeral took place, at my mother's charge; she was deeply distressed by his death and gave orders to spare no expense. She herself did not go to the church, because she did not wish, as she expressed it, to see those two wicked women and that nasty little Jew; but she sent

Kvitsinsky, me, and Zhitkov, whom, however, from that time she invariably referred to as the old woman. Souvenir she would not allow in her sight, and for a long time she was extremely angry with him, calling him his friend's murderer. This disgrace was very painful to him: he would wander ceaselessly on tiptoe about the room next to that in which my mother was; he gave way to a kind of uneasy and abject melancholy, always wincing and whimpering 'immejitly'.

In church and in the funeral procession Slëtkin seemed to me to be quite himself again. He issued instructions and fussed about in the old way, and avidly watched to see that not a copeck was wasted, although his own pocket was not involved. Maximka, in a new coat, also of my mother's giving, produced in the choir such tenor notes that there could be no doubting the sincerity of his devotion to the deceased! Both sisters were suitably clad in mourning, but showed more embarrassment than grief, especially Evlampia. Anna had adopted a humble Lenten expression, but she did not make any effort to weep, only kept passing her dry, beautiful hand over her hair and cheek. Evlampia seemed preoccupied the whole time. That general inexorable condemnation and estrangement I had noticed on the day of Kharlov's death, I seemed to see now also in the faces of all those present in the church, in all their movements and in their looks, but soberer and as it were colder. It was as if all these people knew that the sin into which the Kharlov family had fallen, that grievous sin, had now come before the court of the righteous judge, and that consequently there was no need for them to be disturbed and indignant. They prayed fervently for the soul of the dead man, whom they had rather disliked, and even feared, in his lifetime. Death had struck him down so very suddenly.

'It's not even as if he had been drinking, brother!' said one peasant to another in the church porch.

'You can get drunk without touching a drop,' answered the other. 'The things that happen!'

'He was wronged,' the first peasant repeated the conclusive word.

'Wronged,' echoed others.

'But surely the dead man himself oppressed you all?' I asked a peasant in whom I recognized one of Kharlov's serfs.

'Everyone knows he was a hard master,' answered the peasant, 'but all the same . . . he was wronged!'

'Wronged . . .' the crowd echoed again.

At the graveside also, Evlampia stood as though lost. She was deep in her thoughts . . . painful thoughts. I noticed that she treated Slëtkin, who spoke to her several times, as she used to treat Zhitkov, or even worse.

Several days later, a rumour spread all over our neighbourhood that Evlampia Martynovna Kharlova had quitted the home of her father for ever, leaving to her sister and brother-in-law all the property that had come to her, and taking with her only a few hundred roubles . . . 'Anna has evidently bought her off!' remarked my mother, 'but you and I,' she added, addressing

Zhitkov, with whom she was playing piquet (he had taken Souvenir's place with her), 'are clumsy-handed!' Zhitkov looked gloomily at his strong hands . . . 'Clumsy, these!' he seemed to be thinking.

Soon afterwards my mother and I went to live in Moscow, and it was many years before I was to see Martyn Petrovich's two daughters again.

XXX

But I did see them. My meeting with Anna Martynovna came about in the most ordinary fashion. After my mother's death, I visited our estate, where I had not been for more than fifteen years, and received an invitation from the arbitrator (throughout Russia at that time there was proceeding, with a slowness not forgotten even today, the determination of the former serfs' land-holdings) — an invitation to be present at the conference with the other landowners of our district on the estate of the widow Anna Slëtkina. The news that my mother's 'little Jew' with the prune-coloured eyes was no longer in this world did not, I confess, grieve me in the slightest, but I was curious to see his widow. She had the reputation of an excellent manager of her estates. And indeed her land and buildings, and the house itself (I involuntarily looked up at the roof, and saw that it was of iron), were all in excellent order, and everything was so neat and clean, so well tended and, where necessary, painted, that it might have belonged to a German. Anna Martynovna herself, of course, had grown older; but that special dry and, as it were, evil charm, that had once so excited me, had not entirely deserted her. She was dressed in country fashion, but elegantly. She received us not with cordiality – the word could not suitably be applied to her – but with courtesy, and when she saw me, a witness of the terrible happening, she did not so much as blink. She might have been dumb for all the reference she made either to my mother or to her father, or her sister, or her husband.

She had two daughters, both very pretty, graceful little things, with dear little faces, and a merry friendly expression in their black eyes; she had a son, too, just a little like his father, and also a fine boy. During the discussion between the landowners Anna Martynovna remained calm and dignified, displaying neither particular obstinacy nor particular avarice. But nobody could have had a better understanding of his own interests, or stated and defended his rights more convincingly; all the 'appropriate' regulations, even the circulars from the Ministry, were well known to her; she spoke little, in a quiet voice, but every word hit the mark. It ended in our agreeing to everything she asked for and making so many concessions that we could only marvel at ourselves. On the way back some of the landowners even heartily abused themselves and all clicked their tongues and shook their heads.

'That's a clever woman!' said one.

'She's a cunning devil!' put in another, less delicate in his speech. 'A smooth tongue and a sharp tooth.'

'And mean besides!' added a third. 'A glass of vodka and a bit of caviare for a neighbour – what's that?'

'What do you expect?' one landowner who had hitherto been silent said incautiously. 'Everybody knows she poisoned her husband.'

To my surprise, nobody considered it necessary to refute an accusation so terrible, and surely baseless. I was the more surprised because, in spite of the abusive expressions I have quoted, everybody, not excluding the coarse-tongued landowner, respected Anna Martynovna. As for the arbitrator, he was positively eloquent.

'Put her on a throne,' he exclaimed, 'and she'd be another Semiramis or Catherine II! The discipline of her peasants is a model. The upbringing of her children is a model. What a head! What a brain!'

Leaving Semiramis and Catherine II out of it, there was no doubt that Anna Martynovna was leading a thoroughly happy life. Inward and outward satisfaction, the pleasant serenity of spiritual and physical health, seemed to radiate from herself, her family, and everything around her. How far she deserved this happiness is a different question. Such questions, however, are asked only in youth. Everything in this world, whether good or bad, comes to a man not according to his deserts but in consequence of certain as yet unknown, but logical, laws which I will not undertake even to indicate, although it sometimes seems to me that I dimly apprehend them.

XXXI

I inquired of the arbitrator about Evlampia Martynovna, and learned that as soon as she left the house, she had simply vanished into the blue, and 'probably departed this life long ago'.

So our arbitrator expressed himself . . . but I am convinced I *saw* Evlampia, that I met her. It was like this.

About four years after my meeting with Anna Martynovna, I spent the summer in Murino, a little hamlet near St Petersburg, well known to middle-class summer visitors. At that time the shooting near Murino was not bad, and I was out with a gun nearly every day. I had a companion, one Vikulov, who belonged to the tradesman class, a bright and good-natured fellow, but as he expressed it himself, 'a bit of a rolling stone'. There was nowhere he had not been, and nothing he had not done. Nothing surprised him, there was nothing he did not know, but all he cared for was shooting – and vodka. On one occasion, then, he and I were returning to Murino, and we had to pass an isolated house, standing near the place where two roads crossed, and surrounded by a high, close paling. It was not the first time I had seen the house and it always moved my curiosity: there was something mysterious about it, something secretive, uncommunicative, something reminiscent of a prison or a hospital. From the road nothing was visible but its high-pitched roof, painted dark red. In the whole fence there was only one pair of gates, and these seemed to be hermetically sealed; no sound ever came from within them. You felt, nevertheless, that somebody must live in the house; it had none of the appearance of an abandoned dwelling. On the contrary, everything about it was so strong and solid and sturdy that it might have withstood a siege.

'What fortress is that?' I asked my companion. 'Do you know?'

Vikulov screwed up his eyes knowingly.

'An odd sort of building, isn't it? It brings in quite an income to the local constable!'

'How is that?'

'It's like this. I suppose you have heard of the sect of Flagellants – you know, that haven't any priests?'

'Yes.'

'Well, this is where their chief "mother" lives.'

'A woman?'

'Yes, the mother; what they call a mother of God.'

'What on earth . . . ?'

'I'm telling you. She's very strict, they say. A regular martinet! And simply rolling! I'd just like to take all these mothers of God . . . But what's the use of talking?'

He called his Pegashka, a wonderful dog with an excellent nose, but with no idea of pointing. Vikulov had to tie up her hind leg, so that she wouldn't bolt so wildly.

What he had said stuck in my memory. I used to go out of my way on purpose to pass this mysterious house. Then, one day, I was just coming up to it when suddenly, marvellous to relate, I heard a bolt rattle inside the gates, a key grated in the lock, the gates themselves opened very quietly, there appeared the head of a powerful horse, with a plaited fringe, under a gaily decorated yoke, and a small cart of the kind used by horse-dealers and travelling merchants rolled slowly into the road. On the leather-cushioned seat nearer to me sat a man of some thirty years old, of strikingly handsome appearance, in a neat black coat, with a black peaked cap pulled down low on his forehead; he was sedately driving the broad-backed horse, as fat as butter; next to him, on the farther side of the cart, sat a tall woman, as straight as an arrow. A costly black shawl covered her head, she wore a short olive-green velvet jacket and a dark-blue merino skirt; her white hands, primly crossed, lay on her bosom. The cart turned along the road to the left, and I found myself less than two yards from the woman; she moved her head slightly – and I recognized Evlampia Kharlova. I recognized her at once, without a moment's doubt, and indeed there was no room for doubt: I have never seen anybody else with such eyes as hers or, especially, such a turn of the lip, haughty and voluptuous. Her face had grown longer and less youthfully rounded, her skin was darker, here and there wrinkles were visible; but the greatest change was in the expression of that face! It is difficult to convey in words, but how self-assured, severe, and proud it had become! Not merely confidence of power, but satiety of power, showed in every feature; the careless glance she let fall on me spoke of the old-established, inveterate habit of encountering only awe-struck, unquestioning obedience. This woman evidently lived in the midst not of followers but of slaves; she had evidently forgotten the time when any order or desire of hers was not instantly fulfilled! I called her loudly by her name and patronymic; she started very slightly, looked at me a second time, not with alarm, but with contemptuous anger, as though to say, 'Who dares to disturb me?' and, barely opening her lips, uttered a word of command. The man sitting beside her gave a start and brought the reins down on the horse's back with a great sweep of his arm that made it break into a swift strong trot – and the cart disappeared.

I have never met Evlampia since then. How Martyn Petrovich's daughter came to be a mother of God among the Flagellants I cannot even imagine; but, who knows, perhaps she has founded a sect which will be, or is already, called after her, the Evlampians? Anything may happen, anything is possible.

That then is what I had to tell you of my Lear of the Steppes, and of his family and his deeds.

The story-teller said no more, and after talking for a while, we went our several ways.

Weimar, 1870